A
BARGAIN
OF
SHADOWS

NORTHERN LIGHT PRESS
TORONTO

F.M. ADEN

Part One

The Opera House

The world was carved in threes
as the favored number of the Three Kings.
Each world was given to a Fate to oversee.
The Land of the Living,
the Land of the Unseen,
and the Land of the Dead.

Devotionals No. IX, Verse 2.
Excerpt from *The Last Scripture* 250 AD.

Chapter One

The Opera House was filled with a sea of strange faces. The gilded dressing room backstage smelled of fine powder and the overwhelming scent of perfumed begonias that had been sprayed upon the decolletage of the young girls. Élisabeth Bellacourt wrinkled her nose, swallowing back the urge to sneeze.

Élisabeth sat in her velvet chair, waiting for the stagehand to direct them onstage. All the dancers wore matching white tulle dresses. The thick, spidery cloth hung over the hips of the slim-boned girls like a curtain, giving their narrow physique the illusion of a wider frame. It hid the dreadful truth that they were all poor and starving. Most were deep in debt from paying for lessons at the Royal Academy of Dance. The girls rarely spoke to Élisabeth, but she didn't take their cold shoulder to heart; after all, her father owned the glittering National Opera House of Prasin. A reminder that she would never understand their struggles, and a fact that didn't endear her to the other girls.

However, they were different around her half-sister Louise. They adored Louise Bellacourt. Everyone did.

The soothing tinkle of charms dangling above the various dressing stations caught her eye. Some of the trinkets were dedicated to Laos, the Bringer of Light, some of them to Pras, the Hunter, and others to Mòrge, the Misfortunate One. The High Trinity. The sacred protectors of their continent Annthès.

She could see the serpent with the fake gold coin between its pointed teeth representing Laos, the silver stag representing Pras, and the crow with the single eye that sparkled like a rosary bead representing Mòrge.

Mòrge was said to protect one from misfortune and envy. So, his charm was naturally the most popular choice among the dancers. Élisabeth had a bracelet with the one-eyed bird on her wrist, which was gifted to her by her father.

A delivery boy passed their dressing room, carrying a bouquet of fresh peonies in his thin arms. For a moment, her heart had swelled at the thought that Charles had sent it for her —she adored peonies—but then the young boy passed the hall, heading towards her sister's private fitting room.

Louise was the only dancer who had her own dressing room. She was also the lead in all their ballet performances. Her face was printed on the posters that decorated the streets of the capital city of Prasin. Papa had said it had cost a fortune at the printing press, but good advertisements boosted ticket sales and Louise was a lucrative investment. Especially with King Alphonse's latest interest in ballet. In the last few years, the arts, mainly poetry, literature, and dance soared in popularity in Prasin.

"Ready, girls," Madame Dupont called, with a clap of her hands. Her multitude of rings clacked loudly with the gesture. She wore one of her fancy red ballgowns with puffed sleeves and a low-cut neckline that was all the rage this season.

Behind her was the foreboding, wiry shape of Pierre, their ballet master. His spectacles hung on the bridge of his slightly bulbous nose as he walked back and forth, inspecting them like cattle.

While Madame Dupont had a naturally graceful disposition, Pierre was as surly as a stray cat. He was renowned for his impeccable productions that drew inspiration from Lionel Carmouche, one of Prasin's greatest operatic composers. Carmouche was said to have performed his famous composition *The Little Knife* at the Grand Palace when Queen Honorine ruled during the Erudition Era. Carmouche's work also tended to fill out all 1979 seats of the Opera House.

Élisabeth dusted her face with powder even though she would be wearing a masque. All the girls would be concealed tonight, all but Louise.

Tonight, they were to perform *The Girl*. It was a tale of an orphan who rose to riches using her wit. The girls swarmed out of the room in a fit of nervous chatter like a colony of bees. Élisabeth was the last to step out. Most of the dancers kept a wide berth from her. Not *only* because she was a Bellacourt. The circumstances of her birth had been a scandal, and it seemed that even after nearly two decades it still haunted her, wrapping its ghostly fingers around her throat. She had been born out of wedlock and was of foreign blood from a continent that despised Annthès. The northern continent of Annthès had always had an oily relationship with the southern nation of Tezrik who had closed their borders to supply a decade ago. They were in negotiations, but it was clear to see that it was going rather poorly, and tensions were rife. At any moment the civilians expected to hear the shattering crash of cannons and watch the air go dark with smoke.

Tezrik refused to supply them with the oil, gold, and rare minerals they used to sustain their economy. There were whispers of a war on the horizon. But Tezrik had a military that would put theirs to shame. Her mother was from a small coastal village in Tezrik and had come here on a short trip when she'd met her father.

Some days Élisabeth felt entirely other, like a stuffed doll whose head had not been stitched on quite right or a book that had been folded with the pages creased.

Louise arrived in a worn ballet dress to depict the poor status of her character. Even in the stained garbs, her beauty radiated like a jewel held against the sun. She was only fourteen, a prodigy, while Élisabeth was eighteen. It was the curse of being a woman. Your life was a ticking clock. A silent progression towards an inevitable drop. Men were celebrated as they aged. Wisdom grew on the branches of their life tree. And women were forgotten the moment their youth and beauty faded.

As the years passed Élisabeth had begun to feel that despite everything, she would never find her way into the spotlight. It often felt like she was doomed to wither in the background like a child's discarded toy, while the young dancers dazzled at the front row. As much as she had tried to love Louise when she was young, Louise's mother—Élisabeth's stepmother—had successfully driven a wedge between them.

Élisabeth stepped onto the stage, and her eyes immediately shot upwards to the shadows that consumed Box Five. Her father had never told her which patron sat there. The last time she'd asked his skin had grown deathly pale and he had changed the topic so swiftly it made her head spin.

She felt a strange prickle of nerves. As if she were an insect stuffed beneath a glass jar. The feeling was both eerie and oppressive.

As the first string of the piano began Élisabeth lost herself to the motions of the performance, finding her footing in the distance far from the bright lights that washed over Louise like the moon, coughing its droplets of silver light onto her.

"You are the fly on the back of a gazelle," Pierre would say to her anytime her dancing seemed to outdo the other girls. "You are the one Louise carries, you do not carry her."

Sweat dripped down her nape as she twirled and leaped in the background. She could feel a wintry, impenetrable gaze on her and when her eyes snapped upwards there was nothing but a mass of shadows staring back at her.

"Splendid performance girls," Papa said.

He pulled her and Louise to his chest, pressing sloppy kisses to their foreheads. Louise complained about him ruining her powder, but Élisabeth did not mind. Her father was the only person who loved her.

She braced her shoulders when her stepmother arrived, carrying a bouquet of summer-bright tulips straight from their gardens.

"Louise, darling," Delphine said in her high-octave voice. "Marvelous performance. Your best yet!"

Élisabeth was not surprised that she did not compliment her. Delphine had married her father when Élisabeth had just turned four years old and it had been the worst day of her life. She had cried for hours and begged her father not to do it. She had known that afternoon when her father introduced her to Delphine in their parlor room that the woman was a serpent. The kind that bit you, and you realized hours after that the bite was lethal, and by then it was too late to do anything of note.

"Babette did magnificently!" her father said, staring at her with sparkling gray eyes. They were filled with pride and Élisabeth felt her heart swell under his warm gaze. "I could pinpoint her moves among all the other girls. Her dancing is nothing short of ethereal. Simply sublime!"

Élisabeth watched Louise's face twist in jealousy.

"What about me, Papa?" she asked.

"You already know you are talented, Louise," he said. "And if you don't, your mother shall remind you in five minutes."

"Hugo," Delphine said, aghast. "Louise is nothing if not a paragon of humility. It is Élisabeth who is hungry for flattery. Vanity is a rather ugly trait, Élisabeth."

"Your rouge is smeared," Élisabeth said with a sharp smile. One that was full of teeth.

She enjoyed watching Delphine fret over her appearance. Louise ruined her fun by telling her mother that she was lying.

"Vanity is an ugly trait, Delphine," Élisabeth said rather sweetly.

"It is these childish pranks that I cannot stand, Hugo," Delphine retorted.

Her pale face grew red and blotchy with each word.

"Babette has a youthful soul," he said dismissively. "Do not take her jests to heart."

His words were enough to silence Delphine.

And Élisabeth enjoyed the silence while it lasted.

Élisabeth snuck out to the parade that night to partake in the Prasin Carnaval which took place every year on King Alphonse's birthday at the start of the Spring Equinox. It was a festival for the working class that Delphine had called gauche and vulgar. Élisabeth was of the frame of mind that anything Delphine despised was destined to become her greatest pleasure. That night she had come across a fortune teller sitting at a street booth. Her face was layered in wrinkles like a rumpled petticoat. At least, the parts that were unconcealed by her masque were. Everyone was in masque as was customary for the celebration.

Her crooked fingers danced over a set of chipped cards.

Élisabeth did not believe in magic. It was said that a long time ago magic existed between the three realms. There was the realm of the mortals, the realm of the dead, and the realm of the Fates. Each king in the High Trinity had made a Fate, a being of high power to oversee each realm. But as the centuries passed the magic had vanished and it was said that when the mortals abused it Laos had withdrawn the light of magic and left it to the other realms alone.

Élisabeth had been drawn to the old lady. It was as though her fingers spun a lute to a song that only Élisabeth could hear. She wondered if in the fables this was how the innocent maiden was trapped in a faery ring of bramble and mushrooms, by drifting towards something that called to them even against their better judgment.

"Welcome, my dear," she said. "Have a seat please."

Élisabeth sat down warily.

"You look lost," the woman said.

She eyed her olive skin, waist-length dark-brown hair, and bejeweled masque. It was clear to see that she did not share the pale coloring of the northerners. Perhaps the woman thought she was the daughter of one of the diplomats who often arrived at the behest of the Emperor of Kirath, the capital city of Tezrik to continue the never-ending negotiations.

"I mean no offense, but I am not one to believe in the work of soothsayers and clairvoyants," Élisabeth said. "This is rather unlike me."

"Many who sat upon that chair said the same words you just did," she said. "They always leave here as believers."

"How much?" Élisabeth asked, opening her velvet pouch.

"Four Annès," she said.

Élisabeth gave her five and the woman tucked the coins swiftly in her pocket. Her frail fingers returned to toy with the cards in her deck. She slowly plucked three and laid them down.

The fortune teller's eyes widened, blue orbs staring at Élisabeth with horror. The woman's fingers shook when her battered nail grazed the peeling paint of the first card. It was a small creature with a forked tail. Black fur covered its hide like paint.

"This is the Devil card," she said. "There is someone vile and wretched who will make you question everything."

"You speak of my stepmother, Delphine," Élisabeth replied. "She *is* a rather vile woman."

"No," the woman mused. "You have yet to meet the Devil."

Élisabeth shuddered at her words. Someone worse than Delphine—why, the thought alone was simply chilling.

"This one," the woman continued, flipping a second card. It was a woman peeling back the jaws of a lion. "This is good. This is Force. It means you shall possess great strength in the ordeals ahead. I see a dark adventure before you. One that will change you completely."

Perhaps this meant Élisabeth should speak to her father about her plans to leave Prasin. The idea had haunted her mind for quite some time. They had a townhouse in Harford and she would not have to worry about accommodations. She could swiftly begin her search to join a new ballet company. And it was close enough to Prasin to satisfy her overprotective father.

"This last one," the woman said, voice shaking like the

wind rustling a thin branch, "it is darkness incarnate. This is Death."

Her heart stuttered as she stared at the iridescent card. It was the Shepherd of Death ferrying a boat across a sea filled with bones.

She felt foolish for letting her words affect her. The woman had likely told half of Prasin they would die. It was a con. And a good one at that. The woman was a seasoned actor.

"Someone will die?" Élisabeth asked suspiciously. "Will I die?"

"Your future is difficult to read," she said. "It is like a veil covers you. One that I cannot see through. But I believe it to be someone close to you."

Her heart tightened. "My father?"

"I cannot say," she said.

"Well, what can you say?" Élisabeth asked sharply.

"I have told you all I see," she said. "You walk a dark path filled with mistrust and shadows and death. It hovers above you like a cloud, and you will be tested in more ways than one."

It was bleak and disheartening and Élisabeth made a promise to herself to never seek out a fortune teller again.

As she walked home, her mind drifted to the impending conversation she sought to have with her father.

Tomorrow night she would tell her father that she was done.

That she was leaving behind Prasin and going to Harford

She would run and she would not stop.

Not until the shadows that chased her disappeared.

Chapter Two

Élisabeth sat stiffly at the dining table, trying to ignore the grating sound of Delphine's voice as she shared the latest society news and what she had read in the *Inkling Herald*, a pompous and tawdry gossip column. Charles Auclaire sat across from Élisabeth in a pressed verdant-green coat, a gleaming cravat, and an embroidered vest. He was the son of the King's Chancellor and Élisabeth had always been half in love with him. He had a tone that bespoke confidence and a smile that made most girls' cheeks grow as red as an apple. Not to mention he was charming and kind. It was impossible to be anything but smitten with him.

When she had first met him last year, for a moment, he seemed interested in her, but then Delphine had gotten wind that he was the most eligible bachelor and was suddenly determined to parade Louise before him at any chance she got. It hadn't been long after that his attention had swayed to her younger sister. It didn't matter that their father would not allow her to wed until she was sixteen. Louise was determined to enjoy a long courtship.

Charles nodded politely as Delphine rambled about one sordid tale after the other

while Élisabeth stifled a yawn, taking another drawn sip of her onion soup. Louise sat beside him, using any opportunity to place her gloved fingers on his elbow to capture his attention. She knew that Élisabeth liked him. It was why she partook in these pathetic displays. Louise had found her old journal when she had been snooping around Élisabeth's bedroom. The realization that Élisabeth had wanted him was the main reason she was interested in him. Louise had liked another boy before, one whose name she could not recall for the life of her. One that doted on her, but the second Louise had discovered Élisabeth wanted Charles that poor boy had been swiftly rejected, and suddenly she was open to Delphine's matchmaking.

Once the dreadful meal was behind them, they drifted towards the parlor room. The Bellacourts lived in a lavish townhouse just south of the River Frelles. It was a grand brick home with gold molding running across the walls and palatial ceilings that one had to crane their neck to see. The boiserie floorboards gleamed with a shine that reflected her appearance. The swan-white walls were hung with many portraits of her grim-faced ancestors. Men with feathery mustaches and women with sharp collarbones and shrewd stares.

Servants poured them glasses of wine and Élisabeth swiftly made her way to her father. She had gotten her height from him and her eyes. The rest, he said, was her mother, who had been born in Lupaz—a miniature island on the coast of the continent of Tezrik—and had been part of a traveling troupe. She had only been in Prasin for three days and the second time she'd returned had been with a child in her arms.

"She was dying, Babette. She caught the Yellow Fever," her father had whispered to her whenever she was sad. "I was there with her in the end, and she never stopped loving you. Not once."

Élisabeth missed her most days. She had long ago crafted a vision of what she was like, and that image had stuck with her. She imagined her to be tall like her, with glowing brown skin and a smile like a candle that burned even on the coldest of nights. Strong, resilient, and talented.

"May we speak, Papa?" she asked, pointing towards the balcony.

"Yes, my dearest," he said, offering her his elbow. "Come along."

There was a chaise that Delphine had spoken of replacing, but Élisabeth liked that it was worn. Even in the dark, she could see the tufts of sponge protruding from the shredded covering like a hare slinking between the dirt.

"How much?" her father asked.

"What?"

"You have called me here to give me a heart attack, no?" he asked with a deep sigh. "Have you opened another account?"

She did have a bit of a problem when it came to her spending habits. She had accounts at many of Prasin's renowned boutiques where she tended to buy the latest dresses of the season which was unfortunate for her father because they were never cheap.

"You have such little faith in me," Élisabeth said with an innocent smile.

"My troublesome daughter," he said, shaking his head fondly. "What do you need?"

She took a deep breath. "I want to go to Harford."

Harford was just a train ride over the mountain pass that was ruled by Duke Silas. It was another formidable country within the continent of Annthès. She didn't think her father would allow her to travel past the continent.

"On a trip?" he asked. "My schedule is booked I can't possibly—"

"No," she said quickly. "Not us. Just me."

"I suppose a weekend would not hurt," he said. "So long as you are properly chaperoned. Perhaps, you and Louise can take a trip. You two should spend more time together."

"No, I..." The words were sticky, clinging to her throat like honey.

It was a frightening thing to seek a fresh start. But she wanted to take her ballet seriously, as it was the only thing that made her feel alive. It drowned her, drawing her under its dark lullaby and she was more than willing to follow its haunting call. Even now her mind was on that stage, feeling a network of eyes on her and that nervous lurch of her stomach as she danced on the tip of her toes. She had never led a performance on the Prasin stage. Pierre had said she wasn't ready even when she begged her father to make him let her. Her father would always say that he deferred to Pierre's expertise and that her time would come.

"It will be just me," she said, clearing her throat. "I wish to debut in Harford. At the Theatre Royal."

Her father stilled. "But you work for the National Opera House."

"I have not seen a dime for my work," she said.

"Because I give you a monthly allowance that far surpasses what the other dancers make," he said.

"I am not under contract," she pressed.

"Where is this coming from, Babette?" he asked. "Is this an attempt for me to increase your allowance? Or are you unhappy?"

"I don't want to live in the shadows," she said. "I don't want to live in this gilded cage anymore."

She wanted to become a shining star. A force to be reckoned with. She wanted to dominate the world, not just Prasin. If she got a fresh start in Harford she could thrive without Louise's overpowering fame and carve out something of her own. Nobody would let her lead in Prasin when she had been in the background for far too long. Somewhere new would give her the chance to build a reputation and finally have the career she longed for. And who knew what would come after? Maybe she could travel the continent or even visit her mother's country and search for her family. The possibilities were endless.

"There is something that I must tell you, Babette," her father said.

He sank into the cushion beside her and the heavy look on his face filled her with unease. She could not leave without his blessing. One because she depended on him financially and two because she loved him. More than anyone in this world. He never looked at her like she was a failure, as Delphine often did.

"I have carried a burden for the last two years. You are the eldest and you shall inherit the Opera House one day, and you should know something in case anything ever happens to me," he said. "Do you remember the day my parents died?"

Élisabeth didn't think she would ever forget February 19th. It had been snowing and they had been unbearably cold in their tiny apartment when a messenger had knocked on their door. A boy with a grimy face and holes in his gloves with a folded letter stood in the corridor, staring at them expectantly. A thick, creamy envelope with a red wax seal.

It had been a letter that conveyed that the Bellacourts had been killed in a carriage accident. As the next of kin, her father had been summoned to claim his inheritance.

It had been the first time her father's smile had reached his eyes. His parents had disinherited him when he'd claimed Élis-abeth. Left him out on the street to fend for himself. They had refused to taint their reputation with rumors of a foreign, bastard child.

Her father worked on the docks to support them, but it had been difficult for him to go from ballrooms and wine to hard labor.

When they'd arrived at his family's townhouse they had run down the empty hallways as he drank to his heart's content. He had let Élisabeth jump on the fancy coverlet with her shoes on and gave her a sip of wine when she begged him. They had laughed and danced in the grand atrium, and for the first time in a long time, her father's smile wasn't the sad one he'd wear when he was trying to cheer her up about their terrible circumstances.

His smile then had been open and bright and filled with vivacity.

Élisabeth felt a flash of pity, as he hunted for the right words to explain what burden weighed him down.

"I thought it was a gift, this townhouse, the Opera House, the servants and carriages," he said. "A plea for forgiveness from my parents, but I should have known better. It was nothing but a mirage."

"What do you mean?"

"The Opera House is not what it seems," he said. "We are the owners, but we bend the knee to a stronger force."

The word *force* chilled her. It reminded her of the fortune teller's cards.

"A long time ago the Bellacourts were hungry and poor, and they lived in the empty attic of the Opera House until they struck a bargain with an entity that lived in the catacombs," he said. "My father used to tell me this tale and I'd always thought it was a ghost story meant to spook me and prevent me from exploring the cellar and tunnels below."

A shiver trailed down her back as he spoke. The Opera

House had once been a church and the catacombs had been used to store corpses.

"It was cold and damp down there, and something always stopped me from delving into the shadows; perhaps it was his story or rather some sense of preservation."

"You yelled at me when I went down one day," she said.

She had been fourteen at the time and she had never seen her father so angry. His pale face had reddened to a monstrous shade. Fingers tightly gripping her shoulder.

"You never, ever go down there, Élisabeth!" he roared. "Do you understand?"

It had been so unlike him to lose his composure, that Élisabeth had promised to obey him.

That hadn't been the only time when she'd sensed something amiss about the Opera House. She'd have nightmares often when she fell asleep in the dressing room. A single nightmare on a never-ending loop that only ever plagued her at the Opera House. As if the beings that terrorized her mind were closer there. As if they lived behind the stone walls and underneath the floorboards.

She would find herself drowning in darkness, watching as the opera seats unraveled like it was one giant rug that had been shaken ferociously.

A dark entity would stare down at her from Box Five, watching her with void eyes. The floors were always covered in white roses, their petals stained with blood. And when she'd look at the stage, she'd see Delphine and Louise hanging from an overhead rope. Their necks were crooked, and their vacant eyes stared off into the distance, their limbs lax and stiff as if they had been in that position for a long time. Finally, that slippery, oily voice near her ear would speak to her. Masculine and dark and haunting. His voice had a musical cadence to it like it had been made for sopranos.

"If they are gone, you can have everything you ever dreamed about," he whispered.

Posters unraveled from the broken rafters with her face printed on the glossy cover and beneath the headline were the words in golden script.

Élisabeth Bellacourt
Opening Night
The National Opera House

"You only need to say the word," he breathed. "And all of this can be *yours*."

She could not tear her eyes away from the poster. Big and shimmering and hers. It swayed as if a pair of invisible hands were holding it, and an ache built in her chest. She wanted it so terribly her fingers reached for it as if she could touch it.

"Say the word, and it is yours," he echoed.

She tried to turn her neck to face him, but it was like her muscles were locked in place.

Could it be as simple as a word?"

"Ye—"

A hand shook her awake that day and her father had stood over her, warning her to never sleep in the Opera House again. For some odd reason, she had listened. As if she knew even then that he had saved her that day, saved her from making a terrible, wicked decision. Those vivid, sorrowful dreams had felt so real, so tangible, almost as if she only needed to reach her hand out and capture his promises.

"That day you snuck off to the catacombs; I wanted to protect you from a fate that you did not deserve," her father said. "It preys on fear and weakness and insecurity. It strengthens it like a healing balm pressed upon a festering wound."

"What do you speak of, Father?" she whispered.

In some hidden crevice of her soul, she felt as though she knew the darkness that he spoke of.

"I do not know what he is. Only that he is not human," he said. "My ancestors called him the Phantom."

Shivers wracked down her back.

"What does he want?" she asked.

"We pay a price," he said. "On October the 8th we offer him a soul."

That was three weeks from today.

"Whose soul?" she whispered.

"It varies," he said. "I don't think my parents cared who it was. It is why there is always infamy around the Opera House. A missing debutante, a servant who was never seen again, a violinist whose violin was found abandoned between the aisles. But they happen so far apart nobody has realized what is occurring. You must understand Babette, they had no choice, and their curse has followed me. It is now my burden to carry. Mòrge, give me the strength to bear it!"

Bile coated her throat, and her fingers shook. Élisabeth had a strong constitution. She'd never been someone who fainted over ill happenings or emptied her stomach when she heard a gory tale. But she suddenly wanted to at that moment with the hope that it would satisfy this strange, torn feeling inside her.

"I only send people who are unworthy," her father whispered. Guilt weighed his shoulders down. "Thieves and liars and cruel men who do not deserve mercy. But I grow tired of this curse. I will end it before it ever comes your way, Babette, but you must know in case anything ever happens to me."

"Why don't you just sell it?" she asked. "Sell the Opera House."

"I tried," he said. "But that was when the fuses were

somehow cut, and a fire began on stage. We lost three staff members because I wanted to run away."

As angry as she was that he had kept this secret from her, she could see the pain in his eyes. She remembered how near the end of the year he was always withdrawn. The light in his eyes would fade to wisps of nothing. He always said it was the end of the year accounting and sorting out the books that tired him, but she knew now that it was this looming darkness.

This entity that fed on the misery of the Bellacourts.

Élisabeth reached for his hand, wrapping her fingers around his.

"How can I help, Papa?" she asked.

"Go to Harford," he said. "And don't look back."

"I can't leave you, not now," she said.

"I'm going to end it, Babette," he said. "I will not leave you this twisted legacy. You deserve so much more. You deserve the world."

Élisabeth would not let him lose his life. He was all she had. The one person who had always loved her unconditionally. She would never forgive herself if anything happened to him.

"I won't leave," she said. He opened his mouth to protest. "Not until the 8th. Whatever plan you have I need to know it is safe and that you are well."

He wasn't pleased by this decision, and he opened his mouth to say as much. Élisabeth caught his hand again, holding tight.

"I won't abandon you, Papa," she said fiercely. "Nothing you say will change my mind."

His shoulders slumped. "I should not have told you. I wanted you to know in case I fail, in case I—"

"Shh," she said, frightened by the idea of losing him. "I

don't want to hear another word. You will outsmart it, whatever *it* is. It is no match for you."

She refused to walk away when his life could very well be in danger. October the 8th was close. She had waited long enough for her dreams, and a few more weeks wouldn't hurt.

It hit her then that the fortune-teller had been right.

Her life had indeed taken a bleak and frightening turn.

Chapter Three

It had been two weeks since she'd spoken with her father. She did not know what he intended to do to end this curse on their family. Élisabeth had spent her morning in the chapel behind their manor sitting in the pews as she stared upon the old statue of Pras. There were two statues on the dais. One was a man with clever eyes and beside him was a stag the same height as him. All the High Trinity had an animal form and Pras' was the Silver Stag. They were also known in fables as the Three Kings and were the rulers of the unseen realm before they had spread and conquered other realms.

The city of Prasin had been named after him. Most regions had their preference for which of the three they favored. But here in Prasin, most chapels were dedicated to Pras who was known in the Last Scripture as being something of a trickster. There were tales of him disguising himself as a beggar and punishing those who mistreated him. There had been a time when the High Trinity had existed and ruled the realms but many suspected that they were trapped in the Drowning—a tomb beneath the seas of the unseen realm, leaving the realms to the charge of their chosen Fates. Some heretics had begun to call them the blasphemous title of the "Sleeping Kings."

Painted on the stained mosaic glass were the three Fates. Each of their palms were flat upon the other's palm. In the center, bronze-skinned and glowing was Lune the Unbending, who oversaw the Graylands, the realm of the dead, on the right stern-faced with a long blond beard was Aldéric the Measurer, who oversaw the unseen realm, and on the left was Berthe the Spinner, her raven hair piled in a dark crown, milky skin gleaming like fresh snow and who oversaw the mortal realm.

The wind whistled through the crack in the window, and the spindly branches of the elm tree scraped along the glass with its crooked fingers, as she whispered her fervent words in a circle of hope.

Let him live.

Let us live.

On the days leading up to the 8th Élisabeth noticed that her father had a strangely resolved look in his eyes, and his shoulders were braced as if he were going to war.

"Do you need my help, Papa?" she asked.

She had a performance tonight, but she was willing to skip it to help him with his plan. Élisabeth had debated going down to the catacombs ever since he had told her about the twisted bargain. To break his one rule and see this phantom that haunted them. To confront their adversary and demand that *it* leave them alone. But anytime she climbed down the curled staircase that led to the cellar and she stared at the worn door with the heavy padlock, she'd feel a terrible sense of unease. The hair would stand on end on her arms and her limbs would tremble and she'd have to return upstairs to catch her breath.

Once she worked up the courage again, that same fear would wring her dry once more. It was a vicious cycle of bravery and cowardice, tangled like the laces of a corset.

"No," Papa said. "Focus on your performance."

So, that was what Élisabeth did. She went on the stage, and she performed as she always did. But neither her mind nor her heart was in it. Now that she knew the significance of the night, she could feel this malice in the air. Almost as if the Phantom were here, watching her, rejoicing in her misery. Just before the intermission, Louise stepped on a nail in the floorboard, and her startling cry echoed terribly along the high ceilings. She was quickly ushered towards the velvet curtains by an alarmed Madam Dupont.

The dancers followed their distressed leader and Élisabeth wondered if she should find her father. He was not sitting in the front row as he always did and she assumed he was down in the cellars, confronting the Phantom.

The show would likely be canceled, and refunds would be issued now that Louise was hurt. Élisabeth wouldn't have to face the wrath of Pierre for disappearing.

"Bellacourt," Pierre snapped.

It took Élisabeth a moment to realize he had spoken to her. Louise was "Louise Bellacourt" to him, and she was simply "Bellacourt" as if he could not be bothered to say her full name.

"Yes, sir?"

"You are taking the lead," he said.

"What?" she whispered.

"Are you deaf?" he asked. "Your father is not here so I don't give a damn about his rules. You are leading the rest of this performance."

"What rules?"

"Speak to him about it," Pierre barked. "Change into Louise's costume and take center."

Madam Dupont pulled Élisabeth into Louise's dressing room. Her sister sat in her brocade chair, sniffling away her tears, a crumpled moss-green handkerchief tucked in her fist.

"No," Louise cried when Madam Dupont pulled the dress that she was to wear for the second half from the wardrobe. A beautiful coral number with crystal beading stitched into the bodice and a soft tulle skirt. "She can't wear that, because it is *mine*. I am fine. I can finish."

"And bleed all over the floor?" Madam Dupont demanded. "This is a tale of romance not horror."

"But Élisabeth is not ready for this," Louise said. "She has never led a performance of this scale. There is a delegate of the King's office who is looking for someone to perform at court. It is an important night! Where is my mother?"

"Can't fight your battles without Delphine?" Élisabeth asked with a quirked brow.

"Shut up, Élisabeth," she said. "You will ruin Father's reputation with your subpar performance if you take the stage and sales will plummet. We will never recover. We will be ruined."

"You know what?" Élisabeth said. "I am leaving. I do not need this. Not tonight."

If all went according to plan, she would be on a train to Harford first thing tomorrow morning. Her ticket was booked, and her trunks were all packed. She did not need to hunger for something that was not hers in a city that had never chosen her. It was time to find her father and ensure that his mysterious plan had succeeded. She could scarcely focus without knowing the outcome of this confrontation. Her stomach was tight with worry. She should have gone with him; why did she always obey him?

Élisabeth spun on her heels, feeling a strong sense of determination. She would find her father, and protect him as she should have done. Her steps faltered at the sight of Pierre. His face was red and blotchy, mustache twitching in the way it did when he was livid. The girls would often joke that a rat lived under his mustache, and it only showed its signs of life when Pierre roused it from its slumber.

"Why are you not dressed?"

"Because I just quit," she said. He opened his mouth, but she cut him off before he could get a word in. She would have never done such a thing a few weeks ago but knowing that she was leaving emboldened her. "My father knows. I told him weeks ago. You can end the show."

"Pierre Clement does not cancel his shows," Pierre snapped. He grabbed her by the elbow just as Madame Dupont stepped out with the dress. "Undress her. Here and now."

He released her, turning his back to give her some privacy. She was trapped between him and Madame Dupont who stared down at her like a hawk.

"I will tell my father about this," she warned, as she snatched the dress from Madame Dupont. It didn't take her long before she had unwillingly pulled it on, and Madame Dupont hastily pulled the silk strappings in the back to tighten the bodice.

Pierre led her to the stage and Élisabeth was both nervous and frightened at the thought of leading. Her eyes instantly darted to Box Five. Even though she could never see the mysterious owner, she could always *feel* them. But tonight, there was nobody there and she felt a sense of disappointment. She hadn't even realized that she was comforted by that one regular.

Élisabeth tightened her core, her arms floating fluidly into position. As she spun, her pointe slippers barely seemed to graze the floor. The world blurred as she spun like one of those statuesque horses designed for children and placed on a twirling podium. Her balance was an anchor amidst the storm of motion. She leaped into the air and settled with grace on the polished parquet floor. Sweat dripped down her forehead as she rotated, twirled, and soared. She performed her variations, and the lack of dancers behind her should have frightened her, but she liked dancing alone under the great light fixture.

It made her feel like she was the only person in the world.

Élisabeth felt her mind fall back into that place of hunger and hope and madness. She wanted this so terribly that it hurt. The room fell in silence, and when she completed her final pirouette the crowd stood, the cheers and applause so loud it made her ears ring. Flowers were thrown from the stalls, and orchids and marigolds lay at her feet, surrounding her in a crescent of petals. Their green stems tickled her ankles as she stood front and center. Pierre was beside her holding her hand. Madame Dupont grabbed her other hand and the rest of the dancers joined them.

She felt a trail of tears slip down her face as she stared out at the crowd.

"Élisabeth Bellacourt," he called. "The greatest dancer of her generation."

Pierre rarely praised anyone. His words felt like the grandest compliment she had ever heard.

"I have to go find my father," Élisabeth said when Pierre opened his mouth.

The applause thundered as she made her way backstage, but her joy was short-lived as she thought of her father. Guilt ate away at her, as she rushed through the room that was bustling with aristocratic men in their finest tailcoats embroidered with either their regal crest or the latest floral motifs. All of them were affluent patrons who held season tickets and therefore were permitted access to personally meet some of the famous dancers. Her father had despised the idea when pitched to him by his friend, a fellow business owner, but Delphine had overheard the conversation and thought it a splendid idea. How else would the girls meet honorable matches? She'd said.

"Perhaps someone will tolerate Élisabeth's unfortunate birth and take pity on her," Delphine had added.

"Like my father took pity on you?" Élisabeth had shot back. "I heard you were penniless, and your father could barely pay your dowry because of his gambling debts."

It had been enough to silence Delphine, who hated to be reminded of her humble background.

Someone grabbed her wrist, and she spun around prepared to chastise the fool for stopping her, before her annoyed gaze landed on Charles' brown eyes.

"You were simply marvelous, Babette," he said warmly. "A feast for the senses."

She felt her cheeks heat. It was hard to ignore him when he was so kind and generous with his compliments.

"All my friends have been pestering me for an introduction, but I must admit..." He leaned down with a twinkle in his eyes. He reached for her hand, holding it in the cusp of his smooth palm. "I don't feel much like sharing your company. Would you like to join me for dinner?"

Élisabeth blinked, confused by his invitation. She could see many of the gentlemen on the outskirts looking at her with interest as if they had never seen her before in their lives. The other girls did not seem pleased by their lack of attention. Even though many of them would never gain a proposal from these men, there were a few who still held out hope. Delphine called the girls vultures and prostitutes to seek the men's attention. But it had been her insistence to accept these men backstage, either out of greed to pocket their money or in the hope that Louise would receive multiple marriage proposals.

Louise stepped outside of her dressing room. Her foot was wrapped in a white cloth, and she limped forward on her good one. Her gray eyes instantly shot towards Élisabeth's wrist where Charles held her, and her pale lips tightened.

A gentleman stepped forward, one that she assumed was Charles' close friend, William. Charles had mentioned that he was visiting Prasin at dinner the other night.

"Well, Charles, will I wait all night to make the acquaintance of the woman who stole the show?" he asked.

Her mind spun from the attention. This was the last thing she needed right now.

She could feel Louise glaring daggers at her before she stormed away, likely to find Delphine. It was strange to be the one envied.

Élisabeth opened her mouth to politely excuse herself when Charles began to speak.

"Élisabeth, this is William Fairfax, he is visiting from Harford," Charles said. "William, this is Élisabeth Bellacourt, the woman of the hour."

Around the corner, she caught her father's mop of dark hair as he made his way to the back of the stage where the offices were located. Her stomach flipped with joy. He looked perfectly fine. Perhaps he had broken the curse, and they were all safe.

"Bellacourt!" Pierre barked before she could shake William's offered hand. "My office. *Now.*"

"How about we all have dinner together?" Charles pressed. "Tomorrow night?"

"I'd love to make your acquaintance," William added.

Élisabeth felt dizzy, caught under their rapt gazes.

"Dinner works," she said.

Élisabeth walked down the corridor to Pierre's office. She came to a halt just short of the door, surprised to see her father hunched over Pierre's desk.

The door had been left ajar and Pierre and her father had yet to see her enter.

"What is going on, Pierre?" her father demanded.

"That is the reaction to Élisabeth's performance, your daughter, who has the talent to bring this company renowned fame!" Pierre said. "I do not care what your reasons are for hoarding her like a thief, but I want to focus on Élisabeth."

"Élisabeth is not to take center stage," her father said sharply. "Those are my rules."

Élisabeth felt her heart drop. It sounded like they'd had this argument before. It sounded like Pierre wanted to give her a shot. Pierre believed in her and from the sounds of it, he always had.

"I do not care," Pierre snapped. "Whatever it is—"

Pierre's head turned and her father looked at her. His eyes were wide with sadness and guilt.

"Babette—" he began.

Élisabeth turned on her heel. There was a backdoor that went out to the alley, and she stepped out. Her dress felt unbearably tight. Louise had smaller breasts than her, and the suffocation felt chest-deep, both from the corset and this strange, grating pain that filled her. It was as if her lungs had forgotten how to work.

"Babette, darling," her father said. The door slammed shut loudly behind him. "Slow down. I am too old to chase after you."

Élisabeth knew she should have inquired about the outcome of the curse and the Phantom, but she could not shake off this betrayal.

"Pierre advocated for me and you just...you refused to give me a chance," she said. She felt the hot slide of tears trickle down her cheek. "I always thought it was Pierre who didn't believe in me, but I never suspected that it was my own father."

He winced. "It is complicated, Babette."

"Was it Delphine?" she demanded. "Did she force you to pick between me and Louise? Did she make you cast her as the lead?"

"Of course not," he said. "I was scared."

"Of what?" she yelled. She'd never shouted at him before, and it felt both wrong and satisfying.

"The Phantom," he said. "It took me a long time to realize that it was you that drew him out of the shadows. I was afraid that he'd hurt you or steal you away, so I hid you in plain sight. I told Pierre to not let you lead despite his protests that you were brilliant. I knew in my heart you were simply extraordinary, but I couldn't lose you. You know how much I love you."

There were tears in his eyes. He hadn't cried even when his parents died, and the sight filled her with fear, sympathy, and anger.

"You are my entire world, Babette," her father said. "That is why I refused the Phantom tonight. No more people. No more feeding this beast. I will be a better man and father. You have my permission to go to Harford and if Pierre wishes to follow you, I will end his contract. I want you to soar. To live the life you dreamed of. The one I was too afraid to give you."

Her heart twisted with his words, and she wiped away her tears. It was foolish to be upset with him when he was so distraught. He had done what he thought was best for her and had been forced by circumstances outside his control.

"I forgive you," she whispered.

How could she be angry at him when he looked so small and sad? He suddenly seemed old, as if the weight of the years had caught on to him.

He wrapped his arms around her in a tight embrace and she rested her head on his shoulder, feeling the strength of his grip and assuring herself that all would be well. The worst of it had passed them. Her father had taken a stance, and she was proud of him for it.

"Will he leave us alone?" she whispered. "Are we safe?"

"Time will tell, but you must go and live your life, Babette," he said.

"Will you visit me in Harford?" she asked.

"I'm afraid I will visit so often you will tire of me," he said.

Her mouth softened in a smile, as her fears and doubt floated away until there was only the ripe taste of a fresh beginning.

Chapter Four

Élisabeth stood in the foyer surrounded by all nine of her trunks. Her maid, Charlotte, had said she would have the rest sent to her in a week. Delphine had been sour all morning, both by the positive reception to Élisabeth's performance, and the steady realization that all the capital was intrigued by her. There were rumors that the King's court would be reaching out soon to the ballet company. For a moment, Élisabeth had debated staying, but the idea of a fresh start was far too tempting to resist. Deep in her chest, her father's words had frightened her; she did not want to be the light that lured the dark moth.

Delphine was also rather bitter that Charles' had declined a dinner invitation. Élisabeth had assumed he was upset that she could not join him and William—there had been far too much to do the last few days to spare the time to socialize. More importantly, she didn't have any interest in William even if he was rather handsome. It would be hard to focus on him when Charles was there and that wasn't fair to him.

Louise had blamed all her misfortune on Élisabeth. She

had gone so far as to claim that Élisabeth had planted the nail in the floorboard to steal her role.

The footmen addressed Charles's arrival while she paced the foyer waiting for her father to arrive to wish him farewell. It felt as though she were going on a grand adventure, and she could not ignore the little skip in her heart when she thought of her future. It no longer felt bleak and frightening, but rather bright and hopeful.

"Evening, Babette," Charles said with a wide smile.

"Evening, Charles," she said. "Louise is upstairs, sulking."

She nodded at the servant to go fetch her sister.

"I did not come for Louise," he said.

The servant halted, staring at Élisabeth, as she awaited his next direction.

"You may convey my well wishes when I depart," Charles told the servant.

"Delphine is in the parlor room," Élisabeth said. "*Also* sulking. Perhaps, you wish to brighten her mood."

His eyes widened at the thought of sitting alone with Delphine. She did not blame him, but she could not fathom why he had arrived with no notice if he did not wish to speak to Delphine or Louise.

"Élisabeth, must you twist my hand to reveal my cards sooner than I wished?" he asked. He had that insufferable twinkle in his eye of a man well aware that he was handsome and wealthy, which was a rare currency in Prasin. Most men with true wealth were wrinkled and pockmarked with heavy guts to boot.

Élisabeth had not paid any mind to Louise's despair the past few days that Charles had turned against her. He had sent Élisabeth a large bouquet of red roses the other day congratulating her on her performance. A gesture that had Louise wailing all night.

While such a twist in fate would have had her screaming for joy a few years ago she could not help but be skeptical of it all. Could his attention be so easily swayed?

"William has asked to call on me in Harford," she said. Her voice was cool and aloof. "I may give him the pleasure of my company. He will make a fine suitor, but of course, several others have asked to call on me. I presume the Harford townhouse is simply overflowing with calling cards at this very moment."

Charles grabbed her hand, and a squeal of surprise escaped her when he pulled her along, running to the doors that led to the gardens. Dirt splashed her slippers, and she opened her mouth to chastise him, but he pushed her back along the hedge and she felt the warmth of his lips descend on her.

For a moment, she stilled, surprised by the weight of his mouth, by his hand holding her chin. She was astonished to find that she did not feel the overwhelming desire she had expected. Charles was a good kisser, but it did not awaken a hunger inside her. It didn't make her do anything but raise her hand to his neck. She didn't grip his hair roughly beneath desperate fingers and sway with the feeling of being cherished, nor did she writhe under the hot fingers of desire. It was cold and impersonal.

She felt a strike of disappointment when he pulled away and it dawned on her that she had spent more time building up Charles in her mind. And now the grandeur of her fascinations did not quite match the man before her.

In truth, she realized he was the kind of man who fleeted between sisters depending on who was the most sought-after girl in Prasin. He was a man who wanted the most coveted woman and when that had been Louise, he had doted on her like a besotted suitor. And when Élisabeth had risen to popularity overnight, he had turned to her as if he was merely switching his overcoat, not his woman.

She opened her mouth, but before she could speak a servant ran out. Her hair swayed frantically around her, as she twisted through the hedges.

"Missus," she said breathlessly, not seeming at all surprised by the delicate position she had found Élisabeth in. "Your father...there was an accident at the Opera House. Come with haste!"

Élisabeth's heart dropped to her stomach.

"I have to..." she muttered numbly.

"I'll take you," Charles said. "Get the carriage ready."

He led her outside. Élisabeth felt unbearably cold. She couldn't lose her father. He was all she had. Her fingers shook and she felt Charles hold her hand, but it didn't anchor her. She released his hand, tucking her arms around her stomach during the entirety of the carriage ride, attempting to hold onto the pieces of herself and afraid that if her grip loosened just slightly she would crumble like the dusty flakes of a baked pastry.

Élisabeth ran out of the carriage the moment the door was opened and sped up the stairs tearing through the grand foyer like a storm. She entered the auditorium and was shocked to find him lying on the edge of the stage. Someone had summoned the doctor who was kneeling by him. There was glass, and blood, so much blood. It painted the wooden floor like a blooming red poppy. There were the broken golden arms of the chandelier sitting a few feet away from him, crooked and unhinged from their socket.

"Papa!" she cried, climbing the stairs as fast as she could.

His eyes were closed and his face pale. Glass was stuck in his chest as if he were a pin cushion, and blood seeped beneath his head, staining the wooden floor like a river of death.

"Is he...?"

"He dodged it before it could bludgeon him to death," the doctor said. "He sustained some damage to his head when he evaded it, hence his state, but I believe he will survive, besides some scrapes and surface wounds. If he had not moved in time, I fear that he would not be alive at all."

"How did this...?"

A chill seeped through her bones. She knew the answer before she'd even finished her question. Whatever her father had done last night had angered the Phantom, and this was his punishment.

"I have to go," she whispered.

Élisabeth knew then what she had to do, and her stomach rolled at the thought of facing the darkness that tortured them.

Her father had always worn the key around his neck. The one that opened the door in the cellar that led to the catacombs. She held the blood-covered key, gripping it so tight in her fist it engraved her skin with small teeth marks. The key was large, half the size of her palm, and made of a worn black iron. It looked frightful and gothic and while it was simply a key, Élisabeth could not help but feel a terrible sense of foreboding, caressing it in her palm, as if it were the root of all evil.

She made her way to the staircase that led to the cellar. The room was derelict, cobwebs floated down the ceiling like spring water from a faucet, and discarded barrels of wine sat in the corner collecting dust. Antique boxes of costumes lay atop each other, bent and crooked like an elderly tree, and the faint odor of stale water and moth-riddled clothes filled the air.

At the center of the room was the door with the thick padlock. Dark, weathered wood formed the base, where it had a faded symbol etched across the surface. It was made of intricate lines that looked like an ancient language and tucked between those were vines and serpents that slithered along the letters. She entered the iron key and twisted. The lock clicked and she pried it open to reveal a set of stairs.

The sconces were empty of candles, and Élisabeth found herself submerged in shadows. She could feel inky fingers coil around her throat. For a split second, she had the terrible urge to turn around and flee, but she pushed herself to move forward. The walls closed in, getting thinner and thinner, as though she were being buried alive.

Élisabeth stepped into a cavernous space and to her surprise there was a turbid river that ran in winding lines through the catacombs like a vein. It was a black-green color with a white cloudy film that floated across the channel. It smelled of death and rot. She wondered how the terrible river had existed beneath the Opera House without their knowledge and where exactly it led. Just as she thought this, she felt a strange presence. Something that moved like an oily stain. It was on the other side of the river, its entire form concealed in shadows.

Élisabeth waited for what felt like an eternity for it to speak. At last, when she could bear it no more, she posed her question.

"Are you...are you the Phantom?" she asked.

"What a silly question," he said. His voice was like dark chocolate. Syrupy and thick. Like a hot blanket on a cold night.

"Did you hurt my father?" she asked.

She raised her chin and held her head high as she faced a monster whom she could barely see or understand. In the folktales, it was said that spirits existed in the world. Ones that escaped from the Graylands, the realm of the dead, and returned driven by vengeance and rage. Only those that harbored a wicked intent were strong enough to slip through the cracks of the realm because the realms were stacked on top of each other like a tiered flower cake. The bottom held the Graylands, above it was the mortal realm, and above that was the unseen realm made for divine beings.

"An even sillier question," he said.

"What do you want?" she asked.

"Ah," he said, with a hint of satisfaction. "A question worthy of my ears."

"Enough posturing," she snapped. "Speak plainly."

"Do you wish to save your father from my wrath?" he asked. "After his foolish desire to refuse to fulfill his side of the bargain I have taken matters into my own hands, and decided that he shall not live past the night. I have returned to finish the job."

Fear rooted her to the ground, entangling her in a web of distress.

"I don't want him to die," she said. "Name your price."

"The ferryman will arrive in half an hour," he said. "Give it an earring as payment and it shall bring you to the harbor. I will have someone waiting for you upon your arrival."

She thought she saw a flash of bright teeth.

"I don't understand," she said. "Where does this lead?"

"You will find out soon," he said, rather vaguely.

And then there was only silence.

He had left her alone in this empty catacomb with his vague instructions and this unholy river, speaking words she could not fathom. When he mentioned the ferryman, she had gotten a vivid image of the figure etched into the worn papers of the Last Scripture. The black-robed silhouette of the Shepherd of Death as he led the weary souls to the Graylands.

Her veins ran cold at the thought.

Time felt infinite in the closed, narrow space. The river

followed a serpentine path, disappearing under the archway and into the shadows, making a gurgling sound like a delighted child.

Élisabeth sat with her legs drawn to her chest, awaiting this mysterious ferryman.

Eventually, she heard the splash of an oar and then there appeared a narrow-helmed boat being guided by a figure made of shadow, with empty caverns for eyes. The boat came to a stop beside her and Élisabeth held out her earring as some twisted offering. When his shadowy fingers grazed her hand, it felt like a shock of cold water. He moved aside for her to climb aboard. She sat stiffly on the open belly of the boat while he rowed in solemn silence. She had so many questions. They all pressed together against her head as if a swarm of mosquitoes had slipped into her ear and now resided in the bones of her skull. It was impossible to pluck them apart.

There was an archway ahead that brought them out onto a midnight-blue lake. In the distance, she could make out a deserted harbor. It was strange that there were no other people or boats in sight. Just an emptiness that spanned as far as her eye could see.

The ferryman stopped and Élisabeth couldn't get out fast enough. She practically stumbled onto the wooden dock. She looked out into the distance searching for the person who had been sent to guide her to *him*, to the Phantom. It was strange that the Phantom didn't come to collect her himself or even join her on the boat ride. Perhaps, this was a tactic to frighten her. He had disappeared after he said his piece, so maybe he hadn't even been there to begin with. Maybe this was all a terrible nightmare.

Someone stepped out of the trees. It was a young man. One who was torturously beautiful with lush black hair, a full mouth, and ice-blue eyes. Beside him sprawled on the ground was another man whose neck was twisted at a wrong angle. The sour taste of bile filled her mouth at the sight of the corpse, and a sharp gasp escaped her.

"We need to leave," the young man said. "He will awaken shortly."

"He is dead," Élisabeth said, taking a step back.

"No, he is not," he said. "Just come, I'll explain everything."

"You sound like the Phantom," she said. Their voices were identical. His was beautiful and soothing like a lullaby. Just like *his*.

Suddenly, she felt utterly distrustful of this stranger.

"I am *not* the Phantom," he said. Eyes flaring in anger. "I can help you."

She saw the man beneath him stir. The one that she had been certain was dead. His leg twitched as if the feeling was returning to his flesh, and she knew then that something terrible was occurring before her. The boy could have grabbed her, but he stared at her with desperate eyes, waiting for her to make a decision. It took longer than she'd like, but once the dead man's eyes shot open, she realized he had not lied about the man being alive. Somehow his neck which had been crooked, made a terrible popping sound as it righted itself.

Élisabeth ran toward the boy and snatched his hand. His fingers were freezing. It was so cold almost like she was dipping her hand in a mound of snow. Numbing and tingling all at once. She noticed that he had winced at her touch as if he found it just as discomforting. He led her into the trees just as the man yelled out for them to stop.

The boy yanked her, drawing her close. They ran in the dark. Behind them, she could hear the cracking sound of twigs as the man chased them. It wasn't long before they were spit out onto the cobblestone streets. There were more people here, and it was loud and raucous. The boy pulled her into the crowd of bodies, and she turned back to see if the man had caught onto them, but they had lost him in the stream of people.

"I have a place not far from here," the boy said.

The street looked familiar and when she looked up, she saw the street sign named after one of the Lost Saints. It was said the saints had disappeared when the High Trinity did. The crooked sign read *Sainte Albertine*. It was the same sign she had passed on her trips to the dressmaker and pastry shops.

Somehow, they were in the streets of Prasin. The river had coughed them out into the heart of the city and she felt a sense of relief. For a moment, she had worried that she had fallen into some unknown place. Somewhere that felt nothing like *home*, where shadow-men ferried her across odd rivers and boys cloaked in darkness threatened her father and a dead man awakened without explanation as if his death was one grand performance. It reminded her of those tricks her father would sometimes do, holding a card in his hand and sealing his fist shut, and once he opened it the card would be gone. For a long time, she'd believed it to be magic until he taught her his secret one night while they sat in the library.

"A simple trick of the eye, Babette," he had said.

This had to be another trick.

The boy led her to an old, crumbling building that looked rather ancient even by Prasin's standards. The capital was filled with gloomy buildings cemented with walls of brick as dark as velvet and high vaults. It was rare to find structures that had not been built three hundred years ago. Even the White Palace was only renovated for upkeep; the King was very particular about keeping it in its current state to maintain the tradition and culture of the city.

The front door was peeling, and the paint was thick and layered like an overly powdered face. The boy unlocked it, and Élisabeth stepped inside into a compact space. The stairs creaked beneath them as he led her to the third floor and unlocked his apartment door. The interior was more opulent than she had expected. There was a fireplace concealed behind black bars and a trimmed mirror hung delicately above the mantel with gilded edges that looked like doves. Several art pieces were strewn up on the seafoam blue wallpaper, tilted crookedly across the space like scattered autumn leaves.

He collapsed rather dramatically on the velvet green chaise lounge. Élisabeth sat primly on the opposite chair, back stiff and fingers clasped tightly on her lap.

"Would you like anything to drink?" he asked.

"Some warm lemon tea would be lovely," she said. "With a dash of milk and a teaspoon of honey, if you please."

"I only have wine," he said in a rather dry tone. "Red or white."

"That will do I suppose. Red, please."

The boy went to the kitchen, and she watched as he prepared her drink, making sure he wasn't going to poison her. She had come to a strange boy's apartment, after traveling on a boat that ran under the Opera House that had been steered by a shadowy figure that reminded her of the Shepherd of Death. Nothing made sense. She wondered if perhaps she had been the one hit by the chandelier and her mind was creating these fog-ridden illusions as she slumbered.

"Do you know where you are, Élisabeth?" he asked.

"How do you know my name?"

"Lucky guess," he said, but the words sounded like a lie. "Do you know where you are?"

Her eyes narrowed. She would press that point later.

She did not believe a word from Laurent's mouth.

"Prasin," she said.

"We are not in Prasin," he said. "The second you sat on that boat, you left Prasin."

Élisabeth frowned. He placed her glass on the table before her. His sleeve was rolled up and she noticed that his skin was marked with dark ink. It was that same unknown language she had noticed on the cellar door hidden between the vines and serpents. He followed her gaze and hastily pulled down the fabric, concealing the twisting images and letters from her sight.

"I want to go home," she said. "You must take me back to that harbor."

"That won't be possible," he said. "The Lord of the Below has spies everywhere. It won't be long until they take you to him."

He took a long gulp of his drink. His throat bobbed as he swallowed. He had this strange, haunted look in his eyes as if he had survived a grand nightmare.

"We live in the Graylands," he said. "A purgatory of sorts. Everyone here is dead except for the humans who were sent by the Bellacourts to fulfill the bargain over the years."

"I don't understand," she whispered. "How can the living survive in the realm of the dead?"

"There are gateways that give us access to the world above. There are three to be exact," he replied. "As I said, humans are rare and are used as our thrall. They work in either the brothels or the Lord's court. They are expensive commodities and are in high demand for many reasons, but most of all because their warmth is the closest thing to feeling alive. They don't seem to age once they arrive here. As if time is suspended."

Élisabeth blinked, struggling to wrap her mind around the picture he painted. It was like a dark fairy tale, one that she had no interest in exploring further.

"I see I have shocked you," he said.

His lips tilted in a smile that appeared more mocking than sincere. There was something about him she didn't quite like. He possessed a feral nature that lurked under his polished facade. Like a dog that would chew off its own leg if it set him free.

He wanted something from her. He wouldn't have saved her otherwise.

"So, you are saying that I am trapped here with people who are dead?" she asked, shuddering at the thought. "And humans are nothing but entertainment."

He nodded. "Exactly. I was never one to think much about dying or religious scriptures, but I have been consumed with learning everything I could about this place," he said. He pointed to the wall, and she stared at the sheets of inky paper pinned to the wall. Her eyes widened slightly at the sight of the tilting words written in his frantic handwriting, floating like water lilies across the page.

"I believe it is a pocket in space. A place that exists outside reality and does not go by any length of time. We are all immortal. The Graylands mimics our real world as if it were crafted to be a duplicate but it is run by a force. A force called *aether*."

"My head hurts," Élisabeth said. "Can you slow down?"

"I haven't told you the worst part," he said. "It doesn't matter what bargain you strike with him. You are here which means you are trapped. You forfeited your life the second you came on that boat. The Shepherd of Death only brings souls. He does not return them. And he, like everything here, serves the Lord of the Below."

Fear trickled its icy fingers down her spine. It was like she was stuck in a nightmare. One where the floors made the ceilings, and the ceilings were the floor, and everything was floating around as if a giant's hands had unraveled the weavings that made her life.

"What's your name?" she asked.

"Laurent," he said.

"How did you know my name?"

His mouth twisted as if he were about to share something distasteful. "The Lord of the Below and I are uniquely connected."

"Is the Lord of the Below the man my father calls the Phantom?"

"Yes."

Élisabeth watched him with wary eyes. "In what manner are you connected?"

Anyone who associated with that monster—the Phantom—could not be trusted.

"We are what I call an aberration," he said. He plucked out a coin from his pocket and tossed it in the air as if he needed something to do with his hand. "Aberrations are unheard of in this world. When you arrive, you are dealing with a spectrum of emotions. The realization that you are dead, and everything that comes with it. Sometimes it cleaves the person in half, quite *literally*. It is unbearably painful and when I awoke, he was there, just looking at me, confused, wearing my face and my scars and a crooked version of my grin. Except his eyes were lifeless. *Empty*."

Élisabeth shivered, suddenly feeling a draft. Laurent rose and grabbed a blanket, handing it to her absently. She lifted her cup and felt the bubbles of wine slide down her throat in a slippery path. She took another desperate gulp as if she could erase the taste of all the vile truths he had just told her.

Élisabeth had read a chilling tale once of a farmer who had come out one night to find his sheep and cattle slain, and when he looked beyond the fence all he had seen was a man identical to him, a *shadow walker*, its mouth stained with blood.

"A shadow walker is an omen," she whispered. "In many myths, they are seen as harbingers of doom."

"Nothing good has come from his existence," Laurent said.

He reached towards a drawer in the table and brought out a cigar. "Do you mind?"

He had already lit it when he asked the question which implied it was more about his manners, and that he didn't *truly* care for her response.

"No."

He took a long, slow drag, cheeks hollowing as he sucked in the toxic fumes.

"Do you serve him?" she asked.

"No," Laurent said. "He's been hunting me for as long as I can recall. It makes it impossible to navigate the streets with all his spies."

"Why is he looking for you?"

Laurent's mouth tightened. Smoke slipped from his nostrils in fumes of white.

"To kill me."

Élisabeth blinked in shock.

"You have to return to him, Élisabeth," Laurent said, with a serious expression.

Élisabeth shook her head. "You just said he wants to kill you. What do you think he intends to do to *me*? I want to go home. This was a mistake."

"I told you there is no way home," he said, looking slightly peeved. "Do you not listen?"

"I refuse to accept that," she said.

"You can kill him and see if that helps," he said.

Élisabeth stared at him with her mouth hanging open.

Kill someone? He said the words as if it were akin to taking a trip to the market or distracting oneself with some light embroidery.

"Close your mouth," he said. "Or you'll catch a fly."

She snapped her mouth shut and then frowned, annoyed that she'd obeyed him so quickly.

Now that she looked at him, he seemed tired. There were purple bruises under his eyes and his flesh was so pale it was almost translucent. She could make out the mapwork of indigo veins that ran like a network beneath his skin.

"His existence has been disrupting the laws that govern this place. If he is not killed the Graylands may just become a black hole and swallow the Opera House," he said. "It may destroy your world in the process."

"Why don't you kill him?" she demanded. "You are connected to him, related to him in some perverse way!"

"He is not my child," he said, lips pulling in a snarl. She jumped back and he took a deep breath. "My apologies, I forgot you are a lady. You are just...you are rather infuriating."

"You didn't answer my question," she said. "You simply insulted me."

"I can't kill him," he said. "I've tried. And anybody who I've sent to kill him rarely sur—" Laurent clamped his mouth shut as if he had said too much. "You will need a special blade to do it."

Laurent rose to a stand and walked towards a cabinet. He drew open a drawer and plucked out an ornate box. Sitting on a bed of crimson velvet was a silver dagger.

"Bought this from the black market," he said. "The owner said it could kill the dead."

"If you are dead, how can you die?" Élisabeth asked.

"You ask a lot of questions, Élisabeth," he said. Somehow, she knew those words were not a compliment on her curiosity but rather a dig that suggested he found her to be a nuisance. "And to answer your question we are trapped between the Graylands and whatever lies beyond the Graylands. This is, like I said, a purgatory of sorts. An in-between. There are two ways we can die. One is by the Soulless Ones and the second is by an aether-forged blade. It can poison one and eventually, they will wither to nothing."

There was a screeching sound outside. Something terrible and frightening and beastly.

"He found you," Laurent said. "Or rather his Soulless Ones did. Come!"

Laurent grabbed her hand. His fingers were still shockingly cold as if his temperature did not fluctuate.

Because he was dead. He was a ghost and Élisabeth was trapped here.

"Hide this," he said, giving her the blade.

Élisabeth lifted her dress and slid it into her stockings.

"Look, they won't hurt you," Laurent said, capturing her hand. "But they can't know that we've spoken."

They stepped outside and she noticed that people were fleeing indoors, and curtains were being rapidly shut. She could hear the loud *gong* of multiple bolts being slid in place. The air whistled with a sense of despair, and she was suddenly very afraid of what awaited her on the horizon.

Élisabeth grabbed his hand desperately. "Don't leave me, Laurent. *Please.*"

"I'll try to find a way to see you again," he said. "Be brave, Élisabeth."

She felt something trail down her face. Laurent raised a hand, wiping away the tear with his thumb.

"I'm sorry," he said. "Forgive me."

They were not soldiers, as she had wrongfully expected, but monsters. They floated in the sky, frost covering the windows of the houses they passed. There was a gaping hole in the center of what she presumed were the faces of the creatures and it stretched to make that horrible noise. They were covered in a ribbony sheet of white like the depiction of a ghost in a children's storybook. Except their eyes were hollow caverns of emptiness and their mouths were a stitch of darkness.

They were descending closer when Laurent stepped away from her, hiding behind the alley and diving into the safety of the shadows.

She felt them touch her and then there was only a dark, stifling silence as she fainted.

There was coldness.

So much coldness it drowned her.

And then there was nothing.

Part Two

The Graylands

"My mother, my mother, don't you see?
The spirit who trails me like a stain.
Whose frosty breath tickles my ear,
Mother, mother, don't you see?
He calls me the Spirit-King and he kneels on his bone legs,
Holding a wilted wreath and a blade of silver-ice and to me, he
devotedly begs

The Spirit-King by Arnaud Escoffier

Chapter Five

Élisabeth awoke to a pounding headache. She was in a palatial bedroom. The ceiling was covered in a beautiful mural which was ironic because she was certain she was trapped in her worst nightmare. Silk sheets covered her body, and she realized there was a chain on her wrist that secured her to the bedpost. Only one of her hands was chained, which was a foolish tactic on the part of her kidnappers because Élisabeth was a rather experienced lock picker. A skill she learned as a curious child who lived in an old house with lots of locked boxes and chests. She plucked out her emerald hair clasp and brought it to her mouth, straightening the pin with her teeth. It had a sharp point that would do well as a key.

She pushed it into the keyhole and twisted and turned.

It clicked open and she smiled victoriously.

"Five minutes," a melodious voice called. "And I had been so certain it would take you three."

"La—"

Her mouth clamped shut because the man who stepped forward wasn't Laurent. Physically they were identical in that he had long, darkly luscious hair that fell in thick waves to his nape and lashes that were twice as long as hers. His hair was styled back, and a stray curl fluttered above his forehead, shorter than the rest, which explained why it refused to stay still. A black masque concealed half of his face and his eye on the left side was a milky frost-blue, several shades lighter than the blue on the right as if it had sustained some damage. His masque curved around his full lips.

"Were you going to scream, Lisbeth?" he asked.

His lips were curled in a smile that could only be described as *mean*.

"No," she said.

She would never give him the satisfaction of playing the damsel.

"And my name is Élisabeth, Babette to my friends and family, but you are not granted the pleasure of my pet name. So, you may refer to me as Élisabeth, *not* Lisbeth."

"I will call you what I please, Lisbeth," he said. The words were a slow, lazy drawl. "You will learn soon that I am not someone who is commanded around and certainly not by weak human girls."

"I have come as promised, you said you would leave my father unharmed," she said. "I have fulfilled my side of the bargain."

"I don't recall saying that." He tilted his head. "And besides if I kill him or let him live how will you ever know?"

"Don't play with me," Élisabeth said tightly. "I am not interested in your games."

"A shame," he said, stepping forward.

He rested his hands on the post, his frame tilting forward magnetically. He had the sleek body of a panther. Honed with fine muscle that did not fit the aristocratic intonation of his accent. He was highborn. Or at least he had been when he was alive. She didn't know what death had made of him. Only that there was a cruelty that danced behind his eyes. One that frightened her.

He looked to be a little older than her but not by much. A few years at most, likely twenty or so.

"One month," she said. "One month of service and you free my family from this curse. No more sacrifices. No more tithes. No more contact."

She refused to believe that there was no way back home. He likely controlled the Shepherd and could summon him at will, but he wouldn't tell her unless she offered something in return. A month was a reasonable time to suffer if it freed her father from this curse. He would have done the same for her in a heartbeat.

"How shall we find our thralls to play with?" he asked, raising a brow. "The bargain has been in place since before my rule. The denizens of the Graylands shall revolt."

"No more humans to be used for sport," she repeated sternly. "Those are my terms."

"You overestimate your importance," he said. "You are just a girl. A lackluster one at that."

Élisabeth bit back the urge to insult him. She had to convince him to accept her offer because if he refused, she would have to do as Laurent bid her, she would have to kill him. Her stomach churned at the thought, the cold press of the blade grazing her flesh. A reminder that she would not leave this place without blackening her soul first.

"I am a performer," she said. "I can entertain."

"Are you accepting your role as my thrall?"

"I am not a thrall or a servant," she snapped. "I come from a noble family, the Bella—"

"Do not put me to sleep, Lisbeth," he said in a bored tone. "I don't like impassioned speeches or tantrums."

"Well, what *do* you like?" she asked, voice tittering with sarcasm.

The Phantom smiled. A vicious pull of his mouth that made shivers roll down her spine. He was nothing like Laurent. They merely shared a face. Two sides of the same coin, but while one was polished silver, the other was covered in grime and mold.

"I am an impossible man to please," the Phantom said, disregarding her question. "But I have seen you perform; you are half-decent."

An angry flush crawled up her cheek. "Half-decent?"

"That was me being generous."

"What would you know about the world of ballet and art?" she asked, wrinkling her nose. "You are dead. You are *nothing*. You are less than no—"

"Have you met my wraiths? The Soulless Ones?" he asked. "The smoky figures who brought you to me. Shall I teach you your first lesson about this realm? The wraiths are the only creatures that can erase a person. They feed off one's life force and they are made to do my bidding. Once they have consumed your soul, you are gone. Trapped in a vacuum of infinite darkness and madness. For all of eternity."

Élisabeth heard that terrible screeching sound as if they had been summoned by the mere mention of their name. She could see them floating outside the oval window, pressing their blank faces to the glass. Frost coated the surface where their breaths touched, leaving behind a shining gleam. Her fingers trembled and she folded them under the fabric of her dress in case he noticed the effect his words had on her.

"Shall I permit the Soulless Ones to devour you?" he asked.

He took a step forward as if he intended to unlock the window. Her heart jumped in her throat, making it nearly impossible to swallow. She was putting on a brave front, but she was scared. More scared than she had ever been in her entire life.

"What do you want?" she asked between clenched teeth.

"Respect," he said. "And acceptance of your fate. Forget this attempt to bargain, it is a waste of your time. You do not tempt me enough to truly sway me. You do not hold any power here. It will save you much heartache if you accept that."

He walked towards the door, seemingly done with their conversation.

The door clicked shut ominously behind him.

In his absence, a servant girl entered the room, her head bowed down so low it was a wonder she did not cave inward. Her small and mousy frame made her appear more fragile like the softest wind could blow her away. It was a cruel reminder that this was not a nightmare she would wake up from. This was now her reality.

Élisabeth felt something wet slip from her eyes and she wiped it away furiously. She refused to cry, to acknowledge the fact that she had just realized she had run headfirst into danger, and now didn't have the upper hand any longer. Why hadn't she bargained with him before she came on the boat? Why hadn't she waited for her father to wake up to learn more information? Why hadn't she forced Laurent to protect her instead of feeding her to the wolves?

She had always been impulsive, and headstrong, but she would need better skills now to survive this world of ghosts and monsters.

She could feel the weight of the blade strapped to her lace stockings. The only weapon left to defend herself.

Élisabeth was no murderer, but she would have to cast aside her morals if she had any hope of outsmarting her enemy.

Her long hair was brushed down to the small of her back. The loose tendrils framed her face like the drapes of a curtain. She had tried to speak to the girl, but it wasn't until she had pointed to her open mouth that Élisabeth had realized her tongue was severed. Her stomach churned as the girl dressed her in silence, working with quick, icy fingers. It made her wonder if *he* had done it. And then she felt sick all over again.

A small sigh escaped the girl at the feel of Élisabeth's flesh as if her warm skin soothed her. Her hand would graze Élisabeth's shoulder and spine and it would feel as though someone had blown a cold breath along her body. A reminder that the girl behind her was dead. That Élisabeth was living with ghosts, and the thought had sickened her.

She had been fitted into a tea rose-pink ballet dress. It stopped mid-thigh, and she wore pale white stockings and matching slippers. She felt like a marionette. Something that belonged to someone else, not to herself. It was just her luck that right when she intended to chase the life she dreamed of, everything would take a terrible turn.

She didn't know what to make of *him*. The Phantom. While his smile was cold and scornful, his eyes were empty. Almost as if someone had erased every feeling from the surface. Laurent's eyes had been the opposite. They had been filled with hope, exhaustion, and intelligence. She thought of what he had said about them both having once been a single person and she shuddered. It was like a chapter straight from a gothic tale. One that she had no intention of reading.

She wondered if she'd ever see Laurent again. He promised he'd find her and she hoped he kept his word.

"Can you write your name?" Élisabeth asked. She held out her forearm. "Do you want to spell it here with your finger?"

The girl seemed surprised by her question. As if nobody had ever asked her name before. It took her a moment before she ran her finger over Élisabeth's arm, slowly spelling out each letter.

"Colette," Élisabeth said triumphantly. "That is a beautiful name."

Colette smiled timidly before she nodded to the door. There was a man outside. One with dark hair that looped in beautiful curls and smooth brown skin. Dimples pierced his cheek when he smiled.

"Good evening, madam," he greeted.

"Who are you?" she asked warily.

"General Dakarai but everyone calls me Kai," he said. "I lead the Lord of the Below's armies."

"Why would he need an army?" she asked.

Kai offered his elbow. Élisabeth hesitated for a split second. He smiled again, revealing those twin dimples in his cheeks. He seemed rather harmless, so she accepted. It was impossible not to notice that his offering was not entirely selfless. He seemed to sigh a little when he felt the warmth radiating from her skin. As if she were a walking furnace. Colette had reacted the same way when she'd touched her.

"Territory wars," Kai said, answering her question about the need for an army. "They crop up every once in a while, not to mention the beasts that have been crawling out of the Pit."

"The Pit?" she asked.

"It is a hole that forms often in the woods. It appears unexpectedly and when it does a swarm of beasts climb out. Ones straight from the pages of the Last Scripture," he mused. "The kinds made of old magic."

Her eyes widened in disbelief.

"No need to be afraid, madame," he said. "I am a sworn protector of the Graylands. You are safe with me."

"But am I safe with *him*?" she asked softly.

"I cannot say," Kai said. He didn't ask her to clarify. He

knew *exactly* who she spoke of. "Just don't attract too much attention and he will lose interest. He often does."

"You may call me Élisabeth," she said.

"Élisabeth then," Kai said. "Welcome to the Graylands."

They passed beautiful hallways hung with tapestries of forests and glades and elegant walls with golden molding and marble statues. There were gilt-bronze mounts on decorative bureaus. Long, spindly candlesticks sitting on grim-looking candelabras coated in the gossamer fingers of spiderwebs. The palace was both vibrant and decrepit, not by neglect as there were many servants, but rather a sense of preservation. As if it were holding onto the past with iron fingers.

"Are you from Tezrik?" she asked. His words had a unique accent marking him as a foreigner. Not to mention that anyone from Annthès tended to be frightfully pale and Kai was anything but.

"Ey," he said. "From the south-east coast of Ranova."

"I have been practicing speaking Lupazi—I heard it shares similar vowels and accents to Ranovi," she said a bit too eagerly, switching from speaking Annthèsian. Her mother was born on the eastern coast of Lupaz which bordered Ranova and she'd learned it to honor her.

The continent of Annthès spoke a single tongue to make trade and inner-continental flow easy. But in Tezrik every country spoke its own unique dialect.

She spoke to him in Lupazi, her words cautious and slow, ensuring she accentuated every vowel correctly. "When my father told me my mother was from Lupaz, I bought some old books and taught myself to speak it."

"Your dialect is similar to mine. I can understand you fairly well," Kai said, seemingly pleased by this knowledge. "It is nice to meet a fellow countrywoman."

"How are you here?" she asked. "I thought it was just the people from Annthès or was I wrong?"

"There are three portals in the Graylands that bridge into the three continents. One leads to Annthès, one to Tezrik, and one to Sakrane. Each exit sits on a ley line which is a place of power. In Prasin it is the Opera House, in Sakrane it is the cellars of an ancient ruin and in Tezrik it is the old water temple of Hashren, the sea deity. Somehow the Graylands is a middle ground for all mortals regardless of birthplace. Some streets resemble the old, compact structures of Annthès, some streets have the bright vibrant coloring that echoes the Tezrikan architecture, and others the stark fortresses and keepings native to Sakrane."

In the foyer was a statue of Mòrge the Misfortunate One in his animal form. The giant stone crow stood like a sentry; wings spread widely. It's one immortal eye staring at the front door. Mòrge was also called the Keeper of the Dead.

"I didn't know the dead were faithful," she said.

"We are," Kai said. "We also believe in the Three Fates, but mainly Lune the Unbending who is Keeper of this place. We follow the same belief in the Holy Trinity in Tezrik, but they have different names depending on what country you are from."

They finally came upon a pair of ornate doors. She could hear the loud hum of voices and the delicate sound of an orchestra. She knew exactly who stood behind this door. The person who had her dressed to come and trot at his pleasure like a racehorse.

Élisabeth stumbled backward. The movement was futile because Kai's grip was unbreakable.

"Shhh," he whispered. "You must not show your fear, Élisabeth."

"Who is he?" she whispered back, soft as a feather.

"He has many evolving titles and the most common is The Lord of the Below, but ever since he began to command the wraiths the locals have taken to calling him the Spirit-King."

Élisabeth swallowed, unwilling to face that monster again.

Shall I permit the Soulless Ones to feed on your soul?

What if he called those frightening monsters to her? What if they ripped her to ribbons and devoured her?

Élisabeth dug her feet in, refusing to take another step forward.

"I don't want to drag you in there, Élisabeth," Kai said calmly. "He said to carry you in if you put up a fight."

Élisabeth took a shaky step forward. She didn't know what to expect when the two footmen in their midnight-blue livery opened the doors. On their sheepskin coats was embroidery of an obsidian crow, the body of which came together at the seam so one wing spread on either side. The single, frightful eye watched her like the moon. Cold and relentless.

Chandeliers dripped with crystals, reflecting golden light that multiplied when it flickered along the gilded mirrors. The rustling sound of silk unraveling as the courtiers partook in some licentious kissing made her eyes widen. Élisabeth stood in front of what could only be described as a den of hedonism The powder around the women's mouths had gone thin, revealing their muted skin. Some of the guests spun around the marble floor, men in fine-tailored coats of silk brocade in the favored colors of last season, as if time moved slower here. Women in gowns of amethyst and crimson designed with silk taffeta spun like peacocks.

There was a stage that had been built in the center of the marble floor. And tucked in the corner was an orchestra that held their instruments with calloused fingers. It looked like some of them were bleeding. The blood struck their instruments in a ghastly manner that spoke of neglect and cruelty.

On the dais was the man they called the Lord of the Below, who sat upon a black high-back chair that looked very much like a throne. Two servants knelt on the floor before him. A blond-haired girl and a boy. They looked like they were no older than her and were most likely siblings. Their hands were curled possessively over each of his legs like a pair of starved kittens who fed on his attention.

"Ah, she is here," the Phantom called. "Our treasured ballerina."

Polite claps ensued as avid eyes turned to her. Élisabeth held her chin up high, refusing to cower. The residents of his court looked like flesh and bone. They were not translucent and misty as she had once expected the dead to be. Just frightfully and unbearably cold, as if their bones were made of ice and their souls carried the first breeze of winter. Their faces were unnaturally pale and bloodless. Almost ghoulish. Even Kai's dark skin had a strange, unearthly gray tint to it. As did the other courtiers with brown skin. It was a deviation of all that was good and holy.

Kai released her.

"Go on then," he said, pointing to the stage. "Do not be afraid."

She walked to the stage. Her steps were slow and dragging. She had not received any instructions on what she was to perform. Simply dressed and drawn forward like a guilty person being pulled towards the executioner's axe.

She felt doomed.

The Phantom sat in a lazy sprawl with his desperate servants clinging to him. It took her a moment to realize that some people were marked with a beautiful, bejeweled collar. It took her a bit longer to understand that it was only the humans who had been shackled as if they were expensive chattel. Élisabeth swallowed heavily. She did not want that collar. She would slice her head off before she let them contain her like a wild beast.

The Phantom's ruby lips twisted in a cruel smile as if he could read her like a book. As if he could see the disgust and fear in her eyes.

He snapped his finger, and the orchestra began. It was the opening key of *Dark Dreams*, a tale of a girl trapped in a slumber who fell in love with a man who was nothing but a figment of her mind. It was one of her favorite numbers, and when the vocalist sang the first note, Élisabeth found herself lost in the tale. She spun, allowing her body to feel the rhythm of the music in her bones. She felt that blurry, hazy, almost feverish quality of being lost in a performance and feeling herself embody the character. She could feel the audience getting closer to her, swarming around the stage like ants who'd stumbled upon a crumb. She jolted when a hand touched her ankle. And then there was another hand on her knee like spiders were crawling on top of her. Their desperate, cold hands swallowed her warmth leaving behind nothing but a sticky, damp feeling. She stumbled backward but she miscalculated and lost her footing. She felt them descend on her like a pack of wolves and a scream escaped her.

"Enough," the Phantom called.

The words were a slow, careless drawl, but they jumped away from her as if he had whipped them. Their eyes were slightly wide with fear, and she realized then just how monstrous he had to be for him to rule these vicious people. He was the king of ghosts. And Élisabeth was nothing but his prey. She had never felt so weak before, like a house made of old bones that would crumble at the faintest whisper of the wind. Her fists tightened, anger slithering down her nape like a serpent.

Laurent's words floated through her mind as she glared at

the man who ruined her life. Maybe he was right, maybe there was no other way to escape this cursed place unless she killed the Phantom.

She had been so close to leaving to escaping to Harford, starting a new life, and watching her dreams unfold.

But now all her dreams had been reduced to ashes.

Élisabeth arose on shaky legs and bowed, concluding her performance. She walked to the corner where the eclectic arrangement of food sat. Trolleys with all manner of meats sat on a silver platter: braised lamb, veal tongue, meat pies, beef tenderloin, and roasted chicken. Then there was the turtle soup wafting a delicious scent of clove and nutmeg on another cart. Her stomach tightened as she tried to take as much as she could. It had been hours since she'd last eaten. The dull thud of her stomach had tightened to a pain that felt like someone was stabbing her continually with a dagger. She slipped a long breadstick under her arms, intending to brandish it as a sword if anyone came too close.

"The servants will serve you," his smooth, sensual voice whispered. Élisabeth had been so distracted with taking as much as her hands could carry that she had not noticed him leaving his throne to stand behind her. "No need to grab the food like a thief."

Élisabeth tilted her head to face him. She could feel everyone watching them while pretending to do otherwise. Slowly, unwillingly, she put down her food, except for the bread— that was her weapon.

He raised a brow. "Intend to bludgeon me with that?"

"I don't know if it will work on your thick head," she snapped. "But I am willing to try."

He did not rise to the bait of her insult and simply walked ahead to an empty table.

"We must discuss your purpose in my court," he said. "Sit."

He pointed to the chair across from him while Élisabeth remained standing, just to be difficult.

"I said sit, Lisbeth." His voice was gentle, but there was a thread of warning.

When she didn't move his next response was a direct threat.

"Shall I call my wraiths?" he asked softly.

Élisabeth's lips tightened, and she roughly pulled out the chair and sat down with her arms folded miserably across her chest.

"Good," he purred. "*Very* good."

The servants brought her five courses ranging from appetizers to desserts. And she felt a tickle of shame for acting like a common thief, the buffet was meant for the servants to pile on food for the guests.

"Why are you doing this?" she whispered. "Why do you hate me so much?"

She accentuated this question with a gulp of soup and winced when she burned her tongue. She poured a cup of red wine and sipped heartily. It was all very unladylike of her, but she didn't care to posture before him. She hoped it disgusted him. A glance at his eyes told her he was more amused. The brief flicker disappeared when she met his gaze and his mouth swiftly tightened.

"I despise all of you Bellecourts," he said. His eyes burned as he practically spat the words. He said her surname *"Bellacourt"* like it was foul. As if it sat on his tongue like rot.

He wore a simple black masque that night. One that made his blue eyes shine like gems. He was dressed as a gentleman in a black fitted tailcoat, its brass buttons adorned with that same crow sigil, a cobalt waistcoat, and black trousers. His cravat was loosened as if he could not bear the mask of civility for long. His dark hair had been slicked back with mousse except for that one stubborn lock that dangled above his eye. His polished demeanor hid his vileness and cruelty like a seashell. "They have cost me *everything*. And you will pay the price."

"What do you speak of?" she asked. "My father has not hurt a soul. Or are you referring to my grandparents?"

"That is four questions in two minutes," he said. "I have come to lay down the ground rules. Not to have a conversation. You understand the hierarchy of this place, correct?"

"Ghosts are on top, and humans are no better than cattle," she said.

"Good," he said. "You are a smart girl, Lisbeth. I must warn you against any attempts to escape. An unmarked thrall does not make it beyond a fortnight outside of these walls. The dead hunger for their warmth. They have torn humans limb from limb in their desire to feel an inkling of joy. You will be descended upon much like tonight. You will require a mark to remain safe."

Élisabeth realized then that this was simply one of the many cycles of life. It made sense that the dead longed for the one thing that they did not possess. They ached to feel the hot, rhythmic flow of blood traveling through their empty veins and the golden spark of heat that belonged only to the living. They lived but they were not alive.

"I won't wear a collar," she said, shaking her head furiously. "You will have to sever my head."

"So dramatic," he said with a click of his tongue. "You will be aether-marked. Only high nobles are permitted to aether-mark their thralls. It implies that you are above other humans and will be brought to court if found."

His hand lifted and something with a white-gray hue drifted from his fingertips. It slithered in the air and locked around her throat like a seal. Her fingers tried to grasp it, but they slipped through the wisp as if it were air, even though she could see it. The silvery trail of it remained coiled around her neck. It looked like a necklace with no adornment and fluttered around her throat as if it had a mind of its own.

"Only the dead can see aether," he said. "It is invisible to the living."

"Then why can I see this ugly silver rope around my throat?" Élisabeth snapped. "Take it off! *Now*."

"That is impossible," he said tightly. "No human can see aether."

"I saw it leave your fingers and wrap around my throat," she said. "It is right here!"

His frown deepened. And he rested his elbows on the table, leaning forward.

"You can see it? Truly?"

"Why would I lie about such a thing?"

He looked across the room and curled his finger. Kai left the wall he was leaning on, striding forward. He wore a midnight-blue soldier's coat with black lapels that she presumed signified his regiment color. Other soldiers had burgundy lapels, and a few had silver and some ivory. All of them carried rifles across their backs and stood around various intersections of the Great Hall. It didn't make sense why this place would have soldiers or an army for that matter. Or require weapons. Kai had mentioned something about beasts and her skin crawled at the mere thought.

Kai leaned down and the Phantom whispered something to him. Then the Phantom arose and Kai took his seat.

"Finish eating, Élisabeth," Kai said. "I have a few questions for you when you are done."

Dread filled her stomach, and she knew then that whatever she just said had cast a net of suspicion on herself. It was not what she had intended. Her goal had been to find the perfect time to plunge the blade Laurent had given her into the Phantom's chest and return home.

From Kai's serious expression, whatever the Phantom had shared had erased any ease that she had witnessed earlier on his face.

He looked like he would not rest until he discovered *exactly* what she was hiding.

Chapter Six

He had a name.

One that he had given himself after the incident. He had let the bastard keep their birth name, *Laurent*. In his mind, he called himself *Séverin*. It was sharp and swift. Ruthless and cutting. Something that fit him. Something that belonged to him.

Laurent liked to think he was the original and Séverin was an evil mirage. He liked to think of Séverin as an imposter. Séverin may have carried a different name but he *was* Laurent Moreau. He had all his memories and feelings, dreams and nightmares. And most importantly, he had the scars. Laurent had their old face before the tragedy which was why his theory could not be upheld. How could he be the *true* Laurent if he didn't even have the pain to mark his flesh?

Laurent simply existed now as a grim reminder of his past. Of whom he had been before his life took a miserable turn.

Séverin had been born in the countryside of Normey, not far from the capital of Prasin as Laurent Moreau. He had been the son of a marquis and had been raised in great esteem. His family had been less than perfect; they were a flock of vultures, feuding over land and status. It was why he navigated the politics in the Graylands so easily. He had grown up in a nest of vipers, therefore he had become one himself.

He had fought for the title of the Lord of the Below from the previous ruler, and it had only been because of his strong ties to aether, the power that ran the Graylands, and his mysterious control over the wraiths that had gained him the fear and respect of the people.

Séverin made his way down to the barracks. Around him were cells filled with traitors. The dead could heal their flesh rapidly which made torture a messy and ongoing process. Most of his prisoners were spies from the quarters.

There were four quarters, each overseen by his choice leaders: the Quarter Masters. He had picked them based on who was moving the most weight in those territories. Madame Yvette managed half the brothels on the streets so he'd given her the First Quarter, Florent pushed cigars and smoking pipes woven with aether that acted as a strong hallucinogen into the streets on the Second Quarter, Arata handled weapons on the Third, and Oratile one of the veteran dead who had been here for centuries managed the Fourth Quarter.

Sometimes the Quarter Masters liked to poke at his control and send their spies. They were always fighting over territory like children tugging a toy back and forth. He liked to stay out of it, refusing to pick a side, so they'd often send spies to keep an eye on him who he would then capture and torture. It was a vicious cycle, but it kept things interesting. Séverin did rather fancy organized chaos every once in a while.

He made it to the end of the narrow tunnel and opened the door to the interrogation room. Kai sat across from her with a notepad and a fountain pen, jotting down notes.

Élisabeth Bellacourt's gaze was venomous when she looked

at him. She appeared out of place in the dark, windowless room in her pink dress and long, flowy chestnut-brown hair. She was a pretty girl. A fact that he hated he noticed. High cheekbones, stormy gray eyes, and olive skin. Exactly, the kind of girl he would seduce for a night and forget the next morning.

"Why am I here?" she demanded. "I did nothing wrong."

"I can take over, Kai," he said.

Élisabeth sighed so deeply and dramatically that it grated on his nerves. She had little sense of self-preservation. She was caustic and defiant which both angered and fascinated him.

Kai arose. "Can we speak for a minute?"

Séverin stepped outside and Kai followed him.

Séverin had known Dakarai since he was five years old. Kai had stayed at his family home most summers. His father was a diplomat from Tezrik who was good friends with Séverin's father. While Kai's father attempted to bridge the shaky negotiations of reopening trade which had been sealed for decades after the Five-Year War, Kai would spend his days with Séverin pretending to be soldiers while they chased each other in the nearby forest. Kai had tried to save his life on Séverin's last night among the living. He was the last face Séverin saw before he died. Kai had said the smoke from the fire had burned his lungs, and he joined him not long after in the Graylands.

He died for me.

"Do you think she is a spy?" Kai asked. "For whom?"

"I'm not certain," Séverin said. "But she claims she could see the aether mark I left on her."

Humans could not see or access aether. Aether was the fuel that ran the Graylands. It was a thick, viscous substance that existed around them, and perhaps the closest thing to magic that he had ever seen. It possessed unique properties and could be harvested to become substances that clouded the mind. But it also could be honed into raw power. With aether, he could throw someone across the room with a mere rise of his palm or shatter their insides by simply closing his fist. Not all the dead could use aether to such an extreme. Most could do little parlor tricks, but a rare few like him could do far more.

"The Bellecourts are scum," Séverin said darkly. "I would not have put it past her father to have recruited her in his schemes. He attempted to sever the bargain forged by the first Lord of the Below. He likely thought because I was younger than the rest, I would accept it with no retaliation. Who knows what other foolish decisions he has made since then? Perhaps one of the Quarter Masters came to the catacombs and proposed an alternate offer and he sold the girl to the highest bidder. Maybe she knows far more than we think."

He was certain she could not see his aether. But she knew enough about it to describe it and confuse him.

"She seems innocent," Kai said. "I do not suspect her of such duplicity."

Kai had always had a soft spot for women. He had grown up with seven sisters, of course, he thought the girl was innocent.

"I do not trust her," Séverin said. "She is pretending that she can see aether."

"Test her then," Kai replied.

"Not a bad idea. Wait here."

"Do not kill her, Séverin," Kai said.

Séverin's lips raised, and he saw Kai's brown eyes fill with wariness. He knew that smile. He knew that it meant doom. Even after all these years as friends, Kai did not know him. Not fully. Nobody did.

And that was just the way Séverin liked it.

Élisabeth was pacing the room when he entered. Her movement abruptly stopped when the door sealed shut behind him.

"I would like to speak with Kai," she said in her finest highborn voice. Her chin was raised, hands neatly folded before her. The pale pink ribbon in her hair fluttered in the air, mimicking a waving hand. "If I must answer these silly questions then I will do so with him."

"Afraid of me, Lisbeth?" he asked. His words were a dark purr.

Even though her eyes were filled with misplaced courage, her shoulders shook with nerves. He supposed he could admire her forced bravado. Not many people could look him in the eye and talk back to him. Not if they intended to live to tell the tale.

He summoned aether to his fingers and molded it into a ball of energy.

"Can you see this?" he asked.

"No." She was lying, he knew it. She looked at his opposite hand as if to prove a point. He held the ball of aether in his right and her face had turned to the left to trick him. It proved he could not trust a single word from Élisabeth Bellacourt's devious mouth. She was no better than her father.

"That is too bad," Séverin said. "Because when I throw this at you it will break every bone in your body. If you could see it, you could dodge it, but..." He shrugged. "Goodbye, Lisbeth."

He flung it at her like a wayward lance, and she jumped to the opposite side of the room. It crashed through the wall, smashing the brick into rubble and dust. A gaping hole stared at him and Élisabeth stood on the other side, eyes wide, chest rising and falling rapidly.

"You sick bastard," she said. "You could have killed me!"

"Who taught a girl of noble birth to speak so filthily?" he asked.

"Your mother," she spat.

"That was a stupid thing to say, Lisbeth," he said darkly. "I am rather fond of my mother."

He forged another ball of aether.

"I'm sorry," she said hastily. "I can see your magic. I can evade it."

"This is not a test," he said. "This one is personal."

He aimed it at her once again. She was quicker than he expected. All those years of dancing helped her move with both grace and speed. A flush spread from her collarbones as the wall cracked, fissures running through the brick like the many tentacles of a spider. The door opened and Kai entered, concern etched on his face.

"I didn't summon you," Séverin said.

"I know, my lord," he said. His tone was the proper one he used when they weren't alone. "Is everything fine?"

"Kai, he is mad, he should be locked up, please don't—"

"What did you call me?" Séverin asked.

"Élisabeth do not say such things," Kai chided. "Perhaps we should put a pin on this and pick it up tomorrow. Tensions seem to be running high."

Séverin looked at Élisabeth expectantly awaiting her next set of foul words. She glared at him with such poison it would have burned a lesser man to ashes. She had a rather unique ability to insult him with her eyes alone. Anyone else and he would have carved them for the disrespect. But hers were a unique gray color that reminded him of a rainstorm, and he had always enjoyed the more temperamental weather, when the clouds darkened, and the skies burned with vengeance.

"Tomorrow then," he said. "Bring her to the courtyard at sunrise."

Séverin made his way to the library. It was the oldest room in the Black Palace (a little twist to the naming of the White Palace in the mortal realm). It had been maintained by the last holder of the Seat and was in relatively good shape.

The library smelled of dry ink and shrunken leather broken down by time. Some of the books were so old he wondered if they would crumble to powder in his palm. It was grand with high ceilings and exquisite murals depicting the tumultuous sea and the creatures it protected. Row upon row of goatskin-bound books lay on flat shelves and some special volumes were tucked behind glass cases with fancy latticework. His boots sunk into the thick, floral carpet, the color of a sliced grapefruit.

The library was overseen by the Farrows, a mother-and-daughter duo. The Farrows had been here before he arrived and said that they were the keepers of the Great Library and would continue to be so until the end.

Clarise Farrow was standing on a ladder, hanging precariously off the side. She'd broken her hip before but since their injuries tended to heal overnight it didn't make her exercise any caution.

She looked nothing like what one expected of someone in the field of librarianship. For starters, she had been a convict. Served four years, for what crime he could not say. He'd asked and she simply said she'd tell him one day.

Unlike Kai who enjoyed guessing everything from "she stole a rare jewel" to "she murdered her husband" Séverin did not care enough to attempt a guess.

She had ink markings on her skin, no different from the ones people carried when they survived imprisonment at The Ironhold. One of Prasin's infamous jails.

"My lord," Clarise said. "You make no sound when you move."

"How else will I get people to believe I am omnipresent?" Séverin asked.

Clarise climbed down the ladder. Her steps were slow and cautious.

He'd met Clarise the night he'd taken the palace after he killed Antoine, the last Lord of the Below.

He had burst into the library that night and behind him were the shrieking wraiths, floating in their ribbon-like robes, mouths open wide in hunger. Clarise had come to him, protectively standing before her young daughter Inès, unafraid of the monsters who followed him.

"Laurent Moreau," she had said. Those frail, calloused fingers of hers brushed back his hair. "It is a pleasure to meet you. I am Clarise Farrow, Keeper of the Great Library."

Séverin had flinched when he heard his birth name.

"So young but filled with so much pain," she had said after that presumptuous introduction. "I am sorry, Laurent Moreau."

"You don't know me," he snarled. "Give me one good reason I shouldn't kill you. And my name is Séverin. *Lord* Séverin to you."

"Because our destinies are intertwined," she said. "And I possess the Sight."

His mouth tightened at that revelation. Seers were rare and she likely knew he wouldn't hurt her for her rare abilities.

"Calm down," she said gently.

Her hand brushed his hair again. It was futile. That thrice-damned lock of hair refused to behave. Even the costliest pomade could not keep it slick. Clarise reminded him of his mother. Gentle and soft. Her eyes were bright with kindness and something in his chest had stirred at the touch. Something that had bound him to her that night for better or worse.

"You will kill more before the night ends," she said. "But we are not part of your slaughter. Go do what you must do."

"You won't plead with me to spare them?" he asked.

"No," she said. "My words will not change your course."

Séverin swatted her wrist away, ending that gentle, unnerving touch.

"The next time you touch me I will carve your arm off, understand?" he bit out.

Their skin could heal from wounds, but they could not regrow lost limbs. It was one of the many mysteries that plagued their world.

Clarise had looked at him with a certainty that he would not harm her. And he had been tempted to prove otherwise.

But for some reason, he did not.

Clarise and her daughter Inès had possessed the Sight ever since they arrived in the Graylands. Their eyes had a strange silver halo surrounding the pupil. A marker that they had aether in their blood. Clarise and Inès were aether-touched, unlike most people who were aether-bound. People who were aether-touched were easy to spot by their eyes because their gifts were often mental such as the ability to see into the future or to create illusions. It was incredibly rare for someone to be aether-touched. Whereas people who were aether-bound could physically control aether. Séverin had an aptitude for both principles of magic. Though his physical abilities far surpassed his mental skills.

Clarise had predicted not long ago what Séverin had suspected for quite some time, that the Graylands was unraveling. Clarise said that the balance had been broken and that was the cause of the recent disorder.

The Pit grew an inch wider every day. Many months ago, the hole had been the size of his foot, and the beasts that had escaped resembled serpents with slick bodies that emitted a deadly poison. It had grown steadily wider, and the beasts had mutated. Some possessed wings which made tracking them increasingly difficult and others were the size of grown bears. The wards he had placed on the Pit were like applying gauze to an infection that was slowly eating away at the limbs of the person. The woods grew sickly and diseased as the days progressed. The denizens of the Graylands called it the Blight and it was spreading faster than expected. It was like the aether that coated their world had rotted and turned into something caustic.

"It is getting worse," he said. "Holding up these wards is tiring me."

Inès slipped out from behind the bookshelves, a lily tucked behind her ear and her spectacles half sliding down her nose.

"Good afternoon, my lord," she said cheerily. "Where is Kai?"

Her eyes darted behind him as if she would find the lanky silhouette of his second-in-command. Kai and Inès had this strange situation where both were interested in the other but none of them had the strength to speak it. Séverin found it utterly repulsive. So, he simply ignored it and pretended as if it did not exist, as he did most subjects that he found distasteful.

"Have you found a solution?" Séverin demanded. "I do not pay you both to dust shelves and daydream." The last one was directed at Inès.

Inès frowned. "You don't pay us."

"You exist," he said. "Keeping your life is payment."

Inès looked like she had a clever retort, but with his warning stare, she didn't dare voice it.

He was exhausted. The control he had on the wards that sealed the Pit was wavering. It was weakening, and he felt so exhausted some days it was a wonder he even woke up.

"We've been researching," Clarise said, sitting down at one of the long tables. Séverin took his seat at the head and Inès sat on the opposite side of her mother. "And..."

"And what?" he snapped impatiently. "Do not mince your words, Farrow."

"The cracks in the Graylands happened when you arrived," Clarise said.

"We think it might be connected to the Cleaving," Inès continued. The Cleaving was what Clarise and her daughter called the separation between him and Laurent. They had a phrase for just about everything. It was one of their many quirks. "To what happened between you and...well you."

"He is *not* me," Séverin said tightly. "He is an imposter."

"You and the imposter then," Inès said. "We believe it is causing the rift that is occurring and if we don't fix it, it will swallow us all."

"I've tried uprooting that snake, but he is a slippery one," Séverin said. "I presume his death will fix it?"

Séverin and Laurent had been attempting to kill each other since the Cleaving. It was one of the reasons he had clawed his way to power, why he had practiced his control of aether, and taken his ambition to the court of Antoine, integrating himself into a world of politics and revelry. There had been different Quarter Masters then. People loyal to Antoine, people he had suspected to be allies of Laurent who roamed the quarters building his power.

Ever since he had become the Lord of the Below, Laurent had vanished. Nobody had seen him in a long while. He pretended to be Séverin anytime he was moving through the streets and remained masqued and dressed in his signature dark cloak. So, capturing him proved challenging.

"Perhaps," Clarise said. "You know when we first arrived in the Graylands, Gaspar the last keeper believed there was a book that contained the secrets of the Graylands. He said it was called *The Book of Echoes*. I think it may have some information on the cause of the Blight and the history of the beasts.

Perhaps it might even mention how to seal the Pits permanently and erase the decay."

"And where is this book?" Séverin asked.

"Gaspar had his suspicions," Clarise said. "It might be worthwhile to speak with him."

"Write me his address," Séverin said. "I will pay him a visit."

Chapter Seven

Her new bedroom or rather her latest prison chamber was grotesquely opulent.

An intricately carved rosewood headboard dominated the left wall, detailed with labyrinthine leaves along with irises and swans. The bed was swathed in layers of smooth, golden silk sheets and ruffled pillows. A brocade coverlet was draped on the mattress, caressing the butter-soft base. A crystal chandelier hung from the plaster ceiling with faceted teardrops to illuminate the room. Last night she had sat at the writing table with the delicate mother-of-pearl marquetry, and she had written a sheet of foul insults dedicated to the Phantom, scrawling the page with blood-red ink, her ivory fountain pen quivering under the pressure of her fingers. But the act had done little to soothe her nerves. Not after the antic he had pulled last night when he attacked her so callously.

Someone poked Élisabeth's shoulder, rousing her from her sweet slumber.

"Fine minutes," she mumbled.

It happened again.

"Five minutes."

And again.

Élisabeth sat upright and glared at Colette. Colette silently pointed at the door where Kai stood fresh-faced even though it had not been more than a handful of hours since they last parted. The curtains were slightly diverted, and she could see that the sun hadn't fully come up yet. It was creeping from the horizon like a shy child hiding behind a tree.

"Do ghosts not sleep?" she asked, annoyed.

"I don't like the term 'ghost'," Kai said. "It implies that my job is to haunt which it is not. We exist in the Graylands, and the humans exist in the mortal realm."

"You didn't answer my question," she said.

"We do," he said. "But we do not dream. And we only need to do so every few days. It depends on if we are using too much aether. It can tire us out."

"Where is His Lordship?" she asked. Her voice rang with sarcasm, but Kai didn't seem to pick up on it.

"Something came up, so he won't be joining us," he said. "I have recruited Matthieu, one of my soldiers, to help test out your skills."

"What skills?"

"Your ability to see aether."

Élisabeth sighed. He was being purposefully vague again, just like yesterday. She didn't know why he and the Phantom were determined to believe that she could not see that strange, silvery tint that was their magic. *Magic.* Somehow it did not surprise her that it existed. Not after everything that had occurred in the last several hours.

It was said that there had been a time when magic flowed between the realms like water, traveling through the ley lines in circuits. People had wielded it to great success and the strongest of these wielders had climbed to power, becoming the Three Kings of the three realms. Pras, Mòrge and Laos. To maintain the natural order and ensure that those gifted with magic did not abuse their power they had each chosen a Fate to act on their behalf and serve the realm, but then the Year of the Drowning had occurred and everything had changed. Nobody knew what had made the Three Kings fall into an eternal slumber.

The local folk had all sorts of speculation. Some said the Fates had overthrown them to seek power for themselves while others claimed that their magic grew corrupt and poisoned them. These speculations had led to the Crusade—a divide between those who followed the Fates in rejection of the Kings and those who condemned them, claiming they had killed those they were made to serve.

After the Drowning, the magic had been suckled from the realm leaving behind nothing but a husk of normality.

"Give me twenty minutes," she said.

"Ten," Kai said. Then the door clicked shut behind him.

Élisabeth turned and screamed into her pillow.

Kai straightened when she stepped outside. He frowned when he saw her emerald dress, as if it had caused him some great harm in a past life. Her wardrobe had put her previous one to shame and the sheer number of choices made her freeze. The walnut door had nearly fractured under the weight of silk trains and satins and rigid brocaded bodices stitched with exquisite jewels. Milk-white taffeta gowns and yellow skirts that looked like a cracked yolk stared at her amid pink dresses the color of a fading sunset. Dyed furs of rabbit and vulpine and wolf lay nestled beside the dresses along with cashmere shawls and matching parasols.

It was clear that Séverin saw her as a possession. One that he intended to parade around as he pleased.

"Those are not appropriate clothes for our session," Kai said. "I must advise you to change. I will speak with your maid. Some trousers shall do."

"I will *not* wear trousers," Élisabeth said. "I refuse."

"Why not?"

"It is inappropriate."

"There is no place for propriety in the Graylands," he said. "You could walk down this corridor naked, and nobody would bat a lash."

"No," she said. "That is my final answer."

Kai sighed. "Very well. Come along."

During the day she could admit that the palace was marvelous. Wide corridors with ruby-red walls decorated with gold plaster and hosting a network of fine art and tapestries. Thick embroidered rugs graced the checkered floor. Her slippers sunk into the wool like feathers. Fresco ceilings depicting the Fates in flowing robes surrounded by animals and jewel-tone flowers in a beautiful pastoral landscape. Arched windows flanked with ivory pilasters brought in mild sunlight. The sky was a sickly gray with thick clouds that floated like white pillows.

Kai pulled open a pair of glass doors and led her outside. It had rained last night, and the grass was dark and dewy. Fog escaped her mouth when she breathed and the trees in the distance were feeble and bent, eroded by both time and the fickle weather.

"It was summer," she whispered. "In Prasin."

"This is not Prasin," he said. "It may look like it. Might even feel like it but it is not."

In the distance, she could make out the figure of a young man. His pale hair was overgrown, drifting down to his shoulders, mused and windswept as if someone had run their fingers through it.

"You're not late," Kai said.

"Lost a bet. Traded my night shift for an early morning rotation for the next week," he said.

Kai snorted.

"Élisabeth, this is Lieutenant Matthieu Durand, he leads the Second Regiment," Kai said. "Matthieu, this is Élisabeth Bellacourt, she is…"

"A special butterfly," Matthieu mused. "*He's* never aether-marked any human before."

"Which means she is not to be harmed," Kai said. And then after a brief pause added, "Or flirted with."

Matthieu's lips tilted in a devilish smile. "Lady Bellacourt. You must not believe a word from the mouth of the General—I am nothing short of a gentleman."

He offered his hand in greeting and Élisabeth was not surprised when his lips grazed her knuckles. She could tell he was a dangerous one. From the lazy unkemptness of his uniform to the mischievous glint in his juniper-green eyes. Something about his eyes was familiar, and she had this strange, tilting sensation as if they had met before.

"What are we here to do?" Élisabeth asked.

"To see if you can control aether," Matthieu said. "Kai said you can see it."

Aether, she realized, was what they called their magic. Now that she looked, she could see it around them. It covered the grounds and trees in a silvery hue. As if it were air itself.

"It is simple," Matthieu said. "We will do an observation test and then I will give you my aether to hold. Kai will supervise unless anything goes wrong. Does that work for you?"

"I don't have much of a choice," she muttered.

If she had to tolerate this, at least it was with them and not their wicked leader. The mere thought of him filled her with anger. He had almost killed her last night. Perhaps she should not have made that taunt about his mother, but she had hardly expected the cold, unfeeling beast to care about anyone but himself.

Matthieu performed the same trick as the Phantom had last night. His fingers created that same ball of energy and he asked her simple questions about which hand held it. Thankfully he didn't feel the need to hurtle them at her, he just let it fizz to nothing when she answered correctly.

Matthieu took a step forward with it and she hesitated, glancing warily at Kai.

"He won't hurt you," Kai said. "We are just trying to understand."

"Will it burn me?" she asked.

Matthieu placed his hand beneath hers. "No."

It hovered above them and slowly it lowered and rested on her skin. A tingle spread along her flesh and then she felt a jolt of surprise as it disappeared, melting to nothing. It vanished as if it had been eaten away by acid. Élisabeth stared at the strange web of black tendrils that had wrapped around his magic, choking it to death. And she felt a great deal of unease.

Matthieu flinched and stumbled backward.

Kai leaped forward. "What did you do?"

"Nothing!"

But he did not look convinced. His eyes were narrowed in suspicion.

"Are you okay?" he asked Matthieu.

"Stung a little, it..." Matthieu searched for the right word. "It didn't feel *right*."

Élisabeth used the distraction of their conversation to run.

She heard their voices behind her and the heavy thud of their boots as they gave chase. But she couldn't do this anymore. She could not stand around and get drawn into their world. She did not belong here. Something was wrong with her, she had felt it when his magic had touched her skin. His magic had felt wrong, and she felt something inside her respond to it. She was so busy losing her mind that she did not see him until the strange noose around her neck that they called an aether mark tightened. It choked her, grounding her footfalls to a jarring halt.

"Easy, Lisbeth," he said.

He sat atop a horse with a silky black pelt and wise almond-brown eyes.

Her fingers slipped beneath the necklace, and she attempted to replicate what she had done earlier. She clutched it and watched in satisfaction as it burned to wisps of nothing. She couldn't stick around to admire her handiwork so she quickly dove into the thicket, disappearing under the wet-stained leaves and using the forest's pelt to conceal herself. A green lacewing fluttered by her, grazing the tip of her ear with its papery wings as she kicked up a storm of dirt around her.

"She ran from us, Séverin," Kai called a little breathlessly. "Swift little thing."

Séverin.

That was *his* name.

"I'll get her," Séverin called.

Élisabeth's heart thundered, as she heard him descend.

"Come out, Lisbeth," he said.

She could not outrun him. Not with the weight of her gown. It was a miracle Matthieu and Kai had not caught her with their long legs. And Séverin was a few inches taller than them both; any attempt to flee him would fail. The safest option was to hide. At least until he grew tired of barking his commands.

"I can feel your heat, human," he snapped. "Hiding is futile."

Her breath spasmed. She lifted her skirt, prepared to run, but he stepped in front of her, and Élisabeth stumbled, her back hitting the bark. She hadn't heard him. He barely made a sound when he moved. He took a step forward, and she could smell his scent, a dark ocean breeze mixed with cigar smoke. He grasped her wrists, pinning them high above her head, forcing her to stand on her toes.

Élisabeth was tall, but he was taller. And she hated that.

"You have just become the most interesting person in the Graylands, Lisbeth," he said. "And I do not say that as a compliment."

"Let go of me," she said.

He released her and her eyes darted to the right. Maybe she could...

"If you run and I catch you I *will* kill you," he said. "And that is not a threat, it is a promise."

Something in his eyes made her believe him. He did not strike her as someone who lied. People lied to hide things and because they dreaded the consequences. He did not seem like someone who possessed any inkling of fear. It made her envy him and his strength of character.

"Until I know *exactly* what you are, you will remain under close watch," he said. "Every morning you are to wake up at dawn and practice with Kai. In the afternoon you will rehearse with the other dancers in the ballroom for four hours every day," he said. "Remember what I said about you being a subpar dancer? Maybe I can mold you into someone worthy of reverence, someone worthy of my court."

"I want to go home," she said. "I don't belong here."

"Silly girl," he said with a dry chuckle. "Do you still think you have any say in the matter?"

Anger burned her veins, as he spun on his heels, not even giving her the chance to respond. Élisabeth bent down and picked up a rock, feeling an overwhelming sense of satisfaction when it hit him in the back, falling in a dull thud upon impact. If Matthieu and Kai weren't so close by, she would have attempted to stab him with the dagger.

Slowly, Séverin turned around, his blue eyes unbearably frosty.

"Did you pelt me with a rock?" he asked.

"I was aiming for your head," she said.

He raised his hand, pinning her to a tree. Those wisps of magic, coiled around her like rope. Her hands were stuck to her sides, unable to fry it with her touch.

"Should I go visit your father?" Séverin asked.

Her throat grew dry. "What for?"

"To have a cup of tea."

She frowned.

"To kill him, of course," Séverin snapped. "You are denser than I thought."

Séverin stepped forward to where she hung like a clipped insect, staring at her beneath his strong nose.

"Next time you make a foolish mistake I will bring you your worthless father's head, and then perhaps that dreadful mother of yours, and the bratty sister."

"She's not my mother," she said, between clenched teeth. But inside her skin chilled at just how much he knew about her.

"No?" he asked. "I could have sworn I caught some similarities between you two."

From his sharp-toothed smile, he knew *exactly* the kind of insult he hurled at her by making that comparison.

"Must be the shrill voice," Séverin said at last.

"Shut up!" she said. "Have you been watching us this entire time?"

Élisabeth fell when his gaze dropped, and a shallow scream escaped her as she crumbled to her knees. The thick golden-brown leaves that blanketed the floor eased her fall.

"Come along," he said. "I don't have time to waste."

He hadn't answered her question. And now her mind spun with several other difficult inquiries. Élisabeth could still feel the lingering sensation on her fingertips from when she had come into contact with aether.

Almost as if she were repelled by it.

Séverin pulled Kai away when they returned to the palace. Matthieu had been left to keep guard over her. A curious expression crossed his face when the door clicked shut behind Kai and Séverin while they stood out in the hallway. It was not long after that Matthieu leaned his head on the door. Élisabeth took a step forward to listen in as well.

"No," he whispered with a warning finger. "You stand right there."

"I will tell them you were eavesdropping," Élisabeth said.

Matthieu gave her an annoyed look before he shuffled over to make room for her. Élisabeth smiled in victory.

"You are a devious minx," Matthieu said.

"Thank you."

He scoffed and then they stopped talking to listen.

"It ate away Matthieu's aether?" Séverin asked.

"It did," Kai said. "It reminded me of the Blight. It surrounded it with those same black tendrils. Do you think she has anything to do with the curse?"

"It is not a curse," Séverin said. "There is a rational answer to all of it. Including whatever that Bellacourt girl is. I don't trust her."

"She seemed just as surprised as us," Kai said. "Either she is as accomplished an actor as she is a dancer, or she is just as lost as we are."

"I visited Clarise in the library yesterday. She thinks *The Book of Echoes* will have the answers we seek," he said. "We will pay a visit to Gaspar this afternoon."

"I'll have Matthieu shadow her," Kai said.

"Looks like we're stuck together," Matthieu whispered with a fox-like smile.

"Wonderful," Élisabeth said unamused. "I am over the moon."

"No need to be mean," Matthieu said.

He looked rather offended by her comment and Élisabeth felt the stinging tug of guilt. Being trapped here for a few days had worsened her mood. From the conversation she had overheard, it seemed that Séverin and Kai had no intention of releasing her. She had unknowingly caught their attention which did not bode well for her.

Matthieu took several steps back and Élisabeth didn't get the chance to join him when the door was yanked open.

"Listening in were you, Little Monster?" Séverin asked.

"No," she said defensively. "And you are the monster!"

She looked back to glare at Matthieu. He could have warned her. He simply winked at her, and she had a strong urge to expose him. She opened her mouth to do just that when Matthieu grabbed her elbow.

"Slipped from my grasp," Matthieu said. "I'll keep a closer eye on her, my lord."

"He—"

"See that you do," Séverin said, cutting her off.

He spun on his heels and disappeared down the corner, Kai tight on his heel. Matthieu laughed, a dark, gleeful sound. She tugged her arm away and this time he let her.

"You should have seen your face when that door opened!" he said. "Simply marvelous."

"I hate you," she said. "I hate all of you."

"Oh, it was just a joke, Élisabeth," Matthieu said. "Will you forgive me?"

"No."

He laughed again. She was beginning to despise the sound of that delighted cackle.

***

"He mentioned a library earlier," Élisabeth said. "Can we go see it?"

Matthieu stroked his chin. "You've been ignoring me all day."

"That hasn't stopped you from talking," she said. "So, what is your point?"

Matthieu clutched his chest dramatically. "My weak heart stutters at your cruel words."

"No, your heart stutters at the sight of every maiden with a revealing bodice," Élisabeth said with a roll of her eyes. "I dare say there hasn't been a single woman you haven't flirted with today. I am certain the last two were sisters."

Matthieu smiled wickedly. "So, you *have* been paying attention to me."

Séverin had not been seated on his throne when they arrived at the Great Hall, and she did not catch sight of Kai which meant they were likely on their quest for what they had called *The Book of Echoes*. It was a large part of why she wanted to go to the library. To learn some more from the woman he called Clarise. Maybe she could explain everything since nobody seemed inclined to answer her questions. Even Matthieu refused to tell her what was happening.

Since Séverin wasn't in the Great Hall that evening she hadn't been forced to take the stage. As much as she loved dancing, her desire to perform had faded to smoke the moment she had crossed into this strange subterranean realm. Not to mention the thought of them touching her like they did the other night made her skin break out in goosebumps.

"Library? Where is it?" Élisabeth asked, ignoring his remark.

"I won't do you any favors if you refuse to speak to me and insult me on the rare times you do," Matthieu said, petulantly crossing his arms across his chest.

Unlike Kai whose uniform was as sharp as a knifepoint, Matthieu's was unkempt and disorderly. The collar of his undershirt was loosened, and his coat had been removed earlier. His arm dangled perilously over his shoulder; the fabric hooked to his forefinger. He had drunk so much wine his eyes were glazed. If she had any hope of escaping her captors, it would certainly be under the guardianship of Matthieu Durand.

He stared at her expectantly and Élisabeth sighed.

"I'm sorry for being so...unlike myself," she said. "I did not intend to come off as impolite and cross. It is not you that I am angry at. It is the man you serve."

"I forgive you," he said. "See how easy it is to forgive!"

Élisabeth chuckled and his smile brightened in victory.

"You are unbearable," she said.

"Kai says I'm like a rash," he said. "Clingy and spread far too fast."

Élisabeth snorted. He led her down the corridor and up several flights of stairs until they came upon a set of oaken doors that Matthieu opened with a flourish. They stood in an oval room with forest-green walls.

"Behold the Grand Library. It is the oldest library in the Graylands. Perhaps the only one."

"Not the only one," a feminine voice said when they entered.

A girl floated behind a towering stack of books that concealed her frame except for her shock of gloriously red hair. Matthieu rushed towards her, helping her offload the books onto a table.

"Trying to break your neck, Inès?" Matthieu said. "There are better ways to capture Kai's attention than that."

"I banned you from the library," she said with narrowed eyes. "You spilled wine on a limited edition copy of *The Symbolism of Threes*."

"That is a silly title," Matthieu said. "And you banned me for a month. It has long passed."

"*You* are silly," she huffed. "And the ban was for eternity."

"Shame," he said coyly. "Kai asked me to pass along a message."

Her emerald-green eyes brightened. "Well, what did he say?"

"He said..." Matthieu drawled. "That he wants you to carry his babies and his last name. And he has asked me to officiate the ceremony."

Inès picked up a pillow from the chaise and tossed it at him. Matthieu laughed loudly. It was clear to see that Élisabeth was not the only victim of his teasing.

Inès turned to her as if she had just realized she was there.

Freckles dotted her nose like constellations, a pair of gold-rimmed spectacles hung from her nose, and shockingly, she was wearing a pair of trousers. Élisabeth had never seen a woman wear trousers. "You must be Élisabeth Bellacourt. I am Inès Farrow."

Inès offered her hand. "I've heard so much about you."

"Good things?" Élisabeth asked.

"I'm afraid it was all spoken by Lord Séverin," Inès said.

Élisabeth winced. "Disregard everything you heard."

Inès laughed. "Done."

"This is marvelous," Élisabeth said, staring at the domed ceiling. There were circular windows that reflected the night sky on the ceiling, giving her a view of the stars. They twinkled like gems in the dark.

A spiral staircase led to a second floor. Oak shelves embellished with motifs of acanthus leaves held rows of books.

"Would you like a tour?" she asked.

"I'd love it."

"I'll just stay here," Matthieu said. "Do you have an—"

"No wine or food is permitted in the library," Inès said sharply.

He sighed, collapsing dramatically on the settee. "I'll just stay here, drowning in my thoughts."

"Consider reading a book?" Inès suggested.

"Perhaps not."

"Come, let's leave him to his sulking."

Élisabeth followed her through the shelves. It twisted around them like a labyrinth, enclosing them in a wall of bookcases with dagger-sharp corners.

"The library was constructed by one of the first lords," she said. "Gaspar the last Keeper cataloged seven lords in his record and my mother and I arrived during the reign of Antoine, and then of course, Séverin."

"How did Séverin become lord of this place?" she asked.

The more she learned about him the better her chance of destroying him. She still had Laurent's blade strapped to her thigh, prepared to use it when the opportunity presented itself. Until then she would learn all she could about her enemy.

"He strengthened his control of aether and used it to command the wraiths," she said. "Nobody had ever controlled the Soulless Ones before. They would attack at random, and everyone lived in constant fear. Once you die and come to the Graylands you begin to fear the Second Death. It is what we call the final rest or oblivion."

"How did he control them?" she asked curiously. "How did he gain power?"

"Nobody knows exactly how he controls the wraiths," she said. "He climbed the ranks in Antoine's inner circle and then the next thing we knew we were bending the knee to him. He's cunning and knows how to wield fear like a weapon. But he's also protective of his allies."

She spoke of him with something that sounded suspiciously like respect. Élisabeth did not understand how anyone could see him as anything less than a villain.

"He seems to have some animosity towards me and my family," Élisabeth said. "Do you know why that is?"

"I would never dare to understand the inner workings of his mind," she said. Inès caught her wrist. "Be careful around him. He can be merciless to those he considers his enemy."

Élisabeth swallowed. She knew that Séverin was dangerous. He reeked of malice and cruelty. She thought of that dark interrogation room and the path they had taken to get there. There had been cells on either side of her with prisoners carved like wood. They had been missing limbs and their bloody sockets tilted towards the sound of her shoes, blind to her presence. She thought she would vomit up her dinner that night. Kai had belatedly clasped his palm over her eyes for the remainder of the walk when she gasped. But by then it had been too late—she had seen the horrors of the dungeon.

She would only have one chance to escape Séverin's cruel grasp.

And Élisabeth would not miss it.

Chapter Eight

Séverin went into the city that afternoon to visit Gaspar with Kai. Kai had wanted to bring along a retinue, but Séverin didn't need guards, he simply tugged on the aether chains he had around his wraiths and they floated above them. Their presence cleared out the narrow-winding street as he rode in with his horse. He appreciated the sound of the people's fear as they ran to hide from him, the outdoor vendors had vanished inside their respective establishments and the streets had cleared out within minutes. It was an intoxicating feeling.

"I've been thinking about Élisabeth..." Kai began.

"Don't let Inès find out," Séverin warned.

"Didn't know you had a sense of humor," he replied.

Séverin ignored his remark. He didn't enjoy conversations much, at least not ones he deemed unnecessary. Kai was the only person he knew who could sit in silence without finding the need to fill it with useless words. But he had been rather vocal about his opinion lately—that Élisabeth was innocent and unaware of her gifts.

"I think that she could help us defeat the Blight and perhaps end the curse," Kai said. "I don't believe her to be a threat."

"You are an optimist," Séverin said. "You can't help it."

Séverin climbed off his horse. He stroked Ebony's neck; she was a greedy thing who liked to be touched and she leaned into his palm. Her mane tickled his cheek.

"The only person you look at with adoration is that horse," Kai said with a chuckle.

"And my reflection," Séverin said.

"Careful," Kai warned. "Or I might start to think you are funny."

Gaspar lived in a townhouse on the outskirts of town, far from the bustle of the city. Years of service at court had given him a good sum to purchase a plot of land. Their world ran much the same as the mortal realm. If you wanted to live a good life you worked and perhaps in a few decades or a century, you could retire. They were all immortal. But ever since the Blight those that were centuries old had become what they called specters. Specters were the dead who had been driven to madness and often descended into the woods, shrieking, and mindless in their lonesomeness. They were also dangerous and prone to attacking anyone they came across.

Séverin knocked. His fists struck the wood harder when he was not welcomed within the minute. Slowly it was pulled back by a short, bald man with thick whiskers. He fell into a swift, dramatic bow.

"My lord, you honor me with your presence," he said. "Please, come in."

Séverin stepped inside, removing his leather gloves. "You've done well for yourself."

"Worldly or I suppose unworldly possessions are not my

greatest desire," he said. "Gaspar Gaultier at your service, my lord."

He led them into a parlor room with indigo wallpapers. Gaspar began to quickly unravel the cords that held the damask curtain back to grant them privacy.

"Would you like some tea?" he asked, turning on the lamp beside him.

Séverin shook his head. "We won't be long."

Gaspar sat across from them, palms folded neatly on his lap. He looked erratic or perhaps he simply had a nervous disposition.

"Clarise says you mentioned a book called *The Book of Echoes*?" Séverin asked. "She says it may help us stop the Blight."

"Ah, yes I read about it in a journal entry," he said. "Give me one moment."

He hastily stood upright. His small legs couldn't carry him out of the room fast enough.

"Interesting man," Kai mused when Gaspar disappeared through a secret door like nerve-stricken prey.

"More like he is one year away from becoming a specter," Séverin muttered.

Kai snorted.

Several minutes later, Gaspar returned with a leather-bound book.

"It belonged to a man called Raphael," he said. "He had a deep fascination with understanding our world. And several theories fro—"

"Could you skip to the relevant points?" Séverin asked. "I have a long day ahead of me."

Gaspar cleared his throat. "Very well, he thought that *The Book of Echoes* contained the secrets of the Graylands. It explained the origins of the wraiths and the history of the Graylands and its purpose. Raphael believed that it could also explain how to escape. To cheat death if you will."

"Sounds like a deranged man," Séverin said.

"Maybe," Gaspar said, but it was clear to see he did not believe that. "But I think looking for it is worth a shot."

Séverin arose. "Prepare yourself in two days. We will seek out this book you speak of."

"My lord, I do not..."

Séverin drew the wraiths closer and heard their hungry screeches as their icy fingers clawed against the window. Frost drifted along the glass in a gentle caress visible from the small crack between the curtain. Gaspar swallowed deeply, holding the book close to his chest as if it were a shield. He pushed his spectacles up the heavy bridge of his nose.

"What time shall I be ready?" he asked.

"By sunrise."

Séverin stepped outside. The wind howled around them, and he stared fondly at his wraiths. The Soulless Ones were his only means of control. It helped him wield the fear of the denizens as he pleased.

"Shall Matthieu watch Élisabeth while we are gone?" he asked.

"Yes," he said. "And a rotation of guards to keep her in check as well, she is a slippery one."

He would deal with her when he returned. There was something strange about her magic. Something unnatural. It was almost as if she possessed the same blighted magic that was eating away at his world.

Séverin hoped the answers he sought revealed themselves in this mysterious book because he did not know how much longer he had to save the Graylands.

Chapter Nine

Élisabeth had been forced awake that morning by a pitcher of ice-cold water. She bolted upright eyes wide and fingers clutching her blankets only to find the villain of her nightmares standing by her bedframe with an arrogantly cool expression.

Murderous rage bled through her like ink on parchment, as she stared at the wretched Lord of the Below.

"How dare you!" she yelled.

"Good morning to you too," Séverin said, fists shoved deep into his pockets. "Or should I say afternoon?"

"You never said I had to wake up at dawn," Élisabeth said.

"It was implied," he said. "This is not a relaxing trip to the countryside. You serve my court and there is *always* work to be done."

Élisabeth clutched her blankets to her chest, as he impatiently tapped her foot.

"Go on then," he said. "I won't leave until you've gotten your lazy arse up."

"I can't," she said between gritted teeth. "I am not dressed for polite company. It is terribly improper to enter a lady's room while she is abed."

Séverin chuckled. A darkly, melodious sound.

"Oh, you're serious?" he asked when she didn't join along. "How terribly virginal of you."

Her cheeks burned.

"Five minutes," he said. "Or I'll return to dress you myself."

"So, desperate to see me naked, are you?" she asked. "You are a filthy rascal."

Séverin's mouth tightened in displeasure, and she felt a heavy dose of victory when he spun on his heels and disappeared out the door.

Élisabeth collapsed on the bed, shivering as her damp poplin nightgown clung to her flesh like morning dew.

It felt as though fate conspired to ruin her.

The moment her father had inherited the Opera House had been the beginning of the end.

Élisabeth swore then that she would go down fighting. She would never forget who she was. Or bend to her enemies.

She remembered the misty words of the fortune teller on that warm night. Her smoky voice drifted through her mind like a lullaby.

You have yet to meet the Devil.

Élisabeth was certain that she had met him.

And he went by the name Séverin.

Élisabeth greeted the orchestra members only to be met with silence.

"They do not speak to the dancers."

Élisabeth spun around to find there were three other dancers. One boy and two girls. She could tell they were human, from the flush that crossed their cheeks. The dead's skin was unnaturally bloodless, and they had this eerie stillness about them that unnerved her. Like they could stand for hours and never tire. Like they were statues.

Though the main reason she could tell them apart was because all the humans wore those dreadful collars. It was designed with gems and intricate swirls that were either painted with a letter at the forefront or an animal encased in a circle almost like a sigil. The corners were filled with precious diamonds like it was a festival masque and the sight of it filled her with unease.

The boy's fingers traced the collar almost as if he had forgotten it was there.

"I am Francis," he said, offering her his hand. He looked like a painting, with soft blond hair, bright blue eyes, and the lean physique of a performer. His chest was bare, and he wore white pantaloons. "This is Helene." He pointed at a raven-haired girl whose pale lips lifted in a kind smile. "And this is Marie-Odile."

Marie-Odile had a stern face and looked like she was several years older than her, perhaps twenty-seven or eight. She turned away from her before Élisabeth could make her acquaintance. She was not surprised by her reaction. In every ballet company, there were one or two Marie-Odile's, who assumed everyone was beneath them. At the National Opera House, the role had belonged to her sister.

"Will we perform together?" Élisabeth asked.

Francis nodded.

"I will be leading," Marie-Odile said. "Follow my lead."

Helene nodded sweetly and Francis looked like he would be her pair. Marie-Odile stared at her with sharp eyes.

"There were eight of us a few months ago," she said. "Most

of them are long gone. Not dead. *Gone.* Follow the rules and you may survive a fortnight."

As much as she didn't like the idea of taking orders from Marie-Odile, Élisabeth had no intention of leading. Not in this place. All she wanted was to survive.

***

The crowd tonight was larger than the one last night and she felt a great sense of unease at the thought. It was difficult to navigate the swarm of bodies. The syrupy scent of perfumes—peony, raspberry, orange blossom, and bergamot— twisted in the air like a cloud with an echo of something that burned her lungs. Several of them had cigars with glowing, silvertips in their gloved fingers. Kai had told her that they smoked aether which if consumed could cause strong hallucinations.

There was something utterly hedonistic about the court. Some of the thralls were naked and pleasing their lords and ladies. Desperate hands gripped their servant's flesh, sinking into their warmth. And Élisabeth's eyes widened.

Élisabeth felt stray hands touch her and a yelp escaped her before Kai pulled her under his arm, sheltering her from them. The delicate hair on her nape stood on end. So close, they had been so close.

You are trapped in a court of ghosts who want to sink under your flesh like a blanket.

Élisabeth had always enjoyed tales of horror. Her favorite was a gothic, blood-curling tale called *The Frightful Adventures of Amelia Ashburn.* While Louise had spent her days absorbed with poetry, and memorizing the 24 devotionals in the Last Scripture, Élisabeth had been tucked under her blankets trembling and jumping at the slightest sound.

And now the horror of those pages had bled into her life, staining her with its tainted claw-shaped ink.

She could see *him* on his throne and those two twins at his heel. His head snapped up then as if he could feel the heat of her wrath. His lips pulled in that insufferable smile. He wore a black masque that appeared almost devilish. On the left side it had a painted mouth that held dagger-thin teeth that made him look rather menacing. On one side was his silken soft, male beauty—thinly arched brow as if it had been plucked and shaped to its chosen desire, full lips slightly red with rouge and high, piercing cheekbones that looked like a sculptor had framed them with his talented palms. It was the kind of beauty that was both alarming and uncommon. Like looking at a painting drawn in blood. Darkly sensual and bitingly vicious.

It felt like there was nobody in the room. Just them. Eyes locked together in combat.

He slid two fingers into his mouth, and she stiffened, arrested by the sight until he whistled, and the Hall descended into silence. Kai led her to the stage where Helene, Francis, and Marie-Odile were already prepared in position for their piece. They all wore a black number while Marie-Odile stood in a blistering white ballet gown like her clothes had been sewn from snow.

The orchestra had paused the music as the Phantom's melodic voice filled the air.

"Tonight, we will have a special twist to the performance," he said. "You will all perform solely and the performer with the least crowd favor shall be fed to my wraiths."

Excited whispers and joyous cheers filled the Hall. An odd blood-thirsty sensation tore through the room as the audience prepared to watch them fight for their lives. It was nothing like the underground fights that occurred in the lower districts of Prasin for entertainment. Those fights had never masqueraded as art and beauty. Those fighters had been oiled, their muscles gleaming in the dim light. While the dancers' faces were powdered, their lips painted as they stared at each other in horror, forced to fight a battle they had not prepared for.

Élisabeth straightened her back. Eyes focused ahead. She erased all thoughts from her mind just as she had that night she had filled in for Louise. She was prepared to put everything into her performance, to push herself to the limits. It was the only way she'd survive and she refused to die here in this damp, cold place.

The orchestra began and Helene was first. Each time one of them climbed down the steps from the stage, Élisabeth marked the crowd's cheers. There was a young man with spectacles taking the tally of the sounds, marking it on a book, focused on the reverberation of the applause.

Élisabeth heard her name called. A soft purr from the Phantom's mouth and then she was moving as if something was guiding her limbs against her will.

She let the strings of the harp surround her like a warm blanket as she began her dance.

She pushed herself to a point she never had before. Toes aching painfully as she attempted maneuvers that Pierre had often called revolutionary. Her foot snapped out with sharp precision, swift as a fox diving into the underbrush. Her arms, softly curved, framed her like a portrait.

She forgot about the dead and the Lord of the Below and the Graylands. She was in the National Opera House, and she was proving to everyone who had never believed in her that she was worth more than they had ever thought. She was a force. And she would not be broken.

Her lungs were on fire as she struggled to breathe under the pressure, and she floated above the stage. Her torso tipped forward, her extended leg lifting impossibly high behind her. The pose was executed flawlessly, and she held it for a moment, as if she were a glass figurine, concluding her performance. It was silent. Utterly silent. Nobody applauded or shouted.

Dread crept down her back and then she heard Matthieu shout, clapping widely. And then the room followed suit. She turned her neck and grinned at him and he simply winked at her. Élisabeth dared to look up at the dais. Séverin had a strange look in his eyes. It was not anger or repulsion. It was almost as if he were in awe. Something foreign coiled in her stomach. It took her a second to realize that it was relief that she had shocked him, that she had *impressed* him. And then she chastised herself because it did not matter if she dazzled him, she only needed to gain favor with the crowd and she had.

The response to her performance was deafening.

It took a few minutes for the silence to come to a halt. Séverin impatiently raised his hand, and it grew startlingly quiet. The scorekeeper shuffled up the dais and whispered in his ear.

Séverin looked up and Élisabeth's heart clenched when the wraiths floated down from the ceiling. Their mouths emitted that terrible screeching sound. No name was announced and they drifted towards the stage in a sharp line like a bullet springing through the air.

Her breath tightened in her chest. It was impossible to tell who their victim was, and clear to see that it was intended to be a surprise. It was a terrible feeling, not to know if you would be the one they would devour. The air grew frigidly icy, and fog slipped out her mouth in a wispy tendril when she exhaled. It took her a moment to realize someone had screamed. Helene's head was thrown back as they converged on her. Their forms blanketed her in a vacuum of emptiness. One moment she was whole and alive and the next there was nothing. No blood or torn flesh or broken bone. As if she had never truly existed. As if she were nothing but a memory.

All the dancers were stunned. Their limbs were locked in fear. While Élisabeth did not know Helene well she had been warm and welcoming to her that morning. It was terrible to think such a thing, but she wished that it had been Marie-Odile instead of Helene, and then she chided herself for the thought. She had been here for a few days and already her thoughts were all broken and twisted and wrong.

"You can thank Élisabeth for the idea of this competition," Séverin said. The lie spilled from his perfect mouth like jewels. "It was her brilliant mind that sprung this challenge forth."

The crowd clapped loudly, flooding her with unwanted recognition. All the dancers looked at her with betrayal in their eyes and she realized that this was what he wanted. To paint *her* as the monster and ostracize her from everyone else.

"It wasn't my idea," she said softly.

"Liar," Marie-Odile said. "I knew you could not be trusted."

Francis looked at her with a crestfallen look and her chest ached.

"I didn't—"

He turned his back on her before she could finish, leaving her utterly alone on the stage.

Élisabeth walked numbly to an empty table. The depraved crowd was pleased by her, wrongfully assuming that she had concocted this sickening performance for their entertainment, and she felt their appreciative glances as they appraised her.

Élisabeth filled a plate with food, and then she left the Hall, throat tight with the growing bruise of an oncoming outburst.

Her bedroom was on the highest floor. It was nice to be far away from the revelry down below. To disappear into a well of obscurity and blissful silence. She walked down the empty corridor with her plate of duck liver. Two of the guards stationed outside the Hall were trailing behind her like a mirror reflection. They only stopped following her once she reached her floor and then they remained by the stone balustrade. Eyes locked on some indeterminate point; rifles strapped to their back by a leather harness. It was clear to see her options for escape were slim. Unless she decided to take her chances with the window and risked plummeting to death.

Élisabeth cracked open the closest door. It took her a moment to realize she was not in her bedroom, but rather *his*.

That night when she had first arrived, he had brought her to this bedroom. His bedroom. And when Kai had led her to her room it had been the second door to the left of his. Kai had told her that only she and Séverin resided on this floor.

Séverin clearly intended to keep a very close eye on her.

The way he felt about her wasn't blind hatred. It was rooted in something deeper. Something older than her. Something she assumed had begun the night that the bargain was struck between the Lord of the Below and the Bellacourts. It was tied to the Opera House and in extension, her.

Now was as good a time as any to search his lair. She clicked on the lights and the chandelier illuminated the wide space in golden hues. Dark panels ran along the wall like scars.

There was an ebony lacquered piano in the corner that she had not noticed last time. When she approached it, she found that the keys felt rather worn under her fingertips. There were sheets of music from both renowned composers and some newer names. And behind that were blank sheets with incomplete music. It surprised her to realize the ink was slightly wet as if he had begun to jot it down in a wild frenzy just before he left.

She hadn't played the piano in a long time. Music could reveal the soul of a person, so Élisabeth cracked her fingers and sat on the bench, putting the sheet *he* had written before her. She struck the first few chords and was surprised by the melancholy that suffused the air. The deeper she went the more it felt like she was submerging herself into the bottom of a barrel filled with water and feeling it fill her lungs. It soaked her in its soft despair, drowning her in its miserable arms.

She felt something wet slip from her eyes, and she rubbed it away furiously. She refused to cry anymore, and she certainly would not do so for *his* hauntingly painful music.

Élisabeth stood up abruptly and went to his bedside table. There was a stack of books on a variety of topics. One could learn a lot about someone by their reading habits. There was literature and epic poems from the Spirit Isles in Tezrik. Books about the history of music from Lamuran, a city near Prasin, renowned for its history of birthing the most talented composers. There were books about philosophy and astrology and floriography. Their spines curled like a peeled orange, from the pressure of his strong fingers. The last book was a copy of *The Frightful Adventures of Amelia Ashburn*. He did not strike her as a man who read many fictional titles, so it was an odd coincidence that her favorite book was on his desk. She flipped open the cover and felt slightly dizzy at the words at the front.

The Property of Babette Bellacourt.

Kindly return to me if you find this among your possessions. It is very dear to my heart.

It was written in the handwriting of a romantic twelve-year-old girl. But she had lost this copy last year. She had it with her in her dressing room and then it was gone. Louise had mentioned at dinner that she was always reading the same book and Delphine said one of these days she would throw it in the trash. When it had disappeared, she had yelled at Delphine. It was the angriest she had ever been, and her father had been forced to come between them to soothe the tension.

She had thought Delphine had been lying, but it turned out she was telling the truth for once.

She felt an odd vulnerability looking at the book. At the knowledge that she had scribbled her thoughts in the margins. Some of them coated in childish wonder and horror. Because as a child everything was beautiful and frightening. Children were the only beings who could see something that the world rejected and paint it with whimsy.

And for someone to have read her deepest thoughts was worse than stripping naked and letting them peruse her flesh. Her heart was tucked within the pages of this book.

She grabbed it with possessive fingers. She could not leave it behind. Even if he realized that she had come into his room, she would bear whatever punishment and torment came her way. She would not give him the satisfaction of keeping her book.

Footsteps echoed and her heart thundered at the sound of voices. A deeply masculine voice and a sharp feminine one drifted down the corridor.

Élisabeth fell to the floor, crawling under the bed like a spider. Her breath caught in her throat, and her heart beat a fierce rhythm. She slid the book into the waistband of her stockings, concealing it under her short dress.

The door cracked open and Séverin entered. His footfalls were light and delicate.

"Why are you following me?" he demanded.

Élisabeth stiffened until she heard the soft purr of Marie-Odile's voice.

"You dismissed your servants," she said. "I thought you might enjoy my company."

"How presumptuous of you," he said, in a dry, unimpressed tone.

"You wanted me once," she whispered.

"It is rather easy to catch my eye, Marie-Odile," he said. "But it's impossible to keep my attention."

Élisabeth heard the click of the door being shut rudely, just as Marie-Odile had begun to respond, and she felt pity for the girl. For wanting someone who was broken. And that was what Séverin was. He was broken.

"You can come out, Lisbeth," he said.

Her mind spun. How had he...

"You left your plate full of food on my pianoforte," he said. "It is dripping onto the surface, and you are going to lick it clean."

Her fist tightened beside her, and she grimaced. She would do no such thing. And she would not leave the safety of her hiding spot.

"Fine," he said. "I'll hunt you down myself."

She heard the crack of the armoire. And then the fading sound of his footsteps as he went to the attached bathing room. This was her moment to run. Élisabeth scrambled out from under the bed and raced to the door. Her finger had grazed the doorknob, and a satisfied smile crossed her face, until she felt the cold band of a steel arm around her chest, raising her off her feet. Her nails dug into his arm, but it didn't make him release her.

"Put me down," she snarled, thrashing like a wild animal.

"You simply cannot follow rules can you, Ms. Bellacourt?" he asked. His tone was cold and empty. It pinned her in place like a needle through a cloth.

"I swear to the Fates I will cut your throat out if you don't release me," she warned.

Her voice shook, hinting at her fear. She tilted her neck to confront him, but he was closer than she expected, and her lips grazed his jaw. They both stilled and he released her so abruptly that if she hadn't stretched her legs at the last second, she would have injured her spine.

She was breathing hard. Fists tightened with rage, and he looked just as angry. His lips were drawn into a grim line. His translucent blue eyes stared at her with an iciness that could freeze one's heart.

"Why are you in my bedroom?" he demanded.

"I got lost," she said.

"You made it far past the doorway," he said, pointing to her plate of food. He was right when he said she had spilled her food. Some of the duck sauce had dripped down the sides and sat in a puddle on the surface. "And I was not bluffing when I said you'd lick it clean."

"You'll have to force me," Élisabeth said.

He reached out to touch her, but then his hand stilled, and his face twisted, as if the thought of touching her sickened him. She could still see the shock that had crossed his face when her mouth had accidentally touched his flesh. He had reacted as if he had been attacked. As if some beast was about to maul him.

"Leave," he said coldly.

Élisabeth was not going to waste a good plate of food.

He did not object when she took her plate leaving behind that white dollop of sauce on the glossy surface. It was the least he deserved. If she knew that stain would unnerve him so much, she would have spilled it on the lush carpets as well. It made sense why he was so wound up about it. His room was unnaturally clean. The satin sheets were not ruffled, and the books were rather orderly. He had an even number of books and for some reason, she knew that it was not an accident.

It wouldn't be long before he realized *exactly* what she had stolen.

Élisabeth waited until midnight, the blade cold in her palm. Now, while he rested, it was the time to strike. She could not stay here any longer. His little antic at dinner had proven that he was unpredictable, and it wouldn't be long before his threats came true.

He was already suspicious of her gifts. Élisabeth didn't know what to think of it. She'd never believed in magic, but seeing aether and the proof of its existence, she had no choice but to.

She knew it was inevitable that Séverin would turn on her, if not today then tomorrow. And Élisabeth refused to leave her fate to chance.

Her ear had been pressed to the door for hours. She could hear the guards speaking. It had been several hours since they'd come up and they were long due for a rotation. Minutes trickled by until she finally heard their voices grow distant. Élisabeth slowly cracked open the door and glanced at the stairs. A sigh escaped her when she realized nobody was there.

This would be the only chance she had to escape. Her heart raced as she crept down the halls. Colette had dressed her for bed. So, none of the servants would come look for her, not until the morning. Her diaphanous, pale blue nightgown trailed along the carpet like cobwebs. Her bare feet sinking into the lush, seafoam-green carpet.

Élisabeth cracked his door open. There was a shadowy

form lying on the canopied bed. The velvet drapes were thankfully parted, tied around the wooden beams with a silk cord.

She crept forward, as quiet as a mouse. And then she was hovering above him, blade raised high above his chest. He looked innocent, eyes closed, that infuriating lock of hair grazing his masque. She wondered why he hadn't removed it, but she didn't have time to dwell on the topic. He could awaken at any moment.

It happened fast, so fast it made her mind reel. He lunged for her just as she shot down to impale him with her blade. The sharp head slid between his ribs and his face tightened in pain. At least the side she could see did. It rumpled like a discarded sheet.

"You foolish girl," Séverin snapped.

He tore out the knife and nothing came out. No gushing blood. No muscle and sinew. The wound was gaping and black like his insides were made of rot. Slowly, almost as if someone carried an invisible thread along the broken seam, it sealed shut leaving behind a thin pale scar.

Élisabeth stumbled backward.

He tossed the knife to the floor. His blue eyes were cold and unforgiving.

"It is a myth that a blade of aether can kill us," he snarled. "We are unkillable. Except by the wraiths. And they are *mine*."

Élisabeth swallowed.

"You will regret this," he promised.

Élisabeth spun around, thinking he would chase her, but there was no sound behind her. The guards had been replaced and their brows crinkled in confusion. But they didn't follow her when they realized she was returning to her bedroom. Élisabeth dragged a chair from the dressing table, sliding it under the doorknob. She waited on her bed, knees drawn to her chin, limbs slightly shaking. She had just tried to kill someone.

Granted, he was already dead, but when had she become someone who wielded a blade so efficiently against her enemy?

Now that she was alone, she could soak in the foolishness of her actions.

Séverin would retaliate against her. It wasn't a question of *if* but rather when.

And Élisabeth wasn't certain she'd survive the consequences.

Chapter Ten

It was a few hours before they were to depart to begin their hunt for *The Book of Echoes*. And it was hard to concentrate on his plans when all he could think about was the girl who had stood above his bed in an icy blue nightgown with a blade held above his heart. Her eyes had been soaked in fear and determination. Nobody with any sense of self-preservation would dare to strike him. It was futile and a death wish, but Élisabeth was unlike any person he had ever met before. In a single night, she had managed to invade his bedroom and ruffle through his belongings only to then come around and attempt to kill him. A busy woman indeed.

It was clear to see that he would have to kill her for the slight.

He was rather curious about where she had gotten the blade. It was coated in aether that had been liquidated. It shone with the silvery-gray matter. Another secret Élisabeth was hiding. She had an ally and was full of untruths and deception.

There was a knock on his bedroom door.

"Enter," he said gruffly.

Clarise came in. She had a feverish look in her eyes. The one she got if she was either smoking too much or if she'd just had a prediction. Her visions were spontaneous, but anything she had ever spoken of had always come true. Besides the wraiths, she and Inès were his strongest allies. Their gifts were rare and had proved useful on more than one occasion.

"You can't kill her, Séverin," she rushed. "It will ruin everything."

"You're going to have to be more specific than that," he said. "There are many people that I want to kill."

"Élisabeth Bellacourt."

He stiffened. The mere mention of her name flooded him with irritation and senseless anger.

He was not impressed with her actions. Since she had arrived, she had revealed magic he could not understand, disobeyed him at every turn, attempted to murder him, and tried to turn his second-in-command against him. He saw Élisabeth weaving her lies to Kai hoping that he fell for it.

She was working against him at every turn. And he intended for it to end today.

She was a Bellacourt. She was everything he despised.

He did not need to punish her for the sins of her father. He could simply erase her from this world. And *then* kill her father.

"Why not?" he asked.

"She is important," she said. "To our mission of saving the Graylands."

"How?" he asked. "She's just a young woman. A *human* woman at that."

But even as he said the words, he knew there was so much more to her than that.

"You know why," she said. "She is different."

It was silent for a bit while he fumed. She was supposed to

be *his* dancer. To entertain *his* court. It was his revenge against her insufferable father. Hugo Bellacourt was going to sleep at night knowing that his daughter lived and served him. But now she had become a thorn in his side. She was involved in this, in the matters of his world. The one thing that mattered to him. And worse he couldn't kill her and be done with it.

"Her gift might be what turns the tide," Clarise said.

He opened his mouth to ask how she knew that before he recalled she was a seer.

"What is she?" he asked gruffly.

"I don't know yet."

He was not surprised to discover she was not in the ballroom practicing with the other dancers. It was clear to see that even after he had made an example of her fellow dancer last night to put her in place, Élisabeth had no intention of standing in line and being a dutiful soldier. It both frustrated and amused him. He had faced men who cowered before him, but Élisabeth looked him in the eye with that glint in her stormy eyes that said, *I am not afraid of you.*

"Where is she?" he asked Kai who was perched on the wall, staring at the ceiling. He straightened at his approach.

"In the gardens," he said.

"You didn't stop her?"

"I tried," he said. "With her, it is best to conserve your energy. She doesn't listen after the first few times."

Séverin felt his mouth twitch, but he clamped down on it. He should *not* be finding her antics amusing. It was a blatant disregard of his rules. Soon enough people would think he was someone who could be disrespected. Someone whose rules were not worth upholding. If it were not for Clarise's cryptic message about her he would have ended her. Especially for coming into his room without permission and tainting his sacred space.

"Are the horses ready?" he asked.

Kai nodded. "Gaspar was brought in an hour ago. And the others are waiting in the courtyard."

He nodded and slipped outside, traversing the gardens. Snow trailed the grounds like a shadow, nestling atop tree tops like a wash of foam. Stone statues of old rulers who had left some mark in the hierarchy of this realm stood sentry, staring at him beneath their noses. The groundskeeper had intended to build one for Antoine, but Séverin had forbidden it. This tradition would end. There would be no more rulers to grace his gardens because Séverin refused to fall.

He could sense her inside the heart of the hedge maze. Humans emitted a heat that was easy to follow like blood calling out to a predator. Séverin knew the twists and turns of the old maze like the palm of his hand, and it didn't take him long to find her.

He paused at the sight of her. She was sitting on the ground. The spools of her dress surrounded her like a crown of jewels. She had a book in her hand. He would know that tattered copy anywhere. His fingers had danced along that cracked spine before. He had re-read the young, chaotic thoughts in the margin more than he cared to admit.

"Not surprised you are a thief," he said. "Among other things."

Her spine straightened and she hid the book between the folds of her dress. It was a striking dress. Not as stunning as the ballet dresses she wore, but just as eye-catching. It was a bright pink color the shade of a sliced watermelon with long sleeves, made of a translucent fabric that gleamed under the light. The hem of it was embroidered with flowers. Séverin squinted to make out the design. It was difficult to function with one eye. His other eye had been injured and the vision was so poor it may as well have been blind. Kai had told him to wear an eyepatch because the different sights gave him a thundering headache, but he wasn't yet ready to conceal his eye. It felt like surrender...but to what he did not know.

After a few seconds, he had determined the flowers were a mix of tulips and lilies and cornflowers, sitting in the green blades of grass threaded on the bottom.

"*You*," she said. Her lips curled at the sight of him and she drew her ivory shawl around her like a shield. "Do you not have anything better to do than to sneak up on me, Spirit-King?"

"Do you not have practice, Lisbeth?" he asked.

"It is my day off."

"Says who?" Séverin demanded.

"Says me, tyrant," she said. "Leave me alone. You deserve everything that happened last night. I won't let you hurt me."

She stood up, pathetically attempting to hide her book again as if he hadn't seen it.

As if he hadn't called her out for it.

He ignored her tantrum and focused on what he had come to do.

"Look at me, Lisbeth," he snarled.

Surprisingly she lifted her head to look at him and he raised his hand. A forcefield of power cut through the air, hurtling towards her. It was strong enough to knock one off their feet and her eyes widened. Nails digging into the hardcover of her book. Mouth dropping open in surprise.

She raised her hand to protect her head, but he could feel the force of the energy she had harnessed to build an invisible shield. Except it wasn't aether, it was that dark, tendril of magic Kai had described. Much like the poisoned magic of the Blight. It cocooned her in its dark shade. His aether crashed into the shield, hard enough to rattle it but she remained untouched.

His mouth tightened as he thought of Clarise's words.

Her gift might be what turns the tide.

He hoped Clarise was right because if he suspected for one moment that Élisabeth was a danger to his people and his world he would not hesitate to erase her.

And he would do it with a smile.

Chapter Eleven

Élisabeth did not know what happened. One second Séverin had demanded she look at him with this strange, vicious look in his eyes before he waved his hand, and a rush of silver energy hurtled towards her that looked strong enough to shatter every bone in her body. She felt a strange tingling sensation on her hands as she raised them from her sides to protect her head. It was like she was pulling a cloth over herself, and she felt her limbs shake as his magic crashed into her. But it did not touch her. It simply vanished.

Her hand shook as she stopped cowering. Séverin was staring at her both stunned and angry. His fists were clenched tight by his side.

"Come with me," he said, spinning on his heels.

"What...what was that?" she yelled. "You could have killed me."

"I was testing a theory," he said.

"You could have killed me!" she repeated. "And you've been testing this theory for *days*. What is going on?"

Matthieu usually spent an hour with her each day while

Kai supervised, performing silly tricks, and studying her reaction. She knew they reported it all back to Séverin, so why he felt the need to nearly kill her with these attempts was beyond her. Maybe it was another one of his sick games like feeding Helene to his wraiths.

Élisabeth raced after him, pounding her fists on his stubborn back. He spun around so quickly, it was as if he had disappeared for a split second. He pinned her to the hedges. The leather fabric of his gloves scraped her wrists. Her back collided against the leaves, feeling the prickle of thorns. She flinched and contemplated apologizing, but it was as if Séverin was more beast than man. There was no pleading to be done. Nothing would erase that permanent scowl that pulled at his perfect mouth.

"Don't. Ever. Touch. Me," he said between gritted teeth.

She strained against his palms. "Says the one touching me."

Élisabeth tried to do what she had done earlier—even if she did not understand it, she had done something to counterattack his assault. She tried to draw on that strange, biting sensation.

"You can't do much without your hands," he said. "Not as a beginner at least. I wouldn't waste my energy."

Élisabeth tried anyway and Séverin just stared at her with those eerie blue eyes. She didn't like them. She didn't like how empty they were. As if he were a puppet pretending to be human. She thought of what Laurent had said, that when they had split, he had been standing there with his lifeless eyes, and she shivered.

"Do I frighten you, Lisbeth?" he asked. Voice dropping to a soft cadence. One that was made to soothe but only felt startlingly sinister.

"No," she breathed.

She felt the pressure of his thumb on her pulse as if he intended to silence it.

"Come along," he said, releasing her.

He spun around and this time Élisabeth swallowed the urge to attack him. She followed him, keeping a breadth of distance between them both. At the curved entrance of the maze, Kai waited for them. Dark curls fluttering in the breeze.

"Hi, Kai!" she said, feeling relief at the sight of him.

Séverin's lips moved, and it took her a second to realize he was mimicking her.

"Jealous that nobody has ever greeted you with enthusiasm before?" Élisabeth asked.

"I only enjoy enthusiasm in the bedroom, anywhere else and it is unwanted," he replied.

A dark flush crawled up her throat and she snapped her mouth shut. She was *not* prepared to dignify that response with a comment.

"Hi, Élisabeth," Kai said. "Did you enjoy your walk?"

"Most pleasant to be away from a certain tyrant," she said.

"Give me back my book," Séverin ordered, holding his hand out impatiently.

Élisabeth smacked his hand away.

His eyes darkened and she slithered closer to Kai.

"You will have to rip it off my corpse," she warned.

"You say that like I won't do it," he said. "You say that like I won't *enjoy* it."

Séverin looked like he was debating snatching it from her arms or killing her and plucking it off her corpse as she suggested. She slid further behind Kai who didn't seem comfortable being used as a shield against his friend.

"You may borrow it," Séverin said as if he were granting her a boon by letting her keep *her* book. "But I expect it back within the fortnight. Feel free to write me some new poetic lines in the margins, I shall savor every bite."

The words were said with a sarcastic edge. A callous

reminder that he had read the secrets in her heart. Shame curled in her stomach at the thought that he believed her to be a romantic sop. In many of her earlier observations, she had been just a girl. One who dreamed and who believed the villain was deserving of love and worth saving. It was cruel of him to remind her that he was privy to her innermost thoughts.

Her voice was tight with rage when she spoke. "I hate you."

"I don't even think about you enough to hate you," he replied.

And somehow that was a crueler comment than what he had said earlier.

Nobody had hated her before. Even Delphine who had greatly disliked her had never looked at her with this kind of venom. It was much like acid that could cut through glass, leaving behind nothing but a charred hole in its place.

Séverin led her and Kai to the library. The one she had visited that night with Matthieu.

"I don't understand where you are taking me?" Élisabeth asked. She glanced at Kai. "You said you were leaving in an hour."

"Do not answer her," Séverin said sharply.

"I won't stop talking if you don't answer me," she said. "Better yet I will sing—"

Séverin spun around in his polished boots.

"I have a few questions for Clarise before I leave," he said.

Her eyes brightened. "You're leaving too?"

"Don't get too excited," he said. "I'll be back before you have a chance to miss me."

"Miss you?" Élisabeth said. "I would organize a street festival if you keeled over and died at this very moment."

Séverin's mouth tightened, and she felt a flicker of joy when Kai chuckled. A sound that he briskly hid behind a cough when Séverin glared at him.

The door to the library was drawn open by Kai and Élisabeth was in awe once again at the sheer magnificence of the place. The rows were so high it nearly scraped the domed ceiling. Élisabeth's finger itched to dance along the spines of the books and her foot took a step forward, wondering if she should pick up some copies to read in her spare time. Last time she had been focused on asking Inès a handful of questions to learn more about Séverin and had been far too distracted to do anything else.

Séverin grabbed her wrist before she could disappear.

"Not now," he said sternly.

He released her and looked around. Inès stepped out, decked in her trousers and a vest. Élisabeth was impressed by the lack of social rules their world had. It was equal parts refreshing and fascinating.

"Kai," Inès said, smirking. "Are you here on actual business this time? Or did you come to stare at me?"

Séverin sighed and Élisabeth looked at him with a questioning look.

She didn't think he would answer, but he lowered his tall frame to whisper rather loudly—she didn't think he whispered to be discreet, just obnoxious—and she was surprised he indulged her.

"Inès is a shameless flirt and Kai is too hard-headed to see it," he said.

"We can hear you perfectly well, Séverin," Kai said.

"Oh, good," Séverin said, straightening. "That saves me the effort of repeating myself."

Inès snickered and then she glanced at Élisabeth, before racing forward and clutching her hands with excitement.

"Élisabeth! I saw your breathtaking performance last night. You were like one of those figurines in a music box. So, captivating. I cheered so loudly for you I nearly lost my voice."

"Thank you," Élisabeth said. "It is nice to be complimented. I have only been insulted since I arrived."

She looked at Séverin when she said that, and his mouth raised in a crooked, half-smile almost as if he found her amusing. But that only lasted a second before his smile had drifted like a looming cloud just before a storm.

"Enough posturing, Ms. Bellacourt," he said with a good dose of disapproval. "Some humility would do you good."

"You remind me of my stepmother," Élisabeth said. "You two would get along well."

"I am tempted to go up and meet her," he said. "She must be a sensible woman."

"You should do that," she said. "Maybe she can take you as her lover. You are exactly her sort."

Delphine always got flustered around young men. It was disgusting and offensive to her father. And it pleased her that Séverin grimaced at her suggestion. It *had* been intended as an insult.

"That is enough banter for one day," Kai said, placing a steady hand on both their shoulders. "Shall we call a truce?"

"No," Élisabeth said. At the same time, Séverin said, "*Never.*"

"Where is Clarise?" Kai asked.

"Somewhere on the third floor," Inès said.

Inès went to a bell by the door and rang it. The sound echoed in the room until a woman popped her head up from the railing. She had the same brilliant red hair as Inès and had an air of eccentricity to her. She wore a green dress that revealed the swirls of ink that layered her arm, almost as if it told a story. She had never seen anyone but sailors with ink on their flesh. Something they did to pass the long nights at sea. It was both odd and riveting to see it among polite company. Though she would not use the word "polite" to describe Séverin. There was nothing gentlemanly about him. He was the worst rascal she had ever had the misfortune of meeting.

"Oh, you have brought her," Clarise said, looking at Élisabeth with a warmth in her eyes that made her uncomfortable.

Élisabeth was not used to kindness from older women. Delphine and her friends had always treated her abominably, both because she had her father's adoration and because of the circumstances of her birth. They were an utterly nasty and vicious group of women. So, she could not help feeling a little wary in the presence of Clarise.

Élisabeth regretted her unease because when she approached her, she realized that the warmth that radiated from the woman was sincere. She felt her shoulders loosen when she pulled her into a tight embrace. Élisabeth hesitantly held her. She smelled of cinnamon like she had been baking in the kitchen and her scent soothed her. Clarise smiled at her brightly when she pulled away.

"It's a pleasure to meet you," Clarise said.

"You as well," she replied.

Séverin left her side and withdrew the chair at the head of the table. Élisabeth swiftly slid into the chair at the opposite end. She refused to turn her neck to look at his insufferable face by sitting on his right or left side. She refused to give him *that* much power over her. She thought for a split second that she had caught that wry amusement on his face again, but his brows thundered down as if he was annoyed with himself. *Again.*

"You are both more alike than you think," Kai said with a cheeky grin.

"Shut up," they both said at the same time.

Kai laughed and Inès giggled, sliding into the seat beside the older woman. They looked identical and Élisabeth's eyes slid between them, cataloging their similarities.

"My mother," Inès said, staring fondly at the woman.

Élisabeth felt an odd lurch in her chest. A small flicker of envy. She had never had a mother who looked at her with love and affection. It was a strange thing to witness. She felt that scratchy itch in her throat and swallowed it back. She would never give her enemies any indication that she was weak. Not when Séverin was staring at her so intensely, as if he were trying to figure out what upset her when he hadn't even opened his mouth yet.

"How is it possible?" he asked, looking at Clarise. "That she carries the same blighted magic that taints the land."

"Another twist from the Fates," she said.

Élisabeth stared at them, awaiting answers. She had done something in the maze. Something that had displeased Séverin which was no surprise because everything she did upset him. But it also seemed to shock him. She remembered that arched brow of his rising earlier. She wondered how he'd feel if she told him he was prettier than any girl she'd ever seen.

Élisabeth snickered at the thought.

"Has she gone mad?" Séverin whispered.

Élisabeth's lips dropped and she glared at him.

"You would know a thing or two about that, wouldn't you?" she asked.

His lip twitched in an erratic manner that warned her he was about to do something utterly unhinged to prove her point.

"You need her, Séverin," Clarise said. "She is the key to it all."

Élisabeth didn't know what was unfolding around them. It was heavy, weighted as if the truth would fracture all that she had ever known to be true. She thought of the way her fingers had tingled like they had been struck by lightning. How it had felt like instinct when she stretched that glimmering black sheet over her head. As if it were as natural as breathing.

"It is called aether," Séverin said in a dry tone as if he were forced to lecture a child. "It exists in this realm and is the source that runs our world. It is on every dead thing in this place: the air, the trees, our skin. The only people who are untouched by aether are the living. It is the closest thing to power in this world. Not many can wield it. And those that can often only control small bursts of it."

He nodded at Kai and the young man squinted at the window. He raised a hand, and the window opened so hard the glass shattered.

"Kai," Inès chided.

"Sorry," he said sheepishly. "I've been practicing. I'll fix the window."

"Not enough clearly," Séverin muttered.

"You know if you don't have anything nice to say you could say nothing at all," Élisabeth offered.

"Then I would never speak again," he said.

"*Exactly.*"

"Let us not lose our focus," Clarise said.

It was like she could sense the violence that clouded the air. The need for her and Séverin to claw under each other's skin like beasts. As though nothing would satisfy the other until their enemy met their untimely end. Since he was already dead her options were rather limited, but Élisabeth had a gut feeling that there was a way to end him. Laurent had implied as much. Even if the blade had failed, she would find another way. She would not stop until she was free.

Some days she would dream about Laurent arriving with a true blade that could kill that which could not die. And he would swing it in an unholy arc and cut off Séverin's head and then when he was drenched in the blood of their enemy, he would kiss her.

It was a silly dream, and she'd always had a penchant for glorifying rather mediocre men. Charles had been hungry for fame and yet she had penned terrible, vicious poems in his name. Ones that she had tucked deep in the hidden panel of her drawer in fear that Louise would find it when she snooped. Laurent was not any better; he had given her up to the wraiths, and allowed them to carry her to this dreadful palace and into the arms of a monster whom he knew most intimately. A monster who hunted him as well.

Sometimes she wondered if that was what she believed she deserved. Men who didn't care an ounce about her and would step on her to further their own goals.

A knock sounded on the door. Rough and frantic. Kai rose and Élisabeth straightened when it burst open. Two young men stepped inside. One carried the other in his arms. His face was torn, flesh peeling away like a sliced fruit, revealing the pulpy black interior of its insides. Élisabeth stood up abruptly, chair screeching dramatically behind her.

"My lord," the boy who carried the other said. "We were doing our patrols, and we didn't see it until it was too late."

"See what?" Séverin demanded.

He hadn't so much as straightened at the sight of the mutilated boy and the shaking soldier who held him. They wore midnight-blue coats like Kai and Matthieu did and had rifles strapped to their backs.

"Another Pit opened," he said. "Several miles from here. It is bigger than the last one, and it is spreading fast." His voice shook and his hands struggled to hold the unconscious boy in his arms, as if he could not bear to put him down.

"Is he...?"

"The beast's poison is deadly," Kai said grimly, answering her question. "He will be gone within the hour."

Kai's eyes were crestfallen at the sight of his comrade. He gently took him from the soldier's hands while the boy just stared off into the distance with a blank expression.

"That is impossible," Séverin said.

He looked at Clarise warily and the old woman's lips simply tightened, before she nodded. Clarise seemed to be some type of advisor to Séverin. It struck her as odd because he didn't seem like someone who allowed anyone to guide him.

"We are lucky. It is a far way off. Not anywhere near the town. But you must put up new wards before it spreads."

Séverin cursed.

"Do you recall the way back?" he asked.

The boy was silent, gaze wavering and void of emotion, Kai tapped him on the cheek lightly.

"Our lord has asked you a question, Nicodeme," Kai said.

Élisabeth jolted when she realized the boy who died had disappeared. All that was left behind was the terrible frightful knowledge that he had been there one minute and now he was simply *gone*.

"Where did he go?" she asked.

"There are no corpses. You die. You are gone," Séverin said. He stood up, rising to his impossible height. "Saves us a burial."

Élisabeth flinched at his callous tone.

"Kai, Inès, and you Nicodeme, is it?" he asked. "We will ride out in an hour. Prepare yourselves we will make a stop at the Pit before our journey. Hopefully it will not delay us by much."

Élisabeth felt a strong sense of relief. She would have a few more days now to plot her escape before he returned. While she was sad that someone had died for her to be given this opportunity,

Élisabeth intended to seize it with both hands. It was a good time to slip out now during the chaos before he realized she was still here and had her imprisoned in her bedroom or worse, the dungeon.

Élisabeth was walking backward, hands politely folded behind her back. A paragon of good manners and gentility. It was at that moment when Clarise's shrewd green eyes landed on hers and her mouth pursued.

"You should take the girl," she said. "Kai and Inès might not be enough for you to seal it shut."

Dread slipped down her back. Was he going to sacrifice them to those beasts, feed them while he did his magic and sealed it shut? She would not put it past him to serve his allies to the beasts on a silver platter. She recalled the glint in his eyes when he'd feed Helene to the wraiths. Someone with that level of cruelty was nothing short of a monster, and she could not bear the thought of going anywhere with him.

While the court was not safe it gave her the illusion of civility and rules. Out there in the wilds, there would be nothing but that darkness that trailed across Séverin like a cloak, aching to choke her with its calloused fingers.

She also decided that she did not like Clarise anymore for reminding him of her presence and suggesting she march off to her death. Whatever mayhem that was ensuing here was none of her business. She just had to find her way back to the ferryman. Even if Laurent had said there was no way back Élisabeth chose to believe that there was, and she had every intention of finding it. He had been wrong about the blade, perhaps he was wrong about that too.

Séverin stared at her with cold, distant eyes before he nodded curtly.

"Prepare yourself, human," he said. "You have half an hour."

"You said an hour," she said.

"That does not apply to you."

"I'm not going."

"Either go and pack or Kai can tie you to your horse now without any preparations. It would be wise to pack some food and water. We do not require sustenance so you may starve to death if you rely on us. But alive or dead it is of no consequence to me. Either way, you return to the Graylands. An eternal subject of my court."

A cold shudder ran through her at the picture he painted.

Inès offered her a gentle smile as she disappeared into a door in the corner. There was a bedroom in the library which sounded like a dream. Except nothing in this world was dream-like, everything was bitter and cruel.

Élisabeth decided to take the time to prepare. Sitting here arguing was going to cut into her hour, and she had every intention of taking a *full* hour.

Élisabeth hadn't intended to fall asleep but she did. She had dressed and Colette had brought her some bread, stew, and nuts along with a tin filled with water. She had been fully prepared to venture off into the unknown, but then she had sat down for a bit and then she sprawled down and then she had fallen into a dark slumber.

A hand shook her roughly and she stared into the face of a fallen deity. Angry, beautiful, and proud in equal measures. Her fingers lifted, mind foggy with the residue of sleep and she traced the faint edge of his jaw. He snapped upright with a sharp inhale.

"Don't touch me, human!" he snapped.

Élisabeth was ashamed that she hadn't noticed that it was *him*. But it had angered him, so she didn't regret it that much.

"You won't call me Lisbeth anymore?" she asked hopefully.

"Which one upsets you more?" he asked.

"Lisbeth," she said.

"Human" was impersonal and lacked creativity while "Lisbeth" provoked her rage, reminding her that he *thought* he knew her. He thought he had ownership of her, and that allowed him to call her by a pet name nobody had ever used before. It was always Élisabeth or Babette. Nothing else. It was never Lisbeth. Ever since he had spoken it, she had loathed the name with a passion.

"I shall call you Lisbeth then," he said.

"I shouldn't have answered that," she mumbled.

"No," he said. "But you never do the right thing, Lisbeth. It is why you are here to serve at my will."

"I do not serve you," she spat. "I do not serve weak-willed boys whose hubris shall one day be their downfall."

His lips curled back, revealing those perfectly straight and cruel teeth. Whatever he wished to say was broken by the sound of a knock.

"Come," he called.

Kai cracked the door open.

"The steeds are read—" He paused. "Is *that* what you are wearing?"

It was the second time he had judged her attire and Élisabeth sighed. She wore a beautiful white dress with embroidered peacocks at the hem. The bodice was covered in gems and the corset was snug enough to raise her small breasts to an incredible height. If Élisabeth was going to die in the woods looking into the eyes of creatures that had sprung forth from the pages of a ghastly fairy tale, then she would die amidst the flowers stitched on her magnificent dress.

She would die with grace and beauty.

"Are you certain you don't wish to change into trousers?"

Kai asked. "I think Olivier can spare a pair. He is small enough to fit you."

"Let her be," Séverin said. "If she wishes to dally like a princess through the woods and freeze to death it is of no mind to us."

Élisabeth wrapped herself in a matching fur-lined cloak.

"Here," Kai said, reaching for her heavy pack. There were her spare dresses and her food and water in the pack. "Let me carry that for you."

"Thank you, Kai," she said. "It is so rare to find true gentlemen these days."

Her words were aimed at Séverin who was too busy striking a match against his cigar to listen to her jabs. He pulled it to his fine mouth and sucked deep.

"I don't appreciate men who smoke," she continued. "I think it speaks of a weak disposition."

"I smoke," Kai said, more amused than offended. As if he knew exactly who she was goading with that comment.

"I don't like girls who talk too much," Séverin added. He turned his head and she smelt the sickeningly sweet fumes of his smoke, slipping out his nostrils like twin serpents. "I think it speaks to a desperation that is utterly unappealing."

Élisabeth ignored him, tilting her body to Kai. Pretending as though he was nothing more than his namesake. A mere phantom.

"Did you hear someone speak, Kai?" she asked.

"Very mature," Séverin said. "How old are you again?"

Élisabeth simply smiled, pleased that she'd drawn that frown on his mouth with sheer will alone.

They walked towards a stone fountain where eight thoroughbred steeds awaited them. Everyone stood by theirs. Inès was stroking the neck of a red mare, whispering soothing words to her. Nicodeme had washed the dirt and gore off his body, but his eyes were glassy. She felt a stroke of pity that he had barely had time to mourn before he was pushed into a mission. Matthieu was there leaning over his steed to speak to Inès. There was an old man with spectacles sliding off his crooked nose who shifted on both feet, looking rather skittish, as he eyed Séverin.

Élisabeth felt distaste fill her at the sight of Séverin's twin servants. They didn't simply serve him, they *adored* him which was blasphemous. They stood beside their mares, staring at her with hostile eyes.

"We are a horse short," Élisabeth said.

"Do you think I am going to trust you with a horse?" Séverin asked.

"How will I get there?" she demanded. "Will you drag me behind yours?"

"Tempting," he mused. "You will ride with—"

"Inès," she said desperately.

The girl's head spun to her with a curious look.

"May I ride with you?" she asked.

She couldn't ride with *him*, and she didn't trust anyone else. Perhaps she could handle Kai, but she recalled the excited look in his eyes when he'd seen Inès earlier and she did not want to come between whatever that was. Matthieu was an option, but he was a last resort. He would spend the entire trip teasing her and that was simply unacceptable.

"Of course," she said.

Inès comfortably swung atop in her trousers and Élisabeth wondered if she had made a mistake when she picked her dress. She had presumed there would be a carriage, and she opened her mouth to ask about that before Séverin spoke.

"It is too dense and narrow for any other means of transport," he said. His tone dripped with sarcasm when he next spoke. "You will have to suffer, Princess. Just like the rest of us."

"How did you—"

"You get this haughty look in your eye when you wish to make demands," he said.

Élisabeth felt a flash of annoyance. She was not some spoiled noblewoman. She was a lady raised in good standing. She did not ride horses astride. She suddenly felt utterly out of her depth.

"Here." Inès offered her a hand.

Nicodeme came to her.

"May I?" he asked, pointing at her waist.

"Thank you," Élisabeth said when he lifted her and Inès' strong hand guided her behind her. She was glad to not be given the reins. She was not a distinguished rider. She understood the gist of it, but she did not ride frequently enough to make any great progress.

"It is a six-day journey to the new Pit," Nicodeme said in his throaty, deep voice. His dark hair was tucked behind his ears, and he had the sleek face of a hunter. Someone who was made to destroy and kill. He looked determined as if the thought of silencing the beasts who robbed him of his comrade was his only purpose.

It struck her that she didn't know why she was coming along. It was like bits and pieces were being given to her while Séverin continued to keep her in the dark.

Élisabeth glanced at the old man.

"Who is he?" she whispered.

"Gaspar, the last keeper of the library. He is helping us find a book that might save the Graylands," Inès said.

"It will be a bit of a detour, my lord," Gaspar said, staring at his wrinkled map. "But I can speak on our new course once we come upon the Pit."

Looking into the thicket beyond the grounds and straight

into the hollow nest of trees, Élisabeth felt an ominous presence.

One that pulsed like a living heartbeat.

———

The forest deepened, opening to them like a boar did for a taxidermist's blade. Overhead, mauve light seeped out of the sky and darkness slithered forward until only the sharp, glittering stars guided them like rope.

"Why did your mother ask me to come along?" Élisabeth asked.

Inès and Élisabeth had fallen behind the group. Her mare wasn't the strongest and Élisabeth felt a hint of pity for forcing the beast to carry her added weight.

"How much do you know about the Graylands?" she asked.

"Not enough," Élisabeth said. "I know that you are all dead. Except for the humans who are collared."

She eyed the twins and the heavy gilded collars around their pale throats. She shuddered at the thought of the weight of those things around her flesh. She would unravel if Séverin ever subjected her to it. She would go feral and claw his heart out with her teeth.

"It is very much like Prasin," Inès said. "People are hungry for status, for heat, for *aether*. Aether is everything. It is a substance that exists everywhere but also in people. It allows one the power to do grand things. They can throw you against walls or sever your arms from your body with a slice of their palms."

Élisabeth shuddered at the thought of anyone wielding such power.

"Don't worry," she said. "Most of us can only do small parlor tricks."

She lifted her fingers and a crisp orange-brown leaf floated from the ground. Élisabeth inhaled sharply, feeling it float towards her. It tickled her nose and despite the recoiling sensation in her belly that told her to flee, a surprised laugh escaped her.

"It is nearly impossible to be precise with aether," she said. "It is like a fickle dog that refuses to obey."

"He is pretty strong," she said, nodding at Séverin.

He was several paces ahead of them keeping up with Nicodeme. So, his arrogant self couldn't hear her words.

"He controls many threads of aether," Inès said. "His focus is unlike any I've ever seen. Even better than the last Lord of the Below."

"Lord of the Below," Élisabeth whispered.

It was a fitting title for the ruler of this subterranean realm. The Lord of Ghosts would have been much more accurate.

"The most difficult thing is creating wards," she said. "It is like weaving a blanket. Anytime a Pit opens he requires people to channel from to close the seals. While he can pull from his surroundings, the aether present in people is the purest, rawest source."

"That doesn't explain why I am here," she said.

"You are soaked in something that resembles the woods we are going into," she said, lowering her tone. "It practically seeps from you."

"What does that mean?"

"The Blight," Inès said. "It creeps over the forest in these gauzy, black tendrils. Quiet like the magic you possess."

"Is that a good or bad thing?" Élisabeth asked, unsettled by her words.

"I don't know," she said. "We hope it is a good thing."

Élisabeth was silent, as she contemplated her words. What would Séverin do to her if he found out she was of no use to him? What if he killed her? He hadn't punished her for the attempt on his life.

"Is your mother his advisor?" she asked, swiftly changing the subject to distract her from her bleak thoughts. "I'm surprised he listens to anyone other than himself."

"My mother and I have the Sight," she said. "We see things before they occur. We've always had an aptitude for it. Even when we were alive. It was dim then and has only gotten stronger since we awakened in the Graylands."

"How fascinating," Élisabeth mused.

Inès nodded. "Humans don't carry aether. Only the dead do. But you...you are a curiosity, Élisabeth. It is not aether you carry but something else. I meant it when I said you may be the key to our troubles."

Her heart raced, thudding in her chest like a broken cello string, echoing an unnatural rhythm.

"Is this trouble you speak of what is causing the beasts and the Pit?" she asked.

"Among other things," Inès said. "The Graylands is growing weak and diseased. It is crumbling around us, rotting at this very moment like an infected limb. I don't know how much longer we can keep this place together. It is like ink that has spilled on a piece of paper and no amount of blotting the stain can erase it."

"So, he wants to use me to seal this new Pit?" she asked. "Will it hurt?"

"It will exhaust you and you will be weak for a few days. But the magic you command is different, Élisabeth. And perhaps, it will seal it shut permanently," she said. "But he won't take enough to kill you."

"How do you know that?" she asked.

Inès gave her a smile that was intended to be reassuring but was anything but. It was worse that she broke eye contact and stared straight ahead as if she did not believe her own words.

Élisabeth knew then that she had to escape before they reached the Pit.

What would he do to her *if* she was the key to saving his corrupt world?

Élisabeth did not intend to find out. Whatever twisted idea he had in that mind of his, Élisabeth would be long gone before he got the chance to use her as his pawn. She had to escape the second the opportunity presented itself.

This was not her world, and she was under no obligation to save it.

Élisabeth was only loyal to herself.

Part Three

The Beasts

When the world was born and magic sang its tune, it was said that a coin was tossed among seven high mages, and three were picked among them to rule. There was the golden-skinned Pras with his enchanted bow and arrow, the sharp-eyed, misty Mòrge with his crooked fingers, and Laos with his gold-spun hair and wind-bright smile.

Devotionals No. I, Verse 4.
Excerpt from *The Last Scripture* 250 AD.

Chapter Twelve

They stopped at midnight to rest. Élisabeth's legs were stiff and the bread she had nibbled on was long gone, leaving behind nothing but slick crumbs on her fingers. It had gotten colder at night and for the second time since they departed, she wished she'd worn trousers like Inès and Séverin's human servants: Odette was the girl's name, and the boy was Olivier. They were twins, as she had suspected.

Odette and Olivier began to set up a grandiose black tent for Séverin. One intended for a king. Nobody had brought tents and Élisabeth realized belatedly that they were to sleep outside. The idea was not a tempting one.

Nicodeme knelt down. He had lit a small flame and clutching the wooden trinket around his neck, he prayed to Pras the Hunter that they would make it safely through the woods. There was an odd, haunted look in his eyes as he recited the devotionals. His pale, muted fingers locked around the trinket as if it were a battle sword.

"Are we to sleep with the wolves?" she asked.

"Animals do not feed on our flesh," Kai said.

"We are not tasty enough," Matthieu said, licking his forearm to test his remark.

"And what of mine?" she asked.

Kai was silent.

"We'll keep an eye out," Matthieu said. "Nico, Kai, and I shall do rotations, won't we?"

"We will," Kai echoed.

"And I," she offered. Hoping he did not hear the eagerness in her tone. "I don't think I will sleep much."

Élisabeth intended to flee that night. They were still close to the palace. She had been keeping track of every path they had crossed and every turn they made. She was certain she could find her way back. It would be trickier finding her way from the palace to the city, but once she did, she could look for Laurent and ask him to help her find a way home. Maybe she could bargain with the ferryman. His price would likely be steeper than her first trip. But maybe she could tempt him.

Kai looked at Séverin to see if he would agree.

"If she wishes to be useful, let her," Séverin said. "I doubt she will make the offer again."

Élisabeth felt her chest loosen. It did not matter what happened next.

She had found her opening.

Kai tapped her shoulder and Élisabeth sat upright, alert, and afraid. She raised her hand and she felt that tingly feeling of magic coat her fingers and then she watched in horror as Kai flew several paces back. He was agile enough to land on his feet, boots skidding harshly on the ground, kicking up a storm of dirt and wayward roots and brambles.

Élisabeth breathed hard and stared at her hands in shock.

"Amazing," he whispered.

"I'm sorry," she squeaked.

Nobody roused at the chaos, and she looked at the bodies around them. Séverin had not let his servants rest in his tent, even though it was big enough to fit them all comfortably. It did not surprise her that the selfish boy refused to share his warmth. Even though he did not feel the cold. Not when his bones were made of ice.

It was rather selfish of him.

"Do you think about it a lot?" she asked abruptly. "How did you end up here? What is *here*? The Last Scripture never spoke much about the Graylands. Only that it was the realm of the dead and is overseen by the Fate Lune."

"I am no philosopher," he said. "My guess is as good as yours. Are you good for your rotation?" he asked, swiftly changing the topic. As if he didn't enjoy speaking about his death.

It was clear to see that she upset him.

"I'm sorry."

"It is fine," he murmured. "I miss my family I suppose."

Kai lay down in the empty bedroll beside Nicodeme, and she swallowed back the guilt of bringing up sad memories.

Élisabeth waited two hours for him to fully fall asleep before she slowly sat upright. She decided to steal Séverin's horse. For no reason other than the fact that it would haunt him. It would crawl under his skin, knowing that she had outwitted him. That she had escaped whatever torturous future he had planned for her and done it all on the back of his horse.

A smile danced on her lips as she unraveled the rope tied to the silver linden tree. She was a big beast of a horse with a glossy black hide and intelligent eyes. She whinnied as if she could tell Élisabeth was not her master.

"Shhh," she stroked her neck. "I will be far kinder to you than that despicable man."

The stubborn horse dug her hooves into the dirt, refusing to move an inch.

"Come along," Élisabeth said, yanking gently on the reins, reminding her of who was in charge now. "I'll give you some treats if you listen."

"Bribery," a slow drawl said. "How utterly unoriginal."

Her head spun to see Séverin looming behind her. He wore a loose billowy black shirt tucked into his fitted trousers and a fitted obsidian vest with silver detailing. A strand of dark hair fell onto his forehead sliding between the edge of his masque and skin. It was a simple, black performance masque less frightening than the animal ones he wore with a painted snarl at court during the nightly revels. He looked ethereal and exquisitely beautiful under the moonlight, and she hated that her attention had fractured.

He was a few paces away from her. And the desperation in her chest ratcheted. She would not get an opportunity like this again. Her hands yanked the reins, prepared to heave herself with or without the horse's acceptance when the steed reared back, deadly hooves raised in warning. Élisabeth stumbled back, falling on her behind as she watched those hooves descend. A flutter of panic slid up her chest leaving behind the raw and bitter taste of fear on her tongue.

Séverin grabbed her arm, pulling her roughly just as the hooves of the horse slid into the earth, raising a storm of mud. Her heart was racing, thinking of how her ribcage would have shattered to dust under those strong legs. There was an ache in her arm where he had pulled her, but it was growing duller as she caught her breath.

She couldn't bring herself to thank him. In fact, it was

rather worrisome that he had saved her. It meant that he found her useful enough that she served him better alive than dead.

He still held her elbow. His fingers were wrapped in those leather gloves, and he pulled her along, dragging her mercilessly towards his tent.

"Let go of me," she said, twisting her arm to escape his grasp.

"Your hubris is unmatched, to even think you could steal Ebony and flee into the night is laughable," he said with an unamused laugh. There was a dark edge to it. Something that raised her hackles, and she began to put true effort into her escape. Her elbow collided with his chest, striking flesh that was more muscle than anything else. He lifted the flap of his tent, drawing her into the dark and that faint smell of lemongrass tickled her senses. Most likely his fresh sheets and bedding.

"If you wish to act like a prisoner then you will be treated like one," Séverin said.

He placed her down on the thick spread that made his bed. It was padded and soft. Far better than the thin bedroll that had been given to the rest of them. It took her a moment to realize exactly what he was grabbing when his back turned.

Élisabeth shot up and dove for the tent opening, but he caught her, strong fingers coiling around her waist like a shackle. His leather-clad hands clutched a thin length of rope.

His hand raised and she felt something slip down her. Something with that strange air of mystique and coldness. It draped around her like a cloak and when she tried to lift her leg, she realized she could not move. Nor could she raise her hands.

"What...what did you do to me?" she asked.

"Bound you in aether," he said.

He lifted her limp wrists, coiled the rope around her skin, and did the same to her other hand.

Fear shot up her spine and she felt a bead of sweat drip down her neck. She attempted to fight his hold, to destroy it to shards. She mentally pushed against it, drawing on the seams. Aether emitted a soft gray glow, and she could see where it sealed shut around her ankles.

She used his distraction to focus on freeing her legs. Élisabeth raised her palm, fighting against his hold as she shot a wave of her own dark magic at her ankle.

It took a lot of energy to claw at that one thread, and she felt a sense of victory when it unspooled, falling down her body like water and vanishing from her flesh.

"Impressive," he mused.

Élisabeth tried to unwind her other leg, but he tightened the rope around her wrist stifling any movement. He knotted it swiftly and efficiently as if he tied people up for a living. It was impossible to tear away the aether that still pinned her other leg with her hands sealed together.

"Release me," Élisabeth snarled.

"Rest," Séverin said.

He slid down to the ground against a wooden beam. It had taken the twins an hour to set up his accommodations. And he called her *princess*.

"How long will I be like this?" she demanded.

"Until dawn," he said. "You can no longer be trusted to be left to your own devices. You will spend the remainder of the journey bound during the nights and under my strict supervision."

A chasm opened in her stomach. One that threatened to swallow her whole. It was like she was watching all her dreams wither into ashes. Just as she had languished in the background of the Opera House, relegated to the back, shadowed, and cloistered she was trapped once more. As if she was doomed to never find a sliver of happiness in this world. Cursed to always watch other people live while she stood as still as a frozen river.

She thought of the fortune teller and her dire predictions and realized that perhaps the lady was not a fraud. Perhaps, she was the first honest person she had ever come across in her life.

Élisabeth sank onto his bed. Even though he had not given her permission to do so. She could not be expected to sit upright all night. She enjoyed the flare in his nostrils when she used her legs to slide under his blankets. She hoped she burned her scent into his belongings. She hoped she was a stain upon his life. She hoped he never survived her.

"The rope is too tight," she lied. Even though her brain wanted to surrender, her heart refused to go down without a proper fight.

To her surprise he stood up, rising to his tall height, and loomed over her on the bed. She sat upright, heart racing as she waited for the perfect moment for her attack. He hunched over sliding his finger into the rope, tugging lightly.

"More than enough ro—"

Élisabeth raised her legs and wrapped them around his back, throwing him off balance. She felt the heavy weight of him on top of her, and she used the element of surprise to loop her bound hands around his neck and pull as tight as she could, intending to strangle him. The rope dug into his skin, and she yanked so hard it was a surprise she didn't break the skin.

She recalled how he had not bled even when her blade had struck his flesh, almost as if his insides were made of glass, and she shivered at the thought.

He grabbed her wrists and performed a maneuver that was so lightning-quick it left her reeling. He separated her wrists slightly and yanked them forward, sliding out from under her chokehold. He spun her so she lay flat on her chest, pinning her with his hips. It was eerily silent behind her. Her chest rose and fell violently at the sheer physical energy she had exerted.

"Now where did a well-bred girl learn such nasty fighting moves?" he asked.

She felt his chest press on her back when he leaned down. He was so close she could feel the frost of his breath tickle her ear.

Élisabeth refused to answer. She just lay there impossibly still, hoping he would tire of her and leave. She was all too aware of his presence. Of the sharp pressure of his body against her own, of the heavy weight of his hips, and the sleek muscles that lined his thigh resting flat on the outskirts of her body. Goosebumps danced along her flesh; she had never been this close to a man before, not outside of ballet at least, and even then, it was handholding and acting. It was false and contrived. This was real.

"I can sit here all day," Séverin warned.

She swallowed and spoke against her will.

"I used to walk by the docks in the afternoon just after a long day of shopping," she said. "I would watch the sailors fight, and I suppose I picked up a thing or two."

He spun her around and she felt the slide of his fingers around her throat, grasping her tightly.

"Why should I let you live after that little ploy?"

Élisabeth felt her stomach tighten in unease. Somehow this was worse than when she had been flattened forward. Now she was forced to look into his dreadful eyes both the bright blue orb and the slightly lighter, left one that she suspected was blind. When she had attacked him, she had swung from the left, prepared to prove her suspicions. He hadn't reacted quickly enough, and she assumed that had less to do with his alertness and more to do with his vision. She wondered how it had happened. And what scars lay beneath his masque? His shirt was loose, and she could see the left side of his throat where the skin was rubbery and tight. The sight brought a flash of pity to her stomach.

His eyes darkened as if he knew exactly what she was thinking, and his grip tightened.

"You need me," she said. Her words were a gasp of air.

"I don't need anyone," he said.

"I am important to your mission. That's what Clarise said," she said with her chin raised. "You would not have brought me along otherwise. You won't kill me, so if you are done with your empty threats and posturing then I'd appreciate it if you left me alone."

"Do you think that I won't snap your pretty neck?" he asked.

His thumb pressed against her pulse and she hated that he knew it was racing. He knew that she *was* afraid, but she simply hid it better than he expected.

"Do it," she breathed.

For a moment, she thought he would. There was a cold glimmer in his eyes that frightened her. It was like she had poked at a bear and was now in danger of being mauled.

He slid off her slowly. She could feel the flex of his hard thighs as he stood up.

He marched outside, angrily shoving back the flaps. Élisabeth released a loose breath in his absence. She knew that she had lost her chance to escape, and she wondered if another opportunity would present itself.

She would have to put her head down and convince Séverin that she was not a threat, that she intended to play nice and hope that he fell for the trick.

It would be like a ballet performance. She would fall into the role of the character and lose herself to the music.

And she would wait in the end with bated breath and see if he fell for her honeyed lies.

Chapter Thirteen

Séverin didn't return to his tent until the sun began to rise on the horizon. He kept watch over the camp even though he wasn't supposed to play guard. She was sleeping, elbows tucked to her chest, fingers clasped together almost as if she were praying, but he was not fooled. There was nothing holy about Élisabeth Bellacourt. She was a stray cat who was just as likely to curl up beside you as it was to bite you. On the outside, she was polished and demure, but when provoked her eyes grew alight with rage and her tongue became a weapon of its own making.

He had a thin, skeletal branch in his hand, and he trailed it along her collarbone. She twitched but didn't wake up, which said much about how exhausted she was. He used the branch to stroke upwards. A soft sound escaped her, and he continued his path. The leaf on the end tickled the skin just above her lips and her nose scrunched. It wasn't long before her eyes opened. She shot upright so quickly, that she got dizzy and swiftly fell back down.

"Careful," Séverin said. Lips hiked in a mocking smile.

"What are you doing?" she asked. "Is it a habit of yours to stand above a woman's bed, touching her with a filthy branch?"

"Only the ones I hate," he said evenly. "The ones I like get rose petals."

Her stormy gray eyes burned as if she could incinerate him on the spot. And then she swallowed a deep breath before her demeanor changed. A smile tilted her lips and words that he never thought she'd speak filled the air.

"I am sorry for my reaction last night," Élisabeth said. "It will not happen again."

Séverin's eyes narrowed. Her back was straight in that manner that hinted at a childhood filled with many etiquette lessons. He had never liked girls like her. Even when he was alive, he had despised highborn girls. He hated their practiced speeches and that coy look in their eyes like they were the ones secretly in control.

They were not in control. Séverin was *always* in control.

Élisabeth blinked at him expectantly. Her sweet smile wavered as if it required too much energy to uphold. It was obvious that she had changed her tactic and was attempting another approach. Séverin was amused by how foolish she thought he was. It was almost admirable.

"Do you want me to forgive you?" he asked.

"More than anything," she said, the lie slipping past her mouth with a practiced grace.

The corners of her mouth tightened as if it had cost her soul to speak those words. Séverin felt a shock of amusement that he hadn't felt in a long time. It was the feeling of having a new plaything. Something unique that was made for him alone.

"Say 'Please, forgive me, I was wrong, and you were right as always,'" Séverin said.

He took a step forward, catching her chin and tilting her head up. She intended to murmur the words looking down at her lap, but he would not allow that. This way he could see the fire in her eyes and let it warm him. "Tell me that 'you are a wicked, terrible girl who wants me to guide her.'"

Élisabeth swallowed and he could feel himself growing intoxicated by her internal battle. He could see the turmoil inside her, as her pride fought to take control. Her lip curled in disgust before she schooled her features and was that demure girl once more.

Except her eyes gave her away. Gray and bright and vicious. Like angry, ruinous stars.

"I was wrong, and you were right. I want you to guide me," she said.

"You've cut out many words," he said, tilting her chin higher, feeling the warmth of her breath graze his lips. "Are you a wicked, terrible girl, Lisbeth?"

"Yes," she whispered.

"I am glad that you have admitted it," he said. "I will reward you."

She held out her wrists, presuming that he spoke of freedom.

"No more rope?" she asked hopefully.

He untangled the strands. "The rope stays during the night, but I will teach you how to build a protective shield with your magic in case those beasts slip through the new Pit, so you can protect yourself."

She seemed to like the sound of that. Séverin was going to offer to teach her anyway, but it was funnier to let her think that her little act had swayed him.

It would be interesting to see just how long this act lasted.

They took a break at noon. Gaspar was conversing with Nicodeme who was the only person the old man considered intellectual enough to speak with. Or at the very least the only one who would indulge him along with Élisabeth. Sometimes she would sit and listen to his ramblings.

They were close to the heart of the Blight. The Pit always sprung from the parts of the wood that were diseased, as if it fed off the dark magic. The same magic Élisabeth possessed.

His servants kept to themselves while the rest of them sat in a circle.

"So, who wins?" Matthieu asked.

Kai and Matthieu were singing to Élisabeth to see who could hit the highest notes and who would be deemed the best singer by her trained ear. Of course, Élisabeth was simply ecstatic that she had been asked to act as judge. She sat on a log staring at them both with a serious expression as if she were weighing a political problem of the highest caliber.

"Matthieu has a good cadence," she said. "Very strong lungs indeed."

Matthieu smirked at Kai.

"But Kai's voice has a softness that is rather arresting," she said. "Simply splendid!"

Matthieu's smile dropped as quickly as it had appeared.

"You can't pick us both," Kai said. "I have money at stake."

"As do I," Matthieu said. "And his salary is higher, remember that when you pick, Élisabeth. I could use the money more th—"

"Don't sway her by telling her how poor you are!" Kai exclaimed.

"You've known her longer, she could be biased," Matthieu said.

"I met her several hours before you did," Kai said.

"More than enough time for her to pick favorites."

Séverin turned his gaze from the bickering idiots to Élisabeth who leaned over to whisper to Inès.

"No conspiring with Inès," Matthieu called, pointing an accusing finger at Élisabeth. "She's more biased than you."

"I have made my verdict," Élisabeth said with a solemn expression. "And the winner is..."

She paused dramatically, soaking in their eagerness.

"Matthieu!" Élisabeth said.

"Oh, bollocks," Kai said, kicking at the dirt. He pouted and Inès ruffled his curls which made his mouth tilt in a smile.

Matthieu whooped in joy and rushed to Élisabeth, sweeping her off her feet. He spun her around and she pounded his back laughing, telling him to put her down.

Séverin felt something stir at the sight of her smile. Something that spoiled his day.

He marched towards her, staring at her deeply, before jutting his chin in the direction of the woods. His lips lined in a scowl.

"Come," he said.

Odette and Olivier rose to follow him, but he shook his head.

"Stay," he said. "We will return."

They sat with gloomy expressions. From the way they leaned their heads together, he could tell they were about to start plotting against Élisabeth. He thought of warning her for a second, but then he bit his tongue. Élisabeth was not his responsibility. She was just another vessel for him to use, to stitch his broken world together again.

The Graylands was all he had left. He had no intention of discovering what happens to a ghost that dies. He was not religious even though his mother had been, and he was a terrible person, so it was safe to assume that he was not going anywhere nice. He had built a world here that bent to his will. He had power of the tangible kind that was his Seat and his title as the Lord of the Below. But also, the unseen kind that was his remarkable control of aether.

He refused to give it up.

He wished his wraiths were with him, but they didn't like the Blighted woods. Something about it unsettled the immortal creatures. Some people believed that the wraiths were the dead who died in the Graylands. Each time a wraith claimed a soul it became a wraith. In a cyclical manner of rebirth. But if that theory were true, it did not explain how the first wraith came to be. It was one of the many puzzles of the Graylands.

"Luring me away to skin me like a rabbit?" Élisabeth asked.

"Is that your way of asking me to undress you?" he asked calmly.

Her head spun towards him. Eyes wide as saucers.

"It was a joke," Séverin said dryly. "You would have to pay for that pleasure."

"I could be the wealthiest woman alive, and I would not pay a single cent to spend a night with you," Élisabeth said. "You are not the sort of man I am drawn to."

"And what sort of men are you drawn to?" he asked.

Curiosity bled into his voice and he hated that he showed any hint of interest in her life. He opened his mouth to dismiss the question, but she was quick to answer.

"I like men with fair hair and green or brown eyes who are short," she said. "I also like men with rough voices, the kind that feel like sandpaper on your skin. I like men who do not walk with an over-confident gait as if they own every room they walk into, but ones who are humble. But mostly I like *kind* men."

It did not escape him that she described the complete opposite of himself. His hair was dark, and he was tall. Not to mention Kai had given him much shite over the years about his *lovely* voice. Every sentence was crafted to remind him that he was undesirable, and he did not know why it crept under his skin like poison, but he had a terrible urge to hurt her.

"Is that why Charles chose your sister over you?" he asked. "He must have realized what a nasty piece of work you are."

He had spent many nights in Box Five watching her. He knew *everything* about her.

Her father's little prize jewel.

Séverin had known even then that destroying her would end Hugo Bellacourt. It would be like crushing his fragile heart in his palm. He could only imagine how much the old man suffered knowing that Élisabeth was trapped here with him.

Élisabeth stared at him with those hauntingly wide eyes. Fresh snow had begun to fall, dripping around her in a halo. Her long dark hair danced in the breeze and her cloak was drawn open revealing her snow-white dress and her smooth tan skin.

Only she would prance around the woods in a dress fit for a dinner party. As much as it brought him no joy to think it, Séverin had a single perfectly functioning eye that could see that she was the most beautiful girl he had ever come across. Dark hair and siren eyes. She was tall for a girl and had this swan-like grace about her that likely came from her dancing classes. She was *exactly* the kind of girl he would have been drawn to in another lifetime if it were not for her haughty attitude and spoiled behavior.

"Charles came to me," she said with her chin held high. "Practically begged me to take him back. He kissed me in the garden and—"

"Shut up," Séverin snarled. "Don't make me sick to my stomach."

Élisabeth had that little twist to her mouth she got when she presumed she had won their verbal spar. She didn't win. Séverin relented because he had felt a flicker of guilt at the hurt in her eyes when he'd said that. He knew she didn't get along with her family. Her wicked sister and that devil of a stepmother had done everything in their power to push Élisabeth into the shadows because they knew if she ever came into the light nobody would ever glance twice at her sister, the pathetic, less talented Bellacourt girl.

"I have brought you here to learn to shield," he said. "Not to hear the lackluster details of your love life." And because he could not help himself, he added. "I doubt a man has ever touched you properly."

"I doubt a woman has ever let you anywhere near her," she retorted.

"I doubt a man has ever made you scream," he said.

"What does that even mean?" she demanded.

Séverin smirked, pleased to hold something over her. Of course, a well-bred little girl like her didn't know the first thing about pleasure.

"My point exactly," he said.

She hesitated, torn between asking for an explanation and pretending as if she knew what he meant.

"Let us begin," Élisabeth said, breaking the silence.

Séverin resisted the urge to laugh, and her gaze darkened, almost daring him to give in to his instincts.

"I will be on the attack, and you will be on defense," he said. "It is easier to draw from your surroundings. While we can draw aether from within, it is limited and requires time to be replenished. I presume your gift works the same way."

"Why is it that I have this *gift*?" she asked. She said the word 'gift' the way one would say 'curse'. As if she didn't believe there was anything good about it. In this case, Séverin was inclined to believe the same.

"I'm not certain," he said. "I presume it has to do with your unique connection to the Opera House. It is a ley line. One of those places that has a mystic energy which explains why it is one of the few portals to enter the Graylands."

Séverin crossed the glade and made his way to her.

He pulled on his leather gloves on the off chance he'd be required to touch her for demonstration.

"Do you see it around you?" he asked.

"No," she said.

"Look carefully," he said.

Her eyes scanned their surroundings, but it came back empty. They were growing closer to the areas of the wood that were Blighted. He could feel a strange, void-like energy pulsing from the trees. He could see the dark magic that poisoned the woods, layered like moss on the bushes and ground. It spun around them in threads of black, trailing its rotten fingers across the glade, echoing that same magic that Élisabeth controlled.

Séverin caught her chin, tilting her head higher to look at the trees.

"Slowly," he said. "What do you see?"

"You. Scowling," she said.

"Funny," he said with a straight face. "Try harder."

Élisabeth snapped upright when he placed his hand on the small of her back, guiding her forward.

"Think about how it feels when you're on stage and every-one's eyes are on you and you can smell all the scents that cloud the air, feel the presence of the audience," he said. "Imagine exactly how it feels. How everything feels so alive and tangible. Look around you and recreate that feeling."

Élisabeth took a deep breath, taking a step forward to escape his touch. If it were anyone else, he might have felt offense at the gesture, but with her, he only felt relief. He shouldn't be touching her. He shouldn't even be near her right now.

"I see something," she whispered. "A halo. It is this black

hue, and it is like a smear of color around everything, blocking out the gray-white tint that is aether." Her eyes turned to him and it widened. "There is so much aether around you. It is swallowing you whole."

"I am a rather powerful being," Séverin said. "Do you see the threads?"

"I see lines of it," she said. "Waving in the air like a flag."

Séverin followed her gaze. The world was covered in threads. Not many people could see them, but those who could, could manipulate them. Shielding was the easiest form of using aether and he suspected she could likely shield with her gifts. It seemed to be similar to his, but corrosive when it came into contact. He thought of the way Matthieu had described it: "It was eating away at it, growing stronger as it did so".

"Watch me," he said.

Séverin raised his hand and yanked several threads forward. He raised them over them both, pulling them under the dome of his magic. Inside the air was silent and nothing penetrated their prison. If his shield was weaker, he would be able to pick up sound, but he had ensured it was as strong as steel. "Try it yourself."

Élisabeth raised a hand, but she reached for her own threads. Every person was covered in aether. Just as she was covered in those oily, black tendrils.

Séverin lowered her hand with a sharp look.

"Draw from your surroundings," he said. "You lose energy quicker if you draw from yourself."

"I didn't know it was mine," she said in a matter-of-fact, practically borderline bratty tone. "How was I supposed to know?"

"Of course," he murmured. "Your beauty hides a lack of intelligence. Perhaps this is a waste of my time."

"I didn't hear anything after you said, 'your beauty'," Élisabeth said, rather smugly.

"My point *exactly*," he said.

Séverin took a step away from her. They would have to return to their journey. With each day that passed with the Pit open, they risked innumerable beasts crawling from there. The only good news was that Gaspar said they remained on course to the old library. So, this trip would not take as long as he expected.

Something crackled in the air and Séverin stiffened. Several frantic people crashed through the clearing on horseback.

"They've tracked us," Kai said. "They are a few paces away. We don't have much time."

Nicodeme had his rifle pointed towards some indistinct point. He could sense the oncoming threads of dark magic. It meant there were beasts nearby. And quite a few of them.

"We can't run back," Séverin said. "We need to keep moving forward."

"I can sense their threads, Séverin," Kai said. His voice was tangled in a worried knot. "There are seven of them. And only five trained fighters among us. We could sustain casualties."

Séverin sent a flood of calm towards all of them. More so towards Odette and Olivier who were shaking uncontrollably. He could sway emotions though he rarely used it. He didn't care enough about what people were feeling to alter it. But fear was the cousin of cowardice, and it could easily get one killed.

"Thralls to the back," he snapped. "I'll shield you."

"I'm not a thrall," Élisabeth said.

Even in the middle of a looming battle she still managed to get under his skin. It was a talent she alone possessed.

Séverin walked towards her, footsteps thudding loudly in

the silence. Her back straightened. He caught her chin, raising her head so she could see the raging fury in his eyes.

"You can mouth off to me as you please in *private*, but I won't tolerate any disobedience when our lives are in danger," Séverin said. "So, help me, Lisbeth, if you step one toe out of line and risk our lives, I will kill you myself."

"I will mouth off to you in public too," she said. "Everyone should know what an idio–"

A strange rumbling sound emitted from his mouth. Half growl and half snarl.

"Say that you will behave," he demanded.

He heard the beasts in the distance. Their howls cut through the air with an odd, quivering note. A noise that no animal made. When he turned back to Élisabeth she trembled under his touch. Her eyes were wide and alight with fear. Her fingers were clutched tight before her in a wringing hold like she was drying a wet cloth.

"I will behave," she whispered.

"Sit on Odette's horse," he said. "I'll place the shield on you. If my focus breaks and you are vulnerable, flee and head north, we will find you after."

Élisabeth nodded and went to Odette who did not seem pleased to share her horse, but whatever protest the meek girl wished to speak was swallowed when Séverin shot her a curt look.

"You too, old man," he said to Gaspar. "Stay back and under the shield."

Once the mortals and Gaspar were safe behind them, he turned to the others.

"Rifles to slow them down," Séverin said to Kai, Inès, Matthieu, and Nicodeme. All of them were trained and Inès was a terrifyingly good shooter. Perhaps, even one of the best he had ever met. Better than him that was for certain. "Inès and

Nico take the left. Kai and Matthieu take the right and I will take the center. Weaken them and I will finish them off."

Séverin was the only one who could kill them. They did not die with bullets. It slowed them down enough for one to outrun them. They could only die with aether. And a strong dose of it. Nobody weak and untrained in aether could stop them. It had to come from a practiced user.

They charged through the thicket. Teeth bared and talons digging into the thin sheet of snow. Their yellow eyes were fixated on him with a wild hunger. They always came to him first. They were predators and they sensed him as the biggest threat. Their forms were clawed and hunched, almost human-like. As if a person had been metamorphosed into a beast and kept certain attributes of both species.

Some were curled over with hooked spines and sparse fur that ranged from chestnut brown to black as nightfall, leaping on all four of their spindly limbs. Some had antlers poking from their head like roots, curled and twisting into the air like a pair of outstretched palms, clasped in prayer. Some of them had tattered, web-like wings and those went airborne and were the most dangerous to track and kill.

"Air," Séverin roared.

They were quick and raised their rifles up. Shots rang out and he tossed his hand backward covering the humans in a shield. He flung his other hand forward, throwing out a force-field, watching them fly several feet away, and landing on their backs. All he could see was a curling mass of forked tails, bright canines, and dirt-stained hooves as they collapsed in a heap, shaking the trees like a gust of wind.

Séverin marched forward, hearing the shots ring out.

"They are behind us," Élisabeth said.

He could feel their claws scraping at his shield, searching for a crack. Séverin gritted his teeth against their assault. It felt like their nails were sifting through his mind, peeling it like raw fruit, leaving behind nothing but curled skin.

"Séverin. Left!" Inès called.

He spread his arms, slicing the beast in half. Blood sprayed his face, a sour smell erupting from the wound. Its frayed muscles had been sliced, the webbing of his insides a raw, red shade. Séverin felt slightly dizzy; he'd drawn that from himself, acting quickly under Inès' direction.

He drew on the threads of aether around him and forged a sword. He ran towards them, cutting through their furred hide. Their bones snapped as if they were twigs beneath his boots. Séverin was quick-footed from the years he'd spent in ballrooms when he lived and the training he'd begun the second he died. You could not rule the Graylands if you were not the strongest bastard in the realm.

He felt the shield around the humans begin to waver. He was using too much power to maintain it and fight them off. He was in the middle of four of the beasts. Their snarling mouths close to him.

"Kai," he called. "Protect Gaspar."

He couldn't afford to reinforce the shield and Gaspar was the most valuable person in the group.

He could not take his eyes away from the beasts. Séverin could not risk being bitten. Their bite was fatal even to someone like him.

He heard Élisabeth cry. His head snapped for a split second and that was all it took for him to feel the beast sink its teeth into his forearm. Séverin sliced his head clean off with his sword. He blinked in shock at the wound, at the black bite that left behind puncture wounds. He did not have time to spare to assess it. It was fatal and all he could do now was spare the others from the same fate. He finished off the last three numbly.

Rotten blood coated him and he felt that strange curdle of fear in his chest. He did not want to die. He had already died, and it had been a shite experience. He did not want a taste of the unknown. Not when he had spent so long building a place for himself and becoming the Lord of the Below. He fell to his knees when he had destroyed them, cradling his injured arm.

"Fuck, Sev," Kai said, falling to his knees. "Those bastards in the air fled."

Séverin stared at the bite. It was growing black, tentacled legs across his pale flesh. Blooming like a decaying flower.

"You have to sever it," Séverin said. "Now. Before it spreads."

Inès sat beside him. He could feel the others, lingering, waiting. He didn't dare look up to see if she survived. But Kai answered as if he knew where his thoughts had fled.

"She's fine," he said.

"I don't care," he grumbled. "Just cut the damn thing off."

He shouldn't have even reacted. Gaspar was the most valuable person under that shield. The rest of the humans could die for all he cared. Élisabeth included.

"I don't think I have the stomach for this," Kai said.

"I'll do it," Inès whispered.

"Just hurry before it goes to my shoulder," Séverin said. "Give me something to bite on."

Kai tore off his jacket and cut off the sleeve. Séverin parted his mouth as he shoved the cloth in.

"Here," Nicodeme said. He was the only person who carried a rifle and a sword. The only person who was half as level-headed as him. "It will cut smoother."

"Fates," Matthieu breathed. His skin had taken on a pale coloring. "He is not a fucking cow."

"This is wrong," Kai echoed.

"It is this or the Second Death," Séverin said. "Get a grip

on yourself. Both of you. Not everything is about you two. You can let me be fawned over for once."

"How can you joke about this?" Kai snapped.

Kai's face was tight, and his fists were closed as if he would punch him.

Because if Séverin didn't joke he'd realize that he was about to have his arm sawed off because he broke his focus to look after a girl who hated him. A girl who hadn't said a word since his attack. A girl who probably gloated at his misfortune.

"Wait," Élisabeth called.

She took a step forward and crouched down. Her dark hair fell onto her face, cloaking her expression from him. He had the urge to sink his fingers into the silky strands and pull them aside and see what she was thinking: was she happy? Angry? Sad? Regretful?

"Maybe I can fix it with…" she paused as if the word was ridiculous. "My magic."

"Aether does not heal," he said. "It destroys. It manipulates. But it does not fix."

"You forget that I don't control aether," she said.

"I don't trust your magic; besides, the more time we waste, the higher the poison climbs," he said between gritted teeth. "Inès do it."

"*Please*," Élisabeth said.

He looked up to find her staring at him with a pleading look. There was no secret glee or pleasure at his injured state. And Séverin did not know how to feel about that. Except that he turned away from Inès and offered Élisabeth his arm. Perhaps, this would be the decision that damned him. But he'd been damned the day he met her.

Élisabeth's hand gripped his wrist and the other floated above the wound. She slid her eyes shut, tight and desperate as if she were praying.

"Your eyes need to be open when you command," he said. "Do not shy away from it. Embrace it."

Her eyes shot open, and the fear vanished and was replaced with raw determination. He felt a tingle along his skin. He watched in shock as her fingers emitted a dark glow. It looked like aether, but it was different. He could feel the air grow weighted as he struggled to understand what this thing that felt like aether, but was so clearly not, could be.

There was much that they did not know about the Graylands. It was unexplored terrain. It looked like the mortal realm, but it was not it. Initially, they had suspected it had three continents similar to the mortal realm, and when Kai had gone to sea, he had struggled to map out the unmarked isles he'd come across. Nothing resembled the map of their world. Almost as if this place had been constructed with slippery, mindless fingers. As if the three continents had been pressed together into one big lump of land like clay between a child's fingers.

Now there were the beasts, his vengeful other half running around and plotting against his downfall, and a girl who controlled something that looked suspiciously like the cursed magic that plagued his world. A girl made of darkness and secrets.

He felt a burning sensation at the sight of the injury, and he grimaced. It was like someone had stabbed his open wound. The uncomfortable feeling spread, shooting pinpricks of pain through his flesh. It dulled into a soothing caress, and he watched in a mix of wariness and surprise as the black veins that had spread from the bite retreated, as the beast's saliva was siphoned from his flesh, and the toxin crawled out the wound like a spider. Élisabeth guided it to the snow letting it fall in a wet, black splat.

The wound was sealed shut with a squelching sound.

Élisabeth's hand dropped and she fainted. Matthieu caught her just before her head crashed into the ground.

"How did she...?" Kai began.

Séverin stared at his hand. Relief flooded him at the sight of the healed skin.

"Inès, any ideas?" Séverin asked.

Inès frowned. "I just realized I can't see her."

"What?" Nico asked. "She's right there."

"No, not physically," she said, glaring at him. Nico did not seem phased by her annoyance. "I do not see her future. She is a blank page."

Inès and Clarise could read the threads of aether. Each thread had a story that unspooled in their minds as visions. Séverin had tried to learn how to see the future, but he had given up after a few failed attempts.

"You, Gaspar?" he asked, looking at the man. "Any theories?"

He climbed off the horse and approached them, staring at Élisabeth with fascination.

"No, I am afraid I've never come across someone with such gifts," he said. "A mortal no less!"

"What does it mean?" Kai asked.

"It means that fate either brought her to us to save us or to destroy us," Séverin said.

And he did not know which category Élisabeth Bellacourt fell under.

Chapter Fourteen

Élisabeth awoke to a pounding headache. Everywhere hurt and she stretched her arms, but it was clasped around the knots of a string of rope. Her head shot up to find him crouched on the ground. He spun his hand around a thin blade that looked more ornamental than one intended for battle. It had a needle-thin blade and a handle made of polished ivory with a ruby stuck in the middle of the hilt. A rather old-fashioned relic from the time before rifles and gunpowder.

"Why am I tied up again?" she asked. "I saved your life."

Élisabeth recalled that tingling sense of magic lighting up her fingers, burning away the poison. At first, she thought she was erasing it, but then she realized she was not healing it, but simply luring it out of his body like a snake charmer with a fiddle. The traces of magic that soaked the beast's venom had felt memorable like they were vestiges of her own gifts.

Séverin stood up. The dark froth of his ink-black hair was wet, freshly washed from the looks of it. His black frilled undershirt was rather fancy for their travels. Almost as if he were about to attend a dinner party. The sleeves were drawn up, revealing his pale forearm corded in nets of thin muscle. That one odd strand of raven hair stroked his forehead, while the rest was swept neatly back, making him look *exactly* like the rogue that he was.

"I want to bathe," she said.

Her dress was stained with blood and dirt. The fabric no longer appeared *white*. And her hair looked dull and stiff, hanging limply down her back like seaweed. It would have been nice if she'd been allowed to bring along Colette, so she could help her prepare herself in the morning and night.

His dagger touched her nose and she stiffened.

"What are you doing?" she asked.

"Inès says she can't see your future," he said. "She can read everybody's future. That makes you a loose cannon. That makes you dangerous."

The dagger slid lower, resting on the cushion of her lips. She didn't dare part her lips or speak another word. Any movement and the sharp edge would cut her flesh.

"Sometimes a dog can tear out your throat just as quickly as it can save you," he mused. "Inès has a theory that if you die you may lose whatever gift you have."

Élisabeth should have let Inès sever off his arm. She felt ill even now just thinking of it. The resigned look in his eyes. Inès' fingers gripping the sword so tight, her nails had been half-sunken into her flesh. Kai on his knees, looking like he was about to vomit. Nicodeme with that empty, hard expression on his face as if he could not afford to react while Matthieu had stumbled backwards as if he would faint. And the servants had been huddled in the corner, their whimpers loud in the air as they wept like disgraced saints.

It surprised her that despite being a raging arsehole, his allies cared about him. They had stared at him like he was their world, and it had shoved Élisabeth forward, erasing her shock and pushing her into action. In truth, she had only been five percent certain that she could heal the bite. If Séverin knew how low his odds had been, he likely would not have humored her. She had almost reeled back when he had given her that faint nod. She wondered if he even remembered that.

And now the ungrateful bastard still had two hands and was using them both to torment her.

"How do I know you won't betray me, Lisbeth?" he whispered. "Give me one good reason why I should spare you."

The dagger slid lower, laying slanted across her neck this time. The cool metal caressed her skin.

"I should have let Inès cut off your arm," she snapped. "Or better yet wasted your time until it got into your bloodstream. I should have watched you choke on the poison. You despicable, foul-mouthed bastard."

Her chest rose and fell rapidly with each venomous word she spat, and she felt the dim satisfaction of watching his eyes darken. She had struck a chord. Perhaps it wasn't wise to insult the man who held a blade to her throat, but Élisabeth had never claimed to be wise.

"What happened to your little act?" he asked with a cruel smile. "The 'I'm so sweet and innocent and obedient' act. Couldn't keep it up for longer than a day?"

Élisabeth stiffened. She had forgotten all about that. And now that she remembered she realized that it served her better to fall back into that ploy. It was the only thing that would prevent him from slicing her throat and killing her. Except she wouldn't be truly dead, just trapped here forever as a ghost of the Graylands, caught under his brutal command for all of eternity.

And that was unthinkable.

"I am sorry," she whispered. "You are not a filthy, cursed bastard who deserves to die a horrible and miserable death."

"You never used those insults," he said.

"No," she agreed. "But I thought it."

She blinked at him innocently and let her mouth pull into a soft smile. It was an act. A performance. One that hurt her to perform, but she pretended as if she were on the polished wooden stage of the Opera House, much like that last night when she had stood before the masses. Her face was a smooth shell of grace and kindness. She hoped that he fell for it.

"That smart mouth of yours will get you killed one day, Lisbeth," he said. "Apologize again without the snark and I will consider it."

"Does this amuse you?" she asked tightly.

The words slipped past her lips despite her best effort.

"No," he said. "But I do find it rather stimulating."

She felt the dagger stroke her flesh. It moved in a tantalizing pattern, reminding her that he was rather unpredictable. One twist of his wrist and the caress would become a deadly strike. Her heart raced and she felt herself tremble beneath the blade. He seemed to take pleasure in that reaction. She felt his hand lower, felt the pinprick of his blade along her delicate collarbones. A flush bloomed from her chest, spreading upwards, dazed by the sheer focus in his eyes. She had never seen him look so aptly at anyone and it unnerved her. She realized belatedly that he was tracing the outline of her flushed skin.

"I am sorry," she said.

"For what?" he asked absently.

He didn't seem to be paying attention to her, just staring at her flesh, staring at her reaction. Probably enjoying the fact that he had made her nervous.

"For everything," Élisabeth rushed. "The insults and...and all of it."

"Good enough I suppose," he said.

His hand dropped and she felt a sense of relief.

"Odette will bathe you," Séverin said. "The ropes remain on until I say so."

"No." She shook her head. "She doesn't like me. And frankly, I find her and her twin unsettling."

"Do you wish to remain as you are?" he asked. "Filthy and unkempt?"

"You could have let me bring along a servant of my own choosing," she said. "And not subjected me to yours."

"I take back my offer," Séverin said.

She hesitated. Dirt was caked to her skin like paint and there was absolutely no way she could sleep in this state.

"Fine," she said, between gritted teeth. "I accept your offer."

Séverin did not respond to that. He disappeared out of the tent. For a moment, her spirits lowered, convinced that he was punishing her for talking back, but a half hour later Odette entered with a pail of water, a bar of soap, and a cloth hung off her elbow.

Her pale hair was secured in a tight braid, revealing her sharp face, which was all harsh lines and cruel brushstrokes. Her jaw was boxy much like her brother's and her mouth was tight in displeasure as she surveyed her.

"If you release me, I can bathe myself," Élisabeth offered.

"Do you think I wish to be punished?" she sneered. "I will not disobey my lord."

Élisabeth sighed.

"Now, stand up," Odette said curtly. "Let us be quick about it."

Élisabeth had no issue with that. Her only concern was that her hands were bound, and it made her feel rather vulnerable. She did not trust Odette, but she seemed to want to please

Séverin more than she wanted to cause trouble which worked in her favor.

Odette unlaced her cloak and corset. Next came her dress and she watched as the fabric pooled around her ankles. She sliced the sleeves with a blade which was excessive and unneeded.

Odette ruined a perfectly good dress for that monster.

"Step forward," Odette demanded.

Élisabeth shivered from the cold and stepped forward, the air licking her naked skin.

Odette worked quickly, wetting the rag with water and lavender soap, and working it over her skin. She rubbed viciously as if she was trying to tear the skin off her flesh.

"Is this how you bathe Séverin?" Élisabeth demanded. "I can see why he left me in your care. He wanted me to suffer just as much as he does."

Perhaps, it was not wise to goad the girl, but Élisabeth hated that she was working out her frustrations on her sensitive skin. Odette did not say anything, and the silence felt weighted. When she was done, she grabbed her dress and cloak.

"Stay here," Odette said. "I shall bring you a change of clothes."

Her lips pulled in a smile that reeked of evil intent.

"Wai—"

Élisabeth took a step forward but she had dashed out the flaps before she could catch her. She didn't know what she intended, but nothing good could come from that look she had given her. Perhaps, she planned to leave her here starving and naked. There was a row of Séverin's clothes neatly folded at the foot of the bed. But it was impossible to dress herself with her hands bound so she waited glumly for Odette to return so she could scold her. Just as she thought it, the flaps were drawn back.

"Good, you have retu—"

The words drowned in her throat at the sight of Séverin. The world tilted and time came to an abrupt pause. She could feel the droplets of water on her naked body freeze under the weight of his cold stare. Luckily her hands had been knotted at the front of her body and not behind. They lay flat between her legs, but her breasts could not be concealed.

She remembered Odette's fingers rinsing her hair and laying it flat behind her. Had the devious wench known she was going to humiliate her even then? At the very least her hair could have concealed her chest, but that cursed Odette had ensured otherwise.

Élisabeth couldn't risk raising her joined hands and fussing over it, revealing more of herself to him.

Anyone else and she could survive it. Nicodeme or Kai or even Matthieu would have been bearable but to be so vulnerable before Séverin was a fate worse than death.

"Odette said you were re—" He paused to clear his throat. "Ready."

His eyes were locked on her figure, rather shamelessly perusing her. She wondered if he even knew he was doing it. Or if it was mere instinct because he seemed to come to his senses when she trembled both from the cold and the dark gaze of his eyes.

Her mouth was dry, and no words escaped her parted lips. It was the quietest she had ever been around him. Séverin always brought out an angry, manic side to her, as if he held some invisible strings that forced her to forget the purity of her upbringing and turned her into a wild, insatiable beast who fed on his anger and disapproval alone. But there was nothing disapproving about his gaze then, it seemed almost...appreciative. And the thought made her skin burn.

Séverin turned around abruptly. Shoulders braced as if he were about to march off to war.

"I'll get Odette," he said.

"No," she said quickly. "Inès, get Inès, please."

He took a step forward without any reassurance and disappeared outside. Élisabeth paced wildly. This was the worst situation she had ever found herself in. She paused. In truth, the worst situation was the events that had brought her here. Maybe this was the second. It was in close competition with the night she had met Séverin.

The flaps were pulled back, and she felt her shoulders relax at the sight of Inès' bright hair.

"Fates, Odette is the worst," she said. "Can't believe she took your clothes and told Séverin you were waiting for him."

"Probably wanted him to think I was trying to seduce him," she said. "As if his head wasn't big enough to begin with."

Inès giggled. She drew out her blade and sliced the rope. It felt good to be free. She rolled her wrists, stretching the tight muscles.

"I know you packed a few dresses, but I *also* know you've been cold," Inès said. "You can wear one of my trousers. I don't have a spare shirt, but I'm certain Séverin won't mind if you borrow his. You are both on a rather intimate basis now I suppose."

Élisabeth shoved her playfully and Inès giggled. Élisabeth pulled one of Séverin's fancy shirts over her head. It was black as were all his clothes, and it smelled like him, like the dark foam atop the ocean and cloudy smoke.

"Did he lose his mind?" Inès asked curiously. "When he saw you that is?"

"Too busy drinking in his fill to do anything else," Élisabeth muttered.

Her fist tightened. Now that she wasn't frozen under the allure of his wicked gaze, she was going to destroy him for not reacting quickly. She should not have been surprised that he was *not* a gentleman, and his first reaction had not been to grant her privacy.

"I am going to kill Odette *and* him."

Now was as good a time as any to confront the terrible girl.

Élisabeth stepped outside with a single-minded focus.

Séverin was waiting outside, leaning against a tree, cigar in hand. Head tossed back as he stared at the stars.

"If you kill my servant, Lisbeth, I will use you as her replacement," Séverin warned.

Élisabeth ignored him. Odette sat on a log beside Olivier, their heads bent as they gossiped.

She felt a hard grip on her wrist and spun to see Séverin.

"I don't want any petty drama in my circle," he said tightly. "Drop it."

Élisabeth smiled sweetly. "If you insist."

She waited until his hand released her. Even though his eyes were marked with suspicion, he somehow did not anticipate her next move. Élisabeth slid her knee between his legs, crushing his manhood. He grunted, folding inwards, but Élisabeth did not give him the pleasure of relief. She yanked a handful of his onyx hair, slightly raising him so she could whisper in his ear.

"That is for looking for longer than two seconds," she said, lips grazing his ear. "Did you like what you saw?"

"I'm going to kill you," he said, between gritted teeth.

"You can try."

Élisabeth released him with a shove and continued her path towards Odette.

Nobody had seen her attack Séverin, unfortunately. They

had been tucked away in the shadows and she would have liked to see the other boys flinch in solidarity.

They were sitting in a circle playing cards while Gaspar wrote in his journal. Odette looked up, brushing away the strands of her wheat hair when she noticed her. A satisfied smile pulled at her lips.

"We heard you attempted to seduce Séverin, and he turned you away," Odette said. "I don't know how you can bear to show your face."

"You're not the first pest who sniffed around him to be rejected," Olivier added.

Élisabeth felt her fingers tingle. She thought about what Séverin had said, that magic existed in the air and surroundings, but Élisabeth found it impossible to draw from it, so she drew from within. She yanked on the invisible threads wrapped around her like a cocoon and felt satisfaction as it spread from her fingers in that bleak dark light. She had intended to fling them aside, but instead found herself raising them like leaves fluttering in the breeze, holding them several feet above the ground which was far more satisfying.

She heard Matthieu clap, cheering her on.

"That is it, Élisabeth!" he called. "Make an example of them."

She felt a shot of satisfaction at the sight of their wide eyes and parted mouths. Élisabeth drank that terror like it was a cold glass of water on a sweltering day. It felt good to not be power-less and to have people tremble under the weight of her gifts. To have the others bear witness to her power. To be a force to be reckoned with.

"Apologize," Élisabeth said.

Odette tightened her mouth. Even when she knew Élisabeth could release her hands and let them plummet to their death, fear and stubbornness warred across the young girl's face.

"I said apologize!" Élisabeth snapped.

She could feel him behind her, feel the weight of his hand on her shoulder.

"Do as she says, Odette," Séverin commanded.

Élisabeth felt her anger bleed from her and she felt a sense of sluggish calm. She slowly lowered them both, wondering why she had been so upset to begin with. It had been foolish to attack them. It had been a harmless prank and Odette didn't mean any harm.

"Sorry," Odette mumbled.

It wasn't until his hand dropped that her anger returned. She spun around to face him, her wrath growing tenfold.

"What did you do to me?"

"Made you relax," he murmured. "I tire of your tantrums."

Élisabeth wanted to react to that, but she was too tired to put up another fight. It had been a very long day and using her gifts had exhausted her. She could feel it catching up to her, both from when she healed him and when she'd attacked the twins. It made sense why he said to feed on the magic around them because pulling it from herself weakened her far more than she'd like to admit. Élisabeth spun around to return to his tent. His makeshift bed was a lot more comfortable than the bedroll and she knew he wouldn't let her stay outside with the others. Maybe if she showed her willingness to behave, he wouldn't tie her up. She could hear his hard steps behind her, and when he caught her wrist again there was a glint in his eyes that made her nervous.

"I *did* like it, Lisbeth," he said. "It is a shame you talk so much."

Élisabeth frowned, not quite certain what he spoke of. It

wasn't until she was in the tent, unwrapping her loaf of bread and gingerly biting into it to fill her hollow stomach that she recalled her question earlier when she had him at her mercy.

"Did you like what you saw?"

I did like it, Lisbeth. It is a shame you talk so much.

Fates, she hated him.

Chapter Fifteen

Élisabeth woke up to Inès' face. It was a welcome surprise compared to how Séverin awakened her last time by touching her with a filthy branch. It was like he found her repulsive. Always touching her with his gloves on or some nearby object, as if she were infected. Anyone else and she might have caught offense, but with him, she didn't care much. It worked in her favor that he detested her because she felt the exact same way.

"We are to set out soon," Inès said with a bright smile.

"Where is *he*?" she asked.

"Got bored of watching you sleep I suppose, so he came outside to tell us to pack and get moving," she said.

"At least he spared me the damn ropes," Élisabeth said.

It was dangerous to be bound not only because there were people in their camp that despised her, but because now that she knew the beasts did in fact exist, it meant that she had to be cautious. She could not be left vulnerable if there was another attack.

"Can I ask you something?" Élisabeth asked.

Élisabeth had been thinking a lot about the Blight and the Graylands. She wondered if maybe she offered a solution to this mess, Séverin would let her go. She could not help but think about something her father always said when they were sitting across from each other, solving complex puzzles: 'To know the end of a story one must go back to the beginning'. And the story of their realms had begun with the Three Kings. It was never said why the kings had fallen into an eternal slumber. Some said they faded when magic vanished from the lands. Some said that when people turned to the Fates rather than the Three Kings during the rise of the Crusade that had heightened the popularity of the Fates, it had angered them and made them retreat to the shadows.

Inès sat down before her cross-legged. "Always."

"Do you believe in the myth of the High Trinity?" she asked. "Were there ever Three Kings who ruled the three realms?"

"I've read many books of fables and folklore and religious texts," Inès said. "Strangely, the most truth I ever discovered was in a nursery rhyme my mother used to sing to me when I was young called 'The Sleeping Kings'."

"Will you sing it to me?" she asked. "Please."

Inès chuckled lightly. "I must confess my vocal skills are rather lacking but very well I shall."

Inès cleared her throat and Élisabeth sat as still as a lamb, as the soft, husky words passed her lips.

> There were once three brothers who ruled the
>> lands.
> And to them, three Fates served as their
>> hands.
> The land of the living, the land of the unseen,
>> and the land of the dead.

But a pact was broken, and a dark prince
    emerged.
Chaos descended and the Three Kings were
    submerged.
So, sleep little one, and close your eyes.
Just as the Sleeping Kings were none the wise.

Élisabeth shuddered.

"It is rather bleak, but my mother always had a love for the macabre," Inès said. "I suppose it explains why she sang it so much."

"What do you think it means?" she asked.

"I think it means that history repeats itself," Inès said. "And that the answers are closer than we think."

"Do you think we'll find *The Book of Echoes*?" she asked.

"We will find the library," she confirmed. "But I cannot say if we'll find the book."

Inès stood up. "We should prepare ourselves before Séverin marches in here and drags us out."

"You mean drag *me* out," she said glumly. "He doesn't treat anyone else half as wretchedly as he does me."

"Because he doesn't pay attention to what any of us do." She shrugged. "Whereas he can't take his eyes off you."

"Oh, shut it!" Élisabeth said.

Inès chuckled, the flaps sealing shut behind her, swallowing the raspy sound of her laughter.

Élisabeth left the tent, watching the twins dismantle it. Their glares burned hotter today and Élisabeth smiled because it always tended to provoke her enemies. Just as she expected, their cheeks reddened with rage.

Inès saddled her horse.

"Where is the gremlin?" she asked.

Inès raised a brow.

"Séverin," Élisabeth clarified.

She snorted. "You're the only person who gets away with bad-mouthing him and lives to tell the tale."

"Someone needs to humble him," she said. "He thinks he is untouchable. Did you know he hasn't even thanked me for saving his arm?"

Inès gasped. "How shocking."

They shared a knowing glance before they started laughing.

"Will you share the joke with the rest of us?" Kai asked, untangling the rope that secured his horse.

"Yes, I love a good laugh," Matthieu said. "Is it a dirty joke?"

"We are joking about your friend," Élisabeth said. "You won't join in so it's no fun."

"I might," Kai said.

Élisabeth's eyes widened in surprise. "I didn't know you were rebellious like that."

"Neither did I," Inès said.

"Don't keep us in suspense," Élisabeth said. "Any embarrassing stories to share of him?"

"Well, there was this one time we were at a ball before we died, and he was terribly drunk," Kai said. A twinkle in his eyes. Oh, Élisabeth knew this was going to be good. "He lured a girl behind a curtain—he claims that he thought it was his dance partner—and started kissing her most fiercely only to realize that he was kissing somebody's grandmother. The woman was no less than seventy-five and said that he ought to buy her dinner before he attempted such salacious maneuvers."

Élisabeth laughed and Inès doubled over, grabbing Élisabeth's forearm for support. Even Nicodeme, who was about as fascinating as a wooden plank, smiled in amusement.

"Did he use tongue?" Matthieu asked. "I suppose that is the important question or perhaps we are better off not knowing."

Élisabeth snorted. "He probably did."

"If he did, she wasn't complaining," Kai said. "She made several passes at him after that and Séverin had to leave early."

Élisabeth laughed, struggling to catch her breath. Each time she pictured the scene he painted it made her laugh all the harder.

"Are you all done fooling around?" Séverin snapped.

Everyone straightened and Élisabeth's smile dropped.

"What is so funny?" he asked.

"Wouldn't you like to know?" Élisabeth said coyly.

"They were joking about you," Olivier the rat said.

"No, we weren't," Kai said, casting him a warning look.

"Yes, they were," Odette echoed.

"Shut it," Élisabeth said.

"Kai said—"

"I'm going to scout ahead," Kai declared loudly, swinging atop his horse. "I'll come back if I sense any of the beasts."

Kai had torn off into the distance with a click of his tongue before Séverin could question him. Élisabeth looked at Inès and she nodded. It was time to make haste before the twins revealed all their secrets. Nicodeme and Matthieu went hastily after Kai, sensing the dark wrath that seeped from Séverin, and Gaspar slowly untied his horse, none the wiser of the cloud that loomed over them.

Inès climbed her horse, hand outstretched for Élisabeth to join her so they could flee as well.

Élisabeth took a step forward when he grabbed her hand. Long leather-clad fingers gripping her flesh.

"Let go of me," she said.

"You ride with me," Séverin said.

"I don't want to ride with you," she said. "I want to ride with Inès, and I want to make fun of you behind your back."

"It isn't behind my back if you are declaring it to me beforehand," he said with a roll of his eyes. "I'm starting to think you only bring out the nice act at night when the rope is around. Perhaps, I should bind you during the day. Maybe I should gag you too. Fates, know you have nothing of worth to say and it'll grant me some peace of mind."

Her jaw clenched, and she bit back the poisonous words that filled her tongue. His eyes sparkled as if he knew just how much restraint it took her to remain silent.

He led her or perhaps the better word was dragged her to Ebony. The great black horse stared at her with her intelligent eyes. Élisabeth was still not fond of her for not helping her escape her captor, so she did not rub her smooth neck as she would have done to any other horse.

She opened her mouth to insist on riding with just about anyone else, when his hands slid around her waist, making her mouth snap shut. They somehow fit perfectly around her slender frame. The tips of his fingers brushed each other, connecting at the front of her stomach.

For a second, he didn't move.

"What are you doing?" she whispered.

"Enjoying the silence," he said.

Élisabeth could not find a good comeback to that, and she hated that he fried her brain with a single touch. He lifted her and Élisabeth did not have much chance to catch her bearings before he swung behind her. His powerful thighs enclosed around her body, as he settled in.

He snapped the reins and Ebony began to move, jolting her backward against his chest. Élisabeth straightened until she supported her spine without touching him.

"Why am I riding with you?" she asked. "Inès is fun, and she laughs at my jokes."

"That is not as impressive as you make it out to seem," he said. "Besides, you seem to have the unique ability to heal the poisonous bite of our foes."

He shook his head, as if he were in disbelief. "I can't believe I am going to say this but that makes you *valuable*. Which now makes your survival of importance to me."

"So, no more death threats?" she asked hopefully.

"Just because I can't kill you doesn't mean I can't torture you."

"You can try," Élisabeth said. "But I won't go down without a fight."

"Will you be talking the entire ride there?" Séverin asked with a deep sigh.

"Only until I tire," she said. "I must warn you I don't tire easily."

He looked up to the sky, muttering something that sounded suspiciously like: 'Fates help me'.

"Do you want to know what we were laughing at earlier?" Élisabeth asked. The twins had already revealed that they were poking fun at him. Kai was long gone, and Séverin would likely forget all of it when they stopped to rest. She simply could not resist ridiculing him. She couldn't even wait for him to ask.

"We were laughing at you. Kissing old women at dinner parties. Let me guess—all the girls your age refused to entertain you."

"I'm going to kill him," he said, between clenched teeth.

"We forced it out of him," she said. "If you want to blame anyone, blame me."

"Oh, I certainly do," Séverin said. "Do you think I forgot your little attack?"

"Which attack?" she asked innocently.

"Don't even try that."

He was still upset she had kicked him between his legs. In her opinion, it was the least he deserved for what he put her through.

"Thanks to you I've likely lost the ability to have children," he said.

"It is not like you intend to wed and have a family," she said. "The thought of you as a father and husband is laughable."

"You are one to speak," he scoffed. "You exhibit traits that are the *exact* opposite of an obedient and loving wife."

"And how would you know that?" she asked. "You hardly know me."

"I know that you are self-absorbed and spoiled and silly," he said. "Perhaps, one could consider you as a lover, but as a wife?"

Séverin laughed a bitter, humorless sound, as if he found the idea of anyone wanting her for anything beyond her looks a novelty. And for some reason his words cut her deep. It brought back memories of Charles picking Louise. Perhaps Charles hadn't thought her fit for marriage. Perhaps there was some inkling of truth to his words.

Élisabeth was silent, as a storm waged inside her. She told herself that his opinions of her didn't matter, but somehow his words lingered like a burning fever, far longer than she would ever dare to admit.

The deeper they traversed into the woods the more the trees grew crooked and pockmarked. Their backs hunched in a perfunctory bow. It was as if some terrible illness was spreading, coating its stained fingers across everything. Even the air was rancid and damp, filling her lungs with the sour taste of rot. The trees stirred like prey caught in the trappings of a hunter, twisting, and curling to make their escape. Their gnarled fingers scratched the earth with strong, uneven caresses. The weather-beaten berries had been sucked dry and hung on stems like forgotten souvenirs left for Pras the Hunter.

King Pras' domain was wilderness. Most of his chapels were built in the woods made of the tree bones of his sacred ground. There were trees native to Prasin called Lockedhem, and it was said that the trees were made of his ribs. Each one that he plucked from his chest was replaced by another and with his infinite bones he had marked his most favored woods with the rare trees.

Naturally there were no marked trees as this was not the realm of Pras. The Graylands was the realm of King Mòrge and his chosen Fate, Lune.

She could see the painted footprints of rabbits, foxes, and squirrels as they cut through the undergrowth, as if they sought to outrun the Blight. In the distance, she heard the mournful tune of a songbird as it lamented its woes. Her heart ached for the poor woodland creatures who existed in this vacuum of rot and wrongness.

A cloth was wrapped around her face, protecting her from the stomach-curdling scent and it took her a moment to realize that it was Séverin who had performed the gesture, placing the handkerchief on her face. Perhaps, he felt guilty for his harsh words earlier. They hadn't spoken since that dreadful conversation.

"Thank you," she said, a tad reluctantly.

He picked up on her hesitance and muttered something that sounded suspiciously like "spoiled brat".

"I take it back," she said quickly.

Élisabeth's gaze turned to the decrepit woods.

"How did this happen?" she whispered.

"It began a few months ago. It spread slowly but surely. It's been growing ever since."

The air pulsed with dark tendrils of magic that lay atop what she assumed had once been the aether that Séverin said layered this world. She felt stronger here, as if her magic fed off the tainted air. She shuddered at the thought.

"Cold?" Séverin asked.

"Will you offer me your coat?"

"No, I'd offer up Kai's," he said. Even though the others were far ahead of them, and only the twins trailed behind them, as if they couldn't bear to be far from their master's reach.

"How generous," she said. "Your chivalry knows no end!"

She felt the heavy weight of his coat land on her shoulder. She told herself the gesture wasn't *that* impactful. He was a ghost after all. He did not feel the chill in the air. Still, she could not ignore the trickle of gratitude that slipped down her chest.

This time she didn't say anything and from the small exhale that escaped him, she knew he was glad for it too.

Élisabeth flipped the pages of her copy of *The Frightful Adventures of Amelia Ashburn*. Her father had bought her the book from a little booth in Harford during their visit to their countryside manor. She was unsurprised to discover that Séverin had defaced her property. His scathing comments were written in the margins, critiquing every thought she'd expressed as if he were a wolf who'd come upon a carcass and could not resist pouncing.

There was something wicked about a young man indirectly calling Little Élisabeth stupid because she didn't pick up on the subtext and the rather "obvious foreshadowing that even an idiot would spot a mile away" as he so generously wrote.

Élisabeth had forfeited her posture to lean against him and read. It steadied her so she didn't jostle as much. At any moment she wondered if he would shove her away or bark at her to sit upright, but he didn't say anything. Almost as if he preferred the silence of her reading to her chatter.

She'd talked his ear off, asking several questions about the Graylands until he refused to engage anymore, and she had no choice but to pull out her worn copy and get lost in the gothic tale. She'd even asked him about the necklace he wore. It was a silver chain with a one-eyed raven. He never struck her as faithful, so she didn't understand it. He had tucked it swiftly under his shirt when she asked about it and had ignored her.

"Oh, is it from a lover?" she asked.

"What would you know about lovers?" he scoffed.

"A gift from your parents?"

"You can't carry worldly possessions into the Graylands."

"I know! I know!" she said. "It is from Kai. A friendship necklace. Oh, how sweet of him."

"Just read your damned book."

And that had been the swift end of their conversation.

"We are almost there," he said.

"Your comments are rude and insulting," she said, twisting her neck to glare at him. "You have tarnished my book!"

She miscalculated just how close he was, and she felt her lips graze his smooth skin. He stiffened but surprisingly did not pull away.

"In my defense, I didn't think you would ever read it," he said.

"And if you had known I would read it someday?"

His lips lifted in a grin that would unspool the heart of the most hardened maiden. It was filled with sin and seduction.

"I would have been crueler," Séverin said.

Élisabeth surprised herself when she laughed.

It was such an utterly *Séverin* response that it was almost comforting.

"James Bancroft is the villain," he said.

Her brow raised, surprised that he wanted to talk about the book.

"Not a villain, he has some dubious intent, but his heart is in the right place," she said.

"Yet you are in love with him," he said. "Despite his black heart and roguish manner."

She shrugged. "I suppose I am."

Séverin was silent, and she wondered what he was thinking. For a moment, she had thought to deny it, to protect herself from his judgement. But he'd already consumed her secrets, feasted on them without her permission, and now there was nothing left to hide.

They were one step closer to sealing the Pit *and* discovering the answers that the group sought. Élisabeth wanted to know exactly what she was and how she fit into this world. Even if she did not intend to stick around. It had been three weeks since she'd arrived, and it had felt like *months*. She missed her father and she worried that the longer she remained without practicing her ballet every day the more her muscles would weaken. Pierre had always said that success was equal parts talent and discipline. She had to make a better effort to practice at night, but it was difficult to muster up the energy when she was so exhausted.

And she had to focus on the latter if she ever hoped to return home and pick up the abandoned scraps of her dreams.

Chapter Sixteen

It was bigger than he expected. Like an eye had opened at the center of the world. It pulsed with dark energy and when Séverin looked down it was like he was staring into an abyss. One that blinked back at him. After days of travel, they had finally arrived at the latest Pit that had killed Nicodeme's comrade and Kai's legionnaire. The Pits had begun several months ago. One had opened and then a second and now a third. He had sealed the first two quick enough. Anytime a Pit appeared it gave birth to a new set of beasts who crawled from the gap in the earth and sought to terrorize his people.

Mostly they kept to the Blighted areas of the woods, not daring to venture further, but often they came upon travellers. They had passed several corpses during their journey, their bleached white bones glistening under the rays of light that slipped through the tree crowns. Élisabeth had screamed loud enough to wake the dead. And he'd been forced to slip his palm under her handkerchief and silence her before she awakened any beast that slumbered. Or worse, lured the specters who resided in the woods to them.

The woods, he knew, were made to hide secrets. To bury and swallow and consume.

"This is triple the size of the last one," Kai said. His lips were drawn tight in a frown. "Are we strong enough to close it?"

Séverin glanced back at Élisabeth who hovered under a tree, refusing to come closer. She claimed that she didn't trust the twins to not simply throw her into it, which was a rather valid point. He knew he had to talk with them soon. A part of him had doubted Clarise's claims that Élisabeth was important. Clarise had rather unsubtly questioned him before about his intentions to settle down. In many ways, she was just like his mother when he was alive, pestering him about finding the right woman to soothe his unruly heart. He had wondered if this was Clarise's poor attempt at matchmaking. But seeing what he had after that attack, he knew now that she *was* different. Séverin had suspected it since the day she'd mentioned she could see aether. He had known then that she was no mere mortal girl.

"I don't know," Séverin said truthfully.

"Do you think she can?" Kai jutted his chin at Élisabeth.

"Maybe."

Séverin didn't like that he knew so little. He still hadn't grasped the Graylands. He should have listened to Clarise more when she spoke about "balance" and "rules". It felt like they had angered something with far more power than them and were now suffering the consequences of their actions.

He was thankful that he was not the first ghost to grace the Graylands. It had a functioning society and some semblance of order when he'd arrived which was nice because it meant that all he had to worry about was seizing power. The truth was, if he had been the first Lord of the Below, he would have failed miserably. Kind of like how he was failing now.

"How did she heal you?" Kai asked.

"I don't know," he said absently. "Clarise might know when we return."

Séverin didn't like that there were so many unaccounted variables. His gaze drifted towards Élisabeth. She had her head drawn forward, huddled with Inès, and from her gleeful laughter and the occasional glances at him, he could tell she was in the middle of her favorite hobby: talking shite about him.

"You told her about that old lady I *accidentally* kissed?" Séverin asked.

"She tortured it out of me," Kai said innocently.

"He spilled with little cause," Nicodeme said, joining them.

His lips were pulled in a relaxed smile. It seemed the weight of grief was easing from his shoulders. He had been rather sullen during their travels, but his mood was improving.

Kai tackled Nicodeme and they began to wrestle. Matthieu's head turned towards the raucous.

"Care to place a bet?" he asked Séverin. "I put fifty on Kai."

"I'm not betting on Nicodeme," he said.

Kai already had him on his knees. His arm wrapped around his throat.

Séverin shoved them away from the Pit so the idiots didn't fall to their deaths.

"Enough," Séverin said. "Let us seal this thing and be done with it. Nico and Matthieu keep guard. Inès. Lisbeth. Here. *Now.*"

Élisabeth's mouth moved, mocking him and Inès giggled.

"I have half a mind to throw you in the Pit," he murmured when Élisabeth came to him.

Her piercing gray eyes stared at him as if she could pin him to the spot with her glare alone, and he found himself being swept away in the chaos of her gaze.

"I'll just drag you down with me," she said evenly.

Inès knew how this went, and she held his right hand. Kai took Inès' hand.

"Here," he said. "Hold my hand."

Élisabeth looked hesitantly, at his left hand. He couldn't have any barriers between them while he channeled so the gloves were gone.

He quirked a brow. "Scared?"

Séverin's lips tilted in a sardonic smile, and Élisabeth frowned, clearly not amused by his taunt.

"Must I?" Élisabeth asked.

"Can't control yourself around me?" Séverin asked.

She sneered at him and grabbed his hand. She held it in the style of a formal handshake, but Séverin being Séverin refused to let her be comfortable. He interlaced their fingers even though it was not required for him to cast the wards. He felt her small fingers tighten around his own in a manner that was not *all* unpleasant. She intended to strangle him judging by the crease between her brows, to make the gesture as painful as possible, but the little creature was not strong enough to hurt him. It was almost amusing.

"Séverin!" Inès gasped. "We need to hurry. They are waking up."

Inès had that cloudy look in her eyes. The one she often got when she was in the middle of a vision.

Séverin pulled on the aether around them and began to knot the network of threads along the open mouth of the Pit. It was like weaving a blanket and ensuring that no holes were left for them to sift between. Once he made the first layer, he drew on the threads of Inès, Kai, and Élisabeth. He flattened the small ones that made their aether, but something strange happened when he pulled on Élisabeth's. It burnt through the first layer of the ward.

Séverin snatched his hand away from her.

"Séverin. Hurry," Inès said.

A rumble sounded from below and the clawing screech of nails digging into dirt echoed around them.

"Nico," Séverin growled. "Come here."

Nico was beside him, taking Élisabeth's spot. Séverin would focus on that odd happening later when he wasn't looking into the eye of Death. He had been so confident he could seal this one himself as he had the last. But for one small moment, he regretted not bringing more men. He should have positioned them in the trees to take down any beast that crawled out. Matthieu was an excellent sharpshooter, but he could not protect them alone.

"Nico!" Inès yelled.

Séverin didn't understand what she was screaming about, but then he saw it. Black talons the size of his arm dug into Nicodeme's chest and yanked him into the Pit. Séverin was stunned for a split second.

"Kai. Come here," he called.

Séverin focused on the Pit just as Kai left Inès' side and took the empty spot where Nicodeme had once stood.

Séverin's grip was lethal, but Kai did not flinch.

Nobody else. He would not lose anyone else to this monstrous affliction. He had sealed the tear that Élisabeth's magic made. Just before it closed a beast slipped out. One of the winged ones. It was like a mythical dragon, if said dragon had been drawn by an imaginative child. A limp, almost skeletal black body with reptilian scales and a screech that made him flinch, filled the air like a soprano.

Séverin could not break his focus. If he did the thin ward would shatter. He had to create three folds of overlapping threads for it to be strong enough to keep them contained. He could feel them beating against the wards. Each scratch of their claws and bite of their canines against the shield felt like someone had lit his senses on fire. Goosebumps covered his forearm, and he gritted his teeth, as he weaved the aether to form an unbreakable seal.

Kai had pulled out his gun with his other hand and was shooting in the air, trying to bring down the beast.

"Pull your shield, Élisabeth," Séverin said, between gritted teeth.

"I don't—"

"Do as I say, Lisbeth," he roared. "Or I will kill you myself!"

"I have an eye on her," Matthieu called. "She's safe, just close the damn Pit."

He focused on the Pit and began to weave his second ward. It required more power than he had expected. He felt Kai collapse by his feet, drained of aether, rifle cluttering by his side. He kicked the gun to Inès, holding the thread steady. Soon enough Inès' shots joined Matthieu's as they attempted to bring down the beast.

One more layer. One more layer and he would be done. He hoped Inès could handle it. He could draw from himself if needed, but he didn't want to risk all of them losing consciousness. And it was too dangerous to pull Matthieu into it when he was the last person protecting the humans and Gaspar.

"Séverin, Séverin he's going to die," Inès said shakily. "Séverin, I have to—"

Her eyes were filled with tears. And he knew before she opened her mouth what she had seen. The beast descended towards them; sights set on Kai.

"Don't break the link," he said. His words were little more than a bark. "The ward will snap."

"I won't lose him!" Inès yelled. It was the most fervor he had ever heard in her voice before. "Wards be damned."

He could feel her fingers slipping.

"Wait," Élisabeth called. "I'll save Kai. Don't move Inès."

"Stand down, Lisbeth," he growled.

His jaw tightened. He didn't want to lose Kai, but if he or Inès unlocked their hands the fragile ward would crumble, and they'd all be damned. Kai was his oldest and most loyal friend. Truth be told he was his *only* friend. He had stuck with him and not that imposter Laurent. Even though he'd been uncertain about who to side with, he had picked him, and for that, Séverin would always be grateful. But the fate of their entire realm relied on him and keeping these wards intact.

His throat tightened with a sensation he had not felt in a long time. Not since his boyhood.

Élisabeth came between Kai and the beast. Her hand was outstretched and that dark glow that resembled the Blight slid out her fingers. It wrapped around the beast in a rope, chaining it to her.

"Bloody Fates," Matthieu whispered.

Séverin turned back to the wards. He could hear the beast screeching, but Élisabeth seemed to have it under control if Matthieu's words of awe were anything to go by.

Sweat beaded down Séverin's nape as he unfolded the second string of aether across the flat surface. This one was strong enough to silence the keening sound of their howls and the scrape of their nails. This one was an impenetrable shield. It wasn't until the final ward was placed that Inès looked at him, eyes wide with fright.

"Séverin, you have to be careful," she said "It is not sa—"

Her words faded as she collapsed. Séverin stumbled backward. He felt drained. Even though he hadn't used much of his own storage of aether, creating wards always drained him. He didn't know how many more of these damned Pits he could seal. It was getting more challenging with each one as if they were uniquely made to outsmart him.

He turned around, and Élisabeth stood beside the sickly dragon. It was thin and skeletal with a hollow snout and yellow eyes that glowed under the setting sun. Its focus was on Élisabeth but at the sight of him its snout twitched, and its lips pulled back to reveal a row of needle teeth.

"Shield, Lisbeth," he said sharply.

"He won't hurt me," she said. And then the dreadful girl raised a shaking hand, placing it flat on its snout. Séverin felt sick to his stomach. She would lose her hand. She had saved him an amputation and would be rewarded with her own.

He used the trickle of his aether to shield her. His power was diminished from the sheer effort of weaving those threads. He had no energy and here he was foolishly using it to shield a girl who was treating a beast from the Pit as if it were a stray kitten.

It roared the second he shielded her. Eyes wide and angry.

"No, remove it," Élisabeth said in a panicked voice. "It doesn't like your scent. It doesn't like aether."

"It is not a dinner guest," Séverin spat. "I don't care what it likes."

"I can't control it with the shield," she said frantically. "He will hurt Kai and Matthieu and Inès."

"And me?" he asked. "I suppose my life does not matter to you."

"It was made to kill you," she said. Her eyes were bright with clarity. She took a step back. "I should let it end you. All of it will end. I can be free."

"What are you talking about?" he asked.

It took him a split-second to realize that the beast was not moving and that its unnatural eyes had returned to Élisabeth. Almost as if...almost as if it sought permission. He thought of Inès' words before she had fainted.

Séverin, you have to be careful.

Then the words he had been certain she was about to say: *It is not safe.*

Chapter Seventeen

Élisabeth watched the realization dawn in his glassy eyes. She could see a hint of betrayal, but Élisabeth was not betraying him because she didn't owe him anything.

Magic poured from her fingertips and looped around the beast like a chain. It was a small obsidian creature with thin, skeletal wings and a long snout with pin-like teeth. The second she realized that she could feel the beast submit to her was when she realized that whatever gift she had was the opposite of Séverin's. The beasts wished to devour him, yet they bowed to her. Her magic had burned a hole through his when he attempted to seal the Pit. Anything his magic was made to do, hers was made to undo.

She was the antithesis to him.

"It should end here," she said.

But what she meant was: *you should die here.*

It was her key to returning home, and while the thought of letting this beast go to destroy him sickened her, it was the only way to escape this place and to save herself. She didn't know what she was and from what she'd seen so far, she knew that Séverin suspected that she was a threat, and this scene proved his suspicions. She thought of the time he had held a dagger to her throat; he had barely let her walk away unscathed, and that was the night she had saved him. What would happen now when she so blatantly threatened him?

If she did not end it here and now, he would kill her. That much she was certain of.

"You will only have one shot to kill me, Lisbeth," Séverin said between gritted teeth. "Pray that you don't miss."

He raised his hand, and she watched in awe as he forged a sword of aether. Silver and brutal. He held it tightly with his slim, pale fingers. His ebony hair danced in the breeze. Mouth carved in a hateful line. He looked like a graceful dancer under the fog-coated air. Far too lithe and beautiful to be a warrior. It was fitting that he was a ghost. There was no place in the land of the living for someone so ethereal. Even with the masque and half his face covered, nobody could ever say that he was *not* beautiful.

Élisabeth stared at her beast. It had this odd sour smell like mildew. It was the same scent that layered the Blighted woods. Before she could release the wild-eyed creature to do her bidding, something stabbed the dragon's back. A roar broke from the beast and before she knew it, it had torn off the head of the assailant. Élisabeth watched in horror as Olivier's limp body crumpled to the ground. He had stabbed it with his hunting blade. Odette screamed a loud, piercing wail and she collapsed by her dead brother, hunched over his severed head.

Her stomach churned at the sight of the red stump that was his neck. Blood spurted out from the frayed arteries, staining the grass a horrid dark red color.

She took several steps away from it. And she felt the beast take a step towards Séverin.

"No," she whispered.

The beast hesitated and she repeated the word louder and sterner. Somehow the thought of watching it eat his head sickened her. Fates knew he deserved it, but she could not find the strength in herself to give the command.

"No," she said again. "Don't hurt him."

Séverin looked at her warily and she felt her focus break and her magic return to her fingertips. The cord that held it in place snapped, but to her surprise, the beast didn't attack him, it simply flew upwards and vanished into the mist. Her heart leaped at the sight of Séverin's fingers still grasping the aetherblade. That willful lock lying on his forehead. For a moment, she feared he would still attack her. His gaze was half-drowning with rage, and his knuckles had grown blisteringly white from his grip on his blade. It must have hurt.

He nodded.

She didn't feel it, only saw Matthieu slip behind her, quick as a rabbit. And then his arm was around her neck, she could feel the air being choked from her lungs. Panic gripped her and her hands grabbed his forearm, but before she could truly hurt him, darkness bled into her vision, blanketing her sight.

And then there was only silence.

<hr>

Élisabeth awoke to a veil of darkness and from the tension on her wrists, those infernal ropes were back on her flesh. She blinked in the dark, staring at Matthieu's bright green eyes. His lips were pulled in a jovial smile as if he had not knocked her out earlier.

"Sorry about that," he said. "I do as his lordship commands."

She was in Séverin's tent. *Again.* She was beginning to hate the sight of the black cloth, stretched above her like a mirror reflection of the night sky.

"Where is he?" she asked.

"He is debriefing with the others," he said. "I wonder why they always stick me with you when things get interesting. No offense."

"Offense taken," she muttered. She smiled sweetly. "Will you remove these dreadful ropes? I want to stretch my hands."

"Nice try, but Séverin will have my head," he said.

She sighed. "Fine, at least regale me with a fascinating tale. I don't wish to die of boredom."

"Very well," he said. "Did I tell you about the time I went to a brothel and—"

"Another tale," she said.

He opened his mouth, and the flaps were drawn before he could subject her to a different sordid story. Inès entered with a wrapped cloth.

"I can take second watch," she said.

"Can I stay?" Matthieu said. "Odette has been crying all day, it is unbearable."

"No," Inès said.

Matthieu sighed, standing up. "You are cruel, Inès. I can see why Kai is afraid of you."

"Kai is not afraid of me," she said.

"Want to bet on it?"

"You don't have anything to bet on."

"I have much to bet on," he said. "My services included."

"What ser—" Élisabeth began.

"Don't ask," Inès said quickly. "You don't wish to know. Go. Away." She shoved him towards the flaps.

Matthieu laughed and tossed his head back with a glint in his eyes.

"You know I could help you make Kai jealous," he said. "Might help speed up this torturous romance of yours."

"Thanks, but no thanks," Inès said.

The flaps fell in a whisper when Matthieu left.

"He has a point you know," Élisabeth said with a small grin. "Kai *would* lose his mind."

"I don't know," Inès said nervously. "Kai has had plenty of opportunities to say something, *anything*. I don't know if he's interested."

Kai was always looking at Inès when she was doing menial tasks like braiding her hair or feeding her horse some oats. He looked at her as if she were the most fascinating creature he had ever seen.

"He is," Élisabeth said. "Everyone can see it but you."

Inès smiled softly. She crouched down and removed her ropes.

"I thought I wasn't allowed to be free," she said.

"You're not," she said. "But I think it is fine if you remain so while you eat."

Inès unraveled the cloth to reveal some bread and cheese.

"How angry is he?" Élisabeth asked, tearing a loaf of the bread.

"Livid," she said. "He said you almost killed him. He said you can control the beasts. He never trusted you to begin with, but his suspicions have reached a new level."

"And you?" she asked. "Do you think I'm a monster? Do you think that I am the villain?"

It had crossed her mind before. What if she was the villain of their story? She had this cursed, tainted magic at her fingertips. It was the only explanation they had to work with.

"No," Inès said. "You are afraid, and you are trying to figure things out. Just like the rest of us."

"Thank you for understanding," Élisabeth said.

She would be lying if she said she didn't care about Inès' opinion of her. Especially knowing that Séverin had a terrible habit of bad-mouthing her to the others. In truth, Inès' opinion was the only one that mattered to her.

"I like you, Élisabeth," Inès said. "And I think it is unfair to expect you not to turn on Séverin with the way he treats you. You shouldn't be handled like a prisoner and met with distrust at every turn. You are our friend."

Élisabeth looked down, her throat stretching painfully. She couldn't recall the last time someone had cared. Her father had always cared, but in the last few years, he had been so focused on the Opera House that he hadn't spared a single moment to see how she was handling everything. And when she'd finally spoken to him about her dreams and her future was about to change, she had been thrust into this cold, abominable place.

It was achingly painful to be despised by everyone around her. She was half-afraid to see Odette after what had happened to Olivier. Bile crawled up her throat at the vivid images of his corpse. She hadn't meant for that to happen. Despite her complicated feelings about the twins.

"Will he come back as a ghost?" she asked. She cleared her throat to erase that painful lump. "Olivier, that is?"

She placed her bread down, unable to stomach it.

"Yes," she said. "Odette is upset. Perhaps stay clear from her for the next few days."

"But where did he go?" Élisabeth asked.

"He will awaken at one of the three ley lines. As all mortals who die here do."

"And Nicodeme, I saw him..."

"Gone," she whispered. "We had a vigil for him."

Élisabeth felt a strange sadness at the news. Nobody had seen the beast reach for him. There had been nothing that they could do, but she knew Kai was close to him. They were rather similar. Both were strong, silent, and kind. Except Kai was a bit more lighthearted than Nico. It hurt that she hadn't been invited to the vigil. She felt isolated and alone far more so than the first day she had arrived in this forsaken place. *He* was shutting her out.

They sat in silence for what felt like hours. It was a comforting break, both of them lost to their thoughts. It felt like she was drowning under the weight of all that had occurred in the past few hours. Her gift was beginning to feel far more like a curse.

"Do you have any idea what I am?" Élisabeth asked, staring at her fingers.

"No," she said. "We don't know any more than we did yesterday."

Élisabeth did not find that comforting. Each day that passed Séverin's doubt festered. She worried about when he decided that she was better off dead than alive. She thought of his words the night she had saved him.

Sometimes a dog can tear your throat out just as quickly as it can save you.

And Élisabeth was certain that there would come a day when she and Séverin were trapped in another intense moment, caught between life and death.

She was certain that the next time, she would end him.

She just hoped that she didn't hesitate.

Séverin did not speak a word to her that morning. Dawn crawled like a spider from the crevice of the sky, pooling faint orange light across the decaying woods. She knotted her boots, staring at him warily as his deft fingers untied the rope that held Ebony. It brought a strange bitter taste to her mouth that after Inès' visit last night, he hadn't returned to the tent. Kai came for his round and then it was Matthieu again. He didn't even trust her to stay in the tent alone. She was forced to attempt to sleep while Matthieu obnoxiously ate some biscuits.

"I have a sweet tooth," he said around a mouthful when she had asked him to keep it down.

"Ghosts don't need sustenance," she snapped.

"But my taste is just as strong," he said. "Some things we hold onto with an iron fist. Even death cannot erase my love of sweets. Just as it cannot soften Séverin's temper."

It had been an unbearable night.

Now everyone was acting as if she had been the one to kill both Nicodeme *and* Olivier. She only felt responsible for one of those deaths. Even that had been beyond her control; she hadn't told the beast to attack Olivier, but from Odette's poisonous look she may as well have struck the killing blow herself.

She walked to Kai.

"Do you hate me too?" she asked, switching to Lupazi.

She could see that small vein in Séverin's jaw flutter rapidly. He had forbidden her yesterday from speaking Lupazi to Kai. He claimed she was only doing so to plant seeds of betrayal as if she was some magic whisperer who could turn Kai against Séverin at the twist of her tongue.

"You know he hates it when he can't understand us," Kai said with a loose grin. "Drives him mad. But then again everything you do drives him mad."

"I'm sure it does," she said.

"I don't hate you, Élisabeth," Kai said. "But I don't know if you're a friend or foe. I know that Séverin is not the easiest person to get along with but if the choice is between you and him, I will choose him."

"I know," she whispered.

Kai had known him longer and she could tell that it wasn't

just a relationship built on their roles as lord and soldier, but that they were good friends. Séverin while he was his usual woeful self around Kai would never let any harm befall him and it went both ways. She had seen the fear in his eyes when the beast changed course to come for Kai. Séverin had been devastated.

"Were you truly going to kill him?" Kai asked. He searched her eyes for answers.

"I was never going to hurt you all, and I want you to know that," she said. Whatever mixed feelings she had about Séverin, they did not apply to the rest of them.

It was important for her to maintain Kai's trust. As she saw it, he and Inès were the only people stopping Séverin from killing her.

"I don't know if that fills me with as much ease as you intended," Kai said. "But I suppose I appreciate not being the source of your ire."

Séverin came towards them. Eyes cloaked in suspicion.

"What evil agenda is she sharing this time?" Séverin asked.

"We were deciding what attire we shall wear to your funeral after I kill you," she said. "Kai was going to be respectful and wear black, but I intend to wear white, a color of celebration and hope."

Séverin nostrils flared, and she felt that warm, syrupy sensation slide down her chest as it did anytime she spoiled his day.

She hadn't liked being ignored by him last night, and she did not know what it meant that she cared about his attention at all.

"She jests," Kai said.

"Does she?" Séverin asked darkly.

Élisabeth ignored him.

"There are two horses now," she said. And then she winced

because the words sounded rather callous even if it was true. Nico and Olivier's horses were there for the taking. "I mean we don't have to ride together."

"Those horses were released into the woods," he said.

Élisabeth's shoulders slumped when she realized that he was right. Nico and Olivier's horses were both gone. Séverin walked away and she followed him. The tail of her braid swayed behind her.

"Why?" Élisabeth asked.

"Climb on," Séverin said.

"No." She shook her head. "I want to ride wi—"

"I am hanging by a thin thread, Lisbeth," he said between gritted teeth. "You don't want to test me."

A deep sigh escaped her. She climbed up, feeling strangely faint. Her stomach had been too twisted to eat last night beyond a few nibbles and Inès had told her that the tyrant had only given her five minutes that morning to get ready which she'd foolishly used to plait her hair. Her vision grew spotty and Séverin caught her just as she tilted backwards. She fell in a heap, and his arms coiled around her waist and the back of her knees. Her heart raced at the vivid image of her cracking her skull open and bleeding on the grass. Her fingers had desperately twined around the collar of his shirt.

"Do I need to grab the smelling salts?" he asked. "I thought only innocent maidens fainted, not wicked girls who thrive on disobedience."

"I thought only *gentlemen* caught innocent maidens, not wolfish blackguards with a heart of rot," she retorted.

Séverin placed her down, surprisingly gently.

"When did you last eat?" he asked, dark brows furrowed. She could *almost* believe that he was concerned, if she didn't know him so well.

"Last night."

He left her side, and she saw him go to Odette. Odette frowned and shook her head vehemently but whatever Séverin said next made her hand over the wrapped goods. He returned to her side and Élisabeth was pleased to find that the covering hid a slice of almond cake.

"Oh," she said, pleasantly surprised. "Thank you."

"Is the fare to your liking, Lady Lisbeth?" Séverin asked in a derisive tone.

Élisabeth sighed. "You couldn't be bearable for a minute, could you?"

Séverin didn't respond. He simply swung himself behind her and grabbed the reins. He whistled and the others mounted and then they were trailing behind Gaspar to the old library, to find a book that would answer all their questions.

And hopefully, it would explain *exactly* what she was.

<hr>

Élisabeth stared at her determined pupils. Somehow, she had been able to wrangle the boys and Inès to practice a new dance routine. Matthieu had been more than eager to join so long as he was Élisabeth's partner, but Kai had required some pleading before he reluctantly stood up.

"I have two left feet," he muttered. "And why is Séverin being spared from this torment?"

Élisabeth hadn't even asked him to join her little ballet group. He was sitting a few ways off, scowling at her like she'd murdered his precious horse. He had a cloth in hand and was using it to wipe the rifle he never used. Long fingers delicately traced the weapon as if it was a precious heirloom. Séverin seemed to show a great deal of care towards inanimate objects and animals than he did to humans. He treated his horse Ebony far better than he did her.

Sometimes he'd even shorten their journey if he sensed the beast was tired. But Fates forbid if she was on her last breath, he would sooner let her collapse than take a short break.

"Because he is not my friend," she said. "And he would spoil the good mood."

Séverin stood up then, disappearing into trees with a thunderous expression on his face. Her shoulders softened and a triumphant smile crossed her face, pleased that she'd run him off. It was why she'd spoken so loudly; she *wanted* him to hear her.

"He has feelings too you know, Élisabeth," Kai said softly.

Élisabeth frowned. "He scarcely said more than a handful of words to me this entire morning and he ignored me anytime I asked him anything."

He was punishing her for attempting to kill him. It didn't matter that she had turned the beast away at the last second. It didn't matter that she'd changed her mind. To Séverin, she may as well have finished him off.

"You did try to kill him," Kai said.

"You always pick his side," she said accusingly.

"I can be on your side," Matthieu said, draping his arm over her shoulder. Even though he didn't say it out of any sense of loyalty—he was a shameless flirt—she was glad for his support.

"Thank you, Matthieu."

"Stop distracting her from her lesson," Inès said. "I'm eager to learn."

It was challenging to guide them without music, the right footwear or sturdy flooring. Élisabeth had the sense to pack her shoes with her. She led them through a simple pose and a few other maneuvers and demonstrated the right technique.

"Steady your core," she told Matthieu. "Your balance is abominable."

"I am a soldier not a dancer," he said. "And why is this so hard?"

"You are too old to complain," she said, flicking his nose. "Keep still."

"You're a dictator," Matthieu muttered. "I thought we'd be dancing together, that's the only reason I even volunteered."

Élisabeth had intended to do some duet practice, only so she could force Inès and Kai together, and from the boys' complaints around her, she decided to begin their duet work.

"Fine, come partner with me," she said.

Matthieu grinned widely and she shook her head both amused and outraged by his behavior.

"We will do a simple overhead lift. Kai and Inès, you will follow my lead," she said.

Matthieu lifted her, his hands firmly securing her waist as she posed, holding her balance.

She gave Kai the cue to do the same.

"You look like a swan," Matthieu said. "Like you are carved of marble."

Élisabeth smiled down at him. A genuine smile, because his words were sincere, and his mouth wasn't pulled in his usual smirk.

"Enough of this!" Séverin snapped. His icy voice shattered her focus.

Matthieu slowly lowered her as Kai did the same to Inès.

"We are not here to fool around," he said sharply. He looked at Kai and Matthieu with an unimpressed look. "Both of you go patrol the grounds."

"I'll join you," Inès said to the boys.

Élisabeth went to follow them before his hand latched onto her elbow.

"Go to the tent," Séverin said. "I'll be there shortly."

"I want to go on patrol," she said. "Matthieu can keep an eye on me, if you're concerned I'll escape."

It was far preferable to be with her friends than remain behind with him and his surly temper. Even Inès had been quick to flee. Her and Kai were halfway to the tall trees, heads bowed down as they spoke. Matthieu stayed behind, waiting for Séverin to release her.

"Don't make me repeat myself," Séverin said. "Go to the tent."

Élisabeth glared at him, anger spiking in her chest as if someone had placed hot coals on her flesh. He was treating her like a child and worse he was doing so in front of Matthieu. She was tired of his ill-temper, and his need to suckle every last bit of fun from the air.

"I don't want to be in a tent with you," she said harshly. "I despise you."

Séverin surprised her when he bent down, an arm wrapping around her knee before he swung her over his broad shoulder. A shriek escaped her as the world tilted and Matthieu's frame flipped in her vision. Before he began to walk away from him.

"Put me down, you brute," she yelled. "Put me down. *Now!*"

Élisabeth clawed at his back, nails sinking into the fabric of his coat.

"I will flay your skin," she promised. "I swear it!"

His hand gripped her thigh tight in warning.

"Calm down," he said.

Darkness cloaked them, as they slipped under the flap. Her anger had reached a breaking point, she could feel it choking her from the inside out. The moment her feet hit the ground, her magic coiled in her hand, lengthening to form a gleaming, dark blade.

Séverin had his silver, aether blade in hand.

"Stand down, Lisbeth," he said darkly. "You do not want to make that mistake again."

"I should have let the beast tear you apart," she roared. "I should have made it bring me your worthless heart."

"I will send my wraiths to your father, to your whole damn family if you don't stand down," he said.

"You can't do anything if you're dead," she said.

"You assume they haven't been watching over him this entire time," Séverin said with a cruel twist of his lips. "Try me."

He was bluffing. The wraiths likely could not cross between the realms. But what if it was not a lie? What if she defeated him at the cost of her father?

It was not a risk she was willing to take. Her hand fell, and the magic dwindled as quickly as it appeared. She hated this, hated that he knew her weakness. He had studied her for months, sitting there in the dark and pouring over her like a merchant did his riches. He knew the footprint of her ambitions, the secrets of her heart, the weight of her thoughts. He knew her love for her father, her infatuation with Charles, and just how much she hated Delphine. He knew everything and she knew nothing about him. She didn't even know why he hated her family so much. Or the history of this bargain, a bargain made of shadows and magic. There was a chasm between them, a constant thread of separation, remaining sharp and jagged, like the pointed ends of a tooth. And if she wasn't careful, she would slice herself on it one day, tearing her soul in half.

Séverin snatched the infernal rope from the hook.

"Wrists," he said coldly.

"I hate you," she whispered. "I hate you, you wretched, vile, twisted beast."

"Don't make me repeat myself."

Her throat tightened as she held out her wrists, feeling the rough thread wrap around her skin. Séverin tied the final knot and then disappeared out the flaps.

Élisabeth lay in bed, the urge to cry overwhelming. She could hear the voices of the others outside several hours later when they returned from their patrol. Laughter drifted towards her, and she quickly sealed her eyes shut when she heard footprints close by. She wasn't prepared to speak to anyone, knowing there was a high likelihood that she'd crumble into a thousand pieces.

It was *him*. She could tell by his unnaturally light footfall.

The cold graze of his leather-clad fingers stroked her cheek, and it took her a long moment to realize that a single tear had slipped past her defences, dripping like a pearl down her skin and Séverin had stolen it. As if it belonged to him.

She resisted the urge to react.

Let him think she was being haunted by her nightmares.

The last thing she wanted was for him to know that she was drowning and that he had been the one to toss her into the cold, treacherous waters of despair.

Chapter Eighteen

Séverin felt a strange sensation that morning. It *almost* felt like guilt.

But it had been Élisabeth who provoked his temper; she had no right to distract *his* soldiers. She was a siren with claws made to sink into the hearts of men. How else could she convince his soldiers to learn ballet without making them shoot themselves in the foot, simply to get out of it. There was not a single talented bone in either Matthieu or Kai's body, but yet they had indulged her.

It was like nobody seemed to remember that she had attempted to kill him just a few short days ago. That she was untrustworthy and conniving. She used her big, doe eyes to make people believe she was innocent, but Séverin could see through her lies like a gossamer veil.

He knew poison when he smelled it and touched it. He didn't need to taste it to convince himself of its deathly nature.

That was exactly what Élisabeth was. She was Death wrapped in a silken cloak.

And she had come to destroy them all.

They didn't sense them until it was too late. They should have expected it since specters were often drawn to the Blighted parts of the woods. And they were deep in the thicket of the rot. They were *also* drawn to mortals and tended to claw them apart in a mad frenzy, sinking their fists into their hot, pulsing flesh. They felt the same hunger all the dead did to be near the living, except they were rabid, decaying creatures that did not possess an inkling of sense.

The specter flung itself from the thicket launching itself at Odette. Madness had made a home of the creature, their eyes were wild, rolling around in its sockets like pebbles floating above a river stream. Its clothes were covered in filth and twigs. No traces remained of the person it had once been. A single glance at its manic eyes confirmed as much.

The specter sank its blackened nails into Odette's cheek making her howl in pain. Kai punctured a bullet into its fore-head, but the shot didn't kill it. It did slow the specter down enough for Matthieu to wrestle it to the ground and crack its neck, buying them a few minutes to decide what to do with it. He could see the flash of bloody welts it left behind on Odette. Her raw flesh looked like the wet pit of a peach.

Séverin's head snapped towards Élisabeth. She was in his tent, and he threw a shield on the entire thing. It was excessive and perhaps unneeded, but it bought him time to run towards it. He could make out the fresh prints on the snow. Specters usually traveled in packs and where there was one there was often more.

"Lisbeth!" he called, peeling back the curtain.

He had been too late to call his shield. There were three of them already inside the tent, surrounding her. Élisabeth's hands were raised and the dark tendrils of her magic spun from her fingers, latching onto the chest of each of them. They were standing there still as statues. Séverin blinked in shock. He bypassed them and stood beside her.

"What are you doing, Little Monster?" he whispered.

"Calming them," she replied.

"And then what?" he asked.

Her hand dropped and they walked away. A faint glimmer of clarity in their eyes. Séverin followed them, surprised. Only to find them returning to the woods. They paused before they left and grabbed the wrist of their fallen member and then they were gone.

"That was..." Kai started. "Odd."

"Exceptionally strange," Matthieu said.

Séverin looked back at the tent. Élisabeth stood by the parted fold. She disappeared inside when he met her eye and he turned to follow her.

"Before you ask, I don't know what that was," she said. "It just...it felt right. So, I did it. They listened to me."

And then to diffuse the situation, her lips curled in a smirk.

"Upset that you didn't get to save me?" she asked. "It must annoy you that you don't have anything to lord over my head."

"I don't trust you," he said tightly.

Something about her raised his senses. It was a gut feeling.

That something about Élisabeth Bellacourt was *terribly* wrong.

Chapter Nineteen

Séverin was generously teaching the ungrateful wench how to perfect her magic shield, yet she was glaring at him like he had destroyed her favorite dress. Fates forbid they did anything other than her precious ballet. Her eyes were drowning in frustration.

"This is boring, I want to learn how to kill yo—someone," Élisabeth quickly corrected.

His eyes sharpened.

"You're not even going to make an effort to gain my trust?"

"Nothing I say or do matters," she said. "You are determined to torture me to your heart's content."

Sweat dripped down her brow, sliding like crystals down her doll-like face.

He volleyed power at her so fast, Élisabeth didn't get the chance to strike up her shield and was flung several paces back, falling swiftly on her arse.

"You're enjoying this," she hissed. Tufts of her soft brown hair unspooled from her braid, masking her furious eyes. It wasn't the first time he had distracted her with a conversation to test the speed of her reflexes.

Séverin simply smirked. "Make a quicker shield, and maybe you won't get your arse handed to you so much."

He could see her anger spike, and he should have expected Élisabeth's attack.

Her hand raised and ribbons of darkness unspooled from her fingertips and coiled around his wrist. It felt like fire eating away at his flesh. A small hiss escaped him, and her focus shattered.

Her eyes widened in surprise, as if she hadn't expected to do any great harm. But what else had she expected, a gentle caress? Her magic had left behind a scorching black imprint and his skin peeled like a wilting flower.

"I didn't mean to—"

"No, you knew *exactly* what you were doing," he said coldly. "Not the first time you tried to kill me."

And it certainly would not be the last.

"Maybe if you taught me how to do something other than make this silly shield I would know how to control myself."

"Why would I teach my enemy how to destroy me?" he asked. "And are you blaming me for your impulsive actions?"

Élisabeth glared at him, before she spun on her heels and disappeared under the thicket.

Severin uncoiled the rope he tied her with, staring at her behind cold eyes.

"Can I sleep outside with Inès and the others?" she asked. Eyes bright with hope. "Matthieu offered to keep an eye on me."

He snorted; of course, Matthieu had offered to do so.

"What, you don't like having a padded bedroll with wolf furs and a warm tent?" he sneered.

"It is not the accommodation I have an issue with," she said. "It is the company."

Séverin brushed past her, grabbing one of the spare pillows.

"That is excellent to know, you can sleep on the ground tonight," he said, tossing the pillow at a corner in the tent. He waited with relish, for her to react, but her gaze was locked on his ravaged skin. His wrist hadn't healed yet from her attack. It was a strange and uncomfortable truth to know that there existed a creature besides the beasts who could possibly hurt him.

Guilt flickered across her eyes.

"Can I try healing that?" she asked.

"No," he said.

"Why not?"

"I'm fine," he grunted.

"No, you're not."

Élisabeth walked towards him, placing her delicate fingers on his shoulder, shoving him roughly down on the bedroll. His brows raised in surprise.

"Didn't know you were so eager to mount me like a stallion," Séverin said with a sneer.

"Don't make me regret doing this," she said.

Slowly, Élisabeth turned his hand around, revealing his inner wrist where the damage was the worst. Her head was bent, the trailing finger of her long hair drifting along his thigh like a feather. He could smell her uniquely sweet scent like the insides of a pastry shop. His fist curled so tightly, it ached. He hated this. He hated her.

"I told you I was fine," he muttered, feeling oddly uneasy.

Élisabeth ignored him, brows curling in focus.

"Do you get a perverse sense of enjoyment doing the *exact* opposite of what I tell you?"

Élisabeth grabbed his naked wrist, her warm flesh a soothing balm on his dead skin. Her smooth fingers circled the outside of the cut, trailing the damaged wound, as if she were studying it like a fervent scholar.

"I asked you a question," Severin said, unable to bear the silence.

His irritation spiked when she didn't respond.

"Are you being dense on purpose?" he demanded.

Élisabeth bit her lip, swallowing back the urge to laugh. It was almost as if she knew how uncomfortable he was by her touch and proximity. And she refused to make it easy for him. This game was only fun when *she* was the uncomfortable one.

Her magic fluttered across his skin, and he watched her siphon the dark residue of her gifts from his wound.

"I am almost done," she said, picking up his other hand. "We need not speak."

"I will do as I damn well please," Severin said. "Unless you have a clever way of silencing me?"

"I do," she said. "I'll cut a rag and shove it down your throat."

"Do you want to know what I'll shove down *your* throat?" he asked.

"*No.*"

"My clever tongue," he said. "That is what I will sho—"

Élisabeth clamped her palm on his mouth. The tips of her ears grew red-hot.

"I am a lady of the highest esteem, born of the noblest bloodline," she hissed. "The Bellacourts are one of the oldest and most respected families in the city. You cannot speak to me however you pl—ow!"

He bit her. Teeth sinking into her flesh like the wolf that he was. Her hand dropped abruptly.

"If you read me that silly spiel again I will throw you off the nearest cliff," Severin warned.

Her glare was bright and furious as she turned to his left hand. Her magic slipped out the wound like a fish out of water. He watched in dull fascination as his wound healed, the skin clear and unblemished once more.

Somehow, during each day that passed he had more questions about her magic than answers. Her magic did not heal, it simply reclaimed itself. It was what she had done when the beasts had bit him. Despite his personal feelings about her which were less than positive, he could see the usefulness of keeping someone around that could possibly save them if the beasts attacked.

Élisabeth glanced at the pillow in the corner with a sad, dejected look and a sigh so deep it could have caved the walls of the tent.

"You can have the bed tonight," he said. It would be her reward for fixing her mistake.

She smiled victoriously. A grin that felt like the first rays of sunshine after a thunderstorm, and he frowned at that terrible comparison.

Élisabeth was the thunderstorm *not* the sun.

And he could never forget that.

"No rope?" she asked.

"You wish."

They were hours away from the library and Séverin could feel the tension in his chest fade. It unraveled like a loose needle pulled from a thread. Soon he would have the answers he sought. He would know how to fix the Graylands. He might even learn exactly what the Bellacourt girl was hiding and what these gifts of hers entailed.

He was leaning against a cypress tree, smoking his cigar when he heard a feminine screech. He peered off into the distance to find Élisabeth running like a pack of beasts were descending upon her. He dropped his cigar and forged an aether blade, wondering why no one else was jumping into action.

It took him a long minute to realize that Matthieu was *chasing* her. Something was cupped in his palm that he could not see. Élisabeth ran towards him, crashing into Séverin's arms. It was instinct when he drew her behind him. Her arms wrapped desperately around his torso, fingernails digging into his flesh.

Matthieu covered his hands behind his back and bowed deeply.

"My lord," he said. "May I speak with Élisabeth?"

"What do you have there?"

"He...he has a spider," Élisabeth said, breathlessly. "One big enough to eat me!"

Matthieu threw his head back, his loud, ringing laughter filling the silence. He could see Kai and Inès watching their interaction with avid attention.

"Let me see this creature who is big enough to eat a fully grown woman," Séverin said.

"It is poisonous," Élisabeth added. "Big and poisonous."

Matthieu brought his hands forward, slowly opening his palm to reveal a spiderling with little tentacles crawling on his palm. It could not have been more than a few days old. He could feel Élisabeth shiver behind him.

"See," she said. She stood on her toes, nervously peeking over Séverin's shoulder. "I told you it is dangerous."

"How do you know it is poisonous?" Séverin asked.

"I simply do," she said. "A woman knows these kinds of things."

"That is enough Matthieu," Séverin said. His lip twitched. To think the bravest person he knew flinched at the sight of an infant spider was amusing, to say the least. "We cannot risk her being bitten."

"No, of course not," Matthieu said. Lips tilted in a wolfish smile. "She would suffer an attack of the heart and die not long after."

"Exactly," Séverin said. "Release it far from our camp, we cannot risk it."

"As you wish my lord."

He could feel the tension leak from Élisabeth's body. He felt her fingers soften around him, but they didn't drop, not until Matthieu was a far way off.

"You are safe, Lisbeth," he whispered. "No monstrous spiders are waiting to devour you anymore."

Élisabeth slowly released him. He turned around to face her. Something lurched in his chest at the gratitude that marked her face. At how her eyes were soft and wide, staring at him like he was her savior. It made him feel ten feet tall. It made him feel as though he could conquer anything. Like he could fight a million wars and know that he would always come out victorious if she was standing there staring at him *just* like that.

And then he frowned because why did it matter how she looked at him?

She was one big giant puzzle that he could not solve. Not to mention she had nearly killed him. *Twice.* Unlike the others, he refused to relinquish his anger and forgive her. After all, he had been the victim of her rage. He hadn't felt the need to tie her up in the morning, as he had been considering doing. She had only been able to protect herself from the specters the other day because he had released her to change her clothes, and he didn't trust Odette to not carve her like a wooden trinket. She was still upset that Olivier died because of her. Even though he would awaken in the Graylands once more, her anger remained steadfast.

All he *should* feel when he looked at her was rage and disgust.

"Thank you," she said softly. "For saving my life."

He swallowed the urge to laugh; perhaps "saving her life" was a bit too generous but if it indebted her to him, he would take it. Séverin was nothing if not an opportunist.

"You are welcome, Lisbeth."

Élisabeth left him to go sit with the others and he tilted his head to the corner for Kai to follow him.

"Is something wrong?" he asked. His eyes alert and scanning the treetops.

"No," Séverin said. "But I have a favor to ask."

"Go on," Kai said.

"I want to learn Lupazi," he said.

Kai tossed his head back and laughed.

"She only speaks it to me so much because she knows it gets under your skin," he said. "She says as much when she switches to it."

He knew Élisabeth only spoke it to bait him. She only ever did it the second his attention was on her and from Inès' knowing smirk she had briefed her friend on her little game.

But something about her relaxed posture when she spoke the soft, silvery vowels and the way her attention was focused on Kai alone because none of them could follow the trail of their conversation, made him feel rather isolated. Not that he was particularly involved in the conversations which he *could* understand. He just hated it when they were in their own secret world, and he was watching through a glass. There was an intimacy to sharing a language with someone and he felt an inkling of annoyance that it was Kai who spoke her native tongue and not him.

"Be that as it may I won't give that little monster the joy of knowing something which I do not," he said. "I want to start at the basics. An hour every day. Two hours if we get the chance."

"As you wish," Kai said.

Séverin's head snapped at the sound of her laughter. Delicate and harmonious, like the sway of the chapel bells before morning prayer. Matthieu sat between her and Inès and whatever tale he spun it had the girls falling over themselves. Tears were streaming down their cheeks. And they both held each other's hands across Matthieu's lap as if they were each other's anchor in the midst of a turbulent storm.

"We should ask him for pointers," Kai said. A frown pulled his lips. "He has the girls eating from the palm of his hand."

"I bet I could make them laugh harder," Séverin said.

Kai snorted. "Almost choked on my spit. *You.* Make someone laugh?"

Kai laughed, shaking his head at the mere thought.

"Just made you laugh," Séverin said with a smirk.

"Damn, you're right," Kai said with a frown.

Séverin walked away.

"Well, that doesn't count!" Kai called after him. "You have to try it on them."

As if Séverin would ever do such a thing.

Élisabeth enjoyed laughing *at* him, not *with* him.

The library was an old, crumbling mass of brick with stone stairs that had been eroded by time. The color was bleached to a bone-white shade that looked ghostly, which was rather apt for a building that belonged to the Graylands. The wispy trails of moss coated the left wall, fluttering in the breeze like a strung-up rug and there were mosaic windows punctured into the brick, the pattern concealed by years of dirt and neglect.

Inès drifted towards the sealed doors like the library had reached towards her, pulling her into its embrace. Sometimes he reckoned that the Farrow women belonged as much to the library as any of the books within its hold did. It didn't matter if it was the library in the palace or this decrepit one. They were indiscriminate in their love.

"Ah, here at last," Gaspar said, staring at the building like it was his lost lover. Just as overwhelmed as Inès was. Séverin waited impatiently for Matthieu and Kai to draw the heavy doors open. The wood creaked menacingly; thin gauzy seams of spider-web stretching the hinges like a gruesome smile as it was drawn open.

"Ladies, first," he said, half-teasingly to Élisabeth. A reference to all the times she had called him ungentlemanly.

"Nice try," she said. "Playing at gentleman only highlights how much of a gentleman you are *not*. Besides there could be wild animals inside there, you go first."

Élisabeth shoved him forward, but she did not possess the strength to move him.

Séverin took a step inside the foyer.

Someone flicked on a switch and the rusty chandelier twitched like a dying moth before it illuminated the library. It was smaller than the library in the palace, but just as spacious. Thick bound volumes with leather coverings stood like statues on the hollow shelves. Light glistened off the rare spines carved with shiny gilt lettering. The odor of parchment, leather, and ink tickled his nostrils, as the group separated and began to slowly peruse the space. Matthieu collapsed on the chaise. Long legs dangling from the end as he sighed deeply.

"It will take us ages to find that damned book," Kai muttered, staring hopelessly at the row of shelves.

"Best to get started then," Inès said. Just like Gaspar, she looked like she was at home in the abandoned library. Both their eyes were wide with awe, and Gaspar touched the shelves with his wrinkled palm with a fondness that one often used for animate beings, not a hulking structure of pinewood and rods.

"Let us divide the space," Inès said. "We'll cover more ground that way."

"Matthieu and Gaspar will do the east," she said. "Kai and I will do the west. Élisabeth and Séverin the middle, and Odette you can relax the first day, does that work?"

Odette had been crying all day. Either because she missed her twin or because her face had been ruined by the specter, leaving behind a pair of bloody scars. She hid behind a makeshift veil like a woman in mourning and had been a wreck the entire trip here.

"Must I be paired wi—" Élisabeth began.

"That works," Séverin said. "Come along, Little Monster."

He could hear Élisabeth's frustrated footsteps behind him.

"I. Am. Not. A. Little. Monster," she snarled. "And don't call me that in front of others."

"So, I can call you that in private?" He raised a brow.

"No."

"A shame that I do not take orders from you, Little Monster," he said.

"Stop calling me that!"

"Don't behave so monstrously then."

"I am a respectable woman. A paragon of society," she said with her little nose in the air. "You wouldn't know a thing about civility."

"Because I am a rascal of a ghost who arouses you?" he asked.

"AROUSES?!" Élisabeth screamed.

Séverin's mouth quirked at her reaction. "If people didn't know before they certainly do know."

"Do you truly think that I would ever desire my tormentor and jailer?" she asked. "My enemy."

"You can desire someone *precisely* because they are wrong for you," he said. "You can find someone beautiful and mesmerizing and still want to choke them the second they open their mouth."

Her mouth parted in surprise and Séverin straightened, feeling like he revealed something he shouldn't have.

He unbuttoned his coat, draping it on the chair. He began to roll up his sleeves, slowly and methodically. First the left and then the right. Three times on each side till it reached his elbow.

"Why are you so orderly?" Élisabeth asked.

He looked up at her. Her hair was unspooling, wispy strands drifting along her cheeks in a caress. The end of her braid was also coming undone like a frayed rope. There was something strangely intimate about watching her then as if he had come upon her undressing.

Her eyes were bright and challenging as if she deserved to know. He had the strange urge to irritate her, so he did not respond to her question. He looked down, consumed by his task. He could practically *feel* her anger. It took everything in him to not break out in a smile.

A book fell and then a second. Séverin frowned and picked them up. He looked at the surname of the author and fitted it in its rightful corner, ensuring the spine was aligned.

Élisabeth let out a loose laugh.

"You can't stand chaos!" she said as if she had proven a point.

It struck him then that she had been the disruption that had caused the fallen books and he had proved her point: that he despised disorder. He abhorred it. His skin broke out in chills anytime he noticed anything in his surroundings was amiss.

"Fine," he said between clenched teeth. "I don't like disarray. It drives me insane. Just like you do."

"You could have just said so," she said. "Why must everything be so difficult with you?"

"Maybe I enjoy getting under your skin," Séverin said.

He took a step forward, watching her take a step back. He didn't stop until her back lay flat against the closest bookshelf. They were tucked deep into the shadows, and he could feel her warm breath graze his cheek. He rested his palm on the shelf above her head, feeling the ends of his shirt draw free from his trousers. He could feel the air lick his skin and he watched as her gaze dropped. Thick lashes stroking her cheekbones. A warm flush crawled up her tan skin, filling her with color.

He caught her chin, lazily raising her face to look into her gray eyes. To study her captivating face and wide, innocent eyes. Her gaze was deceptive enough to make one think she was a soft, gentle soul when she was in truth a hurricane. One that would pluck the strongest houses from the earth and leave behind nothing but ruin.

"You won't ever pull anything like that day, will you, Lisbeth?" he whispered. "You won't ever betray me again, will you?"

She stared at him wide-eyed. His proximity, as he had suspected, had silenced her. It was a strange, heady power to know that he affected her so deeply. That he had the same unnameable control over her that she did over him. This strange dark rage consumed him. He had never hated anyone quite as much as he did her. It was a wonder that everyone adored her so much when she was so insufferable.

He remembered that night when he had pitched the idea of killing her before Kai and Inès while Élisabeth was unconscious in his tent.

"We should kill her," he had said, watching as Inès' face grew pale and Kai's mouth tightened. "You both didn't see her. She controlled that *thing*. She is a danger to the Graylands, to us."

"I don't think she would hurt us," Inès said. "You said it yourself, she called it off when it came towards you."

"She's young, Séverin," Kai said. "And she's afraid."

"Plus, you've given her a *million* reasons to send a beast or two after you, don't you think?" Inès added.

Séverin glared at her, and she cleared her throat.

"You know what I mean, my lord," she murmured.

Kai, Matthieu and Inès cared about her. Even Gaspar liked her. She was the only person who spoke to Gaspar ever since Nico died his Second Death. Everyone else found the old man exhaustive. She indulged him when he went on with his theories about the Graylands.

"I won't hurt you if you let me go home," Élisabeth said, drawing his attention. "You will never have to see me again. I will never get the chance to betray you if I am gone."

"Tempting," he said, enjoying how uneven and choppy her breathing had gotten. "But I like you right here where I can see you." He brushed back a strand of her loose hair, tucking it gently behind her ear. "Where I can touch you."

"Hellooooo," Matthieu called.

Séverin took a step backward just as Matthieu arrived.

"Gaspar said I'm more of a hindrance than an asset," Matthieu said. "Seems like he can't concentrate when I talk. And I can't handle doing all that work without talking. Went to

Kai and Inès first but he was busy pulling the old "I'll pick you up so you can reach the higher shelves" trick and I didn't want to disrupt his flow. You know how terrible he is at flirting, almost as bad as yo—" His words drowned in his throat when Séverin glared at him.

He cleared his throat and began again. "So, I thought I'd come see if you'd both killed each other yet."

"Excellent," Élisabeth said, perhaps a bit too eagerly. "We could use your help."

Matthieu's eyes brightened, and Séverin wondered if anyone had ever asked for his help before.

"I can help you reach the higher shelves," Matthieu said, with a flirtatious smile. "Shall I give you a hand?"

Séverin ripped out the first book he could grasp and tossed it at him. It hit him flat in the shoulder.

"Ow," he said.

"Less flirting, more working," Séverin barked.

"You okay, Mat?" she asked.

Since when did Matthieu have a pet name? Who even called him Mat? His name was two syllables while his was three. Nobody called him *Sév*. Well, Kai did, but only when he couldn't help it. Regardless, it hardly made sense for anyone to call him *Mat*.

"Glorious," Matthieu said. "Hard to be upset when you have a pretty girl around to nurse you back to health. Maybe you can massage my shoulde—"

Séverin's gaze was hot enough to flay one's flesh and Matthieu for all his lack of sense seemed to feel the wrath radiating from his corner. Matthieu clamped his mouth shut and began to peruse the titles.

A wise decision.

They worked in silence, as they hunted for *The Book of Echoes*. Gaspar had told them there would be no author name, just the title. He said it was likely written by the Fates in their eternal ink to remain unblemished and undaunted by time. So, they searched the spines. Some sparkled in gem-colored leather while others were dark and threaded.

He and Matthieu did the upper shelves while Élisabeth sat on the ground, flitting through the lower titles. Hours passed as they worked in silence.

"I need a break," Matthieu said, for the fourth time since they started. "Any objections, my lord?"

Séverin sighed. "Just leave."

Séverin looked at Élisabeth.

"You too, go rest," he said. "Matthieu, make sure she doesn't go too far."

Élisabeth ignored him and he waved a hand at Matthieu dismissing him. Matthieu shrugged and disappeared around the corner. She hadn't even *pretended* to acknowledge his words.

"It is one thing to disobey me in private, but I won't have you doing so before my men," Séverin said.

"Does it hurt your fragile ego?" Élisabeth asked.

He took a step forward and her back straightened.

"I understand," she said, quick as a silver bullet. It took him a second to realize she was unnerved by him. It seemed pinning her against the shelf had stirred something in her. "No ignoring you in public. Or insulting you by calling you a dirty—"

"No need to fling insults at me under the disguise of a sentence," he said.

Her lips quirked in a small smile.

"Back to work then," he said.

The quicker they found this book, the quicker they could return home and figure out *exactly* how to save the Graylands.

It was midnight and they all sat at the blackwood table. Matthieu had found an old bottle of wine and heralded it above his head like a trophy. Odette and Gaspar had retired to their chosen corners of the library while the rest of them sat around the rickety table. Séverin had just completed his first lesson on Lupazi a few hours ago with Kai. Séverin had found an empty journal in the library in which he'd carefully written all thirty-nine letters that made the alphabet and how to pronounce it. Kai was a good tutor, patient, and clever. And never short of praise which both annoyed and pleased Séverin. He liked to succeed in every task he put his mind to.

Matthieu had insisted they play at least *one* drinking game before bed that night. And for some reason, Séverin had chosen to indulge him. He sat at the head of the table and to no one's surprise Élisabeth took the other end. As if she were the Lady of the Below and could only ever sit with him as equals. He found it both amusing and infuriating since he had pulled out the seat to his right, so she was closer to him and not Matthieu, but she had snubbed him by walking past him to sit at the head of the table, tapping her little nails on the wood while her lips curled in a vicious smile.

Everyone was a little more fresh-eyed and cleaner. They had found a stream uphill. The brackish water had been thick and sloughy with half-curdled ice. He had been oddly concerned that the humans would catch their death and had advised against it and had told Odette and Élisabeth as much, but his gaze had been locked on the latter when he forbade them. Of course, to no one's surprise, Élisabeth had ignored him and gone off with Inès. It was a miracle they were not cutting off her fingers and toes from frostbite now.

"So, here are the rules," Matthieu said with a serious expression. "We will go in a circle. You pick a person and then you give them a choice: drink or dare."

He placed the bottle in the center.

"I will start," Matthieu said. "Kai."

"Go easy on me," Kai said with a crooked smile.

"Always," Matthieu said. But the glint in his eyes said otherwise. "I dare you to kiss Inès."

Séverin watched with faint amusement as Kai's cheeks reddened and Inès bit back a smile.

Matthieu was practically bursting with glee.

"Very mature, Matthieu," Kai mumbled.

And then to Séverin's surprise, Kai leaned forward and kissed her, slowly and gently, cupping her face as if she were made of glass. It didn't last longer than a few seconds. And when they pulled apart both parties looked like they were praying for a Pit to form beneath their feet to swallow them whole.

Élisabeth's clapping and Matthieu's enthusiastic raps on the table did not seem to help.

"Your turn, Séverin," Matthieu said.

He hadn't finished calling his name before his gaze swung to Élisabeth who groaned dramatically.

"Pass me the drink," she said.

"You haven't even heard what I was going to say," he accused.

"Nor do I want to," she said. "It will likely be a demeaning dare. One intended to humiliate me."

"Coward," he said, when she took a long hearty drag from the bottle.

"Kai, your turn."

"Séverin," he said. "Not a dare but a question, who is the prettiest girl in the room?"

Séverin curled his fingers, indicating to Inès to pass him the drink.

"You won't answer it?" Élisabeth asked.

As if he would ever stroke her ego, by confirming her suspicions.

Inès snickered and he didn't like that she and Kai shared a knowing glance. Now that they'd kissed, he hoped they didn't become one of those insufferable couples who existed in their own pathetic little world. Kai was a competent soldier and a decent friend whom he did not want to lose to something as silly and useless as love.

"Inès," Matthieu called. "You're up."

"Matthieu," she said. "I dare you to strip nake—"

"I forbid that," Séverin said. "*No.*"

He had already seen Matthieu naked at the stream. He did not need to see that again.

Inès snickered, staring at Kai under her lashes to see if he would react to that, and from his furrowed brows he was not pleased.

"Élisabeth, then," Inès said. "I dare you to sit on Séverin's lap."

"Inès." Élisabeth gasped. "I thought you were my friend."

"I am," she said. "But I also like annoying Séverin."

Élisabeth reached for the bottle.

"Oh, come on, Élisabeth," Inès groaned. "You have to do at least *one* dare."

"Fine," Élisabeth said, clearly annoyed.

Séverin leaned back in his chair, watching her approach. He knew his gaze was intense from the little shudder that ran through her shoulders. She had changed into her spare dress as if they were hosting a dinner party. It was a violet shade that made her look resplendent. She had drawn on a diamond choker, the large center pendant hanging beautifully between her breasts. She didn't look like someone who had spent weeks in the wild, but rather a noble girl who had been embroidering and studying the Last Scripture all morning.

Her dark hair fell down her back much like a spinning wheel unraveling silk.

His breath caught in his throat when she sat gingerly on his knee like a lady riding a horse astride. Her back was as straight as an arrow. Fingers tightened before her, lying flat on her knee, the paragon of a genteel upbringing.

"I don't bite, Little Monster," Séverin whispered.

"Wouldn't put that past you," she said.

He was tempted to sink his teeth into her shoulder to prove her right. To feel the gentle scrape of his canines along her flesh.

"Why didn't you let me say my dare?" he asked.

"I would never crawl to you Séverin or fill you with praise," she said.

"Wouldn't you?" he asked. "Sometimes it is liberating to beg. Sometimes it can be rewarding to serve."

"Go on then, do it," she said. "Maybe it will loosen all that tension in your shoulders."

A small chuckle escaped him, and her head snapped back. She seemed surprised that he laughed. And he realized then just how close she was, he could smell the traces of her lavender soap mixed with her unique scent of candied apples. Her eyes searched his face and it felt like time had paused, as they scrutinized each other. He counted the specks of dark blue in her gray eyes. There was a splattering of birthmarks on her slender throat. He counted eight, all sparsely placed like constellations. Something lurched in his throat, an odd, tickling sensation, as his eyes dropped down to her lush, cherry-red mouth. Did he really find this insufferable creature beautiful?

Her eyes widened ever so slightly, and then her head turned, looking away from him just in time for them to watch Matthieu attempt to do a drunken handstand. The bottle passed in a circle; their game long forgotten as they began telling stories. Kai shared stories of the boys in his regiment while Matthieu regaled them with tales of his conquests and the time he had been forced to duel a man whose wife he'd bedded.

Their voices were a faint echo in the background as his mind shifted to the girl on his lap. He was surprised she hadn't bolted from his knees when their game ended. But she was drinking as heavily as the others and slowly her body slumped into him, caving into his chest and folding inward. Her head lay lazily on his shoulder, and before he knew it, she had fallen asleep. She made this little whistling sound while she slept that he, unfortunately, found rather charming.

"I can put her to bed," Matthieu offered.

"No," Séverin said, a bit forcefully. "I got it."

Séverin arose, holding her tight to his chest.

There was a small cottage behind the library. While the others had placed their bedrolls in the library, Séverin had naturally taken the cottage. It was small with no bedrooms, just a tiny open space with a little kitchen and a bed in the corner. There was a fireplace and Kai had cut him some wood at his request. He figured Élisabeth would be here so he could keep a close eye on her and the nights were getting colder. Not that he could tell, his dead flesh did not stir at the wind or the frost that layered the windows. His bones were made of ice, but Élisabeth's weren't.

"No ropes," she murmured. Her head was tucked under his chin. Her warm breath skirted along his flesh like a furnace.

"No ropes," he echoed.

She was too drunk to escape, even if she wanted to.

He lay her down on the small cot, draping the wolf furs over her body.

"I need to change, and my hair must be plaited, or it will

tangle," she said, blinking dazedly. "Can you bring me my shift?"

"Making a servant of me, are you?" he mumbled.

Élisabeth either ignored him or didn't hear him because she began to hum under her breath. And then she was singing softly to herself a lullaby of a fox cub who missed its mother who went out hunting. She had sat up and was attempting to braid her hair, but her drunken fingers kept slipping.

"Thrice damned!" she cursed. "My fingers are as slippery as soap."

Séverin sighed and sat on the rocking chair in the corner. "Come, sit at my feet."

"You can braid?" she asked. Eyes narrowed in suspicion. "Who taught you?"

Before Séverin could admit that he did not know what to do in the slightest, she volleyed several more questions at him in rapid succession.

"Was it a girl who taught you? What is her name? Was she pretty? Will you wed her?"

Séverin chuckled. "Jealous?"

She scoffed loudly. "Hardly. I simply pity the poor girl."

"And why is that?" Séverin asked. "I am a generous lover. I could spend hours between the le—"

"Don't be crude," she said. A blush crawled up her throat. "I do not need a picture of *that* in my mind when I sleep."

Séverin curled his finger. A silent warning that if she did not come to him, he would come to her, and she wouldn't like that.

"I don't find you as frightening as you pretend to be," she huffed.

Élisabeth stood up, she swayed for a second and he shot to his feet prepared to catch her, but she remained upright. She shot him a victorious smile, pleased that she could stand on her own two feet. She took several steps towards him like a newborn colt who was just learning to walk on its spindly legs. She stumbled when she was close to him and Séverin's hands shot out wrapping around her waist.

"Careful," he bit out.

"Yes, sir, no, my lord, my great lord, my...my...vicious enemy, my bitter nemesis, my Séverin...mine," she said. The words were a slur of vowels as she leaned against him. "Nice wall." She patted his abdomen. "Strong wall."

"You are shite-faced," Séverin said.

But all he could think about was: *My Séverin. Mine.*

He wondered what she meant by it. He wondered if she even knew what she meant herself.

He led her to the chair and sat down, guiding her to the ground. She leaned against his knee and Séverin frowned at all her hair. He had tied the braids of a rope before and he figured it could not be any more difficult. The sensible thing would have been to awaken Odette and ask her to take care of it, but ever since Olivier died, she had been shooting Élisabeth venomous stares. He could only imagine what she'd do to Élisabeth if she came across her drunk and vulnerable form. Likely chop her hair off at the root.

Séverin would have to do his best.

Chapter Twenty

Élisabeth was drowsy and lightheaded. She had always had a terrible time with wine which was why she barely drank it, but the bottle kept appearing before her and she'd been thirsty, and truth be told she'd been nervous sitting on Séverin's lap in the library, feeling the lazy drape of his wrist on her thigh and the blistering cold of his body behind her. She had thought of getting up and racing back to her seat, but Séverin would know that he had won. She could *never* let him know just how much he affected her.

And now she was here again, sitting snugly between his legs like a kitten while he played with her hair. It was the only word to describe what he was doing with the strands. He kept lifting it, weighing it in his palm as if he were measuring gold to determine its value.

She bit her lip to swallow back the itch that climbed her throat, but the gesture was futile. Soon enough she was silently giggling, tears slipping down her face.

"What's so funny?" Séverin demanded.

"You. Me. *Us*," she said. "I tried to kill you a few days ago. I was going to feed your entrails to that beast, and you were going to run me through with your blade. And now you're braiding my hair."

"This doesn't mean I despise you any less," he said.

"I hate you too, Spirit-King," Élisabeth said. "Hate you *and* your pretty face!"

It struck her then that the latter remark was supposed to be tucked within the confines of her mind. Séverin chuckled, that melodic, tinkling sound that made her chest ache, thinking about the Opera and the male sopranos. He had a voice that was meant to be revered. A voice that was made to sing.

That was the second time he'd laughed tonight. It was both eerie and comforting. And she could feel the tension in her shoulders melt.

"Where will you sleep tonight?" she asked.

"Don't need to sleep," he said. "Why? Did you want to share your bed?"

"No!"

"Then don't offer."

Élisabeth clamped her mouth shut. He had every intention of misreading her words.

"Well, what do you think?" he asked.

Élisabeth's hand touched the braid. It felt lumpy and uneven. She stared at the ends of her hair. He hadn't bothered to tie it. It just lay in a fluff that would most likely unravel overnight.

"My fingers were too big for the ends," he said, in a defensive tone.

"It's lovely," she lied. "Thank you, Séverin."

She leaned back on his thigh, too tired to undress. The dress was uncomfortable but so was the thought of removing it in this small space while Séverin was here. She could feel a warm flush creep up her neck at the thought of his dark gaze on her while she unfastened her corset. It was clear to see that the wine had robbed her of her good sense.

"Do you still wish to change your clothes?"

"No," she said quickly. "I'm too tired."

"I can—"

"It's fine," she said. Her voice was high-pitched and squeaky, revealing her nerves. "Truly."

"Very well," Séverin said. "Come, let me guide you to bed before you trip on your hem."

The breath left her in a gust of air when he scooped her up, raising her off her feet. It wasn't long before he crossed the floor to the small cot and placed her down gently like she was a delicate box filled with rare gems. It made her chest stir and she caught his wrist before he left. His muted, colorless eyes flared at the feel of her skin on his. For once he did not wear his signature black, leather gloves. He was bared and unguarded. She wished that she could peel away his masque and study the expanse of his face. Even if it was ruined, she wanted to see every inch of him.

"I would have picked Inès too," she said softly.

"What are you going on about?" he muttered.

"When Kai asked you who the prettiest girl was, you were going to say Inès."

She knew he was. He simply didn't want to upset Kai, so he said nothing.

He was silent for so long, that she regretted saying anything to begin with. Maybe he had forgotten the silly game.

"You are such an idiot," he said with a dry laugh.

"I am not!"

She tried to sit upright because having an argument lying down made her feel foolish. But her arms were far too uncoordinated to accomplish the simple task and she fell back down in a dizzy spell.

"Then why is it that you have no idea how wretchedly beautiful you are?" he snapped. "That you are...that you are... there are not enough words to describe how frightfully bewitching you are."

Her heart caught in her throat as she stared at his beautiful mouth which had hardened into a thin line. He was angry at her and for once Élisabeth was speechless. Her mouth was parted in shock. She yanked the blankets over her flushed skin, struggling to control her breathing. She had made him stutter.

He had called her wretchedly beautiful.

He had called her frightfully bewitching.

It was silent for so long and she was certain that he'd left when she heard his voice. Soft as thistledown, soft as candlelight. His voice was lilting and syrupy and otherworldly. Like he was but mere scraps of the night sky sewn into the image of a tortured boy.

"Good night, Little Monster," he whispered.

And then he crossed the floor and returned to his chair, while the creaking bones of the wicker drew her into a gentle slumber and something wispy tilted her lips into a smile.

Élisabeth hadn't expected to be the one to find *The Book of Echoes.*

She was tucked in a little nook with a pile of different texts. The column of books was rapidly growing with each minute, becoming more crooked and threatening with each copy she stacked like a weak-boned house. It could very well drown her in a sea of velvet-black ink and folded pages if she wasn't careful. She had constructed her monument with manuals, poem books, liturgical, and historical tomes. She had even found a rare copy of *The First Scripture* that was said to have been burned during the Crusade when a wave of priests had rejected the Three Kings in favor of the Fates.

Her fingers toyed with Séverin's necklace on her throat. The one with the crow. He had been sleeping on the chair when she awoke, and she had always had swift fingers. She had stolen it from him to simply prove that she could and once she had it, she had kept her treasure. Her father had once said she'd make an excellent pickpocket. And as always, he was right. It hung loosely between her breasts, safe beneath her billowy shirt, another stolen item from Séverin's wardrobe.

Her wrists hurt from holding the mysterious book. It had a heavy leather covering that concealed the title and author on the front and the spine had been covered with a thick brass that ran like a cord from one end to the other. A golden leaf clasp held the pages together, containing the secrets of the book.

She was far away from Séverin and the others. Her skin burned when she thought of last night, of the game and the cottage, and his fingers intertwined in her hair like a ribbon. She shook her head, erasing all thoughts of the boy who was her sworn enemy, and focused on the book on her lap.

Élisabeth curiously opened the clasp and stared at the faded lettering on the title page that read: *The Book of Echoes*. The paper sheets were old and yellowed, emitting a strong smell of dried ink with an echo of a musky floral scent that was likely from the shriveled papyrus sheets. Her fingers tingled when she flipped the page as if the book were wrapped in magic.

She scanned the small excerpt.

In the Beginning.
There were three.

And as such the prophecy began with the three
The Traitor, the Warden, and the Harbinger.
And so it went that every four hundred years
    the Traitor is cleaved, the Harbinger is
    reborn, the Warden guides the lost, and the
    Graylands burn.

Her breath stilled as she flipped the page and came upon what looked to be an old nursery rhyme.

First comes the Traitor, Master of the wicked.
Second, comes the Blight, twisted, and full of
    fright.
Third is the Pit, deep and darkness it emits.
Fourth are the beasts who have come for their
    feasts.
Fifth is the girl with the gifts of night.
Sixth is the Warden with the horn in sight.
Until the balance and order is once more right.

It sounded like a prophecy. She frowned at the bleak, colorless words. All but the last line, which was a candle in a tunnel of shadows, illuminating a small flicker of hope.

She flipped the page and there was a long chapter on the Graylands. Each line of that chilling rhyme had a chapter dedicated to it. A chapter that weaved a story older than time itself. The book was heavy with magic. Not aether, nor her dark nameless magic, but something bright and vibrant and golden. Almost as if it were celestial magic. The magic of the Fates. Gaspar had said the book had been written by the Fates, and staring at the strange words it struck her then that it was not a language she had ever learned. Yet she had consumed the words, swallowing them like it was a delicacy.

Élisabeth turned the pages until she reached the chapter about the girl. Something inside her wondered if it spoke of her. If she was this fabled savior, this chosen one who was supposed to liberate the Graylands from the Blight. As much as she wanted to believe that this was none of her business, it felt like she played a greater role in this mystery. She could control the beasts and even those wild-eyed ghosts who had come to devour her had bent to her will. She had drawn from her surroundings that night when the ghosts had come. She had done as Séverin had taught her and pulled from the threads to control them all at once, to bid them to return to the woods and to harm no other.

She took a deep breath filled with dread and read the chapter.

**Fifth is the girl with the gifts of
night.**
The girl always arrives after the Cleaving.
She will erase the Traitor.
She will do as she is bidden by the Fates and
the Eternal Warden.
Together they will lead the final act.
And only then will the realm be safe once
more.

"You found it then."

Her head snapped up, her heart thudding fiercely. But it wasn't Séverin who stood above her, it was Matthieu. He crouched down, green eyes bright. His mouth was slack in a manner that did not quite fit. Her fingers trembled. She knew with certainty that this girl the prophecy spoke of was her. She was this girl with the gifts of night who had been tasked to save this world.

"I don't know what you're talking about," she said, covering the book with the decoy flap.

"I know who you are, Élisabeth," he said. "I knew the moment I saw you."

Élisabeth swallowed. "I don't understand."

Matthieu sat down, crossing his long legs. His hair was knotted, the blond strands neatly pulled back from his chiseled face.

"The Graylands operates on its own rules," he said. "Every 400 years the Graylands cracks because the Traitor is reborn. And then you come, and you fix it. You correct nature's mistake, and all is right in the Graylands once more."

"I don't understand," she said.

"No, I know you don't," he said. His voice was oddly tender and the way he looked at her unnerved her, as if he had an intimate understanding of every flaw and secret that she had collected over the years. "You know that Laurent and Séverin were cleaved, but I suppose you don't know that they are reborn every four hundred years. Their birth always signifies the collapse of the Graylands."

Élisabeth thought about how the beasts had fled when they had bitten Séverin. Almost as if their work was done. As if he had been their target all along. She thought of those mornings when she had been tucked inside the half-rotted walls of the old chapel in the Bellacourt gardens and forced by Delphine to consume the pages of the Last Scripture and how she'd always been fascinated by the concept of rebirth. How every soul would return in the eyes of another and that strange, echoing feeling of having experienced something before was simply a memory of a past life. She had found it beautiful and had consumed the reading as a rapt pupil would, savoring every bite. She imagined it to be like a decaying tree, collapsing inward until its branches had become roots and the roots became a sapling. Death and life. Winter and spring. The eternal lovers.

"You always arrive shortly after," Matthieu said. "You kill him, and the world is right once more. You are the harbinger but not of doom, of balance. You straighten the scales."

"How?" she whispered.

"It is called the Invisible Sword," he said. "An immortal weapon of the Fates."

"How do you know all this?" she asked. Eyes narrowing in suspicion. It struck her as rather odd that he hadn't conveyed this information to Séverin when he served him. Was this some kind of loyalty test Séverin was making her do? A trap to see if she betrayed him again?

"I am the Warden of the Graylands appointed by the Fates," he said. "I'm also the one who guides you every four hundred years when you are reborn."

It felt strange, but she could sense the thread of history between them both. She remembered when she'd arrived and how it had felt as though his eyes spoke to her in a language only the both of them understood. That there had been something about him that tugged at her.

"I'm your guide," Matthieu said, lips raising in a grin.

"What happens when he's dead?" she asked.

"The beasts return to the Pit, and the Pit is sealed by the Fates. I am *hoping* you decide to stick around in the Graylands because I'm *so* much fun and you have yet to find someone as experienced in the sheets as yours truly—being immortal gives you much time to learn new and exciting tricks," he said. "But usually, you live a human life and then we meet again in four hundred years."

"I'm not immortal?" she asked. "I'm not like you?"

"You are," he said. "But once you return to the mortal world you are no longer immortal. The mortal realm is Berthe's dominion, and she is rather strict about maintaining the balance. All that lives must die and so on."

"My head hurts," she said. "What happens if Séverin finds out that he must die to save the Graylands? He will kill me."

"It won't come to that," Matthieu said with a serious experience. "He can never learn the truth of you nor your purpose."

"Why didn't you tell me sooner if it was such a risk that he could learn the truth before I did?" she asked.

"You wouldn't have believed me," he said. "And that thrice-damned book has a mind of its own. It's sentient. I've tried safe-keeping it, but it always disappears, and finding it again is a headache. You will learn more when you speak to your mot—"

He clamped his mouth shut and then he cursed harshly.

"You were going to say 'my mother'?" she asked. "My mother is dead."

Matthieu stood up. "Hide the book, Élisabeth."

But her mind was stuck on the word he'd almost uttered. It could not be true. Her mother could not be alive. Maybe she was here. She was dead after all. The thought had never crossed her mind, but now that it did, it was all she could think of. Her heart raced at the thought of seeing her. She had only ever seen her in a portrait. Dark skin, brown eyes the color of roasted chestnuts, and a beautiful smile with a pair of twin dimples.

"What happens if I fail?" she asked.

"You kill him, or he kills you," Matthieu said. "Those are the only options. There is no world where the both of you survive."

Élisabeth had retired early that night. Spirits were low because nobody could find the book. She had hidden it under her shirt, tucked in the band of her trousers, and when she'd returned to the cottage and lifted her shirt the infernal book had gone. She had cursed and foolishly kicked the heel of the bed, nearly injuring her toes.

"It's gone again?" Matthieu asked when she'd told him. "That Fates-cursed book, where could it be now?"

"I don't know," she said anxiously. "What if he finds it?"

"He won't," he said. "I won't let him hurt you, Élisabeth. Do you trust me?"

It was strange that she had never given Matthieu a second thought. He was always joking and teasing and was rarely ever serious. Even when the beast had been attacking them, he'd had a wicked grin on his lips as he plummeted bullets in the air. He despised hard work and cared more about finding the closest bottle of wine than anything else. He flirted with anyone who had a pulse and had jokingly told Kai the other night that his dimples made him weak in the knees which had forced Kai to proclaim that he would *never* smile again.

But now that she knew the truth, she could see the glimmer of intelligence in his eyes that remained veiled by his light-hearted nature. She wondered if he acted that way to evade suspicion. If so, it was a brilliant maneuver; nobody ever looked twice at Matthieu Durand.

It made her curious to know about his birth and what exactly it meant to be a 'Warden'.

"I do," she said.

And she believed it. A voice inside her bid her to trust him.

"You must leave," he whispered. "Quietly and without notice. We can't risk him finding *The Book of Echoes* and killing you before you do him. I will distract them."

"Where shall I go?" she asked.

"I will fetch you a map," he said. "Take my horse. He will know who you are. You've ridden him before."

"Your horse is immortal?"

Matthieu nodded. "All animals are undying, but mine was a gift from Lune, the Unbending."

"The Fate?" she asked.

Her mouth dropped open in surprise and he clicked it shut with the tip of his finger.

"Yes," Matthieu said. He plucked out a key from his breast. "There is a house a few hours from here. I'll mark it for you on a map. Wait for me there."

"I'm scared, Mat," she said. "*Really* scared."

The confession slipped past her lips before she could swallow it. This was not the future she had dreamed about as a little girl. She had never wanted to be an instrument of the Fates, to be controlled and manipulated into becoming a weapon. As much as she was at odds with Séverin, she barely could stomach unleashing the beast at him. How could she wield this sword Matthieu spoke of and strike him? Even though she had been tempted to cut his head off more times than she could count, it was different when she was in the throes of anger versus now when she was level-headed. Could she truly plot his murder and go through with it?

"I know," he said softly.

Matthieu lightly tucked a strand of hair behind her ear, and it reminded her of when Séverin had done it that day in the library when he had pinned her against the shelves.

And then she shook her head because everything was as she had always expected. Séverin and her were born to destroy each other.

"I will tell you so much more when we are together," Matthieu promised, dragging her from her suffocating thoughts. "I'll even kiss away all your troubles."

A choked laugh escaped her and from the way his eyes

brightened that had been his goal. He had wanted to make her laugh.

It was nice to have a friend. A protector.

Someone loyal to her and not Séverin.

Élisabeth slid outside the library following Matthieu's cue. She had her clothes packed and had stolen some of Odette's rations since she'd had the sense to bring along far more food than Élisabeth. It was only a matter of time till *The Book of Echoes* revealed itself once more, and she hoped that she was far away from the library when it did. Her mind still spun with all she had learned, and she had every intention of picking it apart when she was alone.

Matthieu was telling some story, spreading his hands dramatically as he re-enacted a scene. Kai was laughing and even Séverin had paused his work to listen. Now was her chance; Matthieu had gathered everything she needed and marked the map for her. She would wait for him to come to her, and they would figure it out together.

She was close to the door. So close to victory when a small, petite figure slipped in front of her.

"Where do you think you're going?" Odette demanded.

Her face was covered by a lace handkerchief that she had attached to the sides of her head with a dull ivory pin. The color was half-peeling, and the paint on the iron was chipped and faded.

"I forgot something at the cottage," she said.

"Matthieu took you there last time. The rules are you are not to be left unattended," she said, raising her nose in the air. Her words were coated in disgust.

"Nobody assigned you as my guard," she said. "Now. Move."

Odette opened her mouth and Élisabeth couldn't risk it. She shoved her out the door before anyone noticed. Odette parted her mouth to scream, but Élisabeth placed her palm on her lips, silencing her. Her blunt teeth sunk into her flesh making her curse. She pushed Odette backward, gaining no satisfaction when she stumbled down the short steps and fell on her behind.

Élisabeth ran to Matthieu's horse and desperately unraveled the tether, hearing Odette screaming for help. Matthieu had saddled the horse and left a bag with water and food strapped to the side, extra provisions if she ran low. Relief drenched her at the sight, and she kicked her heels into the horse's side, tearing off into the distance just as the doors opened and they rushed out. She was not an experienced rider, but Matthieu was right. The beast liked her and didn't hesitate to tear off into the woods.

She could hear Séverin bark something and Élisabeth instinctually flattened herself just as a rope of aether was tossed at her. It tangled in the air, fading to nothing when it didn't meet its target.

She didn't dare look back. Just pushed the horse as fast as she could. If Odette were the reason she was caught and dragged back to Séverin, she would kill the girl. She could hear the thundering applause of hooves behind her, beating in tandem with her heart. She knew the direness of the situation if she were caught. She would never get another chance to escape. She had caught the rush of betrayal in his eyes when he stood atop the stone steps. The sight of it had run down her throat like sour grapes, blistering and distasteful.

She heard Matthieu call out that she had turned left when she had in fact turned right. It was that misdirection that allowed her to escape. She could hear their hooves fading the deeper she marched through the thicket. She paused to pull out Matthieu's map and figure out the best path forward.

At least the sun was shining. Spectrums of bright light

poured through the branches like tea filling a porcelain cup. Layers of beech mast coated the ground, forming a halo around the tree trunk, as she assessed her surroundings. At least she wasn't stuck in one of the Blighted areas; this side of the woods was clear of decay and rotten magic.

Élisabeth took a deep breath and let the forest wrap its arms around her.

Chapter Twenty-One

The violet sky grew ominously darker the deeper she slid into the labyrinth of the woods. Streaks of berry blue, purple, and gray painted the sky depicting a canvas of misery. The woods enclosed her, burying her in a coffin of dirt and tree roots. She could smell the traces of sweetness and rot growing stronger, as she grew closer to the house. She wondered if Matthieu had known that it lay in the Blighted parts of the woods. It would have been a good thing to mention, considering she found the Blight rather unsettling. Mist crawled along the hooves of the horse, rising like foam on the sea, growing so thick she could hardly see where she was going.

In the distance, she could just about make out a wooden frame, short and pointed.

It was a little bigger than the cottage Séverin had stayed in near the library and was just as withered, almost as if the cursed woods had eaten away at its foundation. A pelt of moss and lichen grew on the left wall, seeping into the cracks. Salt was sprayed upon the floor, the three intertwined circles. It was the symbol of the Fates. A protective ward against wickedness.

Frost layered the window leaving behind a gleaming shine like a polished boot.

She tied Matthieu's horse, a beautiful white stallion that he called Silver to the closest fir tree. Her fingers were numb with cold as she plunged the key in and twisted the lock. It was slightly warmer inside, but not by much. There was a bedroom with an attached bathing room, and she was pleased to find that the faucet turned out water. It took a few minutes for the water to turn clear from the brown-green stream that had initially spurted out.

Élisabeth found a stack of timber behind the little dwelling. She started a fire and stoked the flames while she went to wash off the grime. There was some spare clothing that likely belonged to Matthieu in the small mahogany chest and she rolled up the cuffs of the trousers and sleeves. She found a length of rope and knotted the middle, so it stayed upright before she curled on the carpet, face turned to the flames, soaking up the heat while tremors wracked her body. The winter air was brutal as it knocked against the window with its iron fist.

"Hello, Sabeth," a soft voice called.

She spun around to find a woman sitting comfortably on the leather armchair. She was draped in a bright red robe that swept the floor like a bloodstain. It pooled atop the carpet, trickling down in a waterfall. Her robe hid her features while the dim room cast her in a web of shadows. On her chest rested the knitted ends of her plentiful braids. Slowly the strange woman tugged back her hood, revealing a startlingly beautiful face. It radiated with an ethereal glow that nearly blinded her. Her cheekbones were high and proud, and she had eyes as clever as a fox. Something about her made Élisabeth quiver and she had the strange sense that she was standing before something unearthly and seraphic.

"My name is Lune, the Un—"

"Unbending," Élisabeth whispered. "You are a Fate."

"I am," she said. Her voice was euphonious and vibrant. Élisabeth thought of her using it to sing, just as she thought of Séverin's voice. She could imagine it ringing against the high walls of a chapel, glorious and vibrant as she sang old hymns. "I cannot recall the last time someone cut me off."

"I am sorry," Élisabeth said. She fell into a curtsey that didn't feel sufficient, so she dropped to her knees. Head bent, spine trembling in fear. She could feel the weight of her power, pressing down upon her like a hammer made to sculpt diamonds, pressing until it gained the desired shape. Until a block had turned into an oval. A small part of her had always believed it all to be a myth: the many realms, the High Trinity, the Fates. Like scrapes of a tale knitted together by a story-weaver built on awe and desperation and mortal longing.

"You may rise," she said.

Élisabeth stood up on weak legs, uncertain if she should look to the ground while she spoke or her eyes.

"You may be informal in my presence," she said. "You and I are uniquely connected, Sabeth."

Élisabeth didn't feel the need to correct her about her name. It didn't seem appropriate. So, she just stood there awkwardly, staring into the black, hollow eyes of the Fate. There were no pupils in her eyes, just stretches of darkness, pulled like a blanket from one end to the other. Her skin was a warm brown that radiated like gold.

"Come closer, Sabeth," she said. "Come sit by my feet."

Élisabeth walked to her hesitantly and did as she was bidden. Lune's hand reached for her, and she flinched, but her touch was gentle. It stroked her cheek, as light as the softened waves of the sea as it caressed the shores. Élisabeth's skin tingled and she felt the warm flicker of magic graze her face.

Lune's palm glowed with a golden hue. The string of power ran from Élisabeth's forehead to her chin, leaving behind the sticky residue of magic.

"Hmm, close enough," she said.

"What was that?" Élisabeth said.

"You looked a little different as you always do, but you are closer now to your original form," she said.

Élisabeth was afraid to look in the mirror, to see what changes she had made.

"Have I done something to displease you?" Élisabeth asked.

"You have," she said. "But you did not know so I shall tell you and you will not fail me again, Sabeth."

She confirmed the dreaded truth, that Élisabeth had done something so terrible it had forced a Fate to confront her. The Fates lived in the unseen realm and while they managed and oversaw the balance of the realms, they rarely involved themselves in affairs of the living and the dead. There had been a time when they had been more accessible when they would hold councils and solve disputes between kings and tilt wars in their favor. But the days of that were gone and they had not been seen or heard of since the High Trinity disappeared.

For her to have drawn a Fate from recluse and brought her to the Graylands meant that she had broken the balance. It was all that mattered to the Fates: Balance. Scales. Equilibrium. Parity.

And she had disrupted it.

"Your name is Sabeth," she said. "You are a child born of a Fate and a mortal. I am your mother."

"My mother is dead," Élisabeth said.

Somehow, her mind could not wrap around this revelation, seeming far too unlikely to be real. And she worried that she'd upset the Fate by refusing this information.

"Your mortal mother perhaps," she said. "But you were

always mine, Sabeth. It is your undying soul that makes you a Fateborn."

"I don't understand," she whispered.

"Your soul is mine, but your physical nature is determined by the Wheel," she said.

"So, my father...is he my father?" she asked.

"In a sense yes and in a sense no," Lune said. "In this lifetime, yes, but your immortal soul was fathered by another."

Élisabeth found it difficult to wrap her mind around the words she spoke. Each answer she provided was met with another question.

"And my father, my original father," she said. "Where is he?"

"He died," she said. "He was mortal."

"So, he is in the Graylands?"

"No."

Her mind spun and she was silent for what felt like hours. It would take her a lifetime to process this information. She remembered what Matthieu had said—that her mother would explain it before he had bitten his tongue. Had he known that she was the child of a Fate? She had never thought Fates could have children. But it made sense; besides her eyes, Lune looked painfully mortal. Many said the Fates were mortals who had been chosen by the Three Kings and blessed with magic.

"I understand it is a lot to process," Lune said. Her finger rested firmly on her head, stroking her hair. "I will say, Sabeth, that I've missed you. It is always such an agony waiting for you to come home again."

Something twisted in Élisabeth's chest. That odd yearning she had felt as a child when she'd seen Delphine nurture Louise while she watched from the shadows. The feeling pulled her with icy fingers deep into a well of longing and despair. And she was not surprised to find a tear licking a hot path down her cheek. Somehow, it felt like the missing piece of a puzzle had been slotted into her chest, repairing the broken cracks of her heart.

"Do not cry, child," Lune whispered. "You are home. And you may call me Mother."

"Mother," she said softly, trying out the foreign word in her mouth. She hesitantly looked up at Lune to see if she had any objection even if she had permitted her to do so, but her lips were pulled in a soft smile.

"Matthieu knew what I was, didn't he?"

"Mat is a Fateborn like you. His father is Aldéric," she said. "You have known him since childhood, and he is your best friend. You can trust him."

"He said he is immortal," she said. "But I am not?"

"You chose a long time ago to live in the realm of Berthe in the Land of the Living. Berthe is strict about balance and all living things must die," she said. "Mat lives in the Graylands and what is dead cannot die so he remains immortal. If you chose to stay here, in my lands, you too would be immortal."

"Why did I choose to leave then?"

"I'm afraid after all these centuries I cannot piece together the labyrinth of your mind, my darling Sabeth," she said. "As much as I am enjoying our conversation, I know that you came across *The Book of Echoes*, so you are aware of the direness of the situation. It is the Year of the Falling when the Traitor must die, and it is your duty, Sabeth, to destroy him."

"Why am I the Harbinger?" Élisabeth asked.

"Because you asked to be the Harbinger, you wanted to be the one to destroy him," she said. "You were given the power of all three of the Fates to call upon the Invisible Sword. It is a long tale of history but you and the Traitor were always interlocked in the eternal battle. He sits on one end of the scale and you on the other. For there to be balance you must kill him. If you fail it will shatter the Balance and the realms will be in danger. Not just the Graylands."

Élisabeth swallowed, feeling the weight of the worlds on her shoulder. Kill Séverin and save the world or fail and watch everything burn around them. Why had she asked to be the Harbinger? Why was Séverin's soul the price of saving the Graylands and the realms? Why was he called the Traitor? What had he done to deserve this?

Her stomach knotted in unease. There was so much she did not understand.

All she knew was that her enemy was death-touched. And from the firm set of Lune's lips would likely not live past the fortnight.

"Where is the sword?" she asked.

"It will come when you are ready, not any sooner or later," she said. "It was made of the same divine magic that was used to bind *The Book of Echoes*."

"What about the beasts, will their poison kill him?" she asked. "Why is he called the Traitor?"

"The poison can temporarily kill him," Lune said. "But only the Invisible Sword will end him, at least for another four hundred years when he is reborn once more. And to answer your question, he betrayed the Three Kings, and this is his punishment."

She felt a brittle pain slashing at her insides. There had been a time when she'd have done anything to return home.

Even killed Séverin to do so. But everything was a lie.

She was not Élisabeth Bellacourt, she was Sabeth, daughter of Lune the Unbending. Her world was tilting, swaying like a ship trapped in a sea storm, and collapsing into a pit of doom. She didn't want to claim this destiny. She didn't want to be anything bigger than what she was.

"Rest, Sabeth," Lune said. She bent down, placing a cold,

absent kiss on her forehead. "Your magic will grow stronger, and you will not be weighed so much by your mortality."

"Will you stay with me?" she asked desperately.

"I have to go to the Silver Palace, Aldéric has called a council of the Fates to ensure that the Traitor will be neutralized soon," she said. "It is only a matter of time till the Invisible Sword is revealed to you when you are called upon to carry out your destiny."

Lune was gone before Élisabeth could say another word.

Nothing but the faint echo of her divine magic lingered in the empty space.

Chapter Twenty-Two

Élisabeth sat by a nearby stream, studying her face like a willful maiden before her first society ball. Lune had done something to her. She looked more beautiful. An otherworldly beauty that defied nature. Her cheekbones were sharper, keen enough to cut glass and her eyes emitted an unearthly glow like gems were trapped behind her pupils. Her lips were riper as if she had painted them with a tincture of beeswax and dye.

Something cracked behind her and she looked up, her heart pounding in her chest. For a moment, she thought it was *him*. And she feared him. She feared this history that lay between them like a chasm that would not seal. Last night she had been tangled in so many dreams she could not tell her memory from the nightmare. But each one ended with a blade in the chest, sometimes in her chest, and sometimes in his.

As if she were doomed to relive her worst nightmares.

It reminded her of a ballad she had heard once. A rare night when she was not on stage and instead had the chance to sit among the masses. It was of two lovers cursed to die if they fell in love. And so, they had existed on the outskirts of each other's lives with their hearts in their throats. Until they could not resist falling in love and died swiftly after. Élisabeth would feel her eyes tingle at the thought of their doomed love. It felt like she was watching that ballad unfold again. Except there was no love between them, just a cold, distant hate that crept between them like a shadow.

The boy that lurked in the trees wasn't Séverin. It was his other half.

Laurent had found her.

"Not him," Laurent said, hands raised as if he stood before a firing squad. "It's just me."

"Laurent," she said, relief soaking her voice. She stood up and wrapped her arms around his broad shoulders. It had been only two months since they parted, but it felt like years. "How did you find me?"

"Gaspar," he said. "I've known him for some time and would go to him anytime I had a perplexing question that required a scholarly mind. Before he left, he told me that Séverin was hunting down *The Book of Echoes*. He gave me a map with directions to the library and I set off before you all did. I didn't have much time to go through it all before you and the others arrived. I'm afraid I've lost my chance of getting my hands on it before him."

His tone was filled with bitterness, and she found herself shocked by the rage in his voice. She wondered if he could be an ally. If he could help her solve this terrible mess. Maybe Laurent could kill Séverin. Maybe she could place this terrible burden upon his shoulders. What if all she had to do was summon the sword and not kill him? What if someone else could wield it?

Her mouth soured at the thought of killing Séverin, of killing *anyone* for that matter. She thought of him that night, staring at her with those cold eyes. And then those long fingers she had felt in her hair when he'd offered to braid it. She had never imagined someone so harsh could have such a gentle touch.

Guilt flooded her, wringing her from the inside out.

Séverin had been wretched to her, and he had a tendency of always saying the wrong thing. But he hadn't used the ropes on her last night and he had looked after her. Even though he didn't have to. He could have let Odette handle her and likely cut off all her hair to spite her, but he hadn't.

"You look different," Laurent said. "Your face it is...well pardon my straightforwardness but you look more beautiful than I last recall."

"I changed my hair," she said, unimpressed by his backhanded compliment.

"We need to speak," he said. "Come with me."

She noticed four more horses and beside them were four men, covered in dirt with shrewd eyes that watched her. Long-necked rifles swung from their backs, and they carried the rough appearance of hired arms.

"I brought along some allies to help me find *The Book of Echoes*," he said. "Didn't think I could find it alone with such limited time."

"Do you trust them?" Élisabeth asked.

"No," he said. "But I paid them, and they don't get the second half until we return to the quarter so that's good enough."

Light illuminated the small main room as they sat on opposite chairs. It was odd to sit where Lune the Unbending had sat mere hours ago. She wondered how Laurent would react to that information. She wondered if he could even be trusted with the truth—that so long as Séverin lived the Blight would spread and the Graylands would be in danger.

Laurent looked tired. His beautiful face was marked with weariness. Laurent and Séverin were identical, but their mannerisms differed. The way his hands tapped the handrest was rapid and not slow and calculating like Séverin. The way his mouth was upturned was nothing like the firm, immovable set of Séverin's mouth that rarely shifted except when she angered him and it would curl in displeasure or the times when he'd give her that wicked smile.

"Anything exciting happen since you went to his court?" Laurent asked.

"I almost killed Séverin," she said.

The confession tasted sour on her tongue. She had wanted to become a professional ballet dancer, not a murderer. But she was being forced to become something else to survive this harsh world. Something that frightened her.

She was a Fateborn, and her destiny had already been decided for her. All this time she had spent fighting to become her own person only to be trapped under the burden of her birthright. All her life she had catered to other people: to her father, to her stepmother, to Louise, and now her mother. As if she were nothing more than a pawn made to be moved by other people.

She would tell Laurent the truth. All of it. She would let him be the one to end Séverin. It would be cyclical and divine. He could wield the Invisible Sword. He could destroy Séverin. And she could be free.

She didn't owe Séverin any loyalty. If the roles were reversed, he would do the same. Besides how could she let the future of the realms be damned for a boy. It was foolish and she was done making silly decisions.

"The blade of aether clearly did not work," Laurent said. "Gaspar was certain that a powerful blade could end him."

"I didn't almost kill him with that measly toy. I almost

killed him with a beast, but that can't kill him either. Not for long anyway," she said. "Only the Invisible Sword can end him."

"What?" Laurent asked, confused.

Élisabeth took a deep breath before she dove into the mess of the past few weeks.

Strange to think that she had been here for a little longer than a month. It felt like just yesterday she had debuted on the stage of Prasin to high praise, feeling like she was on top of the world.

Now she was in this room being hunted by Séverin, involved in a mess that could destroy the realms, and staring into the eyes of a boy who wore her enemy's face.

Laurent was silent when she finished her recounting. She had told him everything except for Matthieu's role in all of it. That was not her secret to share.

Minutes felt like hours as he stared at her, mouth agape, brows raised to his hairline.

"So, you are the daughter of a Fate," he whispered. "That is...that is big."

"I know. I wouldn't have believed it if she hadn't come to me and said so herself."

"But you said that you have to kill the Traitor, that likely includes Séverin *and* I," he said.

"I never thought of that," Élisabeth said. "Maybe? But maybe it means just Séverin. *The Book of Echoes* says the master of the wicked. That must imply Séverin. Perhaps, it alludes to his title as Lord of the Below."

"Perhaps," Laurent said.

His eyes were distant. His mind leagues away from her.

"Do you know why he hates you so much?" Laurent asked abruptly.

"No," she said. "He seems to either hate or tolerate people.

So, I always assumed he simply flipped a coin and decided that way."

Laurent chuckled before his face smoothened and he leaned forward, hands clasped before him.

"My death was a murder," Laurent said. "A fire started in my home. My father had passed away a few months ago and I had just inherited the Moreau fortunes and barely got to enjoy it before the fire occurred. Kai came to save me since we were meeting for tea that afternoon. During my final moments, I heard a voice whispering beside me and the name Bellacourt was mentioned in conversation."

Élisabeth frowned. "So, you think my father was involved in your death? And that is why he hates me?"

It made no sense. Her father would never do such a thing. He was a kind, sensible man. He was *not* a murderer.

"I unraveled that mystery out of boredom," Laurent said. "I don't feel as intensely as *he* does, so I could remain unbiased about the situation and figure out the truth rather than simply latch onto the easy answer."

"Was it my father?" she asked. Even though she knew the answer. It could not be him, because her father had no interest in Séverin's fortune. He was a wealthy man.

"I came across one of our old housekeepers here in the Graylands," he said. "A man by the surname of Bellacourt who confessed that he was hired by my uncle, the weasel-eyed Guerrier Moreau, to gain our fortune. My uncle figured the house was a small price to pay for my death. He made certain to put out the fire after I died; the house didn't fully crumble, only the left wing was wrecked, and with some renovations, it was as good as new. His accomplice, this Bellacourt fellow, had called him to say that the neighbors had rung for the fire department. And that was the name I heard when I died."

"So, everything was a lie," she whispered.

Séverin had punished her for no reason, simply because it was easier to hurt her family than to hunt for the truth. Anger coiled in her gut, as she realized that he had ruined her life, for nothing. At any point, he could have confronted her about these accusations, and she could have cleared her name, but he had preferred tormenting her instead. All that guilt that had flooded her earlier burned to ashes, as her fist curled in her lap.

"I can't help wondering if it was all predestined: you being drawn here, him mistaking the culprit, his hatred for you," Laurent said. "It seems we are all puppets of the Fates. Even you, Élisabeth."

Élisabeth was silent as she contemplated this new piece of information.

"Will you help me?" she asked. "Will you kill Séverin if I summon the blade?"

Laurent looked up, staring at her with those sapphire eyes. Keen and clever. Élisabeth realized then that if he refused her, she would do it herself. She would not stop until she enacted her vengeance. He had ruined her life, he had tormented her father for *years*, and he would die for his sins.

Laurent nodded. His words were void of any feeling. And his eyes reflected twin flames of anger. He needed this just as much as she did. They both hungered for the same dark outcome. For Séverin's ultimate demise.

"I will," he said in a steel voice. "The Spirit-King shall fall."

His words were a vow. One that she clutched with both hands and cradled close to her chest, hearing it whisper its bloody melody, promising her that the Lord of the Below would die soon.

Chapter Twenty-Three

The wind whistled its braying tune, rustling the branches with each stroke of its song, as they made their way through the dark woods. Moonlight slithered between the crowns of the trees, soaking the floor with its luminous touch.

Élisabeth felt a sense of unease the deeper they traversed into the sickly woods. Laurent was beside her on his steed while his four men trotted behind them. Their cold faces stared ahead with greedy eyes as if they could see their next payment at the end of their travels.

"I don't know if this is a good idea," she said.

"You said it yourself, Élisabeth," Laurent replied. "Hiding that book protects us all. We will go in while they rest and steal it, but first, we need an army."

"I told you everything it said," Élisabeth said, frustrated. "And he might not find it. It's sentient. We might not even find it."

"Séverin is in the dark now but if he finds *The Book of*

Echoes, he will know *everything*," he replied. "He will kill you before we kill him."

"How will returning to the Pit help us?" she asked. "I don't know if I can control all of the beasts."

"We only need them in case we require a distraction," Laurent said. "You are a Fateborn, you are more powerful than you think. This is your mother's realm, *your* realm. Nothing can harm you."

There was a chance that she could not control them and then they would be free to hurt anyone as they pleased. It was the reason she had spared Séverin to begin with, because killing him was not worth seeing Kai, Matthieu, and Inès get hurt if she lost control of the beast. And a small part of her could admit that she had not been ready to kill him then.

But now that she was ready, she had to decide if it was worth putting her friends in danger. They did not deserve to fall for Séverin's ill-doings.

"We need to think this through," she said. "Or I need to learn how to control my gifts. Séverin was teaching me—"

"Stop," Laurent said. His tone was sharp and left little room for disagreement. "You will follow the plan, Élisabeth. It is sound. We rally the beasts; we steal the book and if it comes down to it, we attack his little friends."

"What are you talking about?" she asked. "We never agreed to hurt them."

She could sense the Pit. And hear it. The cold, unwelcome nature of the abyss, staring at her with its open maw. The howls and screeches from below raised the hair on her forearms. Morbid depictions of Nicodeme's death assaulted her senses. Those sharp, brutal claws sank into his chest like a hook capturing a fish.

The Pit reeked of the darkly pleasant smell of Séverin's magic, drowning out the acrid scent of corrupted magic. She could make out the silvery threads he'd used to seal the Pit. It floated in the open air like a blanket. Her heart was beating rapidly like a galloping deer escaping its predator, and she felt a terrible sense of foreboding. What if it got out of control? What if the others got hurt? How would she live with herself if this plan went sideways and the people she cared about suffered as a result?

"They won't hurt anyone," Laurent said, in a softer tone. "They will be fed. It will be easier for you to control them."

Élisabeth watched as the four men stood in a line and one by one fell into the Pit. Darkness swallowed them whole, and she could hear the miserable echo of their screams. Then there was only the grating crunch of limbs being torn like weeds from a plant. Her eyes widened in horror and her head spun to stare at Laurent. He had a calculative look in his eye.

"Hopefully that will keep them somewhat satiated," he said.

"Why did they...?"

"I told them once Séverin dies I shall bring them back," he said. "That I will be the new Lord of the Below."

"How?" she whispered.

Laurent rolled his eyes. "It was a lie."

"You tricked them," Élisabeth said.

Laurent simply blinked. And she realized how painfully little she knew about him. She knew more about Séverin. She knew Séverin was a pianist, and that he was also a composer. She knew that he was friends with Kai and Inès. She knew that those loyal to him would die for him. She knew that everyone seemed to see a side of him that she caught only rare glimpses of. She knew that he was as his namesake said, severe but also austere and thoughtful.

She barely knew anything about Laurent. It should have concerned her that the first time she met him, he had sold her out to the wraiths and told her to kill a man who could not be killed so easily. She felt foolish for trusting him. For telling him secrets that could doom her.

"I am leaving," she said softly.

Laurent cut her off. "I'm afraid I can't allow that."

"I won't burn the wards," she said. "I won't release them. Not without proper control of my magic. Not if I think for a second that my friends will get hurt."

"We are all dead, Élisabeth," he said. "It does not matter what fate befalls the dead. You should know this better than anyone. You are a Fateborn. You should be upholding the Balance."

"Well, let me be clear," she said. "I won't replace one evil with another. You are worse than him."

Élisabeth turned to leave, but he grabbed her forearm.

"You know, Élisabeth, if you are not my weapon, I won't let you be his," Laurent snarled. "What happens if you decide to kill me instead of him? Maybe I am the Traitor that dies?"

"I told you it is him," she said. "It specifically said—"

"Prophecies are fickle and hold many meanings."

Somehow, the thought had never crossed her mind. And now that it did there was nothing she could do to erase the folly of trusting the wrong boy.

She twisted in his arms, but he was stronger than he looked. In the dark, she could see the mad gleam in his sapphire eyes. It was cloaked in chaos. A strange, destructive need that she had never noticed before. "It is not the end, Élisabeth. We will see each other soon. Perhaps, if you are dead and have nothing to lose, you will be able to do what needs to be done. Maybe if you care a little bit more about the Graylands imploding you will find it in yourself to make the hard choices."

"What about Séverin?" she asked desperately. Rocks crumbled beneath her sliding feet, she was so close to the edge. So close to death. Her heart thudded fiercely, banging against her ribs. "We can kill him. *You* can kill him. It is what you want. It is what you've always wanted."

"I don't trust you, Élisabeth," he said tightly. "You will use me to fulfill this prophecy and I refuse to be the one who dies. *I* will be the one who wins this time."

"Why would I help you when I awaken if you betray me?" she snarled.

Laurent's mouth curled up in a frightening smile. "Because you lose your memories when you die in the Graylands. It is different than dying in the mortal realm and I will be more than pleased to mold you into a better soldier. You will summon me that blade and you will kill anyone that gets in our way. Those pathetic allies of his included."

The words were like a shock of cold water on her nerves, shattering everything she had ever believed to be true. Dread filled her as she stood on the precipice of the Pit, and before Élisabeth could attempt to plead or fight or kill him, he had released her with a forceful shove, pushing her into the dark.

A scream escaped her as she fell into the Pit, deep into a place made of monsters and death.

And then there was only a bleak, miserable darkness.

Chapter Twenty-Four

Kai returned a day after Élisabeth had left without the girl in sight.

"If you keep that up you will grind your teeth to dust," Kai said unhelpfully.

"How could she just disappear?" he asked.

"It rained and any prints that were there were washed away by the rainwater," Kai said.

Séverin reached for his necklace, a thing he did any time he was frustrated until he recalled that she had stolen it. Élisabeth assumed that she had been as slick as a snake, but her warm fingers had jolted him awake. He hadn't intended to sleep, but the power he'd used rebuilding the wards had tired him.

Séverin had kept his eyes sealed shut, curious to know what she was doing, to see if she was foolish enough to attack him. He had felt her slip his necklace off his throat and heard her giggle to herself in victory. A gesture that had surprisingly amused him, far more than it angered him which was an odd reaction. He should have been furious, should have cut her hand at the wrist for daring to steal from him. But he had done nothing, he hadn't so much as confronted her. And he regretted it because that small conquest had foolishly made her think she could win the war.

"You never take that necklace off," Kai said, eyeing his bare throat. "That chain and Ebony are your most prized possessions."

Séverin had found the chain, hidden in the Palace. It felt soothing in his palm. As if it were a keepsake he had once lost and now stumbled upon again, and he hadn't taken it off since. It had always felt like he was *meant* to find it.

"Élisabeth stole it," Séverin said.

"And you let her?"

Séverin frowned. "She did it to irritate me. Why would I give her the satisfaction of reacting?"

Kai laughed, a small, surprised sound.

"What?" Séverin demanded.

"Nothing."

"Maybe I should take a look?" Matthieu offered, pushing forward from the tree he leaned against. "I might have more success."

Matthieu had been the first to insist that he go after Élisabeth, but since it was his misleading call that had lost them her trail, Séverin could not help but be suspicious of him. He wasn't certain if Matthieu was simply infatuated with Élisabeth or if it was something more. But he would not give him the chance to try anything grimy.

"No," Séverin said. "Our efforts should be focused on finding the book."

He looked to Matthieu, waiting for him to skulk back to the library. Once the oaken doors clicked shut, he turned back to Kai.

"Do another sweep," he said. "She can't have gone far."

With Élisabeth gone and Kai searching her trail, it meant

they were two people short in their search for the book. A part of him had considered that maybe Élisabeth had stolen it.

It was why he needed Kai to find her. If the little monster had indeed stolen it, she would not survive his wrath. He had been foolish to let his guard down. To let her rest with no rope, to hold Matthieu back from trailing after her like a whisper. She had taken advantage of his leniency and he would not make that mistake again.

When he found Élisabeth Bellacourt she would regret making a fool of him.

Inès stood before a lectern carved to resemble a raven in flight. Her palms rested on either side of the black marble as she stared at the thick tome before her, brows knitted in concentration. Her mouth was tight in a grim line.

"Is that *it?*" Séverin asked.

"No," she said. "It's a copy of the First Scripture. Every copy in existence had been burned by the Crusaders. It is fascinating. There is so much that was lost during the reformation. So many answers to questions that had plagued my mother and I."

Inès and Clarise had always been devout. Clarise said she'd grown up in an abbey and had been training to become a High Priestess before she had come to the capital and committed whatever crimes had led to her arrest.

"Did you know that there were Four Kings? Laos, Pras, Mòrge, and Ren?"

"No, but I don't particularly care," he said.

His lack of interest did not deter Inès.

"Ren is the Lord of Chaos. He is also called the Endless," she said. "It is said that he was the prince and son of Mòrge the Misfortunate One and on his Nameday Mòrge had gifted him the Darklands. A realm that the rulers used as a prison to punish the wicked. Back then you either came to the Graylands or the Darklands. One made for the good and the other for the rotten folk."

"Why does any of that matter?" he asked.

"Because there is a reason this was burned, Séverin," she said. "I think this is bigger than the Graylands. I think the Fates are involved in whatever is happening."

"You believe that they exist?" he asked. "Nobody has ever seen them. For all we know they could be a myth."

"I do." She nodded firmly. "And maybe this is the missing piece of the puzzle."

Séverin crossed the room and sat down on the crimson sofa. He had learned to never dismiss any of Inès feelings. Even if it was not a vision, her feelings could be just as strong, just as instinctual as her gifts.

"Okay, but how does this fix the Graylands? How does this stop the Blight?" Séverin asked.

"Ren, just like the other kings, had a chosen Fate," she said. Her green eyes stared at him, bright and knowing. "The Fate's name was Sévère the Judger."

"So, we share a namesake." Séverin shrugged. "What does that have to do with anything?"

Séverin wasn't even his real name. Simply one he picked for himself. It couldn't be more than a coincidence.

"Ren had gotten powerful, and his magic was creeping into the other realms. The Three Kings were afraid, so they tied his soul with Sévère's to weaken him and they stripped Sévère of his power which likely fragmented his memories. Fates are mortals with divine magic so without it Sévère was just a man, a vessel made to hold the Lord of Chaos. He was banished to the mortal realm and upon his death he came to the Graylands where he was cleaved to dissolve his power. The Graylands exist just below the Darklands, so he is stronger here, but not as strong."

Séverin listened silently. Matthieu arrived in the middle of her explanation, and he had this unreadable look in his eyes.

Matthieu laughed, the sound rather forced. "Really, Inès? Shouldn't we spend more time looking for the book than being bored to death by these tales? I could hardly listen to the priest during my boyhood, but this is simply insufferable."

"It explains everything, Séverin," she said, ignoring him. "It explains why you chose that name. It explains why Laurent and you cleaved. You are the Fate and Laurent is the Lord of Chaos."

"This is silly," Matthieu said. "You can't possibly believe this."

"No, it is not!" Inès said. "Why is Séverin the most powerful being in this realm? Why can he alone control the wraiths? Why is he the only one who can seal the Pits?"

Matthieu was silent, as was Séverin. It was a lot to consider. And as ludicrous as it sounded it was the first thing that seemed like answers. He contemplated what this could mean and felt a flare of annoyance that he was the Fate and not the Lord of Chaos. Laurent that fool wouldn't know how to rule a realm if it came before him on both knees. No wonder the other kings had rallied against him and defeated him. He was weak-willed. He was a coward.

Séverin was falling deeper into this theory. He could feel himself accepting this as truth.

"So, how do we stop the Blight?" Séverin asked. "Do I sacrifice Laurent, because I am comfortable with that approach?"

"Maybe," she said. "I don't have all the answers yet." Inès frowned. "Something is missing."

It was late when Séverin went back out to the woods. Kai had returned empty-handed and Séverin's frustration had grown with each passing minute. Élisabeth, he was certain, was tied to all of this. He should have asked Inès if she had learned anything about her.

He found himself unraveling Ebony from the hazel tree and descending into the woods. Inès, for some odd reason, had bid him to go to the Pit; she couldn't say why, only that he had to go there. He didn't feel the Pit snap open, he just felt something odd graze his wards. A sensation he could not quite pinpoint. As if someone had fallen into it, causing the faintest of ripples. And there was only one person who could affect his wards. *Élisabeth.*

Kai had insisted on coming along, but Séverin dismissed him. He had his rifle strapped to his back and his aether sword in his hand. He couldn't sense the beasts close by, so the ward wasn't fully dissolved.

It was silent when he arrived. He tested the wards, pressing on it with threads of aether to hunt for any cracks. It was solid, but a bit thin. As if it was worn out. The damage was not so terrible that he had to return for Kai or Inès to funnel him their aether. He could fix it on his own.

He heard a soft whimper below and froze. It was silent. Perhaps, too silent. He could not hear the beasts, just a small, feminine sound. Before he could wonder if he lost his mind, he heard a small cry of pain and then a familiar, infuriating voice.

"I'm going to kill you, Laurent," she yelled. "Do you hear me? I am going to kill you! You wretched, conniving bastard!"

Séverin unclasped his rifle and spun around. That bastard was here. He was going to end him. He could make out the tracks of a few horses and a few scuffed boot marks. He must have come with other riders and fled when he heard his approach.

Coward.

Séverin swung the rifle over his shoulder and returned to the edge of the Pit.

"Your knight in shining armor left you for dead," he said dryly. "Rather unsurprising if you ask me."

"Shite!" she yelled. "Not *you*. Not now."

He was impressed and a little flattered that she could tell their voices apart.

"Your filthy mouth grows worse with each passing day," he said. "What company have you been keeping?"

"I was with your terrible half," she said. "Fates, I hate you both. I think my arm is broken."

"Pity," he said. "Well, I have dinner plans. I should be on my way."

She cursed louder, making his lips twitch. Only she could paint his vision red with fury one minute and amuse him the next. He walked a few ways off, and her curses grew louder at his retreating footsteps.

"Wait," Élisabeth called. "Please, don't leave me. None of them can fly. And the wards frighten them. I...I am too weak to shatter the wards. Everything hurts. Please, don't leave me."

"What will you give me if I save you?"

"Anything," she said.

"Get on your knees," he said.

"I don't have time to pray," she said in a snarky tone.

He had half a mind to leave her for death. But despite commanding his feet to move—to abandon her as she would no doubt abandon him—they remained stuck to the ground.

"Did you do it?"

"Yes," she said softly.

"Say 'I am sorry for attempting to kill you and for plotting against you with the pretender and for running away'," Séverin said. "Say 'I am a foolish, half-witted girl who will obey you from this moment forward'."

She repeated his words between gritted teeth.

"Why did you leave?" he asked.

"It doesn't matter," she said.

"Something frightened you," he said, "pushed you to turn to Laurent, what was it?"

"I can help you save the Graylands," she said, ignoring his question. "I am the answer to your prayers."

"How?" he asked.

"Help me and I'll tell you."

Séverin was silent. He was tired of half-truths. He would not lift a single finger till she told him what she knew.

"I have *The Book of Echoes*," she said. "Here with me, now."

"Liar," he called.

"There is a prophecy," she said. "It explains everything, but you need to bring me up."

He didn't even acknowledge her pathetic lies. He knew better than to fall for her honeyed words. Laurent would have never let her keep the book. It was clear to see Laurent shared his suspicions that Élisabeth was nothing but a serpent. It explained why he had turned on her so swiftly—she must have given him a good reason too.

"Fine!" she said. "I don't have the thrice damned book, but I read it and then it disappeared. It is sentient, but it is in my mind."

That part did not sound like a lie. He was getting better at telling when she was lying to him. Her voice went up the slightest bit whenever she lied. A hint that she was not a trained actor.

"I'll go fetch a rope then," he said. "Was that so hard?"

"Hurry," she said. "It hurts."

"Don't move."

"I can't move even if I wanted to."

"I know," Séverin said. "It was a joke."

"Your humor needs work," Élisabeth said.

"What did you say?" he asked. "I didn't quite make that out. It sounded like you said 'please, leave me for death, I do not need your help'."

"Nothing," she mumbled.

"As I thought."

Séverin went through the satchel on his horse, unspooled the length of rope, and slid it down the Pit. He waited a bit but when he didn't feel a tug, his brows creased.

"Little monster?" he called. "You alive?"

It was silent and he frowned. He was not going in there. There was no world in which he risked his life to save the girl who betrayed him and constantly lied to him. If she didn't respond in the next few minutes, he would accept that he'd been too late. That she was likely dead and would reappear as a ghost not long from now. If she died it would likely neutralize her unique abilities. Clarise had suspected that it was a gift that could likely only be wielded by the living and not the dead. This was a boon. And he had to accept it for what it was.

"Lisbeth!" he snapped.

He heard nothing. His fist clenched the rope.

Don't do it. It could be a ploy. She intended to kill you only a few days ago and has been plotting with your nemesis behind your back. She possesses magic that is the antithesis of yours. The magic of the Blight; the ruin and destruction that is eating away at your world.

The reasonable voice in the back of his mind faded as he tied the rope around the trunk of the nearest tree and wound the other end around his fist. He clenched his teeth as he slowly descended into the dark. His feet grazed the dirt wall and rocks crumbled beneath the heel of his boot. Out of all the idiotic decisions he had ever made, saving a girl he despised at the risk of his own life made it to the top of the list.

He heard their rumbling roars and snapping jaws. The cacophony of noise grew into a frenzy the lower he got. What if she died and there was no body to recover anymore? Just him and the beasts who ached to tear into him.

What if it was all for nothing?

It was pitch-black, but he could make out the lump of a body. They surrounded her in a ring. Their wild eyes danced between him and Élisabeth. Their stance was protective as if they were prepared to lunge at him at the smallest provocation. Séverin raised his hand to show that he had come in peace. Even though his finger itched to wield his aether sword or at the very least unclip every bullet in his rifle at the beasts.

"I'm not going to hurt her," he said.

They snarled when he took a step forward.

"Lisbeth," he whispered sharply. "Now is not the time to play at being a damsel."

They were inching closer, leaving her side to tear him limb from limb.

"Lisbeth," he repeated.

He watched her stir, blinking slowly. He noticed that her arm was cradled to her chest, and she winced when she sat upright.

"Good," he said when she looked at him. "Call off your loyal dogs."

She sat upright, rubbing her eyes. She held out her good arm and wisps of her dark magic spilled from her fingertips wrapping around them like a leash with dozens of strands curling around their throats. There had to be at least sixty of them. Ugly and bestial and hungry. He could make out dead bodies plucked clean to the bone. Other misfortunate souls who had fallen into their lair. In a matter of hours, there would be no bones, just a void of a person who had once existed.

"You look good when you need me," Élisabeth said with a smirk. And then she winced as her movements jostled her arm. "Should I make you beg me? Make you fill me with praise and insult yourself as you always make me do."

"Your victory will be short-lived once we reach the surface," he said tightly. "Do not let your hubris get the best of you."

Élisabeth stood up, dusting herself with her good hand, as if even in the middle of danger the best thing to do was to ensure her appearance was prim and proper.

Séverin picked up the rope with his hand. She walked towards him. One hand still holding back the trembling beasts. He could feel the strain it was causing her to exert such power when she was injured and tired.

"How do we do this?" she asked.

"Wrap your arms around my neck and legs around my waist," Séverin said. "And don't let go until I tell you."

"Can you help?" she asked. "My hand hurts."

He could tell it cost her a lot to ask for his help again. So, he swallowed back the urge to tease her and simply nodded.

"And...and hurry. I don't know how much longer I can hold them back," she said.

Séverin placed his hands on her narrow waist and lifted her, letting her tangle her long legs around his waist and her good arm around his neck. She used her injured hand to maintain the threads on the beast, even though it hurt her. He was impressed by her strength.

"You're doing good, Lisbeth," he said. His tone softened. He could not recall the last time he had spoken to someone with such gentleness.

It was as though she knew how rare it was for him to praise

someone because her back straightened then and she stared at the beasts with renewed focus, chin firmly set. Almost as if she refused to let them hurt him. Her gray eyes had a strange glow to them. Not silver like aether, but something else, something darkly divine.

Her jaw was tight as she maintained her focus. Even when her fingers spasmed and her elbow nearly collapsed.

"You are doing splendidly," he continued. And then because he couldn't help but overdo it, and likely because the talking distracted him from the beasts breathing down his neck, he added. "I'm proud of you."

Élisabeth shuddered as if she had wanted to hear those words for a very long time.

Séverin climbed upwards, hoping that the rope held their weight. Rocks crumbled beneath his heel and there was a second where his foot lost purchase on the crevice and they stumbled. Élisabeth lost control and he heard the thunderous sound of their hooves and claws as they tore through the ground to reach them. Séverin renewed his climb, hearing them ascending upwards, viciously snarling behind him.

"I'm sorry," Élisabeth said, clutching him tightly. "I broke focus...I don't know how to control them. They move so fast, I don't know—"

"I got this," Séverin said, cutting her off. Even though he could feel them behind him, feel the wet, slick rot that was their breath, feel the tainted air curl around his ankle like a brand. He was not far from the opening. He just needed to climb upwards, and the wards would repel them. "Relax."

He felt one grab onto the flaps of his coat. The fabric screeched as it was torn off and then they were on the edge of the Pit. Séverin heaved them both over, falling over onto the ground.

Élisabeth still clung to him, shaking from the shock of it,

sprawled flat on top of him. Séverin itched to tear her off as she clung to him tightly, her entire body trembling. Instead, he raised his hand up to awkwardly pat her back instead. The odd gesture seemed to calm her down, so he laid his palm flat and began to stroke her spine. Up and then down like she was a wild mare. She liked that far more than the hesitant pats because her limbs relaxed, and her breathing softened to a whisper.

"I could have broken my neck," she whispered. "I could have died."

"Serves you right for trusting that pretender," Séverin said. "What exactly were you thinking?"

"Yell at me later," she murmured. "I'm too tired to pretend to care."

"We need to return to the library," Séverin said. An unsubtle hint for her to get off him.

"You said not to let go until you told me to," she said.

"Are you saying that because you are an obedient girl all of a sudden or because you enjoy being a smartass?"

"You tell me," Élisabeth said.

Séverin felt his mouth twitch, but he shook his head, refusing to give her any sign that he found her funny.

Her head would get too big.

And then there would be no stopping her at all.

Élisabeth was oddly silent as they rode back to the library.

"Laurent told me that the reason you forced me here is because you believe my father had something to do with your death?" she asked. "You believe that he is the reason you are in the Graylands?"

Séverin stiffened. He wondered how much he'd told her. Somehow during their hunt for the book, he had forgotten to focus all his attention on how much he wanted to punish Hugo Bellacourt. He knew that he had something to do with his death. He had heard as much when the acrid taste of smoke burned his lungs to ashes and flayed his flesh with its cruel touch.

Bellacourt.

The name that had made him hunger to rule the Graylands so he could oversee the bargain the first lord had struck with the owners of the Opera House to supply them, humans, in exchange for peace.

"Laurent said it wasn't my father," she said. "He sai—"

"I don't believe a single word from that imposter's mouth," he snapped. "And I'm surprised you do after what he did to you."

"He had no reason to lie," she said sharply. "He said that he met a servant that worked in your home. One who shared my surname and was hired by your uncle who wanted your title and fortune!"

Uncle Guerrier was his father's only brother and had always been a bit of a snake. In truth, Séverin should have suspected him, but now that she said it, it made a bit of sense. Guerrier had always been jealous of his father and his status as a second son had made him rather bitter. Not to mention he'd never liked Séverin.

Séverin clenched his jaw and refused to say a word. Even if it was true, what difference would it make now? He had upturned her entire world and tormented her father in retaliation. Their innocence would not erase his actions and admitting that it was a possibility would only push her further away. And for some inexplicable reason he did not want that.

"You refuse to admit that it could be true," she said accusingly. "That I was never supposed to be here, and you should have never hurt my father."

"And what will any of that change?" he snapped. "Regardless of me luring you here, your father had a bargain with many lords before me to supply the Graylands with our human thralls. He still disrespected our bargain. He still deserved to be punished."

"He didn't deserve any of that," she said loudly. "And I will never forgive you for it."

Séverin gritted his teeth but didn't say a word.

"You will never let me go home, will you?" she asked. The words were a whisper.

He was silent, refusing to acknowledge the truth before them.

"You know what I think, Séverin?" she snapped. "I think it never mattered what the bargain was or your revenge against the Bellacourts or even teaching my father a lesson. I saw you watching me every night. I saw you in Box Five!"

"And, what?" Séverin whispered darkly. "Say it, Little Monster."

Élisabeth was painfully silent, swallowing back the words that neither of them was prepared to speak.

The dark, twisted truth that he would have *always* stolen her away to his world. And that perhaps he had fallen for her spell long before he had ever spoken to her.

"You don't seem all that angry at her anymore," Kai said, staring at him with squinted eyes.

Élisabeth lay on the chaise lounge as they packed and prepared to head home. She had refused to speak a word to him, sitting in her sullen, cold silence after their argument. Inès had made a splint for her injured arm using the hard-shell spines of different books that looked like a beetle's carapace, but from Élisabeth's pain-laced face it was clear she needed proper attention from a medic. And while they didn't have a medic at court Clarise was knowledgeable about these things and could help her. Her time in prison had taught her a thing or two about broken bones and healing.

The Book of Echoes was not here. Out of all Élisabeth's lies he knew that when she said it was sentient, she meant it. But Élisabeth had read it, that much he was certain of.

"You know, I'm beginning to think you would forgive Élisabeth for anything," Kai said. "I've never seen you give somebody so many second chances."

"She claims to have read *The Book of Echoes*," he said. "She is of use. For now."

"So, we're giving up our search?" Inès asked.

"No, Gaspar will remain behind to continue going through the catalogue," he said. "Élisabeth read it. She will tell us what she knows."

"You trust her to tell us the truth?" Kai asked. "Did she say why she left? Why is she working with Laurent?"

"She is still full of secrets," he said. "But she needs to heal, and we have to return to court before I can drag all of them out."

"I'm glad she's safe," Inès said. "You did a good thing, Séverin."

"I didn't do it for her," Séverin said, folding his arms across her chest. "I did it to save the Graylands."

Inès didn't look like she believed him, but she was wise enough not to say as much.

"Whatever the reason," she said. "I am glad."

Part Four

The Prophecy

The Crusade lasted four years between 1085 and 1089. A swarm of cultists who worshipped the Fates rebelled against the Kings, calling them the "False Ones". Churches and chapels were burned in troves and babes were heard screaming in the night.

A Historical Recounting of the Starless Years, Author Unknown

Chapter Twenty-Five

É lisabeth awoke to the soft sound of music. For a moment, she wondered if she was at the Opera House. She had gotten a fever during their travels back to court, and the entirety of the trip had been a blur of dreams and confusion and madness spun by the crooked fingers of Mòrge. She blinked slowly, gazing at the splint Clarise had wrapped around her broken forearm that had been further encased in a wooden construct.

She could make out the shadowy figure of her tormentor and savior. Séverin sat on his duet bench before the hulking splendor that was his pianoforte like a devoted saint kneeling before its god. He was shirtless, his lily-white, toned chest displayed for her like a marble statue. Lithe and graceful with faint muscles that didn't reveal themselves unless he moved in a specific manner. She watched his long, effortless fingers play a somber, melancholic piece. It wasn't one she had ever heard before. It was not the work of any of the artists she had heard in Prasin, but something unique and wistful and devastating.

Élisabeth slowly sat upright, she must have made some sort of noise because the beautiful keys he stroked came to a crushing, awkward halt.

"Didn't take you for a voyeur," he said.

"Why are you half-naked?" she demanded.

"It is my bedroom. You are the guest, not I," he replied.

"And why am I in your bedroom?" she asked. "I am an invalid, I cannot exactly escape."

"I put nothing past you, Lisbeth," he said.

"Almost sounded like a compliment," she said with a twist of her lips.

"Only you would take an insult to be a compliment."

Élisabeth waited a bit for him to comment on her appearance. Lune had enhanced her beauty and Inès and Kai had said she looked different yesterday. Not to mention Laurent had been rather blunt when he said she looked more beautiful than before which was not an exaggeration. She did look more beautiful. More ethereal. More transcendental.

"Do I look different?" she asked.

"Are you fishing for compliments, Lisbeth?"

"No," she said quickly. A dark flush crawled up her chest.

"Come here," Séverin said.

"I'm angry at you," she said.

He had admitted on the night when he saved her that it did not matter if her father did or did not hurt him. Nothing, it seemed, would have stopped him from bringing her here and she didn't know how she felt about that. It creeped under her skin like vines, ensnaring her organs with its thorn-filled fingers.

"Would you prefer I lie to you, Lisbeth?" he asked. "If I told you that I would have never lured you to the Graylands if it were not for revenge. That I am fair and just and could never hold an innocent person here against their will."

"You said I was a mediocre dancer," she said, glaring at him. "Why not pick Louise for entertainment?"

There was no other reason he would want her here other than to use her for his own entertainment. That was what she was to him, a blank paper for him to scrawl his most merciless dreams on.

"Who?" he asked, brows furrowed in confusion.

It was odd that he didn't recall Louise when she led all their performances. How did he not remember her golden-hair, her jewel eyes?

"Louise, my sister."

He blinked and Élisabeth sighed when she realized she wasn't going to get any answers from him.

He just curled his fingers, beckoning her to him.

She paused when her legs swung off the bed. Someone had put her in a nightgown. A powder blue wispy, ephemeral gown that reminded her of his eyes. But that was not what made her pause. It was the intensity of his gaze, dark and wandering, as she made her way towards him.

There was so much they needed to speak about. Now that Laurent had betrayed her the only sensible thing was to serve him on a silver platter to Séverin. Séverin would find him for her, and she would kill Laurent and the balance would be fixed. Laurent had suspected that he might be the Traitor. So, she would test out this theory, and hopefully the Graylands would survive, and she would return home.

Somehow, she would have to convince Séverin that this plan of action worked in both their favors, and that it was in his best interests to release her once complete.

Élisabeth was surprised when he patted the space beside him. She sat on the edge of the polished piano bench, staring at him warily.

"Are you familiar with musical notation? To read and write them?" he asked.

She could feel the northern wind of his breath, as he spoke, taste the cool mint on her tongue. She was so close to him, it was like staring into the eye of a wild beast and daring it to attack you. His long, fragile lashes fluttered prettily when he stared up at her. Élisabeth wondered if he even knew just how delicately beautiful he was, how extraordinarily symmetrical his face was, like a marble carving.

Élisabeth swallowed, nodding quickly. "I had a well-rounded education and music was always my favorite subject."

"Are you right-handed?"

She had injured her left hand and nodded in response to his question.

"I am creating a new composition," he said. "You will help me write it down."

"What do I get from this?" she asked.

"The pleasure of knowledge," he said. "You must be curious to see the music you perform in the ballet crafted from scratch."

"You trust me to write your notes?" she asked. "I heard composers are rather possessive about their work. And not to mention secretive. Some say they are given to frequent plights of frenzy and madness."

"Trust is a big word, tolerate is better," he said. "I would not trust you to pour me a glass of water without testing it for poison first."

"Your compliments are making me lightheaded," she said. "Careful or I may swoon."

He did something then that both silenced and stunned her. He chucked her chin with two fingers in a manner that would be considered "playful" if done by anyone who was *not* him. But when Séverin did it, it felt intimate in a manner that she could not describe. It made a small part of her wish to see the side of him that he revealed only to those closest to him. To witness the traits that made his friends and allies willing to follow him to the ends of the world and beyond.

"Less talking, more writing," he said.

Élisabeth rolled her eyes but picked up the fountain pen, as his fingers began to drift along the keys. He moved at a slower pace, giving her the chance to write the notes. He played with a flourish that bespoke of a lifetime of lessons. He was a virtuoso. One that would have soared to popularity if he had lived long enough to do so. It saddened her a little bit that he was dead. That everyone here was dead. If she did leave, she likely would never see them again. She didn't know if Lune, her mother, would accept her moving between the realms to visit her friends. From the little she told her there were rules and laws that must be followed.

Hours passed as they lost themselves to the music. Élisabeth had suggested a note that might work better to straighten the melody, and she'd been surprised when Séverin had agreed to change it.

"You are a rather amicable musician," Élisabeth said. "I've never met one so open to suggestion."

"I suppose," he mused.

"How refreshing," she said.

"Don't expect me to change my ways in other areas," he said, giving her a warning glance. "I am a demanding person, Lisbeth. I expect perfection in all areas. Let me see your notes."

He tore them from her fingers before she could clean it up a bit and read her notations with a firm look.

"Adequate," he said. "A most passable effort."

"What does that mean?"

"It means that I've met sailors with better handwriting than yours," he said.

"You scoundrel," she huffed. "Don't forget that I am helping you."

"We'll pick it up tomorrow but before I dismiss you, you owe me some answers," he said.

"Dismiss?" she demanded. "I am no servant!"

Élisabeth reached towards him to shove him, annoyed by his arrogance and his need to command her as if she were his lapdog. Her fingers curled around his naked bicep. His flesh was cold against her own and she stilled. She had always flinched from their unbearably icy flesh, but this time it didn't feel so wretched. It *almost* felt nice. Like laying your palm on a fresh layer of snowfall and feeling the biting touch of winter.

Élisabeth's hand dropped and she thought she caught a glimpse of disappointment, but it had to be her imagination or a trick of the lamp. Séverin did not feel anything but anger and mild annoyance towards her.

"I did find *The Book of Echoes*, that part was not a lie," she said. "And there was a prophecy that stated that once the Traitor that is either you or Laurent dies then the Graylands shall be safe. It also said that the person who will defeat the Traitor is me."

Séverin stiffened.

"It doesn't have to be you," she rushed. She didn't want to think of what he would do to her if he believed himself to be the sacrificial lamb chosen for the slaughter. "It can be Laurent. That cruel, unjust boy deserves to die. The prophecy likely means him."

Rage slipped down her throat like acid, and she wondered if this was what it was like to be the daughter of a Fate. To feel the rage trickle through your flesh, rapidly consuming your insides and pouring out corruption.

She thought of that terrible fall down the Pit. The darkness so thick it choked her, and the loud shattering crack of her bone. One of the beasts had caught her by the collar of her shirt, softening the fall; if it had not, she would have snapped her neck. All because she had trusted Laurent.

"And before Laurent betrayed you it was going to be me," Séverin said, eyes cold and empty. Any trace of that softness she'd caught the night he saved her was gone, replaced by something hollow and mistrustful.

"The realms will collapse," she said. "If the Graylands fractures, the cracks will invade the other realms. You know that, Séverin. You can see the Blight spreading. You can see all these Pits opening. How many more can you close before the Graylands are overrun with them?"

"Since when did you care about the fate of the worlds?" he snapped. "All you've ever cared about was yourself."

Her eyes flashed in hurt. It was clear to see he had such a low opinion of her. And, yes perhaps once she had only cared about her return home and the implications this extended absence would have on her career. But she was not just a girl anymore with hopes and dreams and an ache in her chest that refused to be eased. She was the daughter of a Fate, she was Sabeth Fateborn, the Harbinger and she had been made to protect the Balance. *This* was her sacred duty.

"Since I realized that my role is bigger than I thought," she said. "I have this magic for a reason. I am in the prophecy for a reason."

Élisabeth didn't think it was wise to tell him everything. Certainly, not the fact that this cycle occurred every four hundred years and that she *always* killed him.

"How will you kill him?" he asked. "With the beasts?"

"It's called the Invisible Sword and it'll appear to me when I'm ready," she said.

"The Invisible Sword," he murmured. "We had a replica of it at the great chapel in Normey. It sat encased in glass laying on a velvet pillow, hilt up. In the myths, it was called Kingkiller. It was said to have been forged of the old blood and made to kill any immortal who stood out of line. A blade made for immortals."

"I wonder why it is necessary to kill Laurent," Élisabeth said.

"Inès has a theory," he said. "She suspects there was a fourth king and his chosen Fate. Ren the Lord of Chaos and Sévère the Judger and she thinks I am the Fate and Laurent is the Lord of Chaos."

Élisabeth's mouth dropped. That was important information that she was surprised her mother had not shared. Séverin a Fate was almost, if not more, shocking than her being the daughter of a Fate. She felt the same awe she'd felt in the presence of Lune, to stand before a being of folktales and legend. And she watched as Séverin's eyes flared with an unnamed emotion.

"Are you going to worship me, Lisbeth?" he asked softly. His voice was as sweet as black tea.

"I would never," she said sharply. Shaking her head to erase any sense of reverie. "Why have I not heard of you?"

"It was written in the First Scripture and as you know those were all burned."

The one she'd seen in the library. Inès must have read it. She needed to speak to Matthieu and confirm if that was true. If Séverin was truly a Fate. It meant that Laurent was likely the one mentioned in the prophecy. He was the true Traitor. But there were still pieces missing from the puzzle. How exactly had Laurent upset the Balance? And why were they doomed to repeat this cycle for the rest of eternity?

Nothing made sense and her head hurt attempting to tie all the threads into a neat knot.

"Allies then?" Séverin asked, dragging her from her thoughts. "Will you help me kill my worse half?"

Élisabeth stared at his outstretched palm. It was rare to find him without his gloves. To look in his eyes and not see the thick layer of disgust and hatred. She could still make out a flicker of mistrust and doubt. But none of that revulsion he wore like armor when they first met.

He still does not trust me.

And I do not trust him.

Still, she reached for his hand, feeling his palm lock around hers. His long fingers grazed her wrist stopping a little short of the gauze.

"If you help me destroy him and fix the Graylands I will release you," he said. The words sounded forced. As if it took him great strength to speak it. "I will let you go home."

Her heart paused. She hadn't spoken to her mother about what she was to do when it ended, but she had mentioned that Élisabeth had always favored the mortal realm. Perhaps, that was where she was meant to be, back with her father, back at the Opera House pursuing her dreams of ballet. It was strange but the thought of returning home did not fill her with the same glee that it once had. In truth, she liked spending time with Inès, Kai, and Matthieu. She had never had friends before. She had never had people who were not her blood relatives who cared if she lived or died.

"You don't seem happy by that?" Séverin asked.

His hand was still clasped in hers. His fingertips absently grazed her inner wrist. She thought of when he'd saved her and his palm had stroked her back, and the tremors had stopped as if every muscle in her body was tuned to him. How the blinding pain of her broken arm had faded for a small moment. And the world had stilled like time itself had paused for them.

"That is all you wanted since you came," he continued. "Has that changed?"

Something she could not pinpoint tangled around his voice like a snare. Something that sounded like curiosity mixed with expectation. Did he want her to stay? Did he care?

Élisabeth wanted to ask, but before she could utter a word his hand dropped and his eyes had grown distant and shuttered.

"Doesn't matter," he said. "You can name your price when it is all said and done."

***

Élisabeth was lying awake staring at the ceiling when Séverin returned from the bathing room. His hair was wet and glimmered in the dark and she wished futilely that he would remove his masque. That she could see him, all of him. She didn't know why she felt that bone-deep longing to look at him tonight, but it refused to go away.

"Where will you sleep?" she asked.

"In my bed."

"Oh," Élisabeth said, curled in his bed. "Where shall I sleep?"

"In my bed."

"But there are three extra bedrooms on this floor alone," she protested. "Not including yours."

"As there are three continents in the mortal realm," he said. "Shall we share any more useless facts?"

"Well, I—"

"Do not care to argue this point," Séverin said.

He walked towards the bed and lay flat on the side she had awoken from earlier. Her fever had broken over the past few days, and she felt much improved, even though the pain in her arm still lingered. Clarise had been kind enough to give her some laudanum for the pain.

Séverin folded his arms behind his head, hands sinking into the pillow. The single brow she could see unhidden by his masque was raised in a silent taunt as if to say, 'I dare you to come closer'. She had sat stiffly upright when he'd laid down and now regretted even reacting.

Élisabeth had never been one to shy away from a dare so she laid back down stiffly. She could not turn her back to him because of her injured arm and she refused to face him. Her only option was to lay flat on her back and glare at the ceiling. It would be a miracle if she fell asleep knowing how close he was to her. She could feel the cold of his skin. Even without touching him, it radiated from him just as she assumed he could likely feel her warmth.

She tilted her face to see if he'd fallen asleep but found him staring at her.

"I can't sleep like this," she huffed. "With you just *there*."

"Do I make you nervous, Lisbeth?" he asked. His silky voice, caressing her like a gentle lullaby.

"Don't be ridiculous."

He turned so his entire body was facing her. He rested his hand beneath his head, the featherlike muscle of his bicep straining with the effort.

"Then sleep," he said. "Prove me wrong."

"I know exactly what you are doing," she said with narrowed eyes.

His lips tilted ever so slightly, and it should have worried her that he was amused. Last time he'd been amused he'd killed one of her fellow ballet dancers. And Élisabeth had to remind herself that he was a monster. Just because he had saved her life it didn't change who he was. Even if they were allies now, she could never forget his true nature.

"And what is that?"

"You are challenging me because you know I won't back down," she said. "And by doing so you easily get your way."

"I can't help it if you're so predictable," Séverin said.

"I am not predictable," Élisabeth said, between clenched teeth.

"Do something unpredictable then," he taunted. "Something that would shock me."

"I am not falling for your bait."

"It's a shame," Séverin said. "But you've proved my point so I cannot be too upset."

"And what point is that?"

She hated that she was entertaining his stupid game. She hated that she cared even the tiniest bit about his opinion.

"That you are an unremarkable and dreadful bore of a girl," he said. "You rather remind me of my great-aunt Agathe—"

Élisabeth lunged at him. A near-impossible feat considering one of her arms was strapped to her chest. But she used her legs to swing over his hips and plucked the dagger she had stuffed under her pillow. She'd found it hanging from a glass case in the adjacent sitting room that joined his bedroom. She'd come upon it earlier that afternoon when the sleeping drought had flushed her system. It was one of those decorative weapons with a stiff grip and a dull blade in need of polishing, but it was a weapon nonetheless. It wasn't like she would ever get her hands on a rifle.

"Take that back," Élisabeth snapped. "Now."

"Or what?" he asked. "You'll slit my throat? That won't hurt me."

"I hate you," she said.

"Likewise."

She was shaking with anger. His great aunt? He had just compared her to his great-aunt! Granted she did not know the woman, perhaps she was brilliant and riveting, but Séverin's tone had implied that she was anything but. It was difficult to find an insult that would top that. Though not for lack of trying.

"I hate you," she repeated. "*Very, very* much."

Élisabeth realized at that moment that she was sitting on him. She had been hovering at first, but she didn't know when she had sat down. His hand lay flat on her thigh, slithering just beneath where her nightgown had ridden up. The tips of his fingers were slightly concealed by the bunched fabric. She felt her chest tighten as she realized the rather precarious position she had found herself in. Her skin was on fire and his icy fingers did little to soothe the burn.

It felt like time had paused, and all she could see were his eyes in the dark. Intense and searching. She could never quite tell what he was thinking, so much so that his next question surprised her.

"Did he hurt you besides the fall?" he asked.

It wasn't until his fingers lifted, grazing her cheekbone that she realized he was speaking of Laurent. There was a dark bruise on her cheek, that bloomed a vivid violet shade from the fall. It was tender, but his fingers were gentle and feathery. The cold of it was rather nice against her flushed cheeks.

She shook her head.

"Use your words, Lisbeth."

She hated that she trembled at his commanding tone. She hated that she didn't resist or fight him, but she spoke as he wished.

"No."

"I'm going to destroy him," he said. His hand dropped, fist curling tight. "There will be nothing left of him when I am done with him."

"I would expect nothing less from you," Élisabeth said. And

the words were not reproachful as she intended, but almost fond. "But I will be the one who wields the blade."

She would do it as the Harbinger. It was her role, and a small part of her wished to please her mother.

"Then I shall hold his neck out for you."

The dark promise in his tone made her stiffen. Her eyes were locked on him. Her dark-hearted, vengeful Fate.

Séverin straightened as if he had just realized the shift in the air, and from the way his mouth tightened, he didn't quite like it. She flinched before he even spoke his next words because she knew what was coming before he even voiced it. It was what she would say if she had a lick of common sense if all her faculties hadn't been frayed by his wayward touch and the fact that she was suddenly fascinated by his hateful mouth and its perfect lushness.

"Well, you should get some rest," he said. And then a beat later. "I cannot afford any distractions."

Élisabeth rolled off him so fast, she landed on her injured arm. A whimper escaped her lips, and she felt his hands grab her in an attempt to ease her fall.

His eyes burned in anger.

"Careful," he barked. "Look before you leap."

"I suppose I couldn't get away from you fast enough," Élisabeth snapped.

His mouth tightened and for a moment, she thought she caught a flash of hurt, but then his hands retreated as quickly as it appeared. And he turned his back to her. Élisabeth did not understand why he was upset; he was the one who had started it.

She was glad that he had because nothing good would ever come from something that had been built on lies and betrayal. It was like attempting to grow a plant on infertile ground, hopeless and futile. Séverin had tricked her into coming here, tormented her, and put her in innumerable dangerous situations from simply being in his life. His world was one of darkness, monsters, magic, and mayhem. While hers was of order, brightness, ambition, and glory.

Even if a part of her had buried a fragment of her heart in the soils of the Graylands, she knew wholeheartedly that she did *not* belong here.

Chapter Twenty-Six

The snow fell to the ground, a pearlescent white color like a cracked eggshell. The leaves and the grass had turned jewel-toned, dripping soft and serene flakes to the ground.

Élisabeth stood by the gates that morning, watching her foggy breath twirl in the air like a dancer. Séverin had sent out a hundred men to scour the streets for Laurent. Soon one of his soldiers would find Laurent and when they did, she was to call on the blade to come to her and she would kill him. There was so much uncertainty, but the one thing she knew was that she had to end this. It was the only way to save the realms and to return home.

"How are you feeling?"

She spun around to find Matthieu behind her. His uniform was lopsided. Hair billowing in the breeze like a forlorn sailor.

"Like my arm is broken and I am forced to wear a splint for the next little while," she said.

"Want me to kiss it better for you?" he asked, with a crooked smile.

"Do you ever stop flirting?" she retorted with a roll of her eyes.

His smile dropped. "I tried to come for you. But he was far too suspicious and sent Kai instead. If I knew for a moment that weasel Laurent would find you and hurt you I would have risked everything to come for you."

"I know," she said, squeezing his hand. "I know you wouldn't let anything happen to me. I spoke to my mother, you know."

"The formidable Lune," he said with admiration. "You have her spirit. Did she tell you everything?"

"Maybe not everything," she said. "She didn't tell me that Séverin is a Fate nor that Laurent is the Lord of Chaos."

"She didn't want to frighten you. She didn't want you to fear him," he said. "Did you tell Séverin anything?"

"Just that I would help him kill Laurent," she said. "I didn't tell him much about what we are. What does it mean to be the Warden anyway?"

"It means that I am your guide," he said.

"And the part about the horn? What is your role in the prophecy?"

"Mere formality. It is to let the Fates know that it is done," he said. "That the realm is safe."

"Do you think I did the right thing?" she asked. "This hunt for Laurent, will it fix everything?"

"You always do the right thing, Sabeth," Matthieu said. "Your gut has never led you astray but..."

"But what?"

"You can't trust Séverin," he said. "I see the way he looks at you and it isn't right. Your mother would not approve."

"I'm not a puppet made to do my mother's bidding," Élisabeth said, annoyed that he would imply as much. "Besides, Séverin hates me and I hate him."

"This isn't the first time he's made you fall for his lies," he said.

Élisabeth swallowed. "Nothing he says will make me like him."

Matthieu did not seem convinced, but he shook his head as if it suited him better to ignore the situation. And that calm, lazy grin overtook his face once more.

"If you say so."

He leaned forward and wrapped his arms around her. He smelled of gunpowder and berry wine. Élisabeth fell into his embrace. It felt comfortable, like a favorite coat that one reached for even with its missing button and frayed hem. Nostalgic and bittersweet. She wondered how many versions of her he had seen. She wondered if she was any different to him. Besides her mother, he was the only immortal who knew the intricacies of her soul.

"Am I always the same?" she asked.

"You always look kind of the same," he said. His cold breath drifted along her scalp. "Lune enhanced your mortal beauty, so you look more like *you*. You always have the same personality which is a comfort. That stubbornness and wild temper never failed to arouse me before."

A startled laugh escaped her, and she shoved him back.

"I've missed you so much, Sabeth," Matthieu whispered. "I feel empty when you're gone. Will you stay with me this time? Will you stay with me in the end? We can be in the Graylands, you don't have to return to the mortal realm. You don't have to die again. Maybe it will even break the cycle. Maybe he will never awaken again."

"I don't belong here, Matthieu."

"You do," he said. "This is your mother's realm. There is no place you belong more."

"I will sleep on it," she said. "Give it some more thought."

But she did not think her mind would sway. Her heart was set on returning home. Especially after last night, when Séverin had pulled away, stamping her small heart beneath his polished boot. She didn't know why she cared that he had rejected her. It was not like she would have done anything. Not now that she knew the breadth of their tangled history. Not when she still didn't trust him, even with their recent alliance.

"I will wait for you until then," Matthieu said. "As long as it takes."

Séverin was long gone by the time Colette arrived to dress her.

Élisabeth missed ballet. She intended to perform in the ballroom tomorrow night after her shooting lessons with Matthieu. Matthieu had been teaching her how to handle a rifle. He said it would come easy to her as would most things she enjoyed in her past lives. He said it was why she was such an accomplished dancer and that she had always been drawn to the world of ballet.

Colette tied her corset. It was an exquisite peach gown with no sleeves. It was easier to wear sleeveless dresses than maneuver into fitted sleeves with her plaster and splint-covered arm. Her dark hair fell down her back and even with the cast on her arm, she felt beautiful.

"Thank you, Colette," she said.

She would never get over how her face brightened when she complimented her. It had saddened her to think of how she had been hurt. She still hadn't learned what happened to her tongue. She had asked Séverin if he'd hurt her, and he said if he "cut off girl's tongues for being insufferable he would begin with hers." A remark that had gotten him hit in the chest with a stray pillow.

Élisabeth descended the stairs and walked into the Hall. The room felt alive which was ironic considering most of the courtiers were dead. Loud chatter and tinkling music drifted in the air as the attendants danced and dined.

Séverin sat on his throne, and before him was a wooden table laden with food. Kai sat on his left and Inès on his right. Inès was telling him something which he did not seem pleased about. His lips were pulled in a drawn line.

Élisabeth realized perhaps a bit awkwardly that there was no chair placed for her on the dais and she didn't know who to sit with. She felt a strange, overwhelming sense of sorrow then. A stark realization that this place was *not* her home. Nobody had remembered to set her a seat. Séverin hadn't even escorted her to dinner or asked Kai to. It seemed he wasn't too concerned about her running away now that she had broken her arm and been betrayed by the only person she trusted outside his inner circle.

Matthieu must have been doing his rotations tonight; she did not see his fair hair in the ballroom. That pit in her stomach grew the longer she stood by the door. Her fingers awkwardly tangled before her.

"Did you think you were going to sit with him?" Odette asked.

She sat at one of the tables at the back with a few other humans who all wore those bright, shiny collars.

"Thralls don't sit on the dais," Olivier said. Lips curled in anger. It seemed he still held a grudge which meant Odette must have briefed him on the circumstances of his death. "Maybe if you behave you can sit at his feet."

His collar was gone. As he was no longer marked a human thrall. It seemed his position in their hierarchy was no better than his sister's. He didn't sit with the other dead. Even though his fair skin had that unsettling gray tint to it just like them.

"But he would never allow her anywhere near him," Odette said with a tilt of her head, staring at her beneath her nose. "And you can't sit with us."

"I wouldn't sit with you if you paid me," Élisabeth snapped.

"He was happy when you left, you know," Odette said. "He only sent Kai after you because you are his prisoner."

Odette's smile widened when she flinched at her words. Élisabeth hated that she had reacted at all.

She could lie to everyone else until her throat was dry, but she could not lie to herself.

She cared.

Élisabeth left the Hall, hearing the cackling sound of the twin's laughter floating behind her.

She didn't know where she was going. She stumbled into an empty parlor room. Élisabeth twisted the lock, and the satisfying click of it brought her a sense of relief. She was alone for the first time in a long time. Truly alone. Nobody was looking for her. Nobody cared. She struggled to erase the loneliness that gnawed at her like a manic creature, teeth sinking into her soft flesh like hooks.

Élisabeth fell into a dance routine, refusing to crumble. Dancing was her distraction, it was her faith, her lambent beacon in the dark, her secret language. It was the invisible hands that reached out to her and said *I am here; you are not alone.* Because to be alive was to be seen and she feared that nobody would ever see her. So, she clung to this one, desperate thing that belonged to her alone, clutching it with bleeding nails and a tattered heart and praying that it never let her go.

She spun and twirled and attempted moves Pierre would approve off. She fell an infinite number of times. Her slippers did not have the right grip, and the hem of her dress caught around her ankles more times than she could count, and catching herself with one good arm was far harder than it seemed.

Frustration bled through her veins. A sense of powerlessness engulfed her, drawing her into the depths of its embrace. Élisabeth had never felt so untethered as she did then. Every step she took drew her deeper into the tangled web of her thoughts, luring her into a reverie she could not escape.

She collapsed on the chaise in exhaustion. Her limbs twitched as she struggled to catch her breath, chest rising and falling with the exertion. Her injured arm felt itchy under all the wraps, and sweat dripped down her nape. She felt unbearably alive. For the first time in a long time, she could feel that old hunger rearing its head at the thought of pursuing ballet again. Élisabeth knew then that she had to return home. She had to remember that ballet was her one true love.

And the stage awaited her.

Chapter Twenty-Seven

Séverin paced the length of his room. It was half past midnight and still, there was no sign of Élisabeth.

He had sent his guards to scour the grounds. If Séverin were not already dead Élisabeth would certainly be the end of him.

He could not help but worry. What if Laurent had taken her. What if he hurt her again? And why did his chest tighten at the thought?

Kai knocked on the door.

"No sight of her," Kai said. "I gave the guards orders to continue searching the woods and palace until dawn. You don't think she'd be foolish to leave? Laurent is after her and she's also injured."

Someone strolled in then. Élisabeth. The lady of the hour looked exhausted and bedraggled. Her hair was stuck to her face and the rouge on her lips was smudged. He stiffened. Had she been with someone?

"Élisabeth, thank Fates," Kai said. "Séverin was worried tha—"

"I was not worried," Séverin barked. He pointed to the door. "Leave."

Kai snickered but followed his order. The door clicked shut behind him. Élisabeth didn't look at him. She grabbed the post of the bed and tugged off her slippers.

"Where were you?" he said between clenched teeth.

"I do not owe you any information about my whereabouts," she said stiffly. She glared at him most fiercely. As if *she* were upset at him. The nerve she had. He had worn a groove in the carpet, wondering what harm might befall her. And *she* was upset at *him*.

"I cannot stand you," he said sharply. "You are—"

"Save me the insults," she said. "I don't wish to speak with you."

She spun on her heels. He was close behind her, so close his breath drifted along her nape. He followed her up until the point where she slammed the bathing room door in his face. He grabbed the handle, but it was locked. Séverin pounded his fist against the door.

"Open this door, Lisbeth," he said. "You have five seconds."

"Go away!" she yelled. "I...I never want to see you again."

He paused. Her voice was shaky. In a manner, he had never heard before. It almost sounded like she was on the verge of crying.

Séverin sighed, leaning his forehead against the door.

"Open the door, Lisbeth," he said. And then he added a word he had not used in a very long time. "*Please*."

"Go. Away!"

This was said in a high-pitched voice. One that hinted at an impending breakdown. He swallowed, uncertain of what to do or say. He did not know how to comfort a girl. Let alone one who had conveniently locked him out. He was not equipped to handle these emotions.

"I am not upset," he said gently. It was a lie, of course, he was upset. But the sound of her distress weighed heavy on him. "Not anymore. I should not have reacted so strongly. I just... Kai exaggerated when he said I was worried. I suppose the right word would be disquieted. I was disquieted, Lisbeth."

The faucet twisted. A tactic intended to drown out his voice.

"I am not leaving here until you come out," Séverin said stubbornly.

Her silence was driving him insane, and he refused to pace. So, he sat down, leaning his back against the door, head tilted to the ceiling asking whatever deity watched over them to grant him the patience to deal with Élisabeth Bellacourt.

Séverin shifted, feeling a crick in his neck. Light crept through the parting between the curtains, and he blinked in confusion. His legs were sprawled out and it took him a long moment to realize that he had slept on the floor. He hadn't slept properly the last few nights. Last night he had been watching over Élisabeth. She had a habit of hurriedly turning at night, forgetting about her injured arm, and then a small moan would escape her when she realized it, which would then rouse her from her sleep.

Séverin had put a pillow beside her, to slow down her descent and then he would gently lay her flat on her back. It happened every couple of hours, keeping him awake through the night.

He stared at the bathing room door and swiftly arose. He attempted to turn the knob, but it was locked. Even if it was unlocked, she would not have been able to open the door without rousing him since he'd been resting on the frame. It took longer than he liked to recall that the bathing room had two doors. The other of which led into the secondary bedroom. One that had been intended for the queen of the palace just as his bedroom was made for the king. It was also Élisabeth's old bedroom. The one he had put her in when she arrived to keep a close eye on her.

He left his bedroom and was unsurprised to find that she had placed something beneath the handle of her door. Most likely a chair, to prevent his entrance.

"This is rather childish, Lisbeth," he said. "Don't you think?"

Silence.

"If you don't confirm that you are alive and sulking, and not dead, I will have no choice but to break this door," Séverin said.

More silence.

He cursed under his breath. She was the most vexing creature he had ever met. The bane of his existence. A curse of his own doing.

"Very well," he said calmly. "Don't say I didn't warn you."

He took several steps back, prepared to take a running start.

"I am alive," she said softly.

Séverin paused. "Good, open the door."

"No."

"How long will this tantrum last?" he asked.

"Forever," Élisabeth said. "Now go away."

He cursed some more.

There was no getting to her. Not unless he disregarded her wishes and broke the door down. He turned on his heel and bathed in one of the spare bedrooms since his was being used as a war tactic by Élisabeth, and then he headed straight to the library to gain some answers to solve his latest paradox.

"Séverin, good morning," Clarise said.

"Is Inès around?"

"No, she stepped out for breakfast," she said. "Shall I have her—"

"No."

He didn't want Inès to overhear him and run to Kai and tell him.

"You are a woman, yes?"

Clarise indicated for him to sit near the stone fireplace. He stretched his long legs, tapping his fingers on his knee in a unique mixture of annoyance and something that felt suspiciously like embarrassment because this conversation was rather absurd. He would have never imagined himself in this awkward position.

Clarise was biting back a grin which didn't relax him in the slightest.

"I am a woman," Clarise said slowly. Her lips twitched in amusement. "What is this about?"

"I know a man who is dealing with a woman. An infuriating one. She is of the frame of mind that he has committed some grave ill and he cannot for the life of him think of what he has done wrong. He is an amicable man. Rational and sensible. And she is the utter opposite."

"I see," Clarise said with a nod.

Her eyes sparkled and he did not understand why she looked so joyous.

"She has thrown many tantrums, but this one is the worst because she refuses to engage with me," Séverin said. "With *him*," he corrected hastily.

"Has your acquaintance thought to apologize to this girl?" Clarise asked.

"For what?" he asked. "She refuses to speak about her grievances."

"Hmm," Clarise said. "Sometimes the way to a woman's heart is by performing a gesture. Words can be rather idle if not paired with action. A bouquet of her favorite flowers will do. Along with a heartfelt note."

Séverin felt his stomach tighten with nausea. Flowers? Heartfelt note?

"But what am I apologizing for?" he asked.

Damn it. She already knew he spoke of himself. He would never ask these ludicrous questions on behalf of someone else. And she was a seer, he could not hide much from her.

"Just keep it vague, apologize for your behavior and any offense you have caused," Clarise said. "At the very least it will open the doors for a conversation."

Séverin sighed and stood up.

"Well, I suppose I have work to do."

"Let me know how Élisabeth reacts," she said.

"I never said it was Élisabeth," he said, fixing her with a warning stare.

"Lucky guess," Clarise said.

And then she laughed at her joke, disappearing into the bookshelves she had spent her entire life tending to.

His bedroom smelled like a floral shop. He did not know what flowers Élisabeth favored. So, he had told the servants to pluck all the variety they had grown in their gardens. But then he wondered if maybe she did not like flowers. She always wore such beautiful dresses, so he had Colette run to the nearest seamstress and resize the latest styles to fit Élisabeth. There was a wobbling stack of ivory white boxes by the foot of his bed. And then he recalled that she had a fondness for sweets, so he had asked the pastry chef to prepare a cart with all the finest delicacies.

It was late at night by the time everything had been prepared.

He felt satisfied at the sight of his collection.

"Kai," he called. "Could you escort Lisbeth to my bedroom?"

"Andre said she is in the barracks," Kai said.

"I beg your pardon?"

"I shall retrieve her," Kai said. "I am partly to blame."

"No," he said. "I will. We will discuss this later."

Séverin felt like his skin was aflame as he crossed the courtyard to the barracks. What on earth was she doing in the barracks? His mind couldn't help but fall back to the other night. How she had disappeared. How she had returned looking half undone.

Did she have a lover?

The thought made his gut twist, and he suddenly felt the urge to empty his stomach in the nearest hedge. The thought of someone touching her pushed him forward. He would confront them. No, he would *end* them.

"My lord." The soldiers guarding the front door bowed deeply.

When one of them took a step forward to announce his arrival, he grabbed his shoulder, halting him in place. *"Don't."*

He stepped into the entrance and made his way to the dining hall, hearing the raucous sound of the off-duty soldiers. They were chanting something. Cups banging loudly on the table. It wasn't hard to spot her. She was the only woman in the room. She sat beside a blond-haired soldier whose arm was draped around her. It took him a moment to make out that the broad-shouldered fellow was Matthieu and another longer moment to make out the chant that slipped from their slurred mouths. They were saying the word "kiss" in an unending loop.

The edge of his vision blackened and his fists tightened in retaliation.

"That is a silly dare," Élisabeth protested. "And Matthieu has clearly paid you to say such a thing!"

"Matthieu does not have a penny to his name!" a voice called.

Laughter billowed and Élisabeth tossed her head back joining them in their merriment. Her dark hair flowed down her back, revealing her dainty collarbones. Every man in the room held their breath at the sight of her, and Séverin felt this strange urge to punch all of them, starting with Matthieu.

"Fine, cheek kiss," Matthieu said, tapping his cheek.

Élisabeth rolled her eyes, she leaned forward, and he turned his face at the last second ensuring that their lips brushed. The room grew manic as the men laughed and Élisabeth blushed.

Séverin walked in with a single-minded focus.

"Oi, is that..." one called. And then the loud sound of scraping chairs filled the room as they stood in attention. "We were not expecting you, my lord."

"What are you doing here?" Élisabeth asked warily.

He ignored her, his fist colliding with Matthieu's jaw. Matthieu stumbled backward, eyes wide, fingers rising to cup his flesh.

"My lord, I—"

"You are discharged from service," Séverin snarled. "Pack your belongings and leave within the hour."

"What, why?" Élisabeth asked. "Are you punishing me for locking you out?"

"Not everything is about you," he snapped.

Except it was a lie.

Everything was about her.

Élisabeth took a step forward towards Matthieu.

"Matthieu, don't listen to a word he says."

"I kind of have too," Matthieu muttered. It seemed he had more common sense than Séverin had expected. Kai would not be pleased by this turn of events. He liked the young soldier, but Séverin did not care about Kai's reaction at that moment. All he saw was Matthieu's mouth on *her*, and that blind rage filled him once more.

"If you'll excuse me," Matthieu said. "I have a bag to pack."

"Matthieu, I'll fix this," she called. "It is a misunderstanding."

Séverin turned on his heels. He had to get out of here before he flung the boy with enough aether to shatter every bone in his body.

"Hold on," Élisabeth called. "Stop walking so fast."

Séverin picked up his pace. It took him a split-second to realize that she had run ahead of him and now stood in front of him. His hands gripped her waist just before they collided, and he stilled, fingers locked on her flesh. Her dark hair billowed around her, loose strands grazing her lips. He glanced down at them, plump and ripe, and all he could see was Matthieu's lips against hers.

"I am such an idiot," he said with an unamused laugh. He had been working all day to assort the perfect gifts to win her favor, while she had been interested in someone else this entire time. "How long have you been with him?"

"What are you talking about?"

"Are you in love with him?" He took a step forward. She stilled when he tilted her chin up. "Answer me."

"No," she said. "Why would you think such a thing?"

"Why did you come to the barracks then?" he asked.

"Because he invited me and...and I never know where to sit in the Hall," she said. "All my friends sit with *you*."

"What are you talking about?" he asked. "I had a chair for you last night."

He had a chair for her since she had returned. But she had been too tired the first few nights and had not been up to the task of public dining.

"No, I saw Kai and Inès there," she said. "Don't lie to me."

"I am not lying," he said between clenched teeth. And how dare she imply otherwise. "Inès was there to relay a message. She dined with her mother. She sat for a split seco—wait, is this why you were upset last night?"

Élisabeth folded her arms across her chest.

"I can't believe this," he said. Looking up at the night sky as if it would reveal what sin he had committed to be tortured like this.

"Shut up," she said. A blush slithered up her throat. "Just shut up!"

Her eyes darted everywhere but at him. He could tell she was rather mortified by this entire ordeal. And what a relish it was to see her so ashamed.

His fingers still clasped her chin, and she folded her fingers around his wrist. "Let go of me."

"Fine." He sighed dramatically. "I suppose I will have to return it all."

Élisabeth's eyes narrowed. "Return what?"

"All the gifts I bought to apologize to you," Séverin said. "It is clear to see there wasn't anything to apologize for. I did *nothing* wrong."

Her eyes grew bright with curiosity.

"Gifts?" she asked.

"A shame you won't be receiving them."

"Why not?" Élisabeth pouted.

Séverin frowned, annoyed that it affected him, that it swayed him in the slightest.

"Because I don't reward bad behavior."

"I think you're lying," she said. "There are no gifts."

"Stop accusing me of lying."

"Show me then."

"Fine," he said. "You can see it, but don't you *dare* touch it."

Élisabeth had a disbelieving look on her face as if she could not believe he would ever do such a thing. She had a point—he would never do this for anyone, and he refused to unearth the reason why he had done so for her.

He cracked open his bedroom door and held it open for her. He expected a quip about him finally learning his "manners", but she was silent as her eyes widened. Every possible surface was covered in flowers. Now that he looked at it, he may have gone a bit overboard. His bedroom looked like an untamed garden. Her finger softly drifted along the pink petals of the nearest flower.

"I love peonies," she said wistfully.

Séverin cleared his throat. "I wasn't certain what you liked."

"Well, now you know for the next time you infuriate me," she said. "I have no doubt you will do so within the hour."

She had a warm, teasing smile. One that had him biting back the defensive response he instinctively reached for. Élisabeth did a stroll around the bedroom, sitting on the foot of his bed and dragging the pile of boxes towards her like a child celebrating the festivities of Winter Equinox. It didn't take her long to unravel the shiny, ornate bow and peel off the lids with haste as if he would snatch it away if she took too long.

"Oh," she said, plucking a silver gown with a bodice of crystals. "Stunning."

Her soft gasps as she opened each box and touched the fabric made him feel oddly pleased. He couldn't help but think that looking at her felt a little bit like dying. Violent and devouring and eternal, all in equal measure.

"I want to try this on," she said. Holding up a white ballet dress and matching slippers. "Can you send for Colette?"

"She has been dismissed for the night, but I know my way around unlacing a corset."

Élisabeth scoffed. "Has she truly been dismissed, you scoundrel?"

"No, she has not," he said. "But as I said, I know my way around a corset."

"Well, I am wearing my pannier under," she said. "It is not as though I am naked."

"No, I dare say you are not that interesting," Séverin said.

She stuck out her tongue at him, but obediently turned around to face the wall, giving him her back. If he wasn't so interested in getting under her skin, he would take back his offer to play handmaiden. He was crossing the invisible lines he had drawn between them.

He tugged on the closest string that held her corset. His long fingers made quick work of the strands.

"How did you learn how to undo a corset?" she asked.

"A gentleman never says," he said.

"Then you should be singing like a canary," she replied.

The corset loosened. The strings dangling on the sides. He was perfectly still. As much as he would enjoy the sight of her naked spine, he was glad that she was clothed by her undergarments. Still her proximity and her sweet scent intoxicated him. His fingertips ran along the ends of her hair, and he felt her shiver under his touch. Séverin's hand dropped and he closed his fist so tightly it hurt.

"Will you help me into it?" she whispered. "My arm is... well you can see for yourself."

"Making a servant of me, are you?" He raised a brow.

Séverin grabbed her ballet dress and crouched down to help her into it. He felt her hands grab his shoulders for support and his muscles twitched under her touch.

"I like you like this," Élisabeth said, brushing that one stubborn strand from his eye. He felt his heart lurch at her touch. "You belong on your knees."

"Do not get used to it," he warned darkly.

"Oh, but I already have," she said.

He stood up, towering over her, drawing the fabric over her hips and then he was behind her again, tying the knots of the bodice. His fingers itched to linger, to touch, to study her with all the zeal of a devoted student. It took everything in him to swallow the urge and retreat.

Once he was a safe distance away, he flexed his hand absently by his side, struggling to control his impulses.

"Will you play me something? Something beautiful and secret and haunting. I want to feel like I am dancing with the stars," she whispered.

Her eyes were bright and luminous, as she spoke. And he could not find it in himself to deny her.

He walked towards his piano, fingers itching to do her bidding. He felt like a man possessed and he wondered if she had cast a spell on him.

Élisabeth's eyes narrowed in suspicion.

"I didn't think you'd say yes," she said. "You are being suspiciously amicable."

Séverin slowly rolled up his sleeves. His movements were slow and methodical.

"I am scared," she said. "Your good mood frightens me. What has happened to my Séverin?"

For so long his name had felt odd, like a coat that did not quite fit. But hearing his name pass her lips he realized that for the first time, it fit. Or perhaps that had far more to do with the fact that she had said those words again, she had said *My Séverin* just like that day she had been drunk. As if he belonged to her. He could see his chain dangling between her breasts and he wondered if in some small way she belonged to him as well.

Séverin fell into the music, refusing to explain himself. Some things were better left unsaid. He had revealed his card when he had reacted in front of Matthieu. And then there was the chaotic storm of gifts that lavished his room. He could only bear himself so much in one night.

He played something he had picked up during his years at the Prasin Conservatory. Something plundering and woeful. Something that he was beginning to feel anytime he looked deep into her eyes. It would not feel like drifting among the stars, as she hoped it would. It would feel like the opposite, like crashing and burning. An inevitable, doomed end like a tragic play. He wanted her chest to ache and her mind to spiral like an unwound tapestry.

Élisabeth danced around his room. Like a dove taking flight, she launched into the air, her legs slicing through the air in a flawless split. Then she was twirling, her body curved into a soft bow. Feet grazing the floor in a gentle caress. She looked like those figurines perched atop a music box. Beautiful and untouchable. He recalled his time in Box Five, staring at her from the shadows. He had been nothing but an incorporeal figure, cloaked in darkness, watching the girl who called to him like a moth to a flame.

His fingers flew faster, switching the tempo to a budding crescendo. Élisabeth spun and twisted, brown hair flying behind her like a cape, matching his pace without missing a beat and he felt this strange fulfillment. Like she had been made to dance to his music. Like she was made for him.

Séverin's fingers slipped. A terrible clang erupted around the room. He stood up abruptly, feeling this strange, tense feeling in his chest. As if there was something trapped beneath his ribs, squeezing his insides like a fist. He could feel his thoughts trailing into dark, unknown territories, thinking about things he had no business thinking about.

"*Leave*," he growled.

"What?" Élisabeth asked, chest rising and falling.

She was divinity made flesh, wrapped in her white dress, and he hated that he noticed. He hated everything about this night. He had never felt so uncertain and confused as he did then.

"Take what you need and collect the rest tomorrow," he said. "You may return to your old bedroom tonight."

"But my arm hasn't healed—"

It surprised him that she protested. It should have delighted him that she wanted to stay, but Séverin felt so out of sorts, all he could feel was *fear*.

"I am not your caretaker," he said coldly.

He watched the glimmer in her eyes vanish. The one that had been there since she teased him earlier was gone. He watched as her face grew shuttered and her shoulders straightened. An indifferent mask cloaked her face and he hated that he had put it there. He hated that he ruined everything because he was afraid.

"I don't want Matthieu to be discharged," she said. "He has learned whatever lesson you wished to impart and I'm certain he will not make the same mistake twice. He is one of my dearest friends an—"

Séverin clenched his teeth. "He is your dearest friend?"

"Why are you so upset?" she demanded. "It doesn't make sense."

"You were in the barracks! Kissing a soldier!" he accused. "You are a lady of noble birth!"

Élisabeth snorted.

"Is something funny?"

Great, now she was laughing. Not her small, infuriating giggles but full-blown laughter. She had bent forward, and her eyes gleamed with unshed tears.

"Did you just...did you just call me a lady?" she asked.

His lips tightened. It didn't seem like the question deserved a response.

"Cease this at once," Séverin said.

"You haven't treated me like a lady since the day I arrived," she said, wiping the corners of her eyes. "There was that night Odette stole my clothes, and you refused to look away, and then there was last night when we shared a bed. And just moments ago you insisted upon undressing me and—"

"I did not insist!"

"Fine, you implored *desperately*," she said. "Does that phrase please you?"

A knock sounded, interrupting their intense stare down. She was smirking at him like she knew just how much she got under his skin. Like she knew that nobody affected him the way she did.

"Enter," he called.

"Am I interrupting?" Kai asked, looking at them curiously.

"No," he said. "Lisbeth was just leaving."

"I am not leaving until I know Matthieu's fate," she said stubbornly.

"I came to speak about Matthieu," Kai said. "Did you truly discharge him? On what basis?"

"Do I need to have a reason to discharge my men?" Séverin demanded.

"No, but..."

"Escort him off the grounds, Kai," he said. "That is an order."

"If Matthieu leaves we all leave, me and Kai and—"

"Hold on there," Kai said. Palms raised in defense. "I never said anything about mutiny."

Élisabeth looked prepared to wage a war. His father had always said it was important that he learn to pick his battles with his mother, and judging from Élisabeth's dark look he would regret his course of action if he proceeded. His father's advice was beginning to seem rather sound and then he swiftly chastised himself because Élisabeth was *not* his wife. He shouldn't even be considering changing his stance for her just so he could enjoy a few days of not being at odds. Even though he had no doubt they would find something new to argue about not long after.

"Fine," Séverin barked. "He can remain, but one toe out of line and he will not be discharged, he will be executed. I will feed him to my wraiths."

Élisabeth's shoulders softened in relief, and Kai nodded, seemingly comforted by this new direction as well.

"Thank you, Séverin," Élisabeth said. "I shall take my leave."

"I will send someone to bring you your belongings."

Kai's eyes widened. As if he had just noticed the abundance of flowers in his bedroom. "Are you courting Élis—"

"Get out," Séverin barked. "*Now.*"

Kai left, but his laughter could not be masked, he could hear the echoing sound of his cackle down the hallway.

Élisabeth followed behind him, their heads bent low while they gossiped. He closed the door behind him, rubbing his jaw. He truly was at his wit's end. Between the raging hurricane that was Élisabeth Bellacourt and the fact that his world and everything that he had carefully built was unraveling he had to start focusing on what truly mattered.

Protecting the Graylands. Saving his home.

And not the girl who made him want to forget it all.

Chapter Twenty-Eight

"He won't like this," Kai said, as he led her to the grounds.

"He doesn't have to know," Élisabeth said. "I have to make sure Matthieu is fine. It's my fault he's in trouble. And besides, nobody said anything about my shooting lessons ending."

It shouldn't have surprised her that Séverin had fallen into a dark rage. All he cared about was keeping her leashed like the perfect human thrall. Her teeth gritted at his extreme mood shift. One moment he was kind and thoughtful, and the next he was the surly beast she had come upon the first day she'd arrived. And trying to figure him out was beginning to hurt her head, Élisabeth made a vow then to never cross the line with Séverin. Whatever this blooming attraction was she would tuck it deep into her chest until it wilted and eventually died.

Kai sighed before he led her across the courtyard to where Matthieu waited for her.

"I won't be far," Kai said, in a warning tone.

"I don't need supervision," she said.

"Take it or leave it."

Élisabeth sighed and stuck her tongue out at him when he turned around.

"Very mature," Kai called over his shoulder.

"How did yo—"

"Seen you do it to Séverin more times than I can count," Kai said with a loose chuckle. "Not surprised I get the same treatment when I put my foot down."

Élisabeth laughed, as she made her way towards Matthieu. She was filled with guilt for getting him in trouble. His cheek had healed from Séverin's attack.

"I'm sorry," she whispered.

"Not your fault," he said.

"Isn't it?"

Séverin had reacted so strongly, because of her. He couldn't bear to see her have fun. That was why he'd stormed into the soldiers' mess hall and had the gall to discharge Matthieu from service.

"Séverin's probably wanted to punch me for a while," Matthieu said with a lopsided smile. "You know how insuffer-able I can be."

Élisabeth's face softened. She hoped he said that to ease her guilt, and not because he *truly* believed that he was insuf-ferable.

"You are a rogue, Matthieu," she said. Her hand raised up to lay flat on his heart. "With a heart of gold."

His lips lifted in his signature crooked smile.

Kai cleared his throat. Élisabeth raised an annoyed brow at him when he said "no touching" gruffly.

This was ridiculous. Séverin did not own her. He did not decide who she befriended and how she acted towards them. Defiance bled through her, before it fizzled like a cracked bottle of fine wine when she realized Matthieu would suffer for anything she did.

Her hand dropped limply.

"It's fine, Sabeth," he whispered, so Kai didn't overhear him. And then louder, "Let's begin our lesson."

Matthieu offered her his rifle, holding the end since she couldn't use her injured arm. His fingers wrapped around her elbow for support, and he shot Kai a smug smile that said, 'I found a loophole to your stupid rules'. He was rewarded with Kai's potent glare.

"Tread carefully," Kai said darkly. "He won't discharge you the next time you step out of line. He will execute you."

"Dying for Élisabeth is the noblest way to go," Matthieu said, making her snicker.

"Is this a joke to you both?" Kai said.

"I simply don't understand why he cares," Élisabeth said.

His mood changed like the fluctuating weather. He had apologized for his behavior not in words, but in action, and Élisabeth had felt herself soften towards him before he abruptly demanded she leave. His tone was curt and harsh as if it had all been one big mistake. It would be a lie if she said it hadn't bothered her. But instead of sitting around and mopping about, she would defy him in the only way she could.

"It is not our place to speculate on our lord's actions," Kai said, in his "General" tone.

"He is not my lord, he is a black-hearted villa—"

"Just finish your lesson, Élisabeth," Kai said warily. "You can save your insults for Séverin."

Élisabeth turned back to the tree Matthieu pointed at. Her target for the day. Last time he had lined up bottles, but they were far too tricky to strike so now she just shot at the trees. Élisabeth took a deep breath to steady her rage and focus. It was a wonder that Séverin could sink so deeply under her skin like a squirrel burrowing into the ground.

She squealed in glee when her bullet sunk deep into the thick bark of the tree.

"See!" Matthieu said. "I knew you could do it."

Élisabeth tilted her neck, smiling at him brightly. His face was close to hers and she could make out the shadow of stubble that coated his jaw, outlining the halo of his lips. She faintly recalled last night when he'd brushed his lips against hers and her cheeks burned at the memory.

"No extended eye contact," Kai barked.

Élisabeth snorted.

"His chaperoning skills are remarkable," she whispered. "He could put a society mother to shame."

"Maybe we should do something to truly shock him," Matthieu said with a conspiratorial smile.

"What did you have in mind?"

"No whispering!" Kai said.

"This," Matthieu said.

And before she could brace herself, his cold mouth was planted on hers. A small gasp escaped her, as his fingers sank into her hair, slithering between the thick strands and guiding her head backward to accommodate his height. His mouth tasted familiar and safe. She found herself falling deeper into his arms. Her hand slid up his neck, fingers grazing the rough patch of hair on his jaw. Matthieu groaned under her touch, and she felt a lick of satisfaction travel up her spine, before she was roughly yanked backward.

Kai was furious. His coal-black brows slanted cruelly.

"Is this a joke to you both?" Kai demanded.

"I thought it was pretty funny," Matthieu said.

Kai's fist shook and she stood before Matthieu before he

followed his instincts. Slowly, his arm lowered, but his gaze was furious.

"Come along, Élisabeth," Kai said. "Lesson's over."

He pulled her elbow, and Élisabeth turned back to look at Matthieu who winked at her. A laugh escaped her at his completely unrepentant smile.

"Look ahead," Kai snapped.

"Why are you acting like this?" she asked. "It's like Séverin gave you a course on spoiling the mood and being an utter bore." Élisabeth poked his shoulder. "What happened to the Kai who told us Séverin kisses old women in his spare time?"

"You're playing with fire," Kai said. He paused in the hallway, staring at her. "You know how he feels about you. Why must you provoke him?"

"I know that he hates me and he *also* ruined my life," Élisabeth said. "He was bearable for five minutes last night before he turned back into his monstrous self. He kicked me out of his room like I was a stray dog."

Kai's face softened. "He doesn't know how to express himself. Be patient with him."

Élisabeth folded her arms across her chest.

"I've been treated with abhorrence and ill-will most of my life," she said tightly. "My stepmother Delphine and half-sister Louise never fully accepted me and the boy I wanted more than anything barely looked my way until it suited him. For so long I was trapped in a doorway and each room I entered was filled with people who didn't want me. The war strife with the South didn't make things easier. I refuse to be mistreated. I refuse to be second-best to anyone."

Séverin only wanted her when he suspected Matthieu did. He was no different than Charles who had pursued her only *after* his friend William had expressed interest, and her performance had been celebrated. He didn't care about her and he never would. And she was tired of waiting for the wrong people to choose her.

"I'm sorry, Élisabeth," Kai said gently. "I didn't know things were so hard. You carry yourself so bravely. I can see why Séverin is so fond of you."

"Thank you, but...but just stop putting Séverin on a pedestal. He is *not* a good person," she said. "Matthieu on the other hand is good. So, give him some slack. He jokes a lot, but he has feelings as well."

Kai nodded. "Despite my stern behavior, I am doing this because I care about Matthieu too. What do you think Séverin will do to him if he suspects something between you two?"

"I won't let him hurt him."

"Good luck trying to stop him," Kai said. "One thing about Séverin, anything he wants he pursues with a single-minded focus. Fates, help anyone who gets in his way."

***

Élisabeth was going to perform tonight. A small thrill ran down her spine at the thought of taking the stage. The other dancers weren't pleased to hear that she would be performing solo. Marie-Odile had glared at her during practice as she perfected her routine. It was difficult to dance with her arm still clipped to her side, but she was willing to make the extra effort if it meant she got to perform.

She wore a lace-pink dress that evening with a blooming tulle skirt. Her white silk slippers were fastened, the satin thread coiling around her legs. Her hair was loose and slipped down her back like a waterfall. Colette had tied some of her hair above her head with a ribbon.

It felt different now to perform when she wasn't so afraid.

"Nervous?" Inès asked who'd come with Kai to escort her.

Élisabeth had her arm tangled with Inès.

"No," she said with a wide smile. "Excited."

"You will do splendidly," she said. "Mother is even leaving the library to come and see you and she rarely leaves the library."

"I am honored," Élisabeth said.

Her heart hammered in her chest the moment she stepped outside. Dinner that night was to be hosted in the gardens. Tables had been set, the edges gleaming with roped braids of flowers—drooping irises, starry-eyed chamomiles, and bruise-blue hyacinths. Servants made the rounds with silver platters that held pigeons surrounded with a butter sauce and garnished with lemon, fruits, and vegetables that had been carved to resemble flowers and birds. Apples, oranges, and pears had taken on the likeness of robins, wrens, and doves. Sorbet in glass cups sat in chilled buckets waiting to be served.

He sat on his throne; legs sprawled before him looking like a wicked woodland creature. A faery come to lure her to his world. His ruby-lips gleamed in the dark like they were stained with blood. His embroidered velvet coat was trimmed with golden lines that resembled the constellation.

His head lifted the moment she entered, and he stared at her with his frost-blue eyes. His gaze swept down her body, burning her flesh. She may as well have been naked for the strange desire that marked his expression. Élisabeth's skin heated and she abruptly looked away from him.

Inès giggled beside her, and she elbowed her.

He hadn't bothered to speak to her since last night. She didn't know why he had gone to such lengths to apologize to her if he didn't truly wish to make amends. Even after all these weeks, she still did not understand the inner workings of his peculiar mind.

Élisabeth headed straight for the stage they had constructed for outdoor performances. She could hear the chatter soften to a dull whisper, and she rolled her neck, as she waited for the orchestra to begin her number.

Séverin held up his hand at that moment, and her stomach plummeted when he stood, crossing the small path to the stage. He stopped by the orchestra and whispered something she was too far to hear.

The music switched to a duet she had watched before. Louise had performed it with one of the male dancers before at the Opera House. It was a darkly sensual tale about a girl who fell for the ghost that haunted her. The opening began and Élisabeth took a step backward. She wasn't doing this with him. Not when she was resolved to erase him from her life, to put him behind her like the pages of a bad chapter.

Besides their role as allies to take down Laurent together, she didn't want to have any other relationship with him. She certainly didn't want to perform with him. There was an intimacy to performing with a male dancer, feeling their hands span your waist as they rotated you like you were their doll, their breath colliding with yours, their rough, male cheeks grazing yours as you mimicked desperate lovers. It was why it was so important to establish trust with your partner. And there was no trust between Séverin and her.

"Afraid, Lisbeth," he purred, walking towards her like a tiger on the prowl.

"I didn't know you danced."

"I am a man of many talents," he said.

"I can't do this," she said.

Élisabeth turned to flee the stage, but he caught her wrist. His other fist sunk into her hair and tugged her head back, so she half-leaned on his shoulder. Her gaze fell to the sky, watching in a mix of horror and fascination, as his wraiths swarmed the air, floating in mindless circles looking like drifting clouds.

"Do you see my wraiths?" he asked. "They haven't fed in some time."

"I thought we were past these unoriginal threats," she said, between clenched teeth.

"You never listen when I ask kindly," Séverin said. "You leave me little choice."

"You *never* asked kindly," she said, feeling the sturdy frame of his body behind her. She could feel the sleek muscles of his chest beneath his loose shirt. He'd removed his fancy dinner coat before he came to her, and her breath grew shaky at his proximity. He was far too close for comfort.

"I did," he said. "With my eyes. Must everything be spelled out for you?"

"All your desperate eyes said was "I wonder what Élisabeth looks like under that dress"?" she said. Her words were a taunt. His gaze had been nothing short of lewd.

A dark chuckle escaped him.

"And?"

"And what?"

"And what does Lisbeth look like under that dress?" he whispered. His palm slid down her ribs, stroking her side. It almost made her forget they had an audience before them. That the music was drifting around them like smoke.

She tilted her face to whisper in his ear.

"Why don't you ask Matthieu?"

He stiffened and Élisabeth felt smug when he stepped away from her, but her reaction was rather short-lived when she looked at his eyes. He looked murderous.

"Get off my stage," he said coldly.

"What?" she asked.

"You heard me," he said. "Marie-Odile will take center.

We're not in the mood to stomach your particular brand of mediocrity tonight."

"But this is *my* performance," she said stubbornly. She'd been looking forward to it all day, and she refused to let him rob her of it, she *needed* this. Ballet was her catharsis and the past few weeks had been nothing short of stressful.

The wraiths swooped down and her stomach tilted at their odd screeching sounds. People ran for cover, some crawling beneath the tables for protection. Her heart stilled as they surrounded her, drowning her in their cold.

"Any other protests?" Séverin asked.

Élisabeth didn't dare speak.

"Good," he said. "Now get off my stage."

Her fists tightened by her side, as the wraiths took back to the air and Marie-Odile brushed past her on her way down the steps, digging her shoulder into her injured arm. A small whimper escaped her, and Inès rushed towards her, pity on her face.

"What happened up there?" Inès asked. "For a moment, we thought you'd both undress each other and the next it was pure murder in his eyes."

"I'm done with him!" Élisabeth said.

"Kai," Inès called. "Bring us a bottle of the finest wine. We're getting drunk."

"As you wish," Kai said, disappearing into the crowd.

"Come on." Inès held her hand. "I know a place we can go."

They entered the foyer. Her cheeks burned from being publicly shunned by him. Her throat tightened, and she swallowed back the urge to cry.

Matthieu walked towards them, and relief filled her at the sight of his tall silhouette.

"Did I miss your performance?" Matthieu asked. His

uniform was more haphazard than usual. "I knew I shouldn't have taken that nap."

"You missed nothing," she said. "The tyrant kicked me off stage."

"We're going to get drunk at my secret spot," Inès said. "Feel free to join us. Ah, Kai has returned with our loot."

Kai had three bottles. Two in hand and one tucked beneath his elbow.

"Come on," Inès said, pulling her along. "You won't believe this place."

Inès led them in the direction of the library.

"I thought we weren't allowed to eat or drink here?" Matthieu said.

"Patience," Inès said, climbing to the second floor and then the third.

There was a spiral staircase that led up to a small balcony. From this vantage they could look down on the sprawling oak shelves and if they looked up, they had an excellent view of the sky from the glass that sealed the dome. There were pillows and blankets and it was the perfect place to hide away from the world.

"Well?" Inès asked, pleased with her secret spot.

"It's amazing," Élisabeth said.

Inès shot Matthieu a warning look.

"You can never bring your conquests here," she warned.

"Too late," he said, draping an arm over Élisabeth's shoulder. "She's already here."

Élisabeth giggled as she sat on the blanket and Inès tucked her under her arm.

"We'll sneak to the ballroom later," Inès promised. "And you can perform for us."

"Excellent idea," Matthieu said, uncorking the bottle of wine.

"I love you all," Élisabeth said, draping her arm over Matthieu and Inès. "Get over here Kai."

Kai, who had been leaning on the banister, rolled his eyes, as if it were a chore, but he sat down and let Élisabeth pull him into the hug.

"You know what would be fun," Matthieu said.

"No!" Inès said, at the same time Matthieu said, "If we all started kissing each other. Come here, Kai."

Kai stared at him with horror, as Matthieu grabbed his neck and kissed his cheek. Kai shoved him off, glaring at him. His cheeks grew slightly red.

"We are *not* having an orgy," Kai said, in his sternest voice.

Élisabeth and Inès laughed so hard; they had to hold each other to keep upright.

They passed the bottle back and forth, taking long, leisurely sips of the wine. It tickled her throat, warming her insides as it made its way to her stomach.

"We should all share our darkest secret," Inès said. "Nothing seals a friendship pact like revealing our most dreadful truths. Dakari, what are you most afraid of?"

Kai's head lifted and Élisabeth's mouth twitched. Inès obviously wanted to know everything there was to know about Kai. It was a wonder that they were completely oblivious to each other's feelings.

Kai looked so deeply into Inès' eyes. It began to feel like they were looking into something utterly private, so Élisabeth turned her back to them to face Matthieu.

"What are *you* afraid of, Matthieu Durand?"

"Being a serious bore who takes his duties to heart," he said, leaning down to whisper in her ear. "In other words, being Kai."

Élisabeth snickered. "I'm serious, Matthieu. Tell me!"

His smile softened, slipping away like a feather caught in the wind.

"You, returning home," he said softly. "I am also afraid of being forgotten. My father does a rather splendid job of pretending I don't exist."

"I'm sorry, Mat," she whispered. "Why don't you come with me to the mortal realm? It could be a lot of fun."

"My father would not be pleased, he..." Matthieu hesitated. "Well, he has a bit of a temper."

Élisabeth reached for his hand, his cold fingers sliding between her own. It didn't take much to realize that he both feared and despised his father. Élisabeth wondered how anyone could be upset by someone as bright-eyed and humorous as Matthieu. And that saddened her more, that he had been using his jokes and light-heartedness this entire time as a shield.

"You don't have to hide when you're with me," she said. "You can tell me the truth."

Matthieu pulled his hand away, and Élisabeth felt a deep sense of rejection for the second time that night.

"There is no point in any of this when you intend to leave," Matthieu said. "It simply makes it harder for me, as if it wasn't unbearable enough."

"What am I to do, Matthieu?" Élisabeth asked. "I can't stay here, not when *he* rules this realm. It may belong to my mother, but the Fates do not involve themselves in the lives of mortals. I will be at his mercy."

"Then forget the rat Laurent and kill him instead," Matthieu whispered. "And if he is the wrong target then hunt Laurent. You can summon the blade. You can end this."

"That is too dangerous," she said. "And Kai and Inès would never forgive me."

"What happens if it isn't Laurent? The prophecy is to kill

the Lord of Chaos, nothing changes if you simply kill the Fate," Matthieu said. "What if Séverin is the Lord of Chaos?"

"Then I will have a reasonable cause," she said. "But until that theory is proven, I can't risk it."

Matthieu sighed. "I hate this damned prophecy. And I hate that they made us a part of it. We are trapped in a game run by the Fates."

"I know," she said. "It is utterly unfair."

Matthieu grabbed the bottle, guzzling the wine like water, before he leaned down resting his head on her shoulder. His hair tickled her neck.

Kai plucked out a deck of cards from his pocket.

"Who wants to play a game?"

Élisabeth stumbled to her bedroom, fingers desperately trailing the wall to keep herself upright. Matthieu had offered to carry her to bed, but the likelihood of running into Séverin when they shared a floor was far too high. After their game of cards, they'd gone to the ballroom where she usually practiced. Kai and Matthieu had played a clunky tune on the piano together while she performed a terrible, drunken version of her performance, Inès caught her each time she lost her footing which would bring them to a fit of giggles.

A door cracked open, and her heart dropped to her stomach at the sight of Marie-Odile. Her make-up was all smeared like she'd rubbed it on a cloth. Her powder was splotchy, lipstick cut in a jagged, red line. Bile crawled up her throat when she noticed her in the dark. Marie-Odile smirked, her bright teeth flashing in the dark like the canines of a predator.

"He's all yours," Marie-Odile said. "If he'll even have you, that is. You look wretched."

"Haven't looked in a mirror lately?" Élisabeth spat. "Because I could say the same thing to you."

"I am above the petty retorts," Marie-Odile said. Even though she'd been the one who started it.

She felt a great sense of relief when Marie-Odile disappeared down the corridor, strutting her hips in victory. At least she would not have to listen to the unbearable sounds of their love-making all night. It was some consolation, even though she felt half-sick to her stomach. Her fingers latched onto her doorknob, prepared to erase the visions of Séverin kissing Marie-Odile from her mind with some much-needed rest.

A hiss escaped her when she stumbled inside, hitting her toe on her dresser.

"Where have you been, Little Monster?" Séverin drawled.

Élisabeth straightened, making out the outline of his form in a chair. Her fist tightened with rage. All she could see was him and Marie-Odile tangled in his ornate bed, caught in the dark silk sheets as they kissed ravenously.

"Get out!" she screamed. "Get out or I will kill you myself."

"Shut up," Séverin said. He stood up, crossing the space between them.

Élisabeth ran to her bed and began to gather the many decorative pillows nestled against the headboard, hurling them at him like they were missiles. It was too dark to make him out, but she felt an odd sense of satisfaction when a surprised grunt escaped him.

"Stop that at once," Séverin snapped.

Élisabeth simply renewed her effort.

"Get out or I will bludgeon you to death with these," she warned. "You have five seconds to—"

A shriek of surprise escaped her when she was tackled on her bed. Her breath escaped her in a single whoosh, as the weight of his body pinned her to the mattress. Élisabeth opened her mouth to protest, but her words were forced back down her throat when he tossed a pillow at her head, effectively silencing her.

He snickered. The boyish sound surprised her.

"Did you just—"

"This is kind of fun," he cut her off.

His long arm reached for another pillow, and she beat him to it, hitting him in the ribs. Séverin grabbed two pillows, hitting her lightly on both sides. A double attack, carefully avoiding her injured arm, which she was grateful for. It seemed he did possess a rare bit of sense. Even though he was being entirely unsensible just then.

Élisabeth slid out from under him and grabbed two pillows and began to hit his back. Séverin snatched her pillows from her curled fingers and rewarded her with the same treatment.

"This is ridiculous," she huffed. "I am a lady of noble—"

"Oh, shut up," Séverin said, stuffing a pillow into her face. Her words choked down her throat. "Spare me your self-righteous speech and eat this instead."

Her curses were muffled by the embroidered, peacock-blue cloth, and she tore it off her face. Only to find Séverin's eyes sparkling in the dark. The beast was enjoying himself, and she refused to give him the upper hand. She lunged for him, prepared to tackle him down, but he easily shifted them, using her momentum to slide her under him once more. He yanked her good wrist upward, forcing the trimmed end of her corset to slide lower, scandalously displaying her flesh.

"Is this some grand ploy to undress me?" Élisabeth hissed.

"Don't worry, Little Monster," he said coldly. "You don't tempt me in the slightest."

"Of course, I don't," she said. "You prefer Marie-Odile. I saw her slipping out of your bedroom like a thief in the night."

He preferred women as cold as diamonds, whose tongue

cut just as deep. Élisabeth should have taken comfort that she was not the source of his desire, but her mind was far too softened from the wine to comfort her with a good lie. Instead, she sounded unbearably bitter and envious. Séverin's lips twisted in a sharp smile.

"Jealous?" he asked. "I dare say her performance in the bedroom far surpassed her performance on stage."

Her heart ached at his words. And it took every ounce of her strength to react with anger and not sadness.

"You disgust me," she snarled.

"Are you so delusional to think Matthieu will ask your father for your hand once he's gotten his way with you?" Séverin demanded. "Do you think he truly cares for you, Lisbeth?"

"It doesn't matter what his intentions are," she said with a cold smile. "He is a pretty enough distraction."

Élisabeth should not have been speaking about Matthieu that way, he was her friend, but goading Séverin was far too tempting. Something about the way his eyes darkened and his lips curled like a wild animal, made her want to push his buttons some more. She wanted to make him unravel like a wool string and descend into madness. She wanted him to feel every lick of rage and pain she felt when he'd tossed her off that stage without a second glance, when he brought a girl who despised her to his bedroom to sink under her skin.

It felt like time stopped, as he gazed at her like she was the worst thing that had ever come his way. His frosty blue eyes drifted along her face possessively, cataloguing her features, before stopping at her lips, trapped like a dead moth caught in the stitching of a silk gown.

Her heart thudded rapidly like a broken grandfather clock with the arrows all crooked. The words escaped her unbidden, yanked forward by her drunk tongue.

"Will you kiss me?" she asked breathlessly. Both frightened and curious about the prospect.

What would it feel like to have those plush, red lips crashing down on hers?

Élisabeth presumed it would feel like dying.

Séverin straightened, his hand dropping abruptly.

"Bad girls don't get rewarded," he said, in an icy tone.

Élisabeth sat upright so fast, that her mind spun.

"Good," she said. "Because I would hate it."

Séverin snorted. "Whatever you say."

He walked away from her to the bathing room, using the short-cut to his bedroom. Somehow, she could not erase the thought of Marie-Odile returning to his room for another round of debauchery.

"Where are you going?" she asked, hoping he could not hear just how desperate she was.

"None of your damned business," he hissed.

The door clicked shut behind him, and Élisabeth collapsed back on her bed, grabbing one of the strewn pillows to her chest. She squeezed her eyes shut to erase the feeling of his cold fingers curled around her wrist and the darkly enchanting force of his gaze.

Élisabeth instead thought of his cruelty, and his wretched words until she fell into a deep, dark slumber.

Chapter Twenty-Nine

Séverin had spent the majority of the night staring at the wallpaper that decorated the ceiling. A depiction of the Great Hunt with Pras leading the charge with his holy bow and arrow. There was a similar replica to the bow and arrow hanging in one of the parlour rooms.

He'd gone to one of the spare bedrooms last night. It made sense to move far away from the source of all his troubles, but even here the cursed girl haunted him. He could see her wide eyes, as he'd fixated on her lips. It was a wonder something that spewed such vile words could tempt him so greatly. If he'd had a scribe write down every time she insulted him, he would have a tome as thick as his head by now.

A knock sounded on his door, and he was not surprised when Kai poked his head in.

"You're a difficult man to track down," Kai said.

"Didn't seem to give you much trouble."

Kai sat down on the bedroom bench and stretched his legs out. They sat in silence for several, drawn minutes. Kai hadn't come here to enjoy his rather dull company; there was something on his mind.

"Someone answered our reward call and mentioned a man he suspects is working with Laurent. He accused the human thrall of a small shop-owner," Kai said. "We apprehended the man this morning. He's awaiting questioning."

Séverin swung his legs off the bed. "That's good news. I'll go torture answers out of him."

"This may not be my place, but I should let you know that you were exceptionally cruel to Élisabeth last night," Kai said.

Séverin stiffened. "You're right, it's not your place."

Kai, like most people, did not care for the shift in his tone and carried on undaunted.

"She was looking forward to her performance," he said. "And to replace her with Marie-Odile who has not had a kind word for her since she arrived is rather low."

"Anything that has occurred was all her fault," Séverin said. "And I'm surprised you would think otherwise."

"Really, you're surprised that I think you made a dumb decision, because you are afraid of the weight of your feelings?" Kai asked, with a raised brow. "It is my job to tell you that you are being dumb. You could lose her, Séverin. Does that not bother you?"

"Lisbeth will come to her senses," Séverin said, standing up. He was rather tired of this conversation and the thought of torturing someone made his mouth water. It had been a while since he'd carved into someone.

"And what if her senses lead her to Matthieu?" Kai asked. "The reasonable option."

Séverin paused. "What did you say?"

"Before you threaten to execute him, just know you will truly lose her if you do that," Kai said. "So, how will you beat Matthieu *without* killing him?"

"I thought he was your friend?" Séverin said. "Should you not be aiding him?"

"Well, you are unfortunately my *best* friend." Kai sighed dramatically. "And I really don't want you to start crying on my shoulder when Élisabeth and Matthieu start courting."

"Your advice doesn't really motivate me," Séverin said. "Are you not a virgin?"

"So?" Kai said defensively.

Séverin chuckled. "Relax, I think it's sweet that you are saving it for someone you love. Makes my dead heart skip a beat."

Kai shoved him, and Séverin pushed him back. They tussled for a few minutes, attempting to knock the other off their feet, but none of them could quite manage it. Séverin finally used his magic to sweep his legs out from under him.

"Cheat," Kai grumbled.

Séverin smirked, ignoring the sore loser.

"Where's my prisoner?"

"I did not know who he was, my lord," the man cried, as Séverin plucked out another one of his fingernails. "I thought he was you!"

The lanky, sharp-nosed man hung from a pair of chain cuffs. Blood trickled down his wound, pooling around the ground in a scarlet pond. Kai stepped out of the chamber; he always had a bit of a weak stomach. Even before they died and were mortals, anytime their fathers took them hunting Kai would heave his guts the second Séverin's bullet sliced into the head of the boar or stag they hunted.

It delighted Séverin that the man *was* mortal, that anything he did was irreversible. The dead did not bleed, and it was so much more satisfying seeing the weeping wounds on his prisoner.

"It was mentioned in the reward poster that anyone roaming outside of the palace in my attire is cause for suspicion," Séverin said, slowly, methodically rolling his sleeves. "Your fellow shop owner had to tell me of your deception."

"I...I swear my lord I had no idea," he said, each breath that escaped him rattled in his brittle chest.

"Hmm, the nails and teeth didn't do it," Séverin said, with a cruel smile. "Perhaps, we should begin with some limbs. A finger or two."

Séverin walked to his tool kit, hunting for the perfect knife. One serrated enough to slice through bone.

"He promised I could return home," the man said. The words bubbled out of him, tangled in fear and misery. "I haven't seen my son in years. I just wa—"

"What did he want?" Séverin asked.

"I...I was a priest, and he had all these questions about the First Scripture," the man said. "I was alive during the Crusade. I protected as many copies of the book as I could. My father before me raised me on tales of the Three Kings and the mysteries of the Drowning."

"And what did you tell him?" he demanded. "Hurry."

He had to see Élisabeth, to somehow find it in himself to forgive her for her cruel words. The moment she had told him to ask Matthieu all he could think about was that day when she'd described the men she was attracted to, and it was *not* him. Matthieu looked like that silly fop she liked back in the mortal realm, bright-haired with a loose smile. Her barbed words had brought back all those old feelings of bitterness he'd felt when he'd awakened here, the realization that his life had been cut short, the dooming reality that his pain was marked on his skin, and his life just like his face was ruined. For some foolish reason, he had told himself that she was attracted to him, that the flush that crossed her cheeks when they bickered and her refusal to come close to him was because she secretly desired him, as he desired her.

But her words had crumbled all his beliefs to dust, leaving behind nothing but desolation.

"I told him the story of the old world when the realms were mere babes and magic ruled all. I told him about the pact that governed the Three Kings and how it had splintered, creating what we know today as the Drowning. The tomb that holds that which cannot be held. The silent purr of their absence haunting us like ghosts."

His voice was devout.

"Go on then," Séverin said. "Don't keep me in suspense and cease speaking in riddles."

"There was a pact between the Kings, forged in magic older than you and I. They were to never sire a child. An old priestess said that it would bring about their doom, so they had all performed a ceremony that prevented them from ever spawning a child. And it held as sturdy as a brick, until it didn't. You see Mòrge and Berthe had always been in love, and a Fate is a superior being with far more magic than you and I. Nobody had thought that it would break the binding and that she would find herself with child."

Séverin studied the man's weathered face, hunting for slips of mistruth. He could not fathom why Laurent had any interest in faith and fable, but he silently listened, waiting to hear the conclusion of this tale.

"There were many disputes about what should be done with the child," he said. "The easiest one being that he should be unmade before he was born. But Mòrge refused and Berthe gave birth to the Prince of Princes, Ren the Endless. The Lord of Chaos, the Ruler of the Darklands, the Breaker of the Balance."

"The Fourth King," he mused.

"The one who fractured the Balance," the priest said softly.

"Is that all you told him?"

The man nodded. "And that it was suspected that the Drowning occurred because of the Endless. That the old priestess' prediction had come true, and he had tipped the scales. It is why the Graylands is in danger of coming undone. When the Balance topples, ruinous afflictions arise, realms are endangered, Fates are reduced to mere mortals for all the power they possess in the face of such great upheaval."

Laurent was learning his history. He likely knew just as much as they did. He knew that it would not end until he was erased from this world.

And that Séverin was coming for him.

Séverin was walking down the hallway when he spotted Élisabeth and Matthieu. Élisabeth had a rifle swung over her shoulder, the scene looked rather odd considering she was in an emerald gown fit for a ball. Élisabeth's eyes widened in horror, and it took him a moment to realize his hands and face were smeared with blood. Élisabeth slightly tucked herself behind Matthieu, as if he would attack her next. Dread filled him at the sight of her cowering from him. There had been a time when that reaction would have thrilled him but knowing that Matthieu was the protector in her little fairy-tale and he was the villain did not sit right with him. Kai had been right, Matthieu was digging a path to her heart like the ferret that he was.

"Cutting up some innocent kittens?" Élisabeth asked.

"And puppies," Séverin added, unable to resist this back and forth with her.

She brought out this odd, childish side from him, that he didn't know if he liked or despised.

"Color me surprised."

"Can we speak?" he asked, glaring at Matthieu. "In private."

"Whatever you wish to say can be said in front of Matthieu," she said, raising her chin.

Irritation cut through him.

"Very well," Séverin said. "Shall we discuss how you begged me to kiss you last night?"

Élisabeth's mouth dropped open.

"You dirty liar," she said.

"The only dirty person here is the girl that asked me to shove my tongue down her throat," Séverin said. The lie spilling fluidly from his lips. He got the reaction he wanted. Matthieu was enraged, and Élisabeth was alarmed.

"Fine," she said tightly. "Let us speak in private. Since you will only tarnish my reputation more if I don't comply."

She marched off to the small balcony, tapping her foot impatiently. He felt a smug sense of satisfaction when he drew the curtains closed, obstructing Matthieu's view.

"How dare you tell such vile lies?" she demanded, placing down her rifle. He reckoned they were making some progress if she didn't feel the need to aim it at him. "And in front of Matthieu too. You are shameless."

"Did I embarrass you in front of your newest infatuation?" Séverin sneered.

Élisabeth simply folded her arms across her chest. Something in his chest stirred when she didn't vehemently deny it. One thing about Élisabeth was that she was deeply humiliated by the simple act of feeling. They were alike in that way. So, for her to not speak a word in defence meant that she had feelings for him and the thought sickened him.

A bone-deep sigh escaped her, and her shoulders dropped slightly, as if she were surrendering. The anger melted from her face and was replaced with exhaustion.

"I tire of this, Séverin," she said. "What will it take for you to leave me alone?"

Séverin stroked his chin, as if he were truly contemplating her request, but before he could muster up a perfectly decent, albeit sarcastic response, Élisabeth barrelled on.

"I will go home in a few weeks, Laurent cannot evade us forever. I will keep my end of the bargain," she said. "All I ask is that you allow me to spend my remaining time here with my friends, people who I *actually* care for and love instead of tormenting me with your rotten presence and these twisted games."

"I like our games," Séverin said, sealing the space between them. He captured her chin, running his thumb along her skin, marking her with the blood of his enemy. He watched with dull fascination as it stained her flawless flesh. "*You* like our games too."

"Please, Séverin," she whispered. "Grant me this small mercy."

"I love when you beg," he said, leaning down to rest his forehead on hers. "It almost makes me want to reward you."

"I am not your pet," she said, but her breath was shaky, and her shoulders trembled.

Did she remember his words from last night about the kiss and not rewarding bad behavior? Did she want him to kiss her now? Is that why she was being so good?

He wanted to kiss her; he wanted to drown in her. It was odd to be drawn to someone who brought him so much torment. Much like an insect drawn to the flame of a candle-light, unaware that its touch would incinerate them, but still longing for the gentle caress of the light.

Séverin bent down to do just that when Élisabeth slipped away from him.

"Do...don't," she said shakily. "Whatever ploy this is to infuriate Matthieu I refuse to be a part of it. I am not some toy you can steal. I am not a second option."

Séverin opened his mouth, but her anger had risen again like the crashing tides of the sea. Her fists curled tight to her side.

"I *refuse* to be a second option," she said between clenched teeth.

"What are you talking about?" he asked. "Matthieu is the one using you. He's bedded more women than there are stars in the sky."

"And you've remained abstinent?" she demanded. "Were you and Marie-Odile discussing the weather last night?"

Séverin laughed, an unamused sound.

"I didn't even see her," he said. "I was waiting for *you*. In your bedroom. The entire night."

Élisabeth froze. "But you—"

"I like seeing you jealous." He shrugged. "I find it amusing."

"I have to go," she said softly. "Matthieu is waiting."

Élisabeth rubbed the bloodstain on her chin, desperately attempting to erase him before she returned to her precious knight. Séverin felt a strange hollow sensation in his chest as he watched her pick up her rifle and walk back out to Matthieu.

She didn't even look back at him, as Matthieu escorted her up the stairs. Every bone in his body itched to summon his wraiths and to watch them devour Matthieu's soul. It would be unbearably satisfying to watch him fall in an empty husk before his body disappeared, erased by the fingers of time. But then he thought of the horror that would fill Élisabeth's eyes. Kai was right she would never forgive him for it; she could barely handle it when he discharged him.

He had to find a way to win her over without killing his opponent.

Chapter Thirty

He'd stolen her book. *Again.*

Élisabeth knew it was him, because who else would steal a children's fairy-tale book except the biggest child she knew—Séverin Moreau. She'd also questioned Colette in case it'd been misplaced while cleaning, but she hadn't seen it either. It was clear to see this was another attempt of Séverin's to lure her like a carrot to a horse and force her to speak to him, after she had made it a point to avoid him for several days.

Élisabeth slipped into his bedroom through the connected bathing room doors. It was empty thankfully. The silk bedsheets crisp and tidy. A quick search of the books on his shelf and bedside table, proved unfruitful. She slid her hand beneath his pillows feeling the worn edges of a book spine. A victorious smile painted her face at the sight of her book.

She was just about to leave when she spotted the gilt edge of a frame, peeking like the moon slinking between the clouds. There was a curtain behind his bed, and she had assumed there was a window there, but when she pulled back the damask fabric, she realized that there was a mirror. The edges were covered in dust, except the corner where she could just about make out the shadow of his fingertips, smearing the dust and leaving behind his imprint. Slowly, she curled her fingers around that edge, and drew back the mirror.

Élisabeth reached for the nearby candelabra and plunged into the dark. She entered an old storage room. There were boxes of papers, and when she reached for the top sheet, she realized it was musical notations written in his plain handwriting.

Her footsteps paused at the sight of the painting that hung in the unlit room like a cursed secret.

Her head tilted as she studied the eerie brushstrokes. It was a painting of a shadow-cloaked stage with a single dawn-bright light flashing on a dancer. It wasn't hard to guess whose brown hair and slender frame the dancer was supposed to be. Even though her face was cast away towards the shadows, half submerged in the dark, Élisabeth knew it was her, just as she knew that Séverin had painted this. It felt like him, like madness and obsession and wolf-teeth and corruption.

The paint was smeared across the canvas like it had been done in a mad frenzy. It bled with a strange, oily nature and she could feel that moldy tether that tied her to her villain, her Phantom, her cruel beast, who awakened under the evidence of his hunger, of his wretched mortal need. For all his insults and cruelty, it was an odd truth to know that he stared at her in the dark. She wondered what he felt when he looked at this. She wondered if he hated himself half as much as she hated him.

Her skin flushed with a mixture of awe and anger and something unnamed that curled in her belly like a kernel. One that told her to accept his decaying affection and attempt to nurture it into something bright and plentiful.

Somehow, Élisabeth found it in herself to walk away, to seal back the mirror and soft curtains, and erase the doomed, haunting painting of herself, shoving it deep in the neglected corners of her mind, and sealing it with the same invisible walls he had used to shut her out.

Élisabeth had been brushing her cheeks with powder when she caught the reflection of a shadow in her oval mirror. A startled gasp escaped her until she realized it was Séverin who leaned against her canopy, watching her with rapt attention. It did not surprise her that he did not knock nor announce his presence. His glass-blue eyes were locked on her as if she were performing a most fascinating task.

For some odd reason she had foolishly thought he was respecting her wishes to stay away from her, but it was clear to see that he had no intention of maintaining the carefully carved boundaries she had established.

She thought of that day on the balcony, the cold stone wall behind her and Séverin in front of her. Élisabeth could still feel his dark gaze as he stared at her hungrily. Like a depraved beast who would pounce at any moment.

"Do you ever knock?" she asked.

"Not on doors that I own," he replied.

It was almost dinner time which she'd been having with Clarise and Inès the past few nights. Usually after she'd meet Matthieu in the ballroom and dance for him while he played an off-tune beat. He was a terrible pianist, the music often clunky and awkward, but she was dancing again which was all that mattered, and he was an enthusiastic audience-member.

"I'll be going to a gambling den tonight to speak with some of my spies," he said. "I'll need you there in case Laurent shows his face."

She had opened her mouth initially to cut him off with a quick refusal, but if there was a chance to catch Laurent tonight, it would be foolish to sit by and let the opportunity pass them. Things were getting worse, the Blight was closer to the palace, looming like an impending thunderstorm.

"I've never been to a gambling den before," she said. "I don't know how to play cards."

The tension in his shoulders faded as if he had thought she would refuse him.

"I can teach you a trick or two," he said. "Also, you will need this."

He pulled a velvet box and handed it silently to her.

She found a beautiful glossy white masque with two silver feathers tucked into the end. And beneath it was a heavy diamond choker that looked like a...

"It is safer for you to be seen as my thrall," he said. "Just until we return."

Even though she had a strong urge to refuse it, to simply stay behind, she had a duty to fulfill this realm, to her mother, to herself. So, she grabbed the unappealing gift from his hand. Leave it to Séverin to give her an utterly offensive present.

"At least it doesn't look like a shackle," she mumbled. "I'll pretend it is a necklace."

"I won't be going as the Lord of the Below," Séverin said. "Discretion is key. I don't want Laurent to know that I am asking about him on the streets, it might force him to go deeper underground, so you must not speak my name or call me 'my lord'."

Élisabeth chuckled. "When have *I* ever called you *that?*"

As if she would ever call him by his title. He was far too arrogant as it was.

"I forgot who I was speaking with," he said dryly.

Élisabeth snickered again, feeling some of the tension fade.

So, long as they maintained this rude banter and didn't slip into unchartered waters, she was fine with going along.

"Will Kai join us?" she asked hopefully.

"No," Séverin said, with an unreadable look. "I am afraid not."

"What about—"

"No," he snapped. "Matthieu is not coming."

Élisabeth had the good sense not to push, sensing that he was already on edge. A beat passed before his shoulders loosened and the awkwardness receded.

Séverin reached for the diamond choker, plucking it from the velvet bed where it nestled like a pearl tucked in an ivory seashell.

"May I?"

Élisabeth lifted the thick mass of her hair, holding it above her neck as he slid behind her. Her heart plummeted to her belly, at the light sweep of his fingers along her skin, brushing aside stray strands of her hair. The weight of the choker settled around her throat like an oppressive hand. It was glimmering and cold. And perhaps even beautiful, despite what it represented.

"You could never be anyone's thrall, Lisbeth," he whispered. "You are a force of nature."

"Thank you."

A small chuckle escaped him. "Not a compliment."

Her lips tilted in a wide smile, because for once it *had* felt like a compliment.

And she could bet everything she owned that he had intended it as such.

But then her smile dropped, because this was Séverin, the same cold, indomitable, cruel Séverin who had ruined her life and continued to find new and creative ways to torment her.

She would not let him get under her skin tonight.

"We're just going to do business!" Élisabeth said defensively.

Inès lounged on her bed, resting on her stomach, feet kicking back and forth. Mouth pulled in a Cheshire grin.

"Then why does it matter what dress you wear?" Inès asked coyly.

"Did Kai say something?" Élisabeth asked. Kai made it no secret that he suspected something between her and Séverin. "Because there is nothing going on between Séverin and I. He insulted me just hours earlier and he has lied to me for *days*."

Even though she had lied about Matthieu and her, somehow Séverin lying about him and Marie-Odile was ten times worse.

"Yes, and you will insult him, and he will look at you like he wants to feast on you and lick your bones clean," Inès said. "I know how it goes, Lisbeth. And yes, Séverin said nobody is allowed to call you that but you don't mind, do you?"

"I don't mind," she said. "He shouldn't be claiming my name like it belongs to him."

Élisabeth's brows furrowed, unsurprised that he took something of hers and hoarded it like a dragon sitting over its trove. He was selfish and arrogant and mean, but also wild and passionate and intelligent. He reminded her of one of those turning devices her father had bought her where one looked upon a fragmented glass from a long column and when you twisted the cone, bright prismatic color burst in your vision. Crimson and indigo and yellow light flashing from the glass. Vivid and ever-changing. Séverin was a curiosity. A being of such vast contradictions that she knew she would need several lifetimes to peel away the many layers of who he was. It was a shame that she had no interest in ever finding out more.

Except for that lone day he had treated her to pastries and

dresses and the gift of his music. That Séverin she would have liked to understand.

"You have that look in your eyes," Inès teased.

"What look?"

"Like you're falling in love with him," she said almost gently.

Élisabeth laughed. A high-sprung nervous sound.

"That is ridiculous," she said.

"If you think so," Inès said. "You should go with the silver dress."

Élisabeth's eyes narrowed. "You're not going to try to prove that I am in love with him, as you say?"

"Would you like me to?" Inès asked. Her devious eyes sparkled with joy. She was having too much fun teasing her.

"I just want to know why you think that," Élisabeth said. "I certainly have not been singing his praises."

"Love does not mean that it has to be loud and ostentatious. Sometimes love is staring at someone from across the room in anger with tight fists, furrowed brows, and soft eyes. Sometimes love is marked simply by the way your eyes shift when they enter a room and how your body tilts towards them as if you are two stars, heading towards collision and expecting destruction, but instead creating a beautiful supernova. Burning and brilliant and ethereal. And even if you do destroy yourselves in the process, you made something definitive—something cosmic and divine."

Her chest was tight. "You see that when you look at us?"

"I do."

"I did not know you were a poet," Élisabeth said, attempting to lighten the mood. To erase the unease of her words. It was beautiful and fanciful, but their paths had been designed for them a long time ago. It had been decided by the Fates that they were to be enemies.

Élisabeth dressed, slowly and meticulously as she ensured not a strand of her hair was out of place as she weaved an elaborate coiffure set in place with a gold filigree comb inlaid with turquoise gems. She wore the silver dress Inès had chosen with a beautiful bodice stitched with beaded seed pearls. She frowned at the sight of her splint and then sighed because there was nothing to be done about it. It ruined all of her outfits.

"Ribbons!" Inès said.

"For my hair?" she asked.

"No, silly," she said. "Your arm."

Inès tied an ice-blue ribbon around her splint as if that would make it more appealing. Just as she tied the knot, a knock sounded. It could not have been Séverin because he would not knock.

She felt disappointment stir in her gut when Inès drew it open to reveal Kai. She had expected Séverin to escort her. He did sleep right next door after all. A small part of her had been under the assumption he wished to make amends for his unruly behavior the past few days.

Élisabeth rarely felt the sensation of being overdressed, but now staring at the looking glass, she wondered if perhaps she was tonight. She held her small, bejeweled reticule with her masque tucked inside and stared at her reflection. Her brown hair flowed down her back, shining like the crisp ends of an autumn leaf. Her cheekbones were painted with powder and her lips were lined with a rosy lip paint. She looked alluring and sensual with the bodice of her dress drawn low. The dress she picked did not possess sleeves and she had a lily-white cloak covered in rabbit fur perched on the foot of her bed.

"I thought you were both going to a gambling den?" Kai asked, with a raised brow.

"We are," she said.

"Then why do you look like you're dressed for a ball?" Kai pressed.

"Stop hounding her," Inès said. "And if you must know, Séverin is courting her just like you said."

"Inès!" Élisabeth cried. "That beast wouldn't know how to court a woman if his life depended on it."

"Sorry," she said sheepishly. "I just don't know why it's a big secret."

"I'm not courting anyone," a deep, annoyed voice said.

Séverin stood by Kai. Hands folded neatly in his pocket. She felt her racing heart soften to a dull rhythm when she realized what he'd said. He was right, they were not courting but somehow his words still stung. She didn't know why she put stock in them anymore or cared for that matter. It was like a loose thread hanging from her dress, that she did not possess the scissors to cut, but still she picked at it in a futile attempt to rid herself of it.

His raven hair was slick with pomade, that one gentle lock falling into his eye like a tortured poet. He wore his usual black dinner shirt, waistcoat and trousers. Even with little frill, he was so darkly handsome and captivating it was almost impossible to draw her gaze away from him. His wolfish eyes roved her body. His hand escaped his pocket, and he rubbed his jaw, in that manner he did whenever he was mincing his words. Most often when she got on his nerves. But she hadn't done anything to irritate him. Not yet at least.

"Well, let us go then," Séverin said.

"Shall we wait up for you both to return?" Kai asked teasingly.

He was rewarded with a dark look from Séverin. It was a testament to their friendship that Kai's smile only widened instead of cowering from his friend's black temper.

Élisabeth passed Inès, squeezing her hand good-bye. And

then she was walking down the hallway several paces behind Séverin. It wasn't until they reached the ground floor that he spun around, forcing her to collide into him. Élisabeth braced her fingers on his hips to steady herself.

"You look..." he paused, swallowing heavily. And then his eyes sank down her body, slowly and leisurely with an almost carnal hunger. Her heart thudded, frantically like the wings of a hummingbird. "Did I not say we were going to be discreet?"

"I am discreet," she said. "I brought my masque."

"Nothing about *this* is discreet," he said, waving a hand along her form. "It is the exact opposite."

"Are you upset?" she asked.

"No," he said. Then he cursed loud and harsh. "I cannot think straight, Lisbeth. It is as though there is a cloud upon my mind and every thought flutters away as quickly as it lands. I am constantly caught in a shifting darkness and all I can see and smell and hear is *you*. As if you are the doomed torch sent by some dark deity to guide me to my demise."

Her lips pulled into a wide smile. "Why Séverin, you could have simply said I looked beautiful."

"I am telling you that you are an infection!" Séverin said, frustrated. He wiped a tormented hand down his face. "That you are eating away at me like rot. You are trapped beneath my ribs like a thorn I cannot pluck, enclosed by walls that I cannot shatter. As if you have built a shrine in my flesh. I am saying that you are my worst vice, my most crippling desire, my decaying madness. Do you still think it is a compliment?"

Her smile grew bigger, and she could see him visibly give up with the sigh that escaped him.

"I like knowing that I have cost you sleepless nights. It warms my heart," she said. "It brings me joy to know that I am your worst obsession."

"You are my *only* obsession," he said. "Everything else has been but a drop in the ocean compared to what you do to me. Nothing has consumed me like you do."

His words should have frightened her, but it did the opposite. To her surprise, Élisabeth found that she was delighted by his tortured words.

It was odd that Séverin saying that she was his obsession and that she was eating away at him like rot made her heart twist far more than any beautiful, poetic love declaration garlanded with rose-tinted verses ever would. It was the same sensation she had felt when she looked upon that painting hidden in his lair. Like their souls were mirror reflections of each other's. A tapestry woven with their shared desire and despair and longing, hanging on the walls of a crumbling house.

Maybe they were both wrong and twisted and full of darkness.

Maybe they were nothing but two monsters drawn to the wickedness of the other.

Élisabeth had to be careful that he did not drown her in his sea of shadows, pulling her deep into the abyss.

Chapter Thirty-One

The gambling den was a cloistered space filled with rough-barrel men and fancy women in sequined bodices. Servants in trousers and white-sleeved blouses, drifted along the floor, serving drinks to the women who sat licentiously upon the laps of the patrons. Élisabeth felt Séverin's hand slip into her palm. His fingers were firm and protective as he pulled her behind him. They caught a few stray glances or rather she did. Men looked at her with corrupt eyes and she heard a warning rumble strike Séverin's chest as if he were part animal and then those gazes dropped as swiftly as they arose.

The gray halo of aether clouded the air like fog, erupting from the pipes cushioned between the lips of the patrons. It was a den of darkness and sin. And the deeper they traveled through the ground floor, the darker the lights grew, pulling them into a mass of shadows.

Séverin slid a few coins to the man at the base of the steps and he unraveled the velvet curtains leading them up a dim staircase. One of the guards knocked twice on a door before they were led into an office.

A young man sat before them with a shock of red hair and milky skin. He had fox-like eyes. Clever and striking.

He stood up at the sight of Séverin and bowed deeply.

"My lord," he said. "Wasn't expecting you so early."

Élisabeth stared at Séverin. She thought they were in disguise to trick everyone.

"Florent runs the Second Quarter," Séverin whispered to her. "The disguise is more so for the rest of the city. I don't need word reaching *him*."

"Who is your lovely companion?" Florent asked.

"None of your business," Séverin said. His words were as sharp as knives.

There was a single chair before Florent, and she was surprised when Séverin pulled it for her to sit.

"Didn't take you for a gentleman," she whispered to him. She felt his fingers settle on her shoulders.

"Don't get used to it," he said.

A soft laugh escaped her. It took her a moment to realize that Florent was looking at them as if he noticed something utterly fascinating.

"Shall I ask my men to fetch you a chair?" he asked.

"No need," Séverin said. "Won't be here long."

"I know your men are hunting the streets tracking Laurent. The reward has also incentivized others. As you know my spies are in the mix of it," Florent said. "I have a girl working in Madame Yvette's brothel and she said that he visited there yesterday."

"Didn't take him for one to seek out pleasure," Séverin mused. "Why wasn't this information shared earlier?"

"The girl couldn't leave before her shift ended," he said. "Yvette has a tight leash on those girls."

"Do you think he's working with Yvette?" Séverin asked.

"Could be," Florent said. "Yvette's a snake."

Séverin nodded in agreement. His fingers were gently stroking her bare shoulder as he spoke. His harsh words a contrast to his touch. She wondered if he even knew he was doing that. Élisabeth should have brushed his hand off, but she didn't want to make a scene. And it *did* feel nice, not that she'd ever admit it.

"I'll pay a visit to Yvette tomorrow," he said.

"Good idea," Florent said. "You don't want to parade that one before her." He jutted his chin at Élisabeth. "She'll try to buy your thrall from you. Maybe even sell you one of hers in exchange for her."

Florent's eyes grazed over her in interest and Élisabeth leaned away from him, falling deeper into Séverin's hands.

As if Séverin's cold silence was not answer enough, Florent asked. "*Are* you open to selling?"

"Never," Séverin snapped. "And I'll feed you to my wraiths if you *ever* ask me that again."

Florent raised both palms.

"Just a question," he said. "She is rather exquisite."

"She is sitting right here," Élisabeth said with an indignant sniff of her nose. "Do not speak of me as if I am not here."

"My apologies, my lady," Florent said, pulling on a charming smile. "I did not mean any offense."

"I'll be in touch," Séverin said, offering her his hand to rise.

He spoke the words less as a promise and more as a threat. The words were a mere gnash between his teeth.

"He was pleasant," Élisabeth said, sarcasm dripping from her tone the moment they stepped outside. "Where did you meet him?"

"Florent is a smug bastard. If I didn't have the Graylands

fracturing before me, I'd have him spend a week in my prison chamber while I carved out his tongue for the disrespect."

Élisabeth shivered. "He apologized."

"He should not have uttered the words to begin with."

"I didn't know you cared so much, Séverin," she teased.

He ignored her, walking towards the door.

"I want to play a game of cards," she said.

"Not in the mood," he mumbled.

"You promised!"

"Fine," he said. The word ripped out from him as if he were being tortured. "Where would you like to start?"

Élisabeth tapped her chin, staring at all the tables and eyed one that did not seem particularly complicated. It was the sort of games she would expect to be played in one of those elite gentlemen's clubs in Prasin that the noble men spent far too many hours at. Some of the tables involved complex chips and bartering pieces. But the one that caught her eye looked like a good old fashioned card game.

"It may look simple, but Three-Fold is one of the riskiest games. The price grows steeper with each round," Séverin said. "You have a chance to either make or lose a fortune."

Élisabeth patted his chest. "It is a good thing you are rich, so we won't have to worry about the latter."

Séverin mumbled under his breath about the headache of dealing with an infuriating *and* expensive woman before he led her to the round table.

The card dealer sat at the head. His eyes grew bright at the sight of her expensive gown and the thick diamonds that encircled her collar. While Séverin had been discreet with his dressing style, Élisabeth looked like a walking coin purse.

"Will you partner up or play alone?" the dealer asked.

"Al—"

"Partner," Séverin said. "At least for the first round."

Élisabeth frowned. "But I want to win against you *and* make you a pauper."

"Not going to happen but fine." Séverin sighed. "Deal us both in."

There were three other people at the table. Two men and a woman wearing an exquisite vermillion gown.

Élisabeth listened as Séverin told her the rules. Each round you betted something and played the game. At the end of the round, one person would be at the lowest rung and would be given the choice to either forfeit or continue. If you continued you would have to double your bet, and if you lost you forfeited your initial bet. The person that would win was the one to make it to the third and final round.

The game began and Élisabeth was doing poorly while Séverin took the lead. It made her regret her confident words and from the slight smirk that curled his lips, he *knew* it too, which made it all the worse.

The card dealer kept tossing odd glances at Séverin as if he suspected him of cheating.

"Are you cheating?" she whispered.

"They like to give the win to repeat customers and keep them coming back for more so naturally he's suspicious," Séverin said. "I can make out everyone's tell."

"What's mine?"

Séverin just smirked again, ignoring her question.

Élisabeth lost the first round and the second. And not so shockingly the third.

"I hate this game!" she said, tossing her horrid cards on the table.

The players reluctantly tossed several coin pouches and a gleaming gold timepiece on the table. Séverin eyed her expectantly.

"How will you pay me?" Séverin asked.

His eyes were bright with glee.

"Don't be silly," she said. "I don't have a coin to my name. Not in the Graylands at least."

"There are other ways of making your payment," he said, eyes drifting to her mouth. "I am rather accommodating."

Her skin flushed, and she found herself unable to form a proper rebuttal to *that* proposition.

He laughed, collecting his winnings, and stuffed some of the pouches in her reticule and the rest in his pocket.

"Come on," he said. "I heard there is a parade tonight."

They slipped out the back door and Séverin held her hand as they poured out into the street, falling into the stream of bodies like a river breaking into a lake. The wind slapped their cheeks as they lost themselves in the swarm of masque-covered bodies. She inhaled the smell of perfume and fried street food and that burning tint of aether. Small, glowing cigars were tucked between desperate mouths. From the gleaming silver end, she knew that it was aether they ingested.

All around them, the drums of the performers beat in staccato with her racing heart. The passersby were tangled like rope, arms draped around necks and fingers perusing their partner's body, while greedy mouths explored exposed collarbones. The air was rich with drunk revelry and a woman sang on the street corner. Her ringing voice scraped the sky as bronze light glowed down on her from the street lamps.

Élisabeth grabbed Séverin's hand and pulled him into a spontaneous dance. It was foolish to do so, considering she'd told him to leave her alone only a few days ago, but it was impossible to resist the urge to join the merriment, and she would simply remind him of their boundaries once they returned to the palace.

Séverin's eyes widened, but his limbs moved with a fluid grace like he had grown up in a ballroom. His steps were confident and assured. Even though they spun in a dirty street corner and the music was a mere whisper in the raucous air, as though they were the only people in the world.

Séverin led her with grace, and she wanted to ask him how he was such an accomplished dancer, but it was far too loud for her voice to carry. To speak her words to him she'd have to lean in and whisper in his ear, and the gesture was far too intimate for her, which was ridiculous considering that their bodies were sealed together.

His gaze was locked on hers. And she felt her heart beat wildly and frantically. She felt the dig of his fingers that lay flat on her waist, gripping her with a desperation that was matched by his eyes. He opened his mouth to say something, but by now she knew him far too well to know this was when he fled from her, so it was Élisabeth who drew away first.

"Look, sweets!" she called joyously, heading in the direction of the rich scents.

Séverin followed her, a hint of disappointment in his eyes.

There was a cart filled with all sorts of delicacies. She plucked out several coins from Séverin's winnings and purchased as many as she could carry.

"Matthieu will like—"

The words melted in her throat at the darkness that bled in his eyes. And she quickly swallowed the words. She had wanted to pack Matthieu some. He was the only person who enjoyed sweets like she did, but from Séverin's expression he was not pleased by the gesture.

Élisabeth sat on a bench, nervously chewing on the caramelized crust of her custard.

She had spoiled the mood. She could tell by Séverin's stiff shoulders and unreadable gaze that he was no longer enjoying himself.

"I didn't mean it like that," she muttered.

"And how did you mean it?" he demanded. "First you kiss him, then you spend every hour of the day with him, and then you pack him sweets. What am I to think?"

"He's just a friend," she said. "Like Kai."

"Kai likes Inès and Matthieu likes *you*."

Even if he did, Matthieu knew she was leaving, that there was no point in them starting anything. Matthieu was exactly the type of boy she wanted to be with. Someone with whom she could build something genuine and long-lasting. He was kind and funny and very pretty. And if it were not for the realms that separated them, she would consider letting him court her. She was done picking the wrong boy and suffering for her choices. How many more times would she follow her heart only for it to be ripped mercilessly from her chest by the cruel recipient of her desires.

"Why does it even matter? Would it be more acceptable for you if it was Kai who liked me? Why do you think so poorly of Matthieu? He's funny and he's kind."

Séverin's jaw tightened, and she could feel him growing more agitated with each word.

"It's late," he said coldly. "We should head home."

"No," she said stubbornly. "You go ahead. I'm going to sit here and finish my sweets."

Séverin grabbed her wrist, shocking her when he pulled her upright. He dragged her to a nearby ally. It wasn't the path back to where Ebony had been tied, and she opened her mouth to say as much.

The breath caught in her throat when he shoved her against the wall. His firm, lean body pressed against hers. His pale eyes, were intense and unrelenting as they searched her face as if he would discover all her secrets if he simply stared into her soul. His face was a pale scythe in the shadows.

"Who do you want, Lisbeth?" he asked. No, he *demanded*.

She swallowed the words back like they were a mouthful of fire and her throat remained dry with ash.

His thick lashes swept his cheekbones like a quill on parchment, beautiful and flowery. She could feel the frosty taste of his breath, feel the cold of his death caress her in a frightful embrace. His eyes darkened with desire, and she felt him tilt forward, his chest sealed against hers. His still empty chest, drawing her thundering heart beat into his cavern of still bones.

"I hate you so much." His words were cloaked in venom and anger.

But then she felt him lean forward, as if he were being controlled by a pair of invisible hands. As if everything that occurred from this moment forth was inevitable. Maybe they were always meant to be drawn to each other, to hate each other, to destroy each other, to desire each other.

Élisabeth pressed her palm to his chest, halting his advance. Her heart raced at the next words she spoke.

"I want you to beg me," she whispered.

Her breath escaped her in a sharp, fleeting gust like dandelions caught on the wind, as she watched his mouth press into a firm line. That one singular vein ticking miserably in his jaw. His eyes flared with rage. After all he had made her suffer, it was the least of what she deserved.

"No," he snarled.

"Then you can't have me," she said. Her hand fell limply to her side.

"Is this a game to you?" he pressed.

"No," she said. "But you made me beg you when I first arrived, you mistreated me as your mad heart desired, you tied me up every night and stood over me, as I pleaded with you to release me. And now you cannot bring yourself to beg *me?*"

Séverin stood there. Hands clenching and unclenching by his side. Mouth locked in a grim line.

"Fine," Élisabeth said bitterly. "You clearly do not want me as much as you pretend you do."

He was poison. One that was choking her out and infecting her bloodstream. Nothing pure and worthwhile could ever blossom from rotten earth and that was what Séverin was, he was inhabitable. He would *never* sacrifice his pride for her. It went against the very fibers of his being, and she was foolish to expect otherwise. He had hated her from the moment he saw her and though that hate wavered, it did not dim. The turmoil in his eyes and the click of his gnashing teeth were proof of that.

She realized then how stupid she'd been to lower her guard, to even entertain the idea of losing herself in him. For so long she had wanted someone to call her *theirs*. Someone to dance with her in wet glades and sing to her in the dark. Someone who would choose her and not her half-sister or some other girl, but *her*: Élisabeth. Because their heart longed for her. She had wanted a love so consuming it became the work of poems and ballads. A love written in the stars.

She did not want a boy who retreated from her anytime things got intense. A boy afraid of the breadth of his emotions. A boy who trembled at the thought of *feeling*.

Élisabeth brushed past him, unable to be in his presence any longer.

He caught her wrist. Long, fingers curling around her skin. Cold and possessive.

"*Please*," he said. The words were a silent prayer. It drifted by her ear like the sweetest hymn, and she closed her eyes, absorbing his surrender. "I am yours to command, Lisbeth. I am yours to serve."

Her eyes fluttered closed, but she did not turn around.

Not yet.

"Please, my sweet monster, my most wretched, beautiful

nightmare. Let me drown in you," he breathed. His mouth grazed her ear, and she could feel his lithe body behind her. Wired and prepared to strike, like a looming panther. "I want your siren song to pull me to a watery grave. I want you to fill my lungs. I want you to *destroy* me and to leave me in ruins. And I want to do the same to you."

He spun her around, forcing her to stare at his eyes. Half yearning, half hopeful, half despairing. Her fingers slipped into his luscious hair, as gentle as a hummingbird. He had always been so forbidden, so out of reach, so terribly wrong for her. But at that moment she could not think of a single reason to stop.

Just as she leaned on her toes, she heard glass shattering and they split apart to stare at a drunk man who stumbled into the alley.

"Get out of my house," the man roared.

Séverin was so angry she thought he would kill him, and she grabbed his wrist when he took a menacing step forward. Aether slipped from his finger like weeping water.

"We'll leave you to it," she said, nodding at the strange man. "Lovely home."

She felt a strange sense of sadness that the bench they had sat on had been overtaken by strangers and her box of sweets was nowhere to be seen. Matthieu would not be getting his gift it seemed, and it didn't seem wise to mention picking up some replacements.

They had to retrace their path back to the gambling den to retrieve Ebony. The air felt charged, and she was terribly aware of his palm resting on the small of her back as he guided her through the crowd.

Every time he touched her, she felt that hunger twist her stomach. She could feel the memory of his mouth hovering over hers, dancing mere inches apart. Her skin thrummed when he lifted her onto Ebony and climbed on behind her. He lay the flat of his palm on her stomach as he guided the reins with his left hand.

It felt like hours passed as they rode home, but that was likely because she was aware of Séverin behind her. In a manner she had never felt before. It was as if all her senses were honed in on him.

"When will you finish your notations?" Séverin asked, filling the silence. "I abhor lazy workers."

"I didn't know I was getting paid."

"Maybe do some work and I will consider it," he said.

"Fates, you are insufferable," she said with a shake of her head.

"Insufferably desirable," he said. "You're trembling from my touch alone."

"Because you are cold!"

"Admit it, you simply can't control yourself around me."

Élisabeth turned to glare at him. His mouth was curled upwards.

"Who will you torment when I'm gone, tyrant?" she said.

His smile dropped, and he shrugged.

"Maybe you'll stay," he said.

Élisabeth laughed, the sound fading to a whisper when he didn't join her. Her brows raised in surprise.

"Why would you want me to stay?" she asked. "You hate me."

"Inès and Kai will be upset," he said. Not denying that he hated her. "And I don't want to deal with their whining when you leave."

"I'll miss them," she said. "But I miss my father and my career awaits me."

"You can perform here," Séverin said.

Why did it sound like he was convincing her to stay?

"Because that night you promised I could dance went so splendidly." She laughed bitterly.

"You provoked me!"

"You deserved it."

"You can visit him," Séverin said, going back to their conversation. "Your father that is."

"I can't stay, Séverin," she whispered. "I refuse to be a pawn on your board. To be manipulated as you please."

Séverin was silent, unable to deny that he'd been utterly wretched to her. Even if he had begged her to kiss him, he hadn't apologized for his actions. And she didn't know if he ever would.

The palace's thin spires cut through the clouds like a blade, and the hallway was dark when they entered. Lit candles rested on the lining of the wall, casting flickering shadows against the floral wallpaper. She climbed the stairs with Séverin close behind her, the heavy weight of his palm on her back, guiding her forward. Even though there was no crowd to navigate he still led her as if he refused to break contact.

In the dark, they could bury all the cruel and terrible things they had said to each other in the damp corners of their heart as if the gentle stroke of his thumb that sat layered above the fabric of her clothes could soothe the burn of their mutual hatred.

Séverin led her to her bedroom, from his consuming gaze it was clear to see he had no intention of sleeping. He cracked the door open, and Élisabeth startled at the sight of Inès laying on her bed with a book in hand.

"Élisabeth!" she said. "I stayed up waiting to hear—*oh*, Séverin what are you doing here?"

Séverin released her so abruptly she stumbled. She had almost forgotten that she was leaning back, letting him support her weight. Élisabeth awkwardly took several steps away from him, clearing her throat loudly.

She could feel the burning trail of a blush slither up her neck.

"Nothing," Séverin mumbled. "Just escorting her to bed."

And then a wicked gleam crossed his eye. "You forgot your comb in my bedroom, will you come retrieve it?"

"Her comb?" Inès asked incredulously, staring at the comb on her dresser.

Séverin grabbed Élisabeth's wrist pulling her outside before Inès could ask another question.

"I can't wait another second to kiss you," he said breathlessly. His words made her stomach tighten. Desire swarmed like a hive of bees in his eyes.

He pulled her into his bedroom, the door slamming shut behind them. His hands clutched hers like she was his lifeline.

Their hands dropped abruptly at the sight of Kai and Matthieu lounging in the seating area. Kai had a wine bottle in his hand while Matthieu held out his glass, waiting for him to pour.

"Séverin," Kai said. "We came to have drinks with you. Matthieu's brilliant idea. Something about getting shite-faced before the Graylands unravels."

"Élisabeth what are you doing here?" Kai asked, amused. "Were you two holding hands?"

"No," they said in unison.

"You got some powdered sugar on your face," Matthieu said, pointing to her mouth.

Séverin shocked her by running his thumb along the corner of her mouth and then pulling his finger into his mouth and sucking it clean. His gaze was locked on Matthieu whose lighthearted smile dropped. They had a charged stare-down. And she saw something deadly flicker in Matthieu's eyes, and she wondered if she would have to tear them apart.

"Well..." Kai said, clapping loudly. "Drinks then? Will you and Inès join us?"

"No," she said. It didn't seem wise to stay behind with this odd tension between Matthieu and Séverin. Especially, since it seemed to revolve around her. "We'll have our own little celebration. Night then."

Séverin sighed.

It was clear to see they would not have a moment alone.

"Good night, Little Monster," Séverin said.

Chapter Thirty-Two

There was an earthquake that morning. The palace had rumbled like a starved beast and Séverin could feel the encroaching darkness. Everything that he had worried about was happening. He could feel it. Another Pit had opened and another. Now that he thought about it, all the Pits had opened in a linear line. Almost as if the world were Cleaving.

Something about it reminded him all too much of him and Laurent.

The only way to end it was for Laurent to die his Second Death.

He went to see Clarise before breakfast. Even though he had been tempted to seek out Élisabeth. After Kai and Matthieu left he had been itching to go see her, hoping that Inès had returned to her bedroom, but his eyes had been glazed from all the wine he had drunk. Séverin had been worried about what he'd say when the drink loosened his tongue. Of what dark confessions he would whisper to her like how hating her was the best thing he'd felt in a while. It had nearly broken him to plead with her last night as she demanded. For so long he had built a fortress around his heart, using the vicious bones of his ribs and his cruel tongue as his soldiers to protect the rotten organ. But Élisabeth Bellacourt had come wielding an anvil and he was powerless under her brutal touch.

"I know," Clarise said the moment he entered. "It is happening. We are near the end."

"We have been hunting him for days. After what he did to Élisabeth he went underground—he knew I would kill him, that *we* would kill him. Élisabeth and I," Séverin said. "He's afraid of us."

Clarise sat down. She had a heavy look on her face.

"You know Inès and I cannot see her fate."

"I am aware."

"I always thought that I could see your fate, but I realized that I could only see yours when it was related to someone else's. Your future was always tied to either Kai or Inès or the people at court, so it was easy to read," she said. "I realized now that I cannot see the course of a higher being. And Élisabeth is no mere mortal nor are you."

"But you said she would save us?" he asked. His eyes narrowed. "Was that a lie?"

"When she first came, and you were determined to kill her, I saw that her threads were tied to yours. Inès and I rarely look upon the threads of people. It is a part of being a seer, but not the part that is easy to unravel. Visions are straightforward and clear, but threads are complex. Some people have several threads. It often depicts a lifelong relationship with either a sibling, a parent, a friend, or a soulmate. It is intricate and causes us a great headache to attempt to understand the complexity of human attachments, so we block out that side of our gift. But I was so curious about her that day and when I looked upon your threads it was intertwined so tightly, only a Fate could sever it."

Séverin scoffed. "Élisabeth gives me a headache. I am afraid I shall lose a tooth when I'm around her. Nobody torments me quite like she does. We are *not* soulmates."

But even as he spoke those frigid words, he could feel his chest tighten, feel his body grow alert as if a wild animal loomed nearby.

"It does not change the fact that you belong to each other. I am certain that you will love her someday, Séverin," Clarise said. And then in a soft, motherly voice added. "Perhaps, you already do."

Séverin felt his dead heart stir. It was like the room was tilting, while everything was painfully upright. He did *not* love Élisabeth. That was impossible. It was ludicrous and fanciful and simply out of the question. He desired her. That much he would admit to himself. He had wanted her from the moment he'd seen her dancing in the Opera House and looked upon her bewitching face. A face made to bring men to their knees. He could not recall the last time someone had robbed him of his breath and stolen his most vital senses.

But love? Séverin was not capable of such a thing.

"Take care of her," Clarise advised. "She is tender-hearted."

"This is not the time to play matchmaker, Clarise," he said sternly. "What happens if we don't find Laurent in time?"

"I don't know Séverin," she said with a loose breath. "Perhaps, it is time to make peace with it. It is ending and there is nothing we can do to stop it."

Séverin cursed. He hated people who gave up. It was utterly pathetic, and he was the last person in the world who should be giving impassioned speeches to rile people up. How had he become the optimist?

The world must have truly been ending if he was their bright light at the end of the tunnel.

"Séverin," Kai said, entering the library. "The Quarter Masters have arrived for the monthly meeting. Yvette came along. I was rather clear this morning that attendance wasn't optional."

Kai had gone to Yvette's brothel early that morning to speak to her, but she'd been busy. Séverin's suspicion spiked. What if she was sheltering Laurent? It was the only lead they had since his trip to the city.

Séverin had summoned them to let them know the dire state of things. It was time to issue a mandatory curfew and enhance patrols. Street businesses would have to shut down until further notice. And he personally wanted to question Yvette.

"Make sure the gates are secure," he said to Kai. "Increase the guards at every station."

"Will do," Kai said. He paused for a second. His brown eyes filled with emotion. "And Séverin, whatever happens, I want you to know that you are truly my greatest fri—"

"No heartfelt goodbyes," Séverin said sharply. "The world does not end until I say it does."

Kai chuckled. "I shall say it regardless. You are my best friend and I know despite the snarling and foaming at the mouth I am yours."

"I do not foam at the mouth," Séverin said with a frown. "Élisabeth has been influencing you. And not for the better."

Kai chuckled.

"I'll see you shortly," Séverin said. "There is something I must do."

The world was burning to cinders and Séverin could not help but make a detour to Élisabeth Bellacourt's bedroom. It was as if she were poison, clouding his mind and filling him with a compulsive need to soak in her presence.

There was one last thing he had to do to fix this mess. Something that he should have done a long time ago.

He didn't knock and barrelled inside. The last thing he wanted was for her to accuse him of being a gentleman. Not after the mere thought had brought her to hysterics that night when he'd lost his mind over the kiss with Matthieu and pretended it was only about her reputation.

It does not change the fact you will love her someday, Séverin.

Perhaps, you already do.

He pushed Clarise's words to the corners of his mind. He tucked it so far back that it lay in the cobwebs with all the other things he was too afraid to assess.

Élisabeth sat by the window, staring wistfully outside. Her dark hair was unspooled falling down her body. She wore a yellow nightgown with a frilled collar. He stared at the edge of her beautiful face. At her small button nose and her smooth but firm jawline. She was so beautiful it hurt.

"Morning, Colette, I never heard your knoc—"

She turned to face him, and her spine instantly straightened.

"Séverin, I was just thinking of you," she said. Then her eyes widened, and her next words were a rush of slippery consonants. "Not good things."

"Bad things?" he purred.

"Yes," she said, clearly relieved that he was feeding into her lies.

Séverin walked towards her, enjoying the little shake in her shoulders when he hovered above her. Despite her sweet lies, she reacted to him, and he could admit—perhaps to himself— that he reacted to her as well.

"What kind of bad things?" he asked.

"I won't tell you," she said softly.

Her gaze was lost in his. Like a maiden caught in a labyrinth.

"Will you show me?" he whispered in his sweet voice. A voice that sounded like the whispers of the sea.

Élisabeth shocked him when she reached for his hand and lowered him to sit down beside her. Her movements were slow and gentle as if she were handling a wild mare. And he found himself conceding to someone else, letting her lead him, knowing that each moment he spent in her presence he was losing a piece of himself in return.

His palm was still in her hand. Their fingers were loosely intertwined. She didn't pull away and neither did he. The warmth of her hand made his skin tingle. It felt odd. It felt nice. It felt *right*.

His fingers tightened the slightest bit in case she thought to let go, but Élisabeth gripped him just as tight.

"I know why you are always upset about Matthieu," she said. "I was thinking about it last night and..."

"And?" he pressed.

Her eyes were downcast, almost as if she were shy. He lifted her chin with his other hand, staring into her brilliant steel eyes.

"I would not have liked it if someone was that familiar with you. I didn't like it when I thought you and Marie-Odile were intimate," Élisabeth said in one giant breath.

"It does hurt, Little Monster," Séverin said. "A *lot*."

The confession slipped past him before he could control it. And he realized then that he didn't want to hide it. The Graylands was unspooling like a blanket whose thread had been caught on a hook. If he was to lose everything, he could afford to bear his thoughts to her. Even if it was at the end of their story. He wanted her to be his last chapter. He would *always* want her to be his last chapter. Because she was the only end that he could ever accept.

"I want you to return home," he said. "There is a carriage outside that will take you to the lake. The ferryman has been summoned. His price was rather steep. He has never returned someone to the world of the living. But it is paid for, and it waits for you."

"What?" she whispered. "How am I to leave without seeing this through? I am needed to kill Laurent—"

"You are not," he said a bit sharply. "You are just a human girl."

It was a lie, but what use was she if they never found Laurent?

Her face dropped and his palm felt cold when she drew her hand away.

"I can call the sword," she said. "I am the only on—"

"We'll find another way."

"You don't have the time and you know it," she said. "You know nothing about who I am. The prophecy says—"

"I don't care about the damned prophecy," Séverin snarled. "It is too risky for you to remain here."

"I won't leave," she said stubbornly. "Not until I know my friends are safe. Anything could happen to Inès and Kai and Clarise."

He felt a strange crack in his heart when she didn't mention his name. But at least she did not add Matthieu's name. *That* would have destroyed him.

"I will take care of them," Séverin said. "You have my word."

"Your word," she said with a dry laugh. "As if I trust a word from your mouth. All you have done since I arrived is lie to me. All you do is deceive me and fill me with so much rage I don't know what to do with it. Sometimes I see someone that I would truly like to know, but you push me away the second I get too close. And you are pushing me away now because you are afraid. You are afraid because you want me."

"That is not true," he said.

Élisabeth stood up, she walked away from him, and he felt a clawing sensation in his chest. He took several large steps toward her.

"Lisbeth, don't walk away from me," Séverin said.

He had intended to sound stern, but he just sounded desperate.

With each step she took away from him he could feel that desperation rise. He had thought he was doing the right thing, sending her away to keep her safe. But a part of him wondered if this was because he was afraid of everything that he was feeling. He had always guarded the decaying scab that was his heart from outsiders. Girls were just pleasant distractions and nothing to lose himself over. Yet all his careful shields had crumbled to ashes because of this one, stubborn girl.

He caught her wrist and yanked her backward.

"What do you want me to say?" he asked hoarsely. "Do you want me to say that I think about you every hour of the day? That it is disgusting, and I can't stop? That you have crawled under my skin, and I can't tear you out, and it is not for lack of trying, because believe me when I say that I have tried. I do not know why I feel so much around you. I only know that everything makes sense when you are near me. Even when we're going at each other's throats, and you drive me to my wit's end there is nobody that I would rather be verbally sparring with than with you. You are unlike anyone I have ever met. You are so singularly unique I know that I will never come across someone like you in my lifetime. And Fates, help me but I want you, Lisbeth. All of you and not just the scraps that I am desperately clinging onto until you realize that I am unworthy of you. *I want you.*"

The words had broken from his mouth like a spell.

It did not feel like she was a few feet away, but that there were acres of land between them.

Her eyes were wide, and the silence was so drawn out it choked him. He could feel his fingers loosen and feel that emptiness in his chest expand till it was the size of an abyss. That cold voice inside his mind told him he was an idiot for confessing such a thing, that it would lead to nothing, but her scorn, and his ultimate humiliation.

"Séverin," she whispered. She hesitated for a split second, but it was enough for him to shatter. "I—"

He released her wrist. His shields rose, fortifying against what he knew would be a well-poised rejection.

"You don't have to say anything if you don't want to," he said, the words rushing past his lips. "Forget that I—"

"Shut up," she snapped. "Must you spoil everything?"

His eyes narrowed. But he knew better than to speak when she glared at him like that and tapped her small foot as if he were a disobedient child. He thought of how lucky he was to be the source of Élisabeth Bellacourt's ire. And then he thought of how far he had fallen if he was pleased that she was tearing into him and not some other man. So long as her anger belonged to him, he could handle anything else that came his way.

"You are the most infuriating man I have ever met. You are hot one minute and cold the next. But despite all of that I have found myself inexplicably drawn to you as well," Élisabeth said. "You are...Fates, there are not enough words to describe you."

"Is that a compliment or an insult?" he asked.

Élisabeth laughed and then her smile softened in a way that made his heart clench. He wished she could smile at him like that until the end of time. If the world burned to ashes around him, it would be bearable if only he had that smile focused on him. And him alone.

And then she surprised him when she said, "It *is* a compliment. You are so fascinating, Séverin. It would take me decades to understand you. I want to know everything about you. Even if it is small or inconsequential or forgettable, I want you to give it to me and I will cherish it."

It was the first time someone had said that they wanted to know more about him. He had always been closed off and aloof, and to many, he was simply just not interesting enough to understand. But Élisabeth cared. Élisabeth wanted to learn more.

"I want to know more about you too," he confessed.

He felt her finger graze his masque. "Can I see your face?"

He stiffened. He didn't show his full face to anyone. Not since the fire. He hadn't seen it in a while, but he remembered that it had not been a pretty sight when he'd seen it the first night after the Cleaving. The scars had followed him in death. Most injuries you sustained when you were alive trailed after you into the Graylands. There were people with missing limbs, eyes, and teeth. While injuries that occurred in the Graylands could heal on their own, the same did not apply to those you carried with you in death.

"It won't change anything," Élisabeth said softly. "I just want to see you. All of you."

"I don't know," he murmured. "You may run off screaming for the hills."

"Never," she said. "And if you think that then you must not know me at all."

Séverin felt his shoulders stiffen, as she raised on her toes. Fingers drifting by his masque.

"May I?" she whispered.

He inhaled her intoxicating scent of candied apples and flowers and sunlight. And he could not find it in him to resist her. It was inevitable. He wanted Élisabeth to see him. He wanted the satisfaction of knowing that she cared for every inch of him, even the ruined flesh that made his left cheek.

Slowly, he nodded.

And then the last of his defense against her fell, crumbling to ashes.

Chapter Thirty-Three

Élisabeth slowly removed his masque. Her heart tripped, not because she was afraid, but because this next moment would change everything. For so long Séverin had kept her at arm's length and she was afraid he would never be vulnerable. At least not with her. But now he stood before her his armor lowered, his heart held in his fist, and she could see the miserable organ that he hid so well. His heart reflected the ocean, dark and plundering and soundless.

His eyes were cloaked in fear, and she wanted to show him that she did not care about some scars. She never did.

His masque lowered and she could see the taut skin of his left side. It was raw and the lines of muscles were drawn in criss-crosses. His eyebrow on that side were thinner and not as thick. And his eye was lighter as well.

"Does this hurt?" she asked, drifting her finger down his cheek.

"No," he said. His voice was throaty and low. "It feels... nice."

"And this?"

She drifted her hand down his neck. The results of the burn were not so terrible here, but she could see the hint of flayed flesh. It saddened her that he had been hurt so terribly. She felt an odd need to soothe him. It took her a moment to realize that feeling was tenderness.

"No."

Élisabeth could feel herself swaying towards him. His eyes darkened, growing ripe with hunger and she nervously ran her tongue along her lip. His gaze was locked on her mouth and his hand slid behind her nape, thumb pressed just below her chin, tilting her head back for him.

"Tell me to stop," he said when his lips were a hair's breadth away from her.

"I want this," Élisabeth whispered. "I want you."

"I want you too," he said. "Desperately."

Except when he spoke the words, he had said them in Lupazi. The soft vowels dripped from his mouth like melted butter and her eyes widened.

"Wait, you speak Lupazi?" she asked.

His mouth pulled into a breath-taking smile that made her heart stutter.

"So, you understood me all the times I made fun of you?" she asked.

"Fortunately, no," he said. "I am only a beginner. A shame I couldn't hear what creative endearments you used to describe me."

"You really tested my patience," she said. "I couldn't resist bad-mouthing you."

"I know."

"When did you learn it?" Élisabeth asked.

"A better question I suppose is *why* did I learn it?" he said. "And the truth is I was jealous that you and Kai shared something as simple as a language. I wanted to know everything about you. To listen to every word you spoke. And I could not do that if I didn't understand your language."

His words melted the last of her doubt. Even though she knew that their future was unpredictable and so many questions flooded her mind. Would she return home when the threat was destroyed? Would she choose to remain here? Did she want to stay? Did she want to go?

But at this moment, all she cared about was *this*.

This desperate need to satiate the hunger inside her.

They were so close now. The only thing that separated them was their fractured breaths.

And then there were no more thoughts to ponder because Séverin, her greatest enemy, had kissed her.

Part Five

The Rebirth

Each realm stood atop each other like a ladder or perhaps, more accurately a deck of cards, and if one ever collapsed all the realms would fall to ruin.

An excerpt from *The History of the Realms* written by Southern Scholar, Magan Arale

Chapter Thirty-Four

It felt like he had waited an eternity to taste her. Séverin coiled his hand in her hair, tilting her neck back. He thought of all those times when the world had come to a grounding halt as he looked into her eyes, and how now the world spun around him rapidly at a neck-breaking speed and Séverin did not care anymore if the world was burning, and the realm was collapsing into the void. He would go into the darkness knowing that he had tasted divinity on her lips, and it would be enough. His hand fisted around his necklace around her throat, feeling the jagged wings of the crow dig into the heel of his palm.

Yours, yours, yours.

His mind chanted like a desperate prayer.

His mouth collided with hers, as his eyes sealed shut, and he drowned in the only thing he had ever truly believed in. Not even during his climb to power had he been this ravenous, this pleading, this aching. He would have given her anything in that moment if she had asked it of him. He would have marched to war for her. He would have painted the streets with the blood of those who displeased her. He would have done it all for the simple grace of feeling her hands on his cheek, and the warmth of her breath tickling his skin.

If he had known what it was like for her to look at him like this with tenderness and light and not anger and disgust, he would have not goaded her so much.

"I want you, Lisbeth," he whispered against her mouth. "I long and hunger and despair for you."

It wasn't enough. Somehow, there were not enough words to describe just how much he wanted her. He was not fluent in the language of savage need. How could he tell her that he would crawl inside her if she let him? That he would intertwine their souls and stitch them like silk if she gave him the chance. That he would never let her go, and would instead preserve her like artifacts in a museum, tucked deep in the hollows of his heart.

He kissed her, tasting her sweet mouth, tangling his hand in her luscious hair. He felt her fingers clutch the fabric of his shirt. Séverin stumbled forward, descending onto her bed, hips pinning her to the feather mattress. His mouth trailed the smooth skin of her jaw and collarbone.

"You're mine, Lisbeth," he breathed. "I burn for you. I ache for you. I feel like I am possessed half the time, my body controlled by a spirit I cannot expel. Only *you* are my haunting spirit. You are my captor, and to you alone, I will always surrender."

His mouth was on hers again, before she could respond. He was afraid of what she'd say. He was afraid that she would come to her senses if he gave her the chance. The power was in her hands, and he was nothing, but a starved wolf prepared to kneel at her feet if she demanded it of him.

"You should leave the Graylands," he tried again. "This is not your home. You should not be the one to die for it."

Élisabeth brushed that stray lock on his forehead back, watching in fascination as it fell back down.

"Home is not a place," she said. "It is the people around you that make it a home. And everyone I care about is here."

"Kai and Inès and Clarise, right?" he asked.

He purposefully left out Matthieu's name. So, long as he existed Matthieu would never worm his way into her heart.

In truth, he simply wanted her to acknowledge that she cared for him. That in the end he mattered to her in some small, inconsequential way. If this was the last mark he would leave as the Lord of the Below, if this was to be his chosen legacy, Séverin picked this. He picked Élisabeth Bellacourt staring at him with wide eyes the color of a blooming thunderstorm, lips soft and ripe from his kisses, telling him in her songbird-like voice that she cared.

"And you, Séverin," Élisabeth said.

He smiled and her fingers traced his mouth.

"I've never seen this smile before," she said, soft as a feather. "I like it."

Séverin made his way to the war room, feeling the absence of parting with Élisabeth. There was nothing that he wanted more than to lay on that bed kissing her all day until their lips were as bruised as apples fallen from an orchard, but he had to speak with the Quarter Masters, he had to advise them of the importance of finding Laurent. The fate of the Graylands depended on it. And he had to protect Élisabeth and the others. He felt a renewed vigor to keep the realm safe because Élisabeth wasn't leaving and he would not watch the world burn to ashes with her in it.

He thought of those nights sitting in Box Five, his form

nothing but a muddled shadow. The dead could not stand as they were in the mortal realm. The moment they crossed the river they were incorporeal. They were the truest definition of the term "ghosts".

He thought of that strange, clawing sensation in his chest while he sat in the box as if something inside him were desperate to meet her. Something consuming and writhing and panting. Something that reached for her even though they were separated by time and realms and their very existence. She lived and he was nothing but a faded memory.

He felt a trickle of guilt that he had drawn her into his decaying world. That he had plucked a butterfly from a vibrant garden and brought her to ruins. Someone so lifeless and void like him did not deserve someone so brilliant and alive.

The four Quarter Masters were sitting expectantly in a circle, waiting for his arrival. The servants had brought them wine. Kai usually joined him for these meetings, but his usual seat was empty. He was likely making preparations around the palace to handle the disruptions caused by the growing Blight which all signified that his world was growing bleaker by the minute.

"Our liege lord," they said, rising at once. They didn't sit down until Séverin had.

Madame Yvette was dressed like a performer with her feathered hat, obsidian corset, and deep purple skirt. Florent and Oratile sat opposing each other. They had never quite gotten along and even now they glared at each other. Arata, as usual, was silent and watchful.

"I am sure we are all well aware of the dire state of the Graylands," Séverin said.

"The earthquake this morning destroyed one of my brothels," Yvette said. "The building crumbled like dust. We are lucky that we do not sustain injuries and cannot die from a head wound or I would have lost half my staff. I'm sure I do not need to explain how difficult it was to subdue the panic."

"We all suffered," Florent said with a roll of his green eyes. "You are not the only one whose business was affected by this unfortunate event."

"As we understand the Graylands is in grave danger," Arata said.

Séverin took a sip of his wine, the drink slithering down his throat.

"And you have kept this danger hidden from us all," Yvette said.

"It was no secret," Séverin said. "I have—"

"Nonsense," Yvette snapped.

Séverin moved to sit upright. He was slouching but he could not recall doing so. His vision was blurry, and he knew then that something was terribly amiss.

"Laurent has given us answers," Yvette said, staring at him coldly. "We know now that you are the answer to ending this curse. Your end shall liberate us."

He blinked, struggling to move his tongue. It was heavy and thick in his mouth as if it had swelled.

"You are work..." Séverin couldn't finish his thought.

He tried to clench his fingers to summon his blade of aether, but his mind was fractured. They had poisoned him. It would not kill him, but it would weaken him. It would make him vulnerable. It would ensure that his magic was far from his reach.

"Yo...you...I will..." His words were growing more tangled and less coherent with each attempt at speech. "I will kill..."

And then there was only darkness.

Chapter Thirty-Five

Colette arrived a little after Séverin departed with her usual morning tea and a scone. Élisabeth didn't dine heavily in the morning. She and Louise had always stuck to a curated diet by their chef, a menu that had been designed by Pierre. Even a long way from home she could not shake off the habit. Séverin's chef made the most exquisite dishes, and it was easy to indulge.

She had begun to dance routinely. Mostly for her friends. It was strange to dance for anything other than glory and fame. For so long she had thought she wanted her name to be printed on flyers and for tickets to her show to sell out, but now that she was so far from home she wondered if she still wanted that. Had her dream changed? Or had distance and danger forced her to accept another life choice? One that relied on passion rather than ambition.

"Thank you, dear," Élisabeth said with a wide smile. "And before you ask, I am in a splendid mood. I wish to wear the ice blue dress today."

The one that matched Séverin's eyes. The one that matched that beautifully frightful painting of her.

She felt an odd giddiness that she could not explain ever since that kiss. It was nothing she'd ever felt before.

Colette smiled but then it fell abruptly, and she began rummaging through her armoire for her morning dress.

Élisabeth gingerly took a sip of the tea and sat down.

"Is something the matter, Colette?" she asked. "Do you have your notebook?"

Élisabeth had asked her to bring along a notebook so they could speak to each other more easily, but it seemed she had forgotten it today.

Élisabeth took another sip. Her head felt woozy, and she frowned when her fingers spasmed. The tea fell to the floor, splattering her ankles with a warm hiss. It should have hurt. It should have scalded her flesh, but she felt nothing.

Colette stood in the corner. A guilty look in her eyes.

Before Élisabeth could open her mouth and demand answers the world tilted around her.

And then there was nothing.

Élisabeth awoke to a pounding headache like someone had smashed her head against a wall. *Repeatedly.* Slowly, her eyes opened, blinking against the dim light.

She felt a burst of relief at the sight of the young man before her until she noticed his empty stare. Dread crawled down her throat, settling at the pit of her stomach.

Perhaps later she would ponder as to why the thought of Séverin's presence made her feel as though a weight had been lifted from her chest, and how quickly he had filled her with a sense of safety. Even at his worst, he had protected her in his own confusing ways.

"Hi, Élisabeth," he said.

"Laurent," she whispered. "What are you doing here?"

She tried to move but her hands were knotted so tightly that her flesh dragged against itself painfully, and white-hot pain shot down her injured arm. He had undone her cast to tie her hands behind her back and a whimper escaped her.

She was locked in a moving carriage. The blinds had been drawn so she did not know where they were headed, but she knew if Laurent was guiding her, it could not be anywhere good.

"How did you know it was me?" Laurent asked curiously.

He wore a masque similar to Séverin's, but Séverin would *never* call her Élisabeth. She was always Lisbeth or "Little Monster" but never Élisabeth.

"I know him better than anyone," Élisabeth said.

And then another spasm of pain trailed from her wrist to her shoulder and she hissed. "It hurts."

"I know," he replied. "But it is the only way I can ensure that you don't use your magic. Pain prevents you from focusing which lessens your ability to control your magic."

"You're a bastard, you know?"

"I haven't stopped thinking about what you told me," Laurent said, ignoring her comment. Another thing that Séverin would never do; he couldn't help but react to her slights.

She regretted confessing the truth to him. It was her greatest mistake.

"I met with Gaspar and learned what he overheard from Inès about the Fourth King and his Fate. Gaspar also stumbled upon *The Book of Echoes* when you all left," he said. "I know the truth. All of it."

"I already told you everything," she said. "What more could you know?"

His lips curled in a cold smile. "I will save my truth for the *both* of you."

She didn't know what truths he wished to share, but it could not be good. She hadn't told Séverin about who she was and Élisabeth worried that it would ruin their fragile truce. Trust had been the one thing that had constantly caused a rift between them.

She closed her eyes, trying to summon the Invisible Sword. To kill him before he could betray her again.

Matthieu had said it would come to her when she was ready and she was more than ready now, but all she felt was emptiness. No magic, no weapon, nothing. It remained elusive and out of her reach.

"Nice try," Laurent said. "But pain makes it impossible to focus, your sword shall remain far from your reach."

The carriage slowed at last. From the rocky shift of the wooden wheels, she knew they were crossing uneven ground, and were likely slinking deep into the Blighted woods. The door was drawn open and Élisabeth stared in horror at the state of the land. The Pit was no longer a Pit. It was a thin, gaping seam that seemed to be growing an inch with each passing minute, swallowing brambles, and snow into its maw like a giant, starved beast.

Séverin was tied to a tree. His head slumped forward. Beside him were two men who looked like paid hands. Their clothes were cheap and torn, and their faces were covered in soot. It always surprised her how the Graylands was like an inverted image of their world. There were the poor much like there were the wealthy. And from the hunger in these men's eyes, she knew *exactly* what side of the coin they fell on.

"Séverin!" she cried.

He stirred and blinked slowly.

"Lisbeth," he whispered.

She took a step forward to run to him, but Laurent simply caught the end of the rope that held her. The pressure shot a bolt of pain through her injured arm, and straight to her elbow and shoulder.

A cry of pain escaped her.

"Let go of her!" Séverin growled. His words were a mere rumble in his chest. "I swear if you hurt a hair on her head, you will regret it."

"Tie her up beside him," Laurent said.

"What did you do to me?" Séverin asked.

He was struggling to hold his head up.

"You were given two more doses of nightshade while you rested," Laurent said. "You can't call on your wraiths or fight us with aether. You have no choice but to listen to what I have to say."

"Leave Lisbeth out of it," he said. "Do whatever you want to me, but leave her alone."

"Élisabeth is the root of this disease," Laurent said, pointing his finger at the Pit. "She has been making a fool of us both. Did she tell you *exactly* who she is?"

Fear pooled in her stomach when Séverin looked at her, confused, and whatever he saw in her eyes made his shield rise.

"I shall take that as a no," Laurent said. "Her true name is Sabeth Fateborn, Daughter of Lune the Unbending."

Séverin stared at her with doubt in his eyes.

"You do not know the history of her," Laurent said. "You do not know your own past."

He looked at Séverin with a reverent look. Then surprised them both by bending down on a single knee.

"I did not know who we were, my lord," Laurent said. "Every time we are reborn, we forget our past lives. Gaspar and I have read every page of the First Scripture over the last few days and the entirety of *The Book of Echoes*. Once you read *The Book of Echoes* from start to finish it awakens all your dormant memories. It is why the book is so elusive. It is why it is so willful. It doesn't wish to aid us. Another trick crafted by the hands of the Fates."

"I thought I was the Fate," Séverin said, with narrowed eyes.

"*I* am the Fate," Laurent said. "You are the Endless."

Élisabeth's eyes widened. Séverin looked skeptical, but Laurent would never bend on one knee if he didn't believe it in its entirety. He stared at him with his martyred eyes carrying a devoutness that befitted a priest.

He was much like Séverin: prideful and high-handed. He would not submit if he did not believe it in every fiber of his being.

"It began at the Tribunal when you were declared guilty of plotting against the Kings. The Fates who did the bidding of Laos, Mòrge, and Pras wanted to control you, so they sent Sabeth under the guise of an offering from the Fates to your court to spy on you to prove to the Three Kings that it was time to unearth the Invisible Sword. That it was time to end you. She betrayed you and it was not the first time. She asked to be the Harbinger. To be the one assigned to the Invisible Sword. There can only be one bearer of the sword. And she chose to be the one to end you in every lifetime."

Her stomach churned when Séverin looked at her with betrayal in his eyes. It was clear to see Laurent's words had fit the puzzle in his mind, and fed into all the suspicions that had eaten away at him since the day she arrived.

He knew now the strange origin of her magic that resembled her mother's realm of the Graylands. Her suspicious control of the beasts. Her role as the bearer of the sword.

"Séverin," she whispered. "I don't believe him. I don't rem—"

"Just because you don't remember does not make it false," Laurent snapped. "You are the true enemy."

"We have to stick to our plan, Séverin," Élisabeth said. She did not believe a word from his mouth. "He is our enemy. Not I. Do you not see what he is doing? He is trying to come between us."

"You can break the curse, my lord," Laurent said. "You can regain your power."

"How?" Séverin asked.

"You cannot listen to him, Séverin," Élisabeth said desperately. "He's trying to manipulate you. I don't trust him."

"By killing me," Laurent answered. "They used me to imprison you because you molded me in your image, and I was the only one strong enough to contain you. A fragment of your soul is tied to mine. So, long as I live you will never be at full power. You will always be weak. The sword can only kill you through me, if I am struck you die. But if you unmake me and reclaim your soul you will be free. You cannot let the sword finish me. It must be you."

Her heart stopped. All this time she had thought Laurent was lying to Séverin for some ulterior motive, but when he stood up and unfastened Séverin's ties she wondered if he had spoken the truth. Just moments ago, she had felt like she was on top of the world. Everything had been bright and vibrant, and her chest had been near bursting at the thought of Séverin's words.

She would never forget how he had spoken to her in that breathless, ragged tone.

I want you, Lisbeth.

All of you and not just the scraps that I am desperately clinging onto until you realize that I am unworthy of you.

Élisabeth had felt safe knowing that in the end they had each other, and she was not painfully alone. Anything was better than being alone.

She looked into his eyes, but they were cold and empty. He looked at her as if she were a stranger.

It turned her veins to ice.

"Séverin," she whispered. "Will you release me?"

He ignored her and turned to Laurent.

Something hot and wet slid down her cheeks and it took her a moment to realize she was crying.

"You are certain this will work?" Séverin asked.

"There will be nothing to contain you if I die," Laurent said. "You will be free. I am your only weakness."

"How do I do it?" Séverin asked.

"A blast of power to the chest," Laurent said. "Only your power can free your soul. I hope that you know in the end that I was always loyal to you even if I haven't behaved accordingly in the last few years. I was not aware of our history, but I am your servant now and forever."

Séverin nodded solemnly. "You are forgiven, Sévère the Judger. May your soul live among the stars."

And then he shot him with a blast of gray light that made her instinctually shut her eyes. It tore through the fabric of Laurent's chest leaving behind nothing but a gaping hole. Laurent's eyes closed, a small tear leaking from the corner of his eyes as he shattered, and his body erupted into black celestial dust.

The earth rumbled loud and wailing and Séverin fell to the

ground. His body twitched wildly and uncontrollably. Magic churned around them leaving a bitter taste in her throat. The trees curved in sinuous shapes and spun with no finesse. Séverin's body was shaking, his limbs battering the ground. He was morphing, evolving into something she could not understand. His eyes shot open, and his pupils were gone. A blank white canvas stared at her. Inhuman and chilling. She could hear his bones cracking, and mutating and she watched as the folds of a wing erupted from his left shoulder blade like a butterfly emerging from its cocoon.

The wing had eyes. A multitude of blinking, ravenous eyes. A reversal of Mòrge's one-eyed crow. His hands savagely tore off his masque. His face was changing, growing sharper, more feline, more frightful. In the frosty morning light, he was unendingly, torturously beautiful.

Mayhem bloomed around them, and blood dripped from the sky as something terrible and wicked and monstrous was birthed.

Footfalls sounded in the distance, and she turned her head to see Inès and Kai in the distance. There were what looked to be about twenty thousand soldiers behind Kai, but they were too late—an army would not save them.

Séverin was dead. She knew with absolute certainty that the thing that writhed before her would awaken as something terrible and wretched.

The boy she liked was *dead.*

And the Lord of Chaos had arrived.

Chapter Thirty-Six

"Élisabeth!" Inès cried.

She came to her, nimbly cutting the ropes that bound Élisabeth's wrists. Élisabeth rubbed her aching flesh, wincing at the rush of sensation that traveled up her injured arm.

"Are you okay?"

"I'm fine," Élisabeth said. "How did you find us?"

"I had a bad feeling," Inès replied. "I had Kai gather the army to the Pit when we couldn't find you both."

Kai had crouched a few feet away from Séverin who was twisting and screaming as his body shook with tremors.

"What happened to him?" Kai demanded.

"This is not good," Matthieu whispered. He came forward, hovering behind her. "Where is the sword?"

"I don't have it."

"Because you don't have the intent to kill him," Matthieu said. "You must be clear with your intentions. The Invisible Sword only reveals itself to the Harbinger when it is summoned. You must summon it. Now before he transitions. This has never happened before."

Another wing burst from his back, and she heard the crack of his bones as his spine realigned. Long frightful claws elongated his nails. A bleak dark-gray coloring that reminded her of iron and metal. The world was splitting at the seams. Beasts had begun to crawl forward like spiders from a crevice. She winced at the sight of their curved spines as they slithered out from the ever-growing Pit.

In the distance, she could see robed figures drifting towards them. The beasts were drawn to the woman whose head was shielded by a red robe. The only hint of her identity was the lengthy braids that poured from her hood.

"The Fates," Matthieu whispered. "This is *not* good."

"Did you just say the Fates?" Inès asked. "What do they want?"

"They want to kill Séverin," Élisabeth said.

In her gut she knew it was dangerous to let him live, but how could she slay him when he was in so much pain? How could she let the Fates break him after all the times he had saved her life? After he had crawled into the Pit for her at the risk of his own life. He hadn't known then that their poison would not *truly* kill him. He hadn't hesitated to save her and now she had to save him.

She had to break this cycle of havoc, vengeance, and blood.

It did not matter who Séverin had been in the past. All that mattered was the person he was now. A brave, spiteful, menacing boy with eyes as bright as stars and a tongue as sharp as a whip.

"Protect Séverin at all costs," Élisabeth called. "Do not let the Fates hurt him."

Lune was the first to remove her hood and the disappointment that laced her face nearly brought her to her knees.

"What are you doing?" Matthieu demanded. The soldiers stood in formation as they foolishly brought out their rifles to shoot at the Fates and the beasts who served them.

"Shields," Kai called.

Élisabeth raised her hand, threads of her magic wrapping around as many beasts as she could control. She sent them hurtling back towards the Fates. Lune raised her palm, and they came to a screeching halt and when she twisted her wrist they returned running in the direction of the soldiers, back to them.

Shots rang out and the air burned with the scent of gunpowder as the rotten blood of the beasts filled the air. Yellow, thick liquid poured from their hides, dripping onto the wet glade.

"Stop this, Sabeth," Matthieu snapped. "We must kill him now, fighting your mother is futile. You must do your duty to the realms and the Fates."

"Listen to him, Sabeth," Lune's gentle voice fluttered by her ear. Even though she stood across from her on the battle-field. Her words drifted to her as if she stood by her side. "Do not fall for the Endless' deceit. Kill him while he transforms. Kill him before it is too late."

"I don't want to hurt him," she said. "He saved my life."

"Your mortal life means nothing. It *is* nothing," she said. Her tone was as sharp as blades. "Do not soften for an inconsequential debt. Your life was never in any true danger, or I would have come for you, as I have come for you now. Do not force me to clap my hands and let the chasm swallow your weak friends. Summon the sword. Kill the Endless. And all shall be right once more."

"You would kill my friends," she whispered.

Mistrust tainted her words, and she took a step away from Matthieu as if he had approved her mother's direction.

"I would kill anyone to prevent the rise of the Endless," she said. "The kings were weakened when they bound him to his Fate. It was the only way the sword would work. They are caught in an eternal slumber. We are the last protectors of the realms, and we cannot fight the Endless."

Her eyes drifted to Séverin. And she trembled at the sight of him and those monstrous wings. At the silky length, his hair had grown, falling neatly to his shoulders. Even the burn marks had dimmed, leaving behind nothing but a bleached-white scar that ran from his hairline to his chin in a twisting, corded line like a braid. It cut cleanly through his brows like a scythe. She was witnessing something unholy and heretical. It did not feel godly. It felt monstrous.

Élisabeth walked towards him and fell to her knees. Her fingers skirted his clenched brows, smoothening it out.

"Lisbeth," he groaned between gritted teeth. His eyes were sealed shut, and it should not have surprised her that he knew her touch so intimately. She reckoned he would know her in Death. Nobody knew the secrets of her soul as much as he did. All those years of watching her in the shadows had made him a rapt pupil. A scholar who'd studied the intricate nature of her heart.

"Don't leave me. Please don't leave me," he breathed.

His hand reached for hers. Those rough claws stroked her forearm.

"I need you, Lisbeth," he said softly. "My Little Monster."

"I'm here, Séverin," she whispered. "I know that you won't hurt me."

He was still, and for one wretched moment, she feared she'd lost him. Her throat tightened and before she could lament her woes to the sky, his eyes opened.

Élisabeth knew then that she would accept him for whatever he was: the Spirit-King, the Lord of Chaos, the Endless, the Phantom, the villain of her fairy tale. It didn't matter, because it was Séverin, and his eyes had once been the color of a frozen lake, and his smile had always been slightly crooked and twisted and mean. Except a few hours ago, when it had been soft and sickly-sweet and delicate like a treasured lullaby. She cradled that smile in her chest and told herself that he was *still* Séverin. Even if he didn't look like him, or feel like him, or sound like him. Even if it was rather cruel of him to change everything she was just starting to like about him.

Matthieu gripped her by the elbow, yanking her back as if she sat before a wolf. She opened her mouth to demand that he release her before Lune's despairing voice reached her.

"It is too late," Lune said. And Élisabeth felt her bones chill when she heard the fear that painted her tone. "You have doomed us."

Everything grew unbearably still. The beasts had frozen, and the gunshots had silenced. The Fates vanished. There one moment and gone the next.

Lune left one final directive poised to Matthieu: *Bring her home.*

Matthieu grabbed her arm.

"We need to leave. *Now.*"

"Wait," she said. "Séverin!"

His head turned to her. And she almost flinched at his otherworldly beauty. Séverin had always been beautiful, but now it was a devastating beauty. An ineffable beauty. One made for ruination. His hand lifted; palm upturned for her alone. Deadly claws floating in the air like an offering.

"Come," he whispered. His voice was sharper and more high-strung. As if it were an instrument whose strings had been altered. His teeth were sharper and more pointed. His eyes churned with madness and chaos and unholiness. Blank white windows with no pupil in sight. Grief filled her in the absence of his brilliant blue eyes. She mourned it, the music of her longing so heavy it nearly weighed her down.

Élisabeth took a step forward, blinded by his beauty and drawn forth by the sweet melody of his voice. And a small weak part of her wanted him to protect her, to keep her safe. She hadn't noticed it, but everyone had fallen to their knees. Heads bowed to the ground.

Something trickled down her eyes. It took her a moment to realize it was blood. All around her, the soldiers cried tears of blood as they experienced the supreme magnitude of what it was like to be in the presence of a higher being.

And when the Endless smiled, the skies split open, and blood poured down. The metallic odor burned her nostrils. It dampened her hair, sticking to her shoulders in lengthy clumps.

Before she could hold his hand, Matthieu pulled her back, and the world tilted around her and the Graylands vanished from her sight.

Élisabeth found herself in a hollow throne room staring at the faces of three very angry Fates.

Chapter Thirty-Seven

He had always thought he knew exactly what he was.

A mortal boy born of two parents.

A boy who perished in a fire.

A ghost who lorded over the Graylands.

But he had never expected the magnitude of the truth that lay before him. Centuries of memories had nearly shattered him. He had felt his eyes crack and splinter. Cold salty fluid dripped down his cheek and slid into his mouth. It had healed within seconds sealing like a scraped wound. He could feel the shuffle of his bones and the fissures that ran down his spine as it reformed, unstringing like loose threads and making way for the bones that would support his wings.

Everything about him that had once been mortal, faded, like letters on an old scrap of paper. His memories played before him in a broken loop of his domain the Darklands, his Bone Throne, and his people: prisoners and murderers and thieves. The wicked rot that his father, Mòrge had never wanted in his realm.

He recalled how he had foolishly gifted Lune with his

wraiths, the Soulless Ones to safe-keep her domain, the Gray-lands in return for the gift of her daughter, the beautiful Sabeth.

His Sabeth.

His bitter enemy.

His wickedest foe.

His pride and despair and heart and curse.

Everything that had ever gone wrong in his life was because of her. Her delicate fingers had always been wrapped around his heart, restricting him, shackling him. And he had always been the moon-cursed fool tripping at her hem, following her into gardens of poisonous plants if it meant he got to kiss her. Only to be rewarded with the slicing cut of her blade plunged deep into his chest. The story unfolded in so many different ways, but it always ended the same. It always ended in Death.

He had awoken from his metamorphosis with all the rage that had festered under countless years of torment. Forced to have his soul split when he awakened in the Graylands because he was so close to his realm and power. Made to watch the girl he fell in love with every four hundred years kill him again and again and again.

If it had not been for his Fate he would have died at Sabeth's hands as he always did.

He didn't know why she had spared him in this lifetime. He didn't know why she had chosen him. It was the first time she ever had. He could hear the echo of her words commanding his soldiers to protect him. Even under the whispers of Lune and the Warden's direction she had stood firm by her decision. She had not summoned the sword; she had chosen him.

After a hundred lifetimes of betrayal, she had chosen him.

And she picked him again when she took a step towards him in the end.

His hand was outstretched for her.

"Come," he whispered. "Come to me, my dark heart."

He could see her form fading, waning before his eyes.

"No," he roared when Matthieu cloaked them in his magic, drawing her far away from his reach.

He reached them in a blink of an eye, but they were gone.

Blood dripped from the sky, welcoming him home. He was not in his realm, but he would claim the Graylands from that traitorous Lune. An invisible bridge lay between the Graylands and the Darklands.

"It wasn't you who was the Fate was it?" Inès whispered.

She was on her knees. Just like the others.

"You always were so smart, Inès," he said. "You may all rise."

"Are you still him?" Kai asked. Eyes wide as he looked at him. "Do you remember us?"

"My memory is intact," he said.

Now that he was awakened, he knew what he had to do. He had to destroy the Fates. He would watch them burn for daring to imprison him. And he would use their precious Harbinger to cut out their worthless throats. He would make her *his* weapon. She was the only person who could summon the sword. The only person who could help him slay the Kings and their foolish Fates once and for all.

His body warmed at the thought of the Fates around him broken and crumpled. Their black blood poured from their wounds like a fallen chalice. He thought of Sabeth on the marble floor, blood soaking her train as she lay on her knees, begging him to spare her life, her sweet platitudes pouring from her wicked mouth as centuries of betrayals stood between them like a rift.

He thought of her mouth on his warm, pulsing with her chosen mortality. A decision she had made so she could erase the memories of him and start afresh every lifetime. She was nothing more than a coward, and he would delight in teaching her a lesson.

"Please, Ren," she'd plead. "Please spare me."

The vision was too tempting to ignore.

He raised his hand, and the wraiths came from the Darklands. Layers of their white, diaphanous bodies floated above them. Their void mouths parted in a wretched scream. The beasts around them trembled. Sabeth's precious creatures fell on their heels, staring at him in fright. He had called them from above. From the Darklands. The beasts were outnumbered, and so they submitted to him.

And his wraiths stood strong.

"Come along," Ren said, smiling at his allies. He watched them wince and he could not tell if it was a reaction to his altered state or if it was fear. "We have a war to plan."

Chapter Thirty-Eight

He stood in the dark, cloistered in the shrine of all his old memories and drowning obsessions. Perched on the wall was a painting he had captured one night after he had first seen Élisabeth perform. Her dark hair unspooled like silk from a spinning wheel, mimicking the flow of her short ballet dress. In the actual production, she had been in the back, hidden in the shadows, cast in a dreamless role, trapped in obscurity, but in this painting, she stood front and center. In his eyes, she had been the heart and soul of the Opera House, the raw, bloody organ that kept it afloat. The dark, sorrowful muse who inspired his music.

In a small treasure box, he would keep small trinkets he'd stolen from her dressing room. A sickeningly pale, pink ribbon caught his attention from his collection, and he curled it absently around his monstrous claw.

It made sense that she was Sabeth reincarnated, the one girl who had ever managed to sink her hooks into him. The only person he had ever let come close enough to betray him. His fist tightened claws spearing through his flesh, leaking his black, ungodly blood.

He had let her into the Darklands and had entertained her mother's offering in the disguise of a gift because her beauty and wit and unforgiving tongue had ensnared him. Only for her to use that damned sword to slice his heart and doom him. He was the only being who the Invisible Sword could not fully destroy because his birth was a loophole that upset the Balance. The Kings were never meant to procreate, to pass along their destructive magic. Not only was he the son of Mòrge, but he was the son of a Fate, of Berthe the Spinner.

That made him untouchable.

It made him a threat to their very existence.

And he had every intention of killing them all, his parents be damned. Berthe led this witch hunt against him, and he would watch her suffer. Then he would find out exactly where the weakened kings lay, and he would destroy them.

He needed Sabeth and her sword to accomplish that.

He would make her his weapon. He would make her kill her mother. He would make her set the torch and watch her world fall to ashes. She would suffer for all the torment she had brought him. For choosing the Fates over him. He had promised her the world, and she had chosen to serve his enemies instead.

Maybe she had come to him in the end, but how could the decisions of one lifetime erase all the others?

Sabeth Fateborn would rue the day she was born.

A knock sounded on his door. He sat on the hooked, talon-shaped chair in his bedroom, nursing a glass of wine as his wraiths swarmed the palace windows. They were eager to return to the Darklands, but first, he had to establish a chain of command here.

"Enter," he called.

Kai walked in hesitantly, fingers gripping his sword so tightly it shook.

Ren raised a brow and took a long, lingering sip.

"Come to slay me?" he asked.

"How do I know you're not Laurent pretending to be Séverin who is then pretending to be Ren the Endless?" Kai asked. "None of us were there to witness what happened. How are we to take your word for it? I scarcely recognize you. It is as though I am looking into the eyes of a monster."

Ren sighed, slowly and deeply. The longer he sat replaying the many decisions in his immortal life that had doomed him, the more he could feel the traces of his humanity fading like a cloth that had been stretched too thin.

"Go on then," he said, spreading his arms. "Let's see if your little sword can hurt me."

"You're not going to even attempt to convince me?" Kai asked.

"I've never had much luck changing your mind when it is set," he said. "The truth is you don't *want* to believe that I am the Lord of Chaos, because that would make me the villain, and your morals have always been your weakness. Tell me, Dakarai, do you regret not standing by Laurent that day? He was the good, honorable Fate after all. He was the one who should have lived and I was the one made to be slain."

"Where did your burn marks go?" Kai demanded, refusing to let go of this itching belief that he was somehow Laurent playing a grand farce. "Where did that new scar come from?"

Ren absently touched his cheek.

"This was a gift from your best friend Élisabeth," he said.

"Élisabeth would never do that," Kai said. "You're lying."

"Élisabeth is Sabeth Fateborn, Daughter of Lune and she will do whatever her mother bids her to," he snapped. He pointed his cheek. "She was aiming for my heart when she did this."

"Why did she want you dead?" Kai asked.

"Because she and her mother and the Fates are all cowards."

"So, your scars were magically healed?" he asked incredulously. "Seems rather convenient, Laurent."

Ren shrugged. "I can pick and choose what I keep. There was no need to remember some silly mortal ordeal from a life that I do not care for."

He had chosen to bring back his original scar in its place. His reminder to never fall for the lies of another wide-eyed girl with a blade of death in her hand.

"And what about your friends?" Kai demanded. His brown eyes twisted with sadness and rage. "Are we silly mortals from a life that you do not care for?"

"Do you truly want me to answer that?" Ren asked. "I'd hate to hurt your feelings."

He expected that to be the end of it. For Kai to disappear and leave him to his solitude to plot and scheme, he crossed the room. Ren straightened when Kai grabbed his hand, upturning his palm, staring at the curved white line of an old scar. Ren's jaw clenched, searching for words to dismiss what he saw, to claim that it was a mistake, that he had simply forgotten to erase it in the transformation, but something that looked suspiciously like hope crossed Kai's eyes.

"You're still him," he murmured.

"Don't be ridiculous," he snarled, snatching back his hand. "It was an oversight. Nothing more."

Kai chuckled lightly. "Still afraid of feeling I see."

Ren folded his arms across his chest. He dropped it

abruptly when Kai's smile widened. It was a childish gesture he had always done since his boyhood. Even in different lifetimes, his mannerisms remained untainted.

"It means nothing," he barked.

"It means *everything.*"

Kai disappeared, the door clicking shut behind him. He flexed his hand, regretting keeping the stupid scar. They had been around eight or so at the time, playing in the fields behind his house. Kai had been late that day, his face gleaming with a shiny bruise the size of a small lark. It bloomed an angry, blue shade across his brown skin, covering his cheekbones with its stained wings.

"It was my fault," Kai said, just as Ren opened his mouth to demand answers. "I was late to dinner."

Guilt had twisted his stomach. Kai's father was strict and disciplined and his fist was his chosen method to correct bad behavior. Usually, Ren could swallow the bitter rage that curled in his throat, but Kai looked exceptionally pathetic that day. His curly hair fell into his eyes as if he could hide away from the world if he simply disappeared into himself.

Kai had tried to stop him, he'd begged and pleaded, but all Ren had seen was a blistering red, as he tore into the parlor room where his father sat smoking with Kai's father. He leaped on him, punching him wildly and madly, warning him that he'd kill him if he touched him again. Kai's father had roughly shoved him off him, nostrils flaring, and Ren fell backward, slicing his hand on the cracked bottle on the embroidered carpet.

His father had not been pleased, but he understood why he'd reacted so strongly.

"You shouldn't have done that," Kai said. They had to sneak out at midnight to see each other the next night. Kai's father had forbidden him from ever interacting with him. "It was stupid."

Ren shrugged. "You bleed, I bleed."

Kai pulled out a blade, slicing his palm before he could stop him. He clasped it around his bandaged hand. He had gotten six stitches to heal the wound from that day. Blood soaked into the bandage, as he pressed his twin scar to his flesh.

"You bleed, I bleed," Kai echoed.

Ren stared at the crooked scar then, feeling sick to his stomach. This tormented feeling was what had cost him his life before when he had mistakenly given his heart to the wrong girl. Kai was too good to stand by him, it would only be a matter of time till he betrayed him just like *she* did.

He refused to let anyone get close to him. Ever again.

Chapter Thirty-Nine

The Fates were in the middle of a heated argument when Matthieu and Élisabeth arrived. The walls quaked at the sheer brutality of their divine voices.

"We should have never made her the Harbinger," a man spoke.

He was tall with fair hair and a thick, lengthy beard. Aldéric, she suspected. "Mat would have done perfectly well. I told you he was a good choice."

"Dwelling on the past is futile," a woman with crow-black hair and pale, milky skin spoke. Berthe, she assumed. "We must fortify the wards of this realm and I must return to the mortal lands. There is a war coming."

"Séverin won't hurt us," Élisabeth said.

It was the wrong thing to say because the immortals looked at her with a mix of anger and disappointment. Her shoulders straightened, refusing to cower under their merciless gazes.

"Sabeth didn't know," Matthieu said in her defense. "She can't be blamed for this. He manipulated her."

"And you," Aldéric barked. "You were supposed to guide

her. This is your failure just as much as hers. You were named the Warden of the realms to protect them and we have lost the Graylands *and* the Darklands. The Endless will reclaim his throne and the realms will be broken."

"Maybe I can speak to Séverin," she offered. "Maybe we can come to some agreement."

"That is not his name, Sabeth," Lune said. Her voice was sharp and exhausted. "He is Ren the Endless and he will destroy us all. The Graylands is yours as much as it is mine. He has seized your birthright, and he will take far more before this ends."

"Will the Graylands still come undone?" she asked.

"We don't know," Berthe said. "We have never failed before."

Foreboding filled the air, mixed with trepidation. Élisabeth hated that she had failed them and that the hopeless look in their eyes was because of her. But she also wouldn't hurt him. She didn't care if his name was Séverin or Ren or the Endless, she would not kill the boy she cared about. The boy who had looked at her in the end as if she were his salvation. The boy who had pleaded with her to stay.

Someone pulled her and she realized it was Matthieu.

"Come, we need to go to the White Tower."

"What is at the White Tower?" she asked.

"The Well," he said. "It will help you get back your memories. The scales are tilted in his favor; he knows all about you now and you know nothing."

They slipped out the bronze doors and walked down the hallway. Darkness poured from the oval windows. Outside large, crooked trees stood in formation.

"Thank you for defending me," she said.

"My father can be harsh when he wants to," Matthieu said softly.

He led her outside the castle, onto the stretched green grounds and they walked several paces till they reached a high tower. The stones were a moon-white color, gleaming in the dark like a stack of bones. Matthieu pushed open the heavy iron doors. The air inside was damp, and she didn't protest when Matthieu lifted her to carry her up the stairs. Her lungs would collapse if she attempted to climb it on her own. There had to have been at least a hundred steps.

At last, they reached a well with glimmering water. Matthieu placed her down and picked up a silver cup. He tilted it, scooping up as much water as it could hold.

"Here," he said. "Drink it to the last drop."

"And I'll remember?" she asked.

"You'll remember *everything*," he said. "You'll know why you hate him. You'll know why he must die."

Matthieu paused. "He is a monster, a heretical immortal, a soul-cursed weapon made to destroy us."

Élisabeth hesitated. A small part of her wanted to remain oblivious. To believe that there was good in the world and that the boy she liked wasn't planning on destroying the realms for power, but she could not ignore the fear in the Fate's eyes. They were older and wiser than her and for him to frighten beings of such vast power was something to be concerned about. She glanced at Matthieu, and his lips lifted in an encouraging smile.

"I'm glad you're here with me, Mat," she said, reaching for his hand and squeezing it. "This would all be so much more frightful without you."

"I'm the Warden of the realms, but you've always been my priority, Sabeth," he said. "And now you will know how much you mean to me."

"May I ask you something?" she asked.

"Anything."

"Why do you think I didn't kill him this time?" she asked. "What changed?"

Matthieu let out a sharp breath. As if the words were too difficult to speak.

"I suppose you loved him more," he said. His eyes were sad and forlorn. "You are always drawn to him, but he is always incapable of surrendering his heart. And your affection sours and you kill him. I suppose he gave you what you needed after all this time."

Her throat tightened.

"I think I am in love with him," she whispered, nails scraping the cup, as she stared at her reflection in the water. "And...and I don't know if I want to let that go."

"You were not made to love him," he said. "You were made to kill him."

Élisabeth swallowed hard. "I don't want to be the Harbinger. I just want to be Élisabeth."

"I know," Matthieu said gently. "You will always be, Élisabeth."

Élisabeth stared at the water, dread pooling in her stomach.

"Your heart will remain the same," he said. "You will simply understand your history."

Élisabeth took a deep breath and tilted the cup. The water was cold and sweet as if it had been mixed with honey. It slipped down her throat like velvet, and she tasted the cold drift of magic on her tongue. She placed the cup down and stumbled, falling to the ground. Her head ached as a plethora of memories swept through her brain with the force of a rainstorm leaving behind nothing but pain and debris. Her mind splintered into two halves. On one side it was Élisabeth Bellacourt and on the other was Sabeth Fateborn. And the two halves collided like stars corralling across the sky and twining in a burst of light and stardust.

Matthieu held her as she screamed and screamed and screamed.

It felt like months passed away, curled on that cold floor as centuries of pain, heartache, and happiness ravaged her mind, clutching it with swollen, battered fingers.

And when she opened her eyes, she knew then that she would *never* be the same again.

Acknowledgments

It is a magical feeling writing my fourth acknowledgment letter because I somehow managed to publish four books. I want to thank the readers who have been here from the start and those who are just discovering my work. Thank you for trusting me to tell these stories and embracing them. I don't know where I would be without the book community. Thank you to Gaston Leroux for the *The Phantom of the Opera* not just the book but all the hundreds of iterations it created including musicals and films. This story was a byproduct of my love for gothic litera-ture, and I hope the elements I picked resonate with readers. It is not a retelling but rather an ode, an acknowledgment, a recognition. I want to thank my editor Elizabeth Ward who helped sharpen this story. I want to thank Lola Vagabonde for illustrating the beautiful cover and depicting the elements and characters so beautifully. And lastly, I want to thank my family and friends for their constant support. This would not have been possible without all of you.